A NIGHT
AT THE
KING'S INN

By Alec Arbogast

Ink Smith Publishing
www.ink-smith.com

A Night at The King's Inn

ISBN:

Ink Smith Publishing
P.O. Box 361
Lakehurst, NJ 08733

For my late father,

You taught me what it is to steer life's course with passionate abandon and dereliction of fear. Your unconditional love paved the way to fulfillment and fortitude, for yourself and those whom you loved.

I can still feel your hand on my shoulder, guiding me through the undulations in your silently courageous way.

So, let us raise anchor and hoist sail. And without further ado, dad,

Leeeet's go!

Let the great world spin for ever down the ringing grooves of change.

Alfred Lord Tennyson,
Locksley Hall

ACT I

PROLOGUE

The train's horn blares ahead. Several cars back, the sound manages to rattle the windows of the compartment. The attendee cries "All aboard!" and then hops onto the aft section of the car. The train's chimney bellows curls of black smoke. The gears lurch the object into intermittent motion. The gaslights of the station crawl past the window, illuminating the compartment in splashes of fractured light.

Walter Marley pulls the chain feeding into his pocket and checks the time piece. 2:02 in the morning. He glances one last time at the fading station. The light-drenched Oldham sign and the few stragglers, likely waiting for the dilatory northbound line, becoming mere silhouettes in a constricting swathe of dark.

The feeling of claustrophobia sets in, not simply because of the shrinking of the illuminated world and the enveloping dark, but because of those men… those three men in black trench coats that appeared at the station just prior to the London line's rattling, chortling arrival. *Were they an outside faction of the High Rip Gang?* he wonders. The outward appearance certainly matched. Walter Marley scratches at his beard. He was right to leave the boy in a separate cabin. And he was right to bring a dummy suitcase, nudging the leather suitcase at his feet.

Dozens of sets of wheels roll on the rails below, the driving rhythm of the machine outpaced by that of Walter's heart. He rises and stares out the window, nudging the buttons of his peacoat into their holes. It's a lengthy expanse between Oldham and Birmingham; lengthy and desolate. *A mountainous no-man's land*, Walter thinks, *a topographical nightmare after dark*. He watches as the moon-splashed hills grow in height, pine trees capping their minatory peaks.

The moon hangs low tonight, constantly dipping among the hills and throwing the world into an even deeper black. When it dips out of sight behind an aberrantly tall slope, nothing is visible beyond the brooding glow of the cabins.

Leaving the decoy bag on the cabin floor, Walter throws the strap of his leather satchel over his shoulder. He waits just long enough for the attendee to complete a cabin check, then diminishes the cabin's lantern and steps outside to a deserted passenger car. A lamp hanging at the far right illuminates a placard that reads *Upper Class*.

Walter makes his way to the door with his arms outstretched to compensate for the lurch of the vessel. He pulls the lever and yanks on the door. The exterior din is amplified in the diminutive vestibule and when he throws the door, he is assaulted by the thrashing wind and the grating beat of the locomotive against the rails. He has to avert his gaze from the blur of the passing ground in order to cross the platform joints.

Trains have never been Walter's preferred method of travel—the forced intimacy of passengers confined in narrow spaces for long stretches of time, the interminable cyclical noises of the machinery and, perhaps the most egregious aspect, the nausea caused by tons of amalgamated steel parts disharmoniously galloping forward.

Once he is safely inside the vestibule, he throws the door open and the contrasting hush of the cabin jars his senses. He steps into upper class and moves through the cabin, locking eyes with a businessman whose bloodshot eyes are absorbed in the latest issue of *The Commonweal*. As he passes, he catches a blur of phrases—"October 27th, 1890", and a blot of socialist propaganda entitled, "The End of the Proletariat."

Walter feels the heat of the man's stare even after he has passed, but curbs the desire to look back. He continues through the posh cabin and takes note of its sparse occupancy. *A red-eye to London has the proclivity to entertain far fewer passengers than the day train*, he thinks. A wealthy-looking family of three are the only souls on the car besides the politically-literate gentleman.

The father's frock is stretched neatly across the opposing booth. His dress shirt is hiked up at the sleeves, and he's rolling a dab of amber liquid around a short glass. The daughter, merely a child, is nodding off on the shoulder of her mother, who also looks upon the edge of sleep. The perfunctory, comfortable appearance of the three elicits a curiosity in Walter. *A migratory family?* he wonders.

Seeing the child reminds him of Alger; his grandson must be waiting for him by now. He presses on through the noisy vestibule, and the considerably noisier junction between the cars, and enters the lounge car. An alarmingly lavish bar sits to his right, with a gaunt ginger-haired man at the helm.

He nods to the barman. So far there hasn't been a trace of the three concerning figures at the station. Perhaps they didn't make it aboard. Or, perhaps Walter's mind is slipping from the pressure of his career—of his invention—and merely made a portent out of a benign situation. After all, Burberry coats and bowler hats, while being common adornments of the High Rip Gang, are not one bit uncommon in Walter's ragged hometown of Oldham. The nights there can grow to a stabbing cold; a trait which Walter attributes to the plethora of refineries that line the old waterfront and pepper the town.

The industrial age has turned what was once a meager, and yet wholesome and charming, town into a fertile playground for the conglomerates. Where verdant hills once rolled into the horizon, putrid smokestacks and vapid warehouses now dominate them.

Those as old as Walter can remember when the town of Oldham was comprised of a tightly knit community of but a string of families. Through the century, wealthy and conniving business magnates turned his quaint little town into a regimented production facility, splitting up families and turning ethereal Oldham into the bleak, suffocated work-town that it is today. *Perhaps*, he thinks, *it is best for the boy to start a life in a more propitious environment like London.*

Walter pushes through the lounge car, waving his hand to disperse a thick screen of cigar smoke hovering above a gaggle of businessmen. He hops the space between cars and enters the vestibule to coach. Once inside, he promptly slinks over to the window and peers into the cabin. Economy is slightly more populated than the previous cars, but there is not a suspicious-looking person, not a single anomaly that strikes him as concerning.

Breathing a sigh of relief, Walter turns to the corner of the dark vestibule. Alger is standing against the wall with his arms outstretched. The lad knows how to follow instructions.

"Papa!" Alger exclaims.

Seeing his grandson, even only after twenty minutes or so, is a wondrous event. Walter pulls Alger into a firm embrace, tussling the lad's hair. "Alger, my boy. Oh dear, I'm so sorry." He feels the pins of worry settle into his back, knowing that if he is in fact being tailed, being seen with the boy would ensure doom for them both. "This separation is only for the train ride, I promise you. I simply must take these precautions until we arrive in London, my lad."

Walter pulls away from the boy and looks him in the face. Alger's bowl-cut hair is disheveled, his plump cheeks underlining a set of deep blue eyes. "People might be trying to stop your granddad from sharing his work with the world; alas it is too important a creation not to share with mankind. Now, remember what I told you boy: stay with the trunk in coach, do not let it leave your sight. Do not share words with a single soul that isn't a railcar assistant. Do not, under any circumstances, come find me until we are pulling up to London. Is that understood, lad?"

Alger sniffles and nods his head. "Good boy." Walter gives the young one's hair another tussle. This time, he nearly knocks Alger off balance with his mounting agitation. "I love you, Alger. Never forget that." He exhales, saturnine. "Listen, lad, if…anything was to happen and…you don't find your granddad on the train when you arrive in London, take the trunk and stay with your Aunt Vesper. You remember her address, no?"

The boy nods. "Brilliant, brilliant lad." He dredges the inner pocket of his peacoat and slaps a handful of shillings into Alger's tiny hand. He turns swiftly and heads for the lounge car, foregoing the utterance of another word, or even a backward glance, knowing that if he dallies any longer, he might not have the forbearance to leave the child again.

Walter mounts a creaky barstool and waves through the smog at the ginger barman.

"What can I do ye for, sir?" Given his physical appearance, the man's muddled cockney accent throws Walter slightly—he would have wagered him Irish; but he has more pressing matters on his mind.

"A mug of coffee will do, barman; bitter and black, if you will." The man nods and brandishes an ornate brass brewer that reminds Walter more of his Bunsen burners and anemometers than a coffee maker. He never used siphon brew machines, preferring instead his traditional percolator, an item he has used so heavily the wooden handle has developed an impression of his hand.

Behind him, a group of business moguls pluck at cigar tips with their mouths and blather about investment affairs in London. The barman knocks a pile of coffee grounds into one container, then strikes a match and ignites a wick under another. Over the barman's shoulder blares a tinny, crackly recording from the horn of a phonograph machine.

As the water boils above the wick, the ballad ends, and the barman turns and ejects the cylinder from its housing. He rummages in a drawer for another, inserts it and fondles the stylus until it erupts into a cacophony of mechanical noises. Once he finds the cylinder's groove amidst the churning mottle of air, the horn begins emitting a harsh reproduction of violin music. Walter recognizes it as one of many despondent-sounding Russian pieces.

Seeing the phonograph, or gramophone, as the device is currently being called in the trade, strikes a chord with Walter. His hand plunges into the satchel hanging at his side, retrieves a folder, and flips it open to an articulate illustration of a device. This is a device that he invented precisely two years prior which consists of a single lens camera and paper film, upon which he has finagled a way in conjunction with celluloid and rotating belts, to record movement and project it. Moving pictures, as he calls it. *A rather trite but fitting appellation*, he thinks.

The moving pictures camera is what his contacts in London believe he will be unveiling. Perchance he will attempt again to acquire a patent for it; however, his real creation, a device that is so prominent and ingenious that it truly shall be the zenith of his career, will put his moving pictures contraption to shame. He peels the camera illustration over and gazes upon a blueprint of his other device. Aesthetically it's analogous to a phonograph machine, but his latest invention is so very much more. *Edison be damned*, Walter chuckles.

Prying eyes happened to be present the day that Walter first fired up his proprietary device, one he tentatively titled 'Sonophone.' Since then, word has wafted about like a miasma before a desk fan, and several of England's gangs, as well as lustful corporate wranglers, have sought after him to purloin the technology and be the first to patent it.

"That's quite a sketch you've got there." A voice. To the right—through the haze. An eloquent, proper English accent. Walter throws the folder shut and looks right. A cloud of smoke turns to ribbons—a hand slicing through the air. As the air thins, the figure of a man appears.

It's the dapper family man from upper class. He must be visiting the lounge for a fill-up while his wife and daughter slumber in the other car. A gold embroidered vest shimmers across the man's chest, bouncing light upon his face. Walter shivers at his expression; a contorted snake of a smile underneath eyes that churn with tempestuous determination. His brow is knitted and low, and his hands clenched with white-knuckle intensity upon his sipping glass.

Walter pockets the folder into its sleeve with all too much haste. "Why, thank you." He nods to the man and mocks fascination in the barman, who's now pouring Walter's coffee into a prodigious tin mug.

"Here y'ar, sir," says the barman as he slides the mug along the bar, steam billowing in its wake. Walter can feel the brooding gaze of the family man on him still. He hopes the barman lingers so that he might strike up a discourse with him and mitigate unwanted attention from the strange guest. After giving Walter the mug, however, the barman sets the coffee brewer on the counter and rounds the bar to do some tidying in the cabin.

"Is it often that you dither on a train, sketching arbitrary items?" The glint in the man's eye strengthens. "I do say, sir, that was an immaculate portrayal of a phonograph machine."

"I thank you." With a reticent nod in the man's direction, Walter hoists the mug to his face and takes an intentionally protracted swig of coffee.

"Dare I say, however, that the phonograph you sketched is not a whiff like the one which sits behind the bar?" The man's vicious smirk stanches Walter's blood. "Nay," he continues, "nay, this one has a cylindrical amplifier upon it." He extends his open hand toward the device behind the bar. "Whereas the one upon which I just gazed has a rather ponderous, swan-like neck that blossoms out into an extravagant, peculiarly stamped bell."

How can this be? Walter thinks, his hands squeezing into fists. *I was so thoroughly preoccupied with concern over those three inauspicious gents that I missed what was just before my eyes. The family man is well-trimmed, with an air of opulence about him, a fine grasp of the English language, and, most concerning, an obdurate fascination with my Sonophone. Might he be one of Edison's English associates?*

"That's quite astute of you mister…"

"Friend. I am a friend, to refer to me as such is suitable."

"Well, friend," Walter says somewhat sardonically. "I must entreat you to leave me be, for I have a great deal on my mind and am ill-suited for idle chatter with a stranger on this night. With no offenses meant to you, friend."

To this, the man's disposition lightens, and the barman raises his brow toward them; the intensity of Walter's stare nearly palpable.

"I appreciate your candor," the family man says and looks down. "Barman! Scottish whiskey, neat." The glass barely settles onto the bar before the gentleman snatches it with a near white-knuckle intensity. He swirls the drink once or twice, gulps it, and slams the glass down. "Pardon me, sir, but I have a matter to which I must tend." Walter watches as the man's glimmering vest muddles in with bar smoke and then disappears. Walter shakes his head at the barman, digs in his pocket and tosses the man a two-pence.

Walter tries to scrub the occurrence with the officious man from his mind, but a stout worry, like some carnivorous insect, has dug into his mind and nestled right into its new crevice. All he cares for is Alger's safety, and he can't help but feel the sobering guilt that in his own hunger for innovation and prominence, he has forsaken the boy.

The enigmatic character at the bar could well have maleficent motives, or perhaps he simply fancies the sciences and was taken with Walter's sketch. Perchance he is a neutral party, such as an engineer or architect. *There is no reason as of yet*, Walter assures himself, *to assume him a threat.*

He finishes his coffee with a shaking hand, tosses the barman another coin and heads back to his quarters. The effluvium of dread that follows Walter from the lounge strengthens as he steps into the upper-class car. The wife and daughter of the mysterious man remain in their seats, their slumbering figures sunken into the plush material, but the man's seat is vacant. There isn't a trace of him in the cabin.

Somewhere between Oldham and the train's next stop, Birmingham, Walter remembers there is a tunnel that slices under a rocky hill. If memory serves him correctly, the tunnel grazes the edge of Sheffield Park, which can't be far now. Even on a particularly sunny day the old tunnel is pitch as black. Alas, after dark, stumbling between cars is not somewhere he wants to be. He pushes on.

With trepidation, Walter enters the passenger car. Aside from the constant drumbeat of the wheels circling below, the cabin is hushed and dim. Had he not seen multiple parties entering their cabins at the Oldham stop, he'd be a worried mess that he might be absolutely isolated in this car. Still, if an assailant desired to give him trouble, they wouldn't be without opportunity on the red-eye to London.

If he had not discerned men peering at him through the dusty casements of his warehouse the past several nights—perhaps constituents of another city gang—he would not have left home in such a tizzy. Even today a small group of men, different from those suspicious gits who boarded the train, dithered about his block in a menacing and somewhat presumptuous manner. One of them spied Walter through his high window and the bloke even had the audacity to tip his hat to him.

Perhaps it is all a crude betrayal of his senses, but Walter knows he must be ever vigilant. Alas, just after victuals this evening—which he rushed to provide that the boy might not travel with an empty stomach—Walter packed a few necessary personal effects, bundled up the Sonophone, left it with the boy for precautionary reasons, and abandoned his Oldham home.

He pulls on his cabin door and notices that the latch isn't engaged, even though he succinctly remembers having fully closed the door on his way out. He peels the door ajar only enough to see inside. The cabin is a belly of black; outside the window, a constant whirl of drab, unfeeling nature. He eases the sliding door open and steps inside.

Much to his relief is the discovery that his trunk is exactly where he left it. He can see its brass latches glimmer in the moonlight, projecting a ghostly hue against the dark booth. The cabin is hushed and still, but Walter smells something in the air; something sweet and biting. Whiskey. He feels a wave of nerves fire off through his limbs. The hair on the back of his neck stands erect—the precise sensation he gets when he knows he's being watched.

He feels warm air graze his shoulder and then gently attenuate. The stench increases; someone's breath upon him. He hears a soft commotion behind, and, with supreme deftness, someone slides the door to his cabin until the latch clicks. As he begins to turn, he feels something pierce his side.

"Don't turn or I'll squeeze the trigger and blast you a new kidney." A familiar voice. "What's your name?"

Walter finds his tongue. "Walter…Marley."

"Step into the moonlight." The man shoves Walter against the wall. In the window's reflection he discerns the puffy, scrutinizing guise of the family man. For a moment the two men stare each other down from this perspective; Walter sees terror reflect in his own eyes, and in the family man's, determination.

"It bloody-well is you," the man whispers. "Capital!" Walter feels the sidearm disappear and the man's coiled hands loosen. He turns inquiringly towards the man, but he cannot discriminate much through the darkness.

"Who in the blazes are you, and what do you want with me?"

"Shh, shh. Don't get yourself in a tizzy now." The man is whispering; his voice slightly rattled. "Does anybody know this is your cabin? Have you seen anything suspicious?" he barks.

"Aside from yourself, my good sir, no I can't say anyone should know that this is my cabin. Now what is the meaning of this?"

The man sighs. "You can call me Watters. Douglas Whitby sends his regards."

"Douglas Whitby of Whitby and Sons?"

"Yes, the famous portraitist."

"Now, what could they possibly want with an old sod like me?" Walter feigns naivety regarding the recent splash he has made in the scientific community. He understands that the metastasizing corporations of Great Britain, not to mention the city's supply of independent artists, will surely want in on the fledgling technological landscape.

"His company is utilizing photography instead of oils in their work and is mobilizing towards the concept of creating moving portraits, a la your new moving pictures device," the enigmatic Watters says.

"There's no need to be sheepish with me, my friend, I'm on your side. The business to which I belong, Whitby and Sons, is not alone in divining what you've had your nose in. That youth who was fogging up your window the night you first fired up your contraption was a correspondent with the vicious London Bilge Rats gang. How do I know that he was there, and precisely for whom he was employed? Well, mate, I was there as well. I've been watching you for some time."

His inimical guest cannot see it through the curtain of darkness, but Walter's face is ruddy with surprise and embarrassment. He reaches into his jacket pocket and retrieves a stack of matches.

"No sense in hovering in shadows Mr. Watters, allow me to strike up the lantern." Walter moves towards the object, but a swift hand on his arm stymies him.

"No, my friend. I have been a passenger on this pitching, yawing boat-on-wheels since its point of origin at Thirsk, but I have not yet thoroughly checked each car for anything suspect. Light attracts attention, and it is paramount that we avoid that. I'm an ally, my good sir. You must trust me."

Walter doesn't trust anyone. Putting too much faith in another person is unwise; besides, perhaps, little Walter of course. The child is too young to have developed the false affectations and paranoia that plague the minds of men.

"So, I shall sit in bleak darkness sharing vagaries with a stranger whom I do not have cause to trust, and wait out the remainder of the journey this way?"

"All I can give you is my word, mate. Besides, had I wanted you dead, would you not already be?" Watters asks. Submitting, Walter retires to the booth. Watters sits opposite him and shimmies up to the window. As the moon crests a hill it bathes his face in a muted glow, betraying an expression of what could be exhaustion, but appears more like destitution than anything else.

A *man is more candid when he is intoxicated*, Walter thinks. *This man is either coming down from his inebriation and is remembering the pains that drive him to drink in the first place or is still tangled up in the substance and is thus not concerned with outward appearances.* Walter's own memories are mottled with sorrow, he knows the look on Watters' face all too well.

"Suffer me one question, Watters. Your wife and daughter, why did you bring them along on your nocturnal investigation?"

Silence for a moment from the other man. "To whom are you referring, friend?"

"Those ladies with you in upper class, I presumed you were related to them."

"Ah, the lass and her mother. Simply a kind and welcoming duo, with whom I shared a few laughs and a smattering of stories on the life of the nomad. You see, they were on the way to visit their husband and father in London—do so quite often, so they've said—and here am I, but a lonely mercenary of the night.

"When one chooses a lifestyle as such that I have, they must make haste to rid themselves of any attachments, both physical and emotional. Exchanges like that are the singular instances where I might pretend that I am not quite so alone…"

While he chews on Watters' bitter discourse, Walter sifts through his options, and then it strikes him. Watters has unintentionally provided him with a backup plan for the protection of his grandson.

"I am sorry," he says, rising. "There is something to which I must tend, but I shan't be long." Once more he feels a pawing at his arm. For a drunkard in the dark Watters certainly has an alarming control of his faculties.

"Take this, mate." The handle of a pistol caresses his palm. "In case." Walter has never held a firearm before. He is a man of science and empiricism, not of destruction.

"I'm quite sure I shouldn't," he blathers. "This item is rather extraneous as I shan't be gone long at all. Besides, I wouldn't know what to do with this even if the occasion required me using it." Watters chuckles at this.

"The man reinvents the wheel and he has not the faith in himself to fire a palm pistol. You just point and pull the trigger, friend; hopefully not in such a dim setting as this."

"Thank you." Walter neatly pockets the tiny pistol and strolls down the car. He traverses the vestibule, glides over the gap, and enters Upper Class. The two women with whom Watters was keeping company are still there, still on the cusp of sleep. Walter tentatively nudges the mother, who mutters inaudibly before coming around. She stares at him with a waxy, inquisitive gaze.

"Yes, sir, what is it?"

"Beg pardon ma'am, but with the way you're holding your daughter there you seem like a parent worthy of exaltation, and a nurturing soul to boot," he whispers above the daughter's ear. "There's a little boy two cars ahead. Seems like he's traveling alone, and he's got a dreadfully large trunk with him; commensurate to the size of his body, and nigh twice his weight.

"If the two of you are disembarking at London, would you extend your kindness to the boy and see to it that he gets wherever he needs to go. Perchance he's got family in the city with whom he can stay." The flummoxed look that he receives is hardly a surprise, and Walter doesn't wait for a response before turning back for his cabin.

Even after meeting his supposed protector, Walter is not assured that he isn't still being hunted. He needs assurance that the boy will be all right. Besides, he cannot be certain that Watters is, in fact, benevolent. The man hasn't yet played his hand. He has merely claimed to be working for an opulent artist for whom the Sonophone is a valuable prospect. So, the various gangs of England are on the hunt for the device, as is corporate England surely, and, potentially worse, the eccentric artists—one of whom is aware of Walter's movements.

Walter hastens back toward his quarters. Like the fingers of a spreading evil, long shadows bleed from the corners of the vessel. A killer might be hiding in any of the many dark nooks and crevices. He would never know until it is too late. A paroxysm of dread assaults him; he brandishes the palm pistol, keeping his tremulous finger a distance from the little trigger.

Paranoia mounts steadily as he enters the vestibule. Luckily for him, the room is empty. He throws the connecting door open and just as he preps to leap, the train grazes a bump and pitches left hard. His tentative grip on the gun fails and it is sent clattering to the tracks below.

"Blast!" In a momentary lapse of sagacity, Walter nearly dives for the pistol. That foreign little device might have been precisely what he needed to ensure his and his grandson's protection. *Such a timid fool*, he thinks, making the leap.

As he approaches his personal quarters, Walter discerns a commotion and a damp, muffled noise. *A stifled scream?* Immediately after, a moaning howl. *What on earth is Watters on about in there?* The shades on his cabin windows are drawn taut. He slides the door open. The lantern is lit now, its subdued warmth grazes his cheek; the waxy smell of gas puncturing his nostrils.

"Watters, are you quite all right, I heard—" Three men festooned in long frocks and peacoats, bowlers and ascots crowning their heads, all turn to the door. Watters is perched against the window on a wooden stool, speckles of blood on his gold vest, and crimson trails tease down his face. Beneath him Walter's trunk lies askew. A ream of paper has been tossed asunder, and the diagram of his moving pictures device rests on top.

One of the men bends down and scoops the diagram into his hand. He taps the brim of his bowler just enough to reveal a gaunt, aquiline face. "Well, Doctor Marley, this…moving pictures concept, it really is rather exciting." Piercing through the night, the train's horn blares three consecutive times; a harbinger for something ahead on the tracks. "But it isn't what we have come for. Where is the device? You'll tell us one way or the other." The man nods to his henchmen who, liked coiled snakes, propel toward Walter in a frenzy of coattails.

Just as the men are about to apprehend him, the train car is thrust into blackness, absolute blackness, save the lantern in the cabin. They must be in the Sheffield Park tunnel.

Walter lets out a gasp and throws the sliding door. Nearly tripping over his own feet, he stumbles backward and begins dashing toward the tail end of the car. The utter visual bereavement throws his balance until the men slam open the door, carving a slice of light from inside the cabin. He turns away and scurries down the hall, grunts and footfalls chasing close behind.

"He went that way, mates!"

"I want him alive! We need to find the designs!"

Walter thrusts himself onward until he slams into a wall, the train still black as pitch. He palms the wall for a door and, just as the thunderous footfalls resound ever closer, he finds a latch, his palm striking the cold brass of a door handle. Without a moment's hesitation, he thrusts the door open and instinctively jerks it shut behind himself.

Momentum and panic driving him forward, he nearly tips over the rounded railing of the rear observation deck. A cock-up that would result in a quick, tumultuous death.

An arch of color flurries about him when the train screams out of the tunnel. As the world passes in a textured weave of blotted nature, Walter freezes. He's surely caught, what will happen to him? What will happen to the boy? *Oh god, please spare the boy*. He must press on, he must divine a way out of this, even if merely to protect Alger.

Clawing at the railing, he glances over the side of the train. A ladder to the roof looms just beyond his reach. Grunting in disbelief at what he is about to do, Walter hoists himself onto the railing, inhales sharply, and stretches for the ladder. Walter hears voices amidst the cacophony of mechanical sounds bellowing in his ears. The men are already on the observation deck, and he is caught between the railing and the ladder.

"Where is the old arse?" As soon as Walter makes contact with the outer-rung, he squeezes flush against the train and pulls with all his strength, while driving his heel into the railing. The moment his foot breaks contact, he drives his free hand upward and latches onto the inner-rung of the ladder. He plants his feet firmly and, once safely on the ladder, tries to slow his galloping heart, though there is little time for a respite.

An ugly, sneering face rounds the corner; sallow teeth gleaming in the moonlight. The thug thrusts a fist forward triumphantly. "I've got 'im, chaps! The bloke's tryin' to make a darin' getaway on top. You think you're a gymnast, mate?" he jibes in a choppy Northern English accent. "You're supposed to make us all rich as princes, ye old sod." The thug mounts the railing in pursuit and Walter, rote with nausea and fear, makes for the top of the train.

As he clambers over the final rung, he turns back to find the degenerate ever nearer. The man is younger, more agile, and more reckless than he. Walter stumbles atop the train to find himself barely able to stand. Steam billows from the engine up ahead, sending a barrage of volcanic, black smoke into Walter's face. Where shall he go? What has come of the imbibed agent? He throws himself onward with reckless abandon as the degenerate mounts the roof.

"Where'll you go now, mate?" His assailant grins as he sees his comrades climbing the ladder behind him. Walter watches as the thug's body tenses in preparation to lunge. "You're comin' with me." Walter throws himself downward as the thug pounces. Using his lower center of gravity to his advantage, he thrusts his shoulder forward.

Their bodies collide. Walter is knocked onto his back, the thug flung sideways. Walter watches as his adversary plummets to the ground below, shrieking all the way down until he meets with a boulder, his back contorting into a sickening form. He sees the flaccid body tumble to a stop and disappear in the dark of night.

By the time he turns back the remaining two degenerates are upon him, puffing and panting like wild animals. They too, are in a hard fight to find balance on the slick surface.

"There's nowhere to run, doctor." The leader looks left to right emphatically. "Give yourself up or we'll make this all the more painful for you." Walter's mind is ripe with fear now, but the most glaring issue in his mind is that of his grandson. Oh, the dejection. He has allowed his pride and his hunger for knowledge to drive a wedge between the boy and himself. Not only has he endangered Alger's life tonight, but he has thrown the lad's future to the winds of chance, like a bird with a broken wing.

The lead thug grows impatient and flings himself toward Walter, who instantly freezes. There truly is nowhere to go now. He hurls his body sideways to dodge the impending force, but the man is lithe and cunning. As Walter throws a punch, the man retreats, sending Walter spinning upon the driving force of his own botched attack.

He feels his foot catch a steel guard rail and he stumbles backward, driving down with alarming celerity. His hand connects with the outer casement of a passenger's cabin but is unable to grab hold. He hears a howl from above as the ruffian shouts in frustration. It sounds thin, distant, fleeting. In what must be but a couple of seconds, Walter's mind runs rampant with a deluge of thought. The final piercing visage—the only thing he chooses to cling to as his world goes black—is of his grandson, Alger. Of how much he loves him.

Godspeed, dear boy.

I

Theodore loves his little sister. Her candor, her unwavering morality, her affectations that, to anyone who doesn't know her like he does, are as perceivable as teardrops in a rainstorm. He loves how she is the only person he knows that can continue to puzzle him with her discordant traits. A pervasively complex girl, Alice will forever undermine Theodore's ability to predict her next word, or desire, or decision. The only thing Theodore can count on is her knack for locking him in a state of intrigue.

It's a cool, breezy day, and the sun's waxy beams stream through the buildings. All around, countless sets of fire escapes jut out of the tenements, their boxy figures splicing the sun's rays. The lower west side is experiencing its usual bustle of foot traffic, but something feels different about it. Perhaps it's just the feeling Theodore gets when his sister has a new plan—an ambiguous bud of an idea she proposes to him in order to disrupt the typical wheel-spin pattern she finds life takes.

Theodore is hoping that this is the case today, for every time Alice unveils her latest idea, she does it in a way that manages to appear nonchalant yet somehow salient at the same time; a sort of coy dignity. This is the way things have gone for most of their lives.

When they were children, Alice would procure an adventure out of nowhere. Once, she tiptoed into his room, her eyes alight with the spark of a scheme, and ushered him from bed with prodding, beckoning hands. She told him that it's June 1, the first day of summer, and all the fireflies will be out stretching their legs from a long slumber.

His instinct was to tell his little sister that, no, summer doesn't start for another three weeks, silly head. Then he shelved the retort and joined Alice on her adventure. Because whether or not she knew of what she spoke, his little sister always provided an outlet for him; one where the diffident little boy could go out and explore with his sister, utterly free of judgement or deprecation—from others or from within.

Alice is a grown woman now, and the maturation process hasn't done away with this indomitable trait, it's merely fine-tuned it. Every once in a while, she phones dubious Theodore out of the blue. He's already relinquished himself to her game before saying, "Hello."

His prime directive is to meet her in the lobby of The Diluvial at 9AM sharp. He crosses the busy intersection to the rhythm of his own chirping heart and heads for the archaic steel arches of the hotel's entrance. The building, which must have been there since the Golden Age of music, looks both entirely out of place and right at home nudged against two modern skyscrapers—'sky-sores' as Theodore calls them. *The city does have a capricious charm*, Theodore thinks, *with its dizzying patchwork of old and new*.

The game begins once he is inside the foyer. He is to maneuver himself, via 'methods of reconnaissance,' to paraphrase Alice, to the roof where she will be waiting. As he walks through the lobby, feigning his best casual stroll before the receptionist, he thinks about his last meetup with Alice and hopes that this time he won't almost break his neck in the process of finding her.

He pushes the UP button and, after a sonorous chime, he's in the elevator. The pulleys kick into motion with a grating drag and up Theodore goes. He glances around the ornately decorated elevator, smooth jazz tickling his ears, completing the senescent vibe.

The extravagance of hotels brings a peculiarly foreign sensation to

Theodore every time he's in one. The borderline-sycophantic attitude of the staff; the posh, lacquered interiors; the transitory nature of the rooms and the prodigious assortment of guests they entertain through the years. *If walls could talk,* he thinks to himself.

A ding summons his focus and the door opens to the 11th floor; the last stop in the old hotel. He slides out of the box and peers out a window. The view from just over a hundred feet up is less than stellar—*something one has to get used to, living in the city and all*—Theodore thinks. Brown and red splotches of tenements populate the opposite street. A thick copse of street vendors lay in the wide, old street below.

Theodore plunges into the hallway, guest rooms lining the way. He wonders how many people are checked into the hotel right now, how many he is whizzing by as he makes his way to his sister. At one moment, he might be passing by a local couple taking a one-night getaway, the next, a jubilant foreign family ready to submerse themselves in America's finest city. Perhaps he's wandering past a despondent old businessman who never had time, or the opportunity, to find a woman. A river of jittery nerves cascades down his back. He hopes that man won't be him someday. Although he knows if he is to suffer that fate, it won't be at fault of a career that didn't lend itself to a relationship a la the itinerant businessman; it'll be out of his intensely antisocial and innately distrustful ways. He doesn't relish on realizations like this. In fact, he's usually quite adept at batting them away before they're able to form in his mind.

He takes the first right that presents itself to him and comes upon two more guest rooms, a dead end. And a window. *This must be it,* he thinks to himself, but upon peering out, he realizes the image doesn't gel with Alice's description. He turns and continues down the hall until he comes upon another right turn.

This has to be it. He runs his hand under the crack of the slightly agape window. He peers out to the southern skyline, *yes!* Before him lies the distant form of the Empire State Building. At this precise angle, the Art Deco masterpiece is framed cozily by a prodigious rooftop sign that looms in the foreground, just like Alice described. He can't discern from here which sign it is, but it looks like it might be the big wiry boot sign atop the Clemency Shoe Store.

Glancing left, Theodore sucks in a deep breath to steady his nerves. He knows where Alice is now. He's going to have to clamber out onto the roof and take the ladder to the upper tier. *She's got to be on top of the building,* he thinks. *Why would she make it easy for him, after all?*

He yanks on the window. It slides upward against the frame with a clatter. Taking a brief glance behind to check for prying eyes and seeing none, Theodore climbs out onto the building's sub-roof.

He refuses to look towards the street—to gaze downward at all— nevertheless, he succumbs to vertigo instantly. He never relished the idea of following Alice onto the roof of their family's three-story colonial when they were kids; naturally, the roof was her favorite place to be, and her escape when she needed it.

Wind whipping across his torso and funneling through his ears, he turns and fervently grips the ladder.

He makes the climb up a quick one; turns and shields his eyes from the brilliant swathe of sunlight streaming over the rooftops. This high up above the convoluted city streets it's eerily silent; like there's a massive invisible curtain smothering all the street noise. The sweet scent of morning, the swooning whistle of the wind, the buzz from the hotel's massive neon sign compose the only melody playing for him up here. As usual with an Alice-exploit, he's trudged after her with furrowed brows and rolling eyes, but every time he eventually comes around and realizes that she procures something from deep within him that he'd never find without her silly little adventures. Something meaningful. Theodore pauses in a solitary moment of rapture. *This* was the reason to get out of bed today.

"You're late, Bear," a familiar voice simpers across the wind.

Leaning against a crusty old railing is his sister; a smirk on her face, her arms and legs crossed casually. The sun strikes a fine glow on the crest of her face. He glances down.

"You wore a jean-skirt and platforms to climb a building?" Alice doesn't heed his remark. She turns around to face the city.

"It really is amazing up here, Bear." He remembers back when she used to call him Teddy; likes that name better, but whatever Alice wants to call him is fine with him and endearing in its own way.

"I come up here pretty often these days—especially at night. You should see the way 7th Avenue shines after the curtain of dark has taken it. And if you lean, like this—" Alice strangles the railing with coiled fists and stretches over the edge of the building. Theodore feels his heart gyrate a little in dread but leans at a lesser angle to humor his sister. The giant 'T' in The Diluvial's sign is directly below him, and the sequential letters cascade below in a diminishing, and somewhat nauseating, fashion.

"—you can almost see Union Square Park." With the railing pressing into her diaphragm, her voice comes out squeaky. Theodore nods and then pulls away from the rail. Alice looks at him and withdraws from the edge, smiling. "Très magnifique. Does this remind you of when we were kids?"

"Rain or shine, you would always be up on the roof," he says. "If it was especially bad you would curl up under the part of the roof where it jutted out and wait it out in your little nook." Alice knows he's not merely referring to the weather, and her smile fades a little.

"Remember that old phonograph cylinder we found under the porch?" she says. "When we were kids, we didn't know what it was so we would talk into it like a receiver, thinking there was a magical wish granter listening on the other side." Theodore's head rattles up and down. "Do you still have it?"

Theodore digs in the pocket of his hoody. "I've kept it since we moved out." The austere object rolls back and forth in his palm; its chalky sides rubbed raw. "This baby has seen us through some hard times. I keep it with me wherever I go."

They both stare at the cylinder in an ephemeral daze until a discordant chirp rouses Theodore. He glances over at the railing, where an audacious avian friend is perched, squawking and jutting its head about. "So, you just brought me up here for the excellent pigeon-watching opportunity?" He nods to another squadron of birds that brims the corners of the roof, strutting about in layers of white excrement.

"That is precisely why, my dear brother, because you can't quite capture their majesty until you've seen them at their roost; where they ruminate on the important things in life, like which car to shit on next. That is, when they deign not to defecate on their own turf." She rummages around in the back pocket of her jean-skirt and exhumes two white rectangles, which glisten against the day's light.

Train tickets, plane tickets? Theodore peeks closer, but Alice pulls the items to her chest. "You know how I'm always searching for the next *thing*, Bear?"

"Well, I heard it through the grapevine, aka the internet, about this new old trend that's sweeping New York. People are leasing and purchasing these crumbling old buildings—most of which are historic landmarks—and transforming them into these modern speakeasies, 1920's style.

"You just need to have an *in*, like a secret passcode or an association with the owners…sometimes you have to find the bar, which might be hiding behind clever architecture or something like that. Anyways, there's this one bar that I found online that I'm dying to check out. It's this diminutive space they've revitalized on-site called The Cat's Meow, which was a popular speakeasy in the Prohibition Era."

Reading Theodore's quizzical gaze, Alice grabs him by the arm and stares him down fervently. "Now, when I say landmark, I mean that this place was a posh hotel way back in the 18 and 1900s, and it closed down permanently in like, the '40s." Her free arm is waving emphatically; her face brimming with vigor, her eyes emitting the glint they always do when she's excited.

"So those are tickets to this modern speakeasy?" Theodore points. Alice nods her head. "I'm assuming it's a highly exclusive and expensive club.

How did you swing that, sis?" Alice works at an antique and hobby shop in Chelsea called Vincent's Vagaries. Theodore knows she hasn't two dimes to rub together after rent day. Before responding to his question, Alice's expression changes slightly but retains its equanimity.

"You thought I didn't have a rainy-day fund, Bear?" She dangles the two sheets of paper before him. There isn't a thing on them, save for the blotted bruise of an image stamped on each—the figure of a black cat.

"The, uh, the allure of a speakeasy in the '20s was that alcohol was prohibited. People would line up for the chance to share in some bathtub gin, rotgut," Theodore states. "These bars were used for patently illegal activity…is there going to be any, uh, modern contraband substances at The Cat's Meow? Anything that'll get us arrested like they were at the real speakeasies?" At this Alice shakes her head; waltzes over to the ladder. Hiking her skirt, she mounts it and looks up at Theodore.

"The patrons of speakeasies didn't get arrested back in the day, Bear— only the distributors."

II

Theodore views Manhattan, and the people within, in two disparate ways. There is the Manhattan of the day, where the city seems to be in a massive prolonged inhale; a tense period where it says to itself, 'we can do this, we can get through another day.' A congeries of businessmen and women clogs the city's arteries during the day, as do the daily commuters, who stream in from the various other boroughs and adjacent cities to further congest the vast hunk of concrete. During the early hours, he'll see all the buildings on the lower west side throw open their doors almost simultaneously while the delivery trucks pull up to a halt; a cacophony of screeching brakes resounding down the avenue.

The daytime New York is a cyclical, obdurate machine of progress, the cogs comprised of the millions of residents and workers who, in Theodore's eyes, live in such intimate quarters—quite literally on top of one another—and yet know nothing about each other. Nobody bothers to stop for a moment and immerse themselves in the life of another; a clustered disconnect where time is money, and money is king.

Then, there is the Manhattan of the night. The sun sets, and it always seems to set early in the city—dipping beneath the massive sky-sores and throwing a latticework of twilight down on the streets—a network of yellow squares and rectangles pop into life all around. And the city seems to exhale, expunging the toxins of the day and breathing new life into itself. It's this part of the Manhattan cycle that Theodore admires. The transformation the city undergoes after dark is inimitable. No other place on earth comes alive in quite the same way.

When the hot glare of fluorescent lights bathes the city, a different breed of New Yorker comes out. The intrepid, curious, sociable citizens bust through the woodwork and mingle together in the corners and alcoves; in the dizzying stillness of the tallest towers, and the cramped, clammy cellars below. But despite the apparent social intimacy of parties and clubs, Theodore believes that most people become too blinded by their own insecurities and fears, and guard themselves—as in the masquerade balls of old; only the masks today are figurative and literally skin-deep.

The only thing similar between the two faces of the city, Theodore thinks, is that in each situation people coexist side by side and yet learn nothing about one another, even despite the velvety charms of the city after dark. Sure, an over-stressed pre-med student might take to the city on the weekends to unwind and find a loose drunk girl to fuck, but will he be there when she wakes up the next morning? Will they have gained anything from the ephemeral interaction besides a few moments of awkward, drunken bliss; perhaps a peculiar looking rash that doesn't go away the next week? No, Theodore is obstinate that very few meaningful and lasting interactions happen in the Big Apple.

Theodore knows that he is perhaps too guarded—life has taught him to be so, but he's certain he's better off this way. People cannot be trusted. Except for his little sister, Alice. Mercurial as she may be, she's always there for Theodore. Her love for him is perhaps her only true constant in life.

He watches her as she meanders along the gritty edge of the curb ahead. Being with her these days just reminds him that she's an adult now, in her early 20s, and capricious as she is, she may not stick around the city for much longer now. How long can an intelligent young woman stay working at Vincent's Vagaries? An antique hobby shop can only hold its eccentric allure for so long, especially when it procures a trifle over minimum wage. He may lose his safety blanket to the world at any time now and be utterly alone, seeing as mom and dad are certainly no longer an option for solace. Hell, they never were.

"C'mon, Bear!" Alice calls, fruitlessly competing against the beehive-drone of the cars. Much to Theodore's surprise, Alice is clear across the street now, locking arms with a street sign and doing that upward blowing thing girls do when their bangs fall in their face. She's on the corner of 32nd and 6th, and the greasy beams of the sun are long gone. The city has been consumed by a placid breeze, which espouses the glow of the countless apartment lights to make for a rich and warm atmosphere.

As much as he hates the prospect of socializing with random barflies, Theodore entertains the notion that tonight might be fun. He can feel a tense bundle of excitement build in his stomach. Having an archaic substructure, the city holds many hidden gems in its bowels, and a resuscitated speakeasy will certainly be one to knock off his list.

Alice leads him down several more blocks, until the vertical sprawl gradates into a pit of clustered brick buildings. *New and old, nudging shoulders in the battle for space*, thinks Theodore. Up ahead, his intrepid sister seems nearly to be volleying over expanses of sidewalk; so sure, of herself, and where she is going.

Unaccustomed to peering straight ahead and not down at his loafers while he walks is an exercise in overcoming his entrenched habits of avoidance. He needs to stay in the moment, though, needs to follow his sister. Lewis Carroll got it wrong; Alice is the rabbit, and she is leading him down the hole. *Theodore in Wonderland*, he thinks.

In this section of the city everything feels condensed and packed, like one giant vacuum seal has been placed upon it. Alleyways coil off to the sides of many buildings here; their breadth obscured by the multitude of clothes lines, AC units, and dumpsters that pervade them.

A sense of mystery and intrigue abounds here; a sense that each building harvests the spirits of all who have dwelled within over the years, locking up their secrets and promises—their hopes and fears alike—covering them up with another peel of paint, another layer of mortar and brick, until all that is visible is the ambiguous outer shell that Theodore sees now.

He glances down a side street and sees an apartment building tucked away. Signs of life riddle the windows—shampoo bottles, potted plants—little cues that yes, somebody does live here. Back in that dingy alley, which seems nearly to contract from the titanic city streets, somebody lives there; with probably nothing more than 400 square feet to their name. The congested lifestyle of the city both repulses and intrigues Theodore.

The number of random passersby has attenuated since Theodore and Alice left the financial district, but they aren't in one of the demure and seemingly abandoned family neighborhoods. The occasional group floats past, the men looking opulent in a somewhat rugged, old fashioned way; the women, wearing dresses and skirts of all lengths and levels of discretion. A tangled bramble of figures lines the opposite corner of the street where a saloon-style bar lies, its swinging doors hawing at the sidewalk every time people enter.

"Is that it?" Theodore raises his arm, the sleeve of his slightly oversized hoodie peeling back as he does.

"Really, Bear?" Alice puts her hands on her waist and cocks her hip to the side like she tends to do when pondering Theodore's sensibilities. "A super-exclusive, clandestine speakeasy bar, and they chose to erect it near a patently accessible intersection?" Theodore shrugs. "No, silly, but I think I've found it."

Alice steps off the sidewalk, down a small flight of stairs, and into a narrow walkway that hugs a gaunt brick building. It's one of those buildings that screams old, with peeling strips of mortar surrounding bricks that, even in the evanescing light, show the lashes the sun's given it over the years.

Theodore takes note of the basilic, heavily ornamented entryway. Whatever this building was it was built in a time when craftsmanship was authentic, and structures entirely manmade. *Buildings had character back then*, Theodore thinks, *something this one exudes.*

Alice is up ahead, about midway along the structure, when she pauses. "Look at this, Bear!" She's standing in front of a vintage sign printed on the wall. Chalky and eroded, the sign reads, *Harold's Antiques*. With a look of exaltation on her face, Alice pats Theodore on the back. "We've found it."

"An old sign on an even older building?"

"Yes, to the untrained eye." She begins fondling the brick, her fingers poking and pressing in the grooves like the legs of an insect trying to find a spot to squeeze in.

"But one of these bricks is the key to getting in." She strokes the length of one of the bricks filling out the 'E' in *Antiques* and pauses. The brick looks out of place, with a slightly lighter hue than the surrounding ones. Alice begins to press at one end of the anomalous brick while tugging on the other. The displacement comes with little effort, Theodore notes as he hovers above, scratching his head.

When the loosened brick is fully in her hand, Alice stands and promptly walks to the back of the old building to a spot that is testament to just how archaic the structure is. Standing probably 12-feet high and nearly as wide is an industrial barn-style door. Some of the older structures in lower Manhattan still have these ponderous sliding metal doors, which were built to accommodate horses and old factory cars.

Adjacent to the door is an installation that looks like a mail slot, but with a stout, rectangular opening. The material patently mocks that of the door beside it, and Theodore divines that it's a modern addition that's meant to blend right in. Seeming to have expected each of these peculiar steps, Alice lines up the brick with the slot and, with a coarse, clacking sound, jams it in until it comes to a stop.

Akin to a Hollywood movie where the intrepid underground explorers open the door to an ancient tomb, both Alice and Theodore step back apprehensively. A slosh of mechanical whirring stirs from behind the prodigious door, which then slides open on its rack with an abhorrent grinding noise. *Whoever revitalized this speakeasy certainly had a taste for the theatrical,* Theodore thinks.

He looks at Alice, bewildered and somewhat ecstatic, his heart in his throat. For several seconds after the door opens neither he nor Alice move, they simply hold each other's gaze; on her face, a brilliant pout of self-approval. Peering into the chamber, all he can see through a swathe of black is the flicker of a hallway light.

"We did it, Bear," she says as she steps inside.

"Be careful, Alice!" he urges. "How did you hear of this place again?"

"I...have my social circles online." Inside, her voice produces a hollow echo as if she's in a wartime bunker. "C'mon, Bear, it must be down here."

Reluctantly, Theodore follows. It's gloomy inside and the smell of old pervades the space. Directly ahead is a catacomb-like descent, at the bottom of which is a light fixture emitting a murky hue. This bounces from the hallway up to Theodore and, judging from the meager glow, he is in what used to be a sort of horse stable. *This expounds the existence of the odd door,* he thinks.

They move down the passageway, surrounded by pulverulent brick, and stop at a metal door with a rust-chewed sliding door viewer. *These were common additions to speakeasies in the '20s—this one's probably a relic from the original bar,* Theodore thinks. Alice turns back with a look that doesn't mirror his apprehension—she's practically beaming. He just shrugs. She bangs on the door, a cacophony of duplicate sounds echoing around them.

"Are we sure we haven't stumbled upon a launderer of some sort?" he asks as they wait. "This whole situation is drenched in such an aroma."

"Nonsense, Bear. But, wouldn't that be exciting, too?" Theodore entertains an acute sense of dread right as the door viewer slides open.

A hammy, faux-Jersey accent emanates through the viewer, "State the birth name and pseudonym of alleged child killer who served as hitman under Dutch Shultz during the prohibition." From behind the gatekeeper bleeds the melody of an old jazz song, which sounds dissonant and warbled as it splashes around the stairway.

Al Capone, also probably known as, Allen Capone? Theodore thinks to himself, conceding that his knowledge of old school mobsters is scant at best.

"Mad Dog Coll, aka, Uinseann Ó Colla." Alice crosses her arms and smirks.

"Right on the money, doll face," the already insufferable gatekeeper says, and with a simple click of the latch, the door swings open. While this guy isn't equipped with the most convincing accent, Theodore takes one glance at his outfit and is more than mildly impressed.

Before him stands a man in a double-breasted Chesterfield, which is unfastened to display a vintage vest. It's not one of the austere, chunky-hemmed old-timey vests, but an opulent, ornately designed number that has the gleam of silk or satin. The outfit is complete with dress pants that match the coat, as well as a pair of polished loafers below.

"Entrez-vous," the man practices a foreign dialect this time, failing thoroughly. He then tips his bowler cap to Theodore and Alice, replacing it at a rakish angle on his head, and promptly moves past them and up the stairs. Theodore catches the door.

"Where do you think he's off to?" Alice asks.

"Probably replacing that brick up there so no one else can get in." Theodore smiles and shakes his head.

They enter what looks like a pantry; mismatched shelves zig zag along the walls holding fusty old bottles of liquor. On one shelf is an empty bottle with a decaying label that reads, *Bathtub Gin.* Next to it, a bottle of *Mitchell & Son-Old Irish Whiskey.* Alice points at it.

"These are probably authentic. That bottle might be from early prohibition era, when the Irish gangs ruled distribution." The music croons ever louder now, a rustic wooden door barely containing the intrepid notes.

"When was the last time you went to a bar, Bear?"

"When was the Louisiana Purchase?"

"Stop it," she jibes and knocks him on the shoulder, the commotion teasing his old keepsake out of his back pocket. He pivots and catches the phonograph cylinder just before it collides with the stone floor.

"You brought the gramophone cylinder with you to the bar?" she asks.

"Mhm."

"There's an old gramophone that showed up at my antique store recently. I think it's one of the rare ones that takes cylinders instead of records. We should play that thing sometime and finally hear what it has to say."

Alice throws the door against its hinges. When Theodore sees the bar, he has to retrieve his jaw from beneath him. The walls look they were ripped from a grand hotel, one far more ornate than The Diluvial where he met Alice yesterday—maybe even more so than those in the famed Plaza Hotel. Egg-shell white mingles splendidly with golden accents and warm, moody lighting. Theodore finds his eyes drawn to the back wall, where an old-fashioned bar sits square and proud; a rustic anomaly among the opulence. Hanging above the bar is a neon sign that reads, The Cat's Meow.

"That bar has got to be original," Theodore says, but Alice is already out of earshot. She's making strides toward the back of the room, taking it all in like a glassy-eyed plunderer in a cavern of stashed gold. Strewn around the bar are patrons of varying styles and cultures.

To the right in the surprisingly capacious bar is a man that, perhaps if he were simply strolling about the city and not in a period-themed bar, would be a novel 19th century anachronism. A spindly mustache adorns his gaunt face underneath a top hat and a monocle, the latter of which has to be for show. *Hell, the whole outfit must be.*

A tailored vest and vintage dress shirt make up his torso, and his pinstriped pants hug a pair of glimmering dress shoes. He's in contention with one of the bar's structural pillars, leaning against it with one tensed forearm as he sweet talks a couple of lavishly dressed dames who also look like they were ripped out of a different time period.

To Theodore, the man's attempt at a nonchalant appearance makes his social anxiety even more obvious. The ladies address him with eyes that are far from steamy—tepid, perhaps. *Better step up your flirting game, sir,* Theodore chuckles to himself.

On the bar's left is a gathering of similarly dressed individuals. *These people are proficient at the game of dress-u*p, he thinks, glancing down at himself and shrugging at his own patently casual attire. In front of the bar is the room's largest swelling of bodies. People line the antique booth, some of them making drunken howls to the bartender, who has a surprisingly calm face amidst the squall as he twirls a shaker about.

Theodore catches up to his sister, who is already mingling with a group of strangers—something that would take a cyclopean chunk of courage for Theodore to do but is, of course, second nature to his little sis.

"Bear, isn't this great?" She pulls him by the arm and has to drag him into the social circle, where he is handed a hefty vintage schooner. Inside the mug sloshes a generous helping of clear liquid.

"What's in it?" he asks.

"Gin," replies Alice. Theodore sniffs at the rim, the familiar pungent scent caressing his olfactory. One more sniff. He detects something else mingling with the piney aroma that he can't put his finger on. He takes a sip.

"Well, bathtub gin," expounds Alice, nearly causing Theodore to discharge his mouthful over the crowd. "I guess this guy makes his own bathtub gin, like they did in prohibition days." She points to a tall, ginger-bearded bundle of man standing opposite them in the circle.

The acrid liquor is akin to tap water thinly sprinkled with grain and mixed with a discordant jumble of flavors that results in an overly flat, plain taste. Noticing Theodore's reaction Alice puts a hand on his arm, laughing.

"It's not actually made in his bathtub, Bear. You can do it in large mason jars or metal vats, and it's a rather simple recipe. How do you do it again, Francis?"

"I use high quality water—usually distilled—but at least filtered. I blend it with fermenting sugar and grain in these massive jars, throw in a juniper berry mix and some other flavors, and let it do its thing for a couple weeks.

It's a large-batch stilling concept that mobsters used back in the prohibition days when they needed to keep things on the down-low, brewing all this stuff up in dank cellars and basements with whatever they could get their hands on.

"From there, they would distribute all over, largely to speakeasies like this," he raises his tree-trunk arms and turns his head from side to side emphatically. "Where people would consume even the most ill-prepared liquor just to get hammered and party. So, I'm just trying to emulate that process. Pretty cool, huh?"

Juniper berry mix, *eh? This guy's a winner.* Theodore nods in feigned solidarity and turns to Alice. "I'm gonna go find some real alcohol," he whispers to her, his voice swallowed by the surrounding din before it even escapes his mouth. Alice nods and smiles, then continues talking with a girl wearing a sparkling tiara and a mock flapper-girl dress.

As he weaves toward the bar, Theodore catches an evolving swatch of phrases, little pockets of conversation buzzing about him. A gaggle of girls squeal that, "This place is too cool—the décor is out of this world," and that "It's the most happening place in New York right now," as he passes by. To Theodore, the singular attractive thing about this establishment is the fact that this very space was once an actual speakeasy, many decades ago.

The patronage that had been swarming the bar upon his arrival has dwindled now, with most of the guests gathering in the center of the room where a gramophone with a tulip-shaped horn—probably antique—has been modified and rigged to a modern P.A. system. The gramophone is blaring the rich, splashy tones of a Glenn Miller swing, only this reproduction of the song *In the Mood* is drowned in gaudy, modernized synth, with a heavy drumbeat and layers of post-production muddling it nearly beyond recognition.

Theodore listens to vintage tunes often, and he believes in respecting the classics. *There's nothing more sacrilegious than pitting a monolith like Bach against the electronic keyboard,* he thinks to himself.

He angles himself against the corner of the bar and glances down the lengthy stretch to the other end. It's a coarse, ragged stretch of wood, adorned with weary lines, like pinstripes on a faded suit. The bar itself is certainly the oldest item in The Cat's Meow—splayed knuckles of wood line its edge, the victim of a century's worth of imbibed patrons.

Up above, the silhouettes of countless liquor bottles dance before an intricately backlit cabinet, parts of which may also be original. Theodore flags down the bartender and on the third try succeeds in drawing his attention.

"Old Fashioned, please, and with the sourest of your bourbons." The bartender smiles. "Comin' up, mon Frère." Like the doorman, he too thinks he's bilingual. The Old Fashioned is a simple cocktail and Theodore's go-to drink when he finds himself at a bar, which is by all means an infrequent occurrence.

He watches as the bartender splashes the ice with sugar, kneels some whiskey into the shaker, followed by a jigger of bitters, shakes the mixture, and then transfers it to a fresh glass, grating a thin slice of orange peel onto the pillow of ice.

Good, Theodore thinks, *he made an Old Fashioned the old-fashioned way*. He unfolds what he believes to be an egregious amount of money for a shot of whiskey and hands it to the man. He gives him a little something extra for making the drink right, followed by a nod, and then turns his back to the bar to watch the onslaught of socialites do their thing.

"Are you alone tonight, honey?" A woman creeps up on his left, her elbow trundling across the uneven promontories of the bar. Her eyes are glassy and unfocused. Theodore stiffens reactively.

"Oh, no, I uh..." He scans The Cat's Meow for his sister, and in the swish and swirl of bodies before him, it takes a moment to pinpoint Alice. She's toward the front of the room now, dancing closely with a strange man. Under the diaphanous glow of the bar lights, Alice looks like an angel and, for a moment, he just watches her dance. She's twirling, dipping, laughing and twirling again. His baby sis has grown up so fast, and he's proud of the woman she's become.

"I'm with her." He points Alice out to the tipsy woman. As she spins,

Alice notices Theodore talking with a stranger and winks at him. He knows she's aware of how introverted he can be, but unfortunately, Theodore isn't exactly in the mood to make small talk in a room where even a shout won't rise above the squall. Hell, Theodore knows that even in a room so quiet you can hear the next-door neighbor shit, he doesn't like to engage in idle chatter.

"Oh, she's very pretty," the woman stumbles over her own drunken tongue. Theodore's face turns ruddy with embarrassment.

"Oh, I'm not with her, she's my sister."

"Oh, how fortui-for-fortuity for us. Wanna make out, cowboy?" She hiccups. Annoyed by the garish bluntness of the request, Theodore doesn't respond. He glances right and, tucked away near the corner of the bar, he sees the entrance to a second room that he hadn't yet noticed, and the oddest sensation strikes him.

All he sees is an unassuming doorway, with perhaps a second, more intimate bar, not unlike the ones Theodore has seen in Greenwich Village, waiting on the other side. But he feels he recognizes this scene, and in a deeply embedded way. It's the same feeling he assumes one gets when returning to their childhood home—an intense familiarity despite the changes that have occurred in one's absence. Somehow, that intoxicating sense of déjà vu powers through any temporal perspective, like the augering forces of water through a canyon.

"Um, thanks, but I have somewhere I have to be." His lame excuse doesn't bother him seeing as the girl's probably buzzed enough not to process incoherent thoughts, let alone articulate ones. He slips away and heads for the mysterious back room, partly as an escape from the obnoxious woman, and partly to satiate this curious hunger to be in there.

Inside is a narrow walkway with a musty basement smell. Black and white photos line the walls in what must be the designer's tribute to prohibition-day speakeasies. Theodore glances at a picture of a lavish ballroom riddled with opulently dressed men and women scuttling about the dance floor. The caption reads:

April 22nd, 1920.
Opening Night at The Growler's Ball

Continuing down the hall, he sees a photo of a small rustic bar accommodating several men in matching suits; some propped on barstools and some standing tall with an unveiled air of masculine vanity and pride. The minatory brood are all clutching Thompson machine guns in one hand and stubby cigars in the other, and half of them have their feet propped in a declamatory pose on wooden shipping crates.

The caption to this photo reads:

November 2nd, 1922.
The Cat's Meow's first shipment.

Astonishing. This photo shows what the original bar looked like, which is nothing less than a great visual disparity to the rebranded bar behind him.

One of the last photos on the right on the hall catches Theodore's eye. A richly adorned ballroom is riddled with old-timey folk just as in the other photos, but these patrons are far more decadently dressed and aristocratic in appearance than those in the other images. They're all facing forward in an impressive bunch and smiling to the camera. The peculiarity that caught Theodore's eye is that, in what makes for a thoroughly equivocal and intriguing scene, everyone is wearing a mask of some sort.

Some of the masks are tall and grand, some of them pinched and scantily-adorned. Each and every one of them is a depiction of a wild animal. A slight, oblong man stands front and center with a glass of some effervescing liquid held high in a toast. He's wearing a rat mask that covers the top half of his face. The bottom half is contorted in a massive, crooked grin.

Theodore steps back and regards the peculiar image from afar. The individual components of the image are creepy and unsettling, but the gestalt of the entire scene is downright eerie.

The caption on this photo reads:

December 14th, 1931.
Masquerade Ball at The King's Inn.

As he examines the image, something in the far-left corner of it catches his eye, something that is rather unfitting and, frankly, impossible given the picture's date. Standing towards the very back of the toasting crowd is a slender figure who is wearing a long-sleeved hoodie—one that, in the chalky grain of the old image, looks identical to Theodore's. As his eyes trail upward, his heart thrums in his chest.

The figure in the hoodie is the only one in the room not wearing a mask and, completing the bleeding anachronism, the face above the hoodie looks exactly like Theodore. His heart feels like it has dropped to his balls and then bounced upward.

He squints, shakes his head and squeezes his eyes shut, but when he reopens them, the image of Theodore is still there; pallid, ghastly, and unsmiling. Being that mini-Theodore is so far in the back of what is already a small and faded old picture, it might be a challenge for someone else to deduce that it's certainly him, but one knows oneself better than anyone else. To him, the likeness is beyond that of doppelgängers or chance similar physiognomies.

Fumbling for thoughts after what he has seen is like trying to clamp down a clumsy fist on a slippery eel, but Theodore attempts anyway. How could he be in a picture at some weird masquerade party that he has no memory of attending? Moreover, how could he be in a photo that looks like it was taken in the days when silent film was a nascent industry? The picture was certainly taken long before he was born, long before even his parents were born. Could it be one of his grandfathers? When he was a kid, his officious aunt Silvia, the family chronicler, loved shoving myriad archived photos in his face, like an overeager ticket scalper with a stack of brochures. To his recollection, none of his deceased relatives looked much like him at a young age.

Theodore stares with dubious wonder at the photo, and the longer he stares, the more confused he becomes. He wants to storm down the hall, wrench Alice from that clown with whom she's dancing, and ask if she's ever taken him to a themed party, one at which they ingested a handful of whatever kids use these days to give their cognizance the old heave-ho.

He's one second away from turning on his heels and inquiring to Alice when something peculiar catches his eye—the glint of brass coming from the room at the end of the hall. He feels another pang of déjà vu like he did upon first seeing the secret hallway. Only this time it's stronger, and the immediacy of the sensation is profound. He walks through the open doorway at the end of the hall and finds himself in another bar.

It could be an extension of The Cat's Meow, but this one looks nothing like it. It's tiny and old; the kind of place where Theodore knows he's surrounded by generations of static memories. *If walls could talk*, Theodore thinks once more, looking at the chewed brick hull that surrounds him.

A disheveled and thoroughly inebriated couple stumbles off a barstool and brushes past Theodore, clearly irked by his presence in the otherwise abandoned grotto. He doesn't take heed, though. He's busy gazing around the room in awe of the treasure trove into which he has stumbled. This looks precisely like the bar in the old picture of The Cat's Meow.

And to the left of the bar is the item that drew his eye. Upon a scrappy wooden table is the most beautiful and aberrant-looking gramophone he has ever seen. He straightens his hoodie and tussles his hair. He hasn't seen too many of these, maybe a few on the internet, but this one is unique. It's somewhat analogous to the archaic Edison phonographs, the ones which used cylinders to record and reproduce sound, but it's far more intricate in design than any of the old phonographs Theodore has seen.

It's like an authentic, real world representation of...what is it that young people are so obsessed with these days, Steampunk? That tangent of science fiction that meshes Victorian England style with the steam-powered, brass-cog motifs of the industrial revolution? This gramophone has those features in spades; except for any smoky emissions, although by the looks of it, he wouldn't be surprised if he turned the rig on and it began billowing clouds of cancerous byproduct.

An ornately designed wooden box sits at the base of the antique. Above the wooden housing is a latticework of brass and copper, which serve as mechanical arms of some sort, and are attached at the joints by little cogwheels. Right at the heart of this engineering is a contraption consisting of bolts and clamps, and a narrow cylinder that's meant to fit a phonograph record like a glove.

Hovering over the cylinder is a smudged chrome stylus which has been filed down to a diminutive needle. The sheer technical prowess required for such small-scale craftsmanship is alarming. Attached to this stylus is a cyclopean bell meant for amplifying the sound. This bell is a rich, reflective brass, shaped like the neck of a swan that tried to swallow a traffic cone.

Towards the bottom of the mechanical workings is a cluster of circular dials, like the ones on a modern padlock, only these aren't strictly numerical digits used as a passcode, but they come together to form a specific date. Theodore squints and leans in. The first and largest dial reads: Dec. The second: 14th, the third: 19, with the fourth and fifth completing the number 31. December 14th, 1931.

It's the exact same date as the masquerade ball photo in the hallway. Could this device be somehow linked to that event? He receives yet another silvery finger of nostalgia at the back of his head, this one more potent than either of the previous zaps of déjà vu. It's as if he's become a lightning rod for arbitrary memories, perhaps someone else's, and these things are just jettisoning down from the sky. Only they have no visual representation in his mind as memories would; they're more of an intractable feeling—like instincts.

For all he knows, he's receiving some kind of ambiguous portent—a harbinger, should he proceed, for dangers to come. He's always thought he had a keen sense of intuition. And this sense is telling him to push on, to poke and prod this machine until it spills its secrets like an open diary.

Theodore's fingers grope for his and Alice's old keepsake that's been poking at his ass the whole night. Ever since they learned their discovery was more than just a toy, rather a musical relic from bygone days, he's wondered what it would play, should he ever find the proper device to play it. Alice is right: they should finally listen to whatever song it has to sing.

He glances behind himself to make sure he's still alone and unsheathes the old cylinder record, as one would an ancient scroll on a salient archeological dig. Theodore unlatches a copper seal and then slides the cylinder over the matching tube on the gramophone, returning the seal to its place.

Knowing that he is improvising his handling of the device, he reaches for a brass handle, which goosenecks out of the box's side. He begins gently nudging the aged mechanism into action. At first the crank voices it's disapproval in dissonant metallic groans, and then, as a car engine distributes oil from the pan, it begins to acquiesce and smooth out.

The lever becomes more resistive to the spooling. Theodore hears a mechanical click and the record begins spinning. Off to the side, the lever arm begins trundling through its revolutions opposite the direction he cranked it.

He moves the needle over the cylinder's surface, a cacophony of warbled static bellowing from the device's horn. He steps to the side of the device, lifts the needle, and rubs his traumatized ears. At least he knows the gramophone's operational. Before the spring fully unwinds itself, he scoops up the needle once more and fumbles it into the groove at the left end of the cylinder.

It's an odd feeling Theodore entertains when the record begins to play. All these years and the secret hidden inside this delicate item is about to be divulged to him. There's something equivocally creepy about listening to music from the jazz age in the shadowy corner of an unfamiliar room, all by himself. But the urge to hear it compels him beyond any prohibiting instinct.

He hears a minatory, brooding scratch of notes on a violin as the intro unfurls. The instrument, which sounds like it's playing in a room walled with tin scraps, ascends a scale, leading to a melody break where an accompanying guitar joins in. As the song swells into life, something inexplicable occurs. Theodore feels the hairs on the back of his neck prick up, his hoodie begins to flap like a curtain in a gale. He can feel the blood in his veins stanch and then gather, as if he's plummeting downward faster than his body can react.

The world around shimmers and then peels away into splintered light, evanescing into a hushed glow, like a movie theater when the house lights go down. Directly in front of the gramophone's horn is a vacillating slit of light through which a hazy image appears. The slit increases in size, pulling at the world and sucking it in, like a virulent tear in the very fabric of time and space. Theodore yelps—his legs driving forward against the vortex. His feet scramble to find the floor that's now somehow eluding him, but the soles of his shoes only kiss the air as he tries to backpedal.

He flails his arms, hoping they'll find a solid overhang—anything to pry him from the gaping maw in front of him—but every attempt to escape is thwarted by the power of whatever's sucking him in. Suddenly, as the flaps of his oversized hoodie nearly graze the opening, he plummets, his feet finally finding purchase on the ground. The gale created by the rift settles into a placid vacuum of air that's now only nuzzling him.

The sound of the old record is the only fragment of the world that remains mostly intact, although it too, is altered. The violin sweeps in interminable notes, the guitar's strumming slowed to a discordant drag of vibrations. The gash in spacetime that pulses before Theodore widens and, in what is the most curious development, he can discern familiar objects in the image inside it. It's like peering through a window into another world. Where he was panic-stricken a moment ago, seeing this makes him one big, bundle of curiosity.

He leans forward to see red walls and ornate decorations through the amorphous slit, which begins to widen, allowing for a better scope of the scene. Then it puckers, condensing until he can see nothing of the other side. The familiar fingers of apprehension poke at the back of his mind as he stands at the precipice of choice. Now that he's no longer being sucked toward the rift, he can choose to turn and walk away. Which would be embracing safety and familiarity. But for the first time in his life, Theodore chooses to engage. He chooses opportunity over safety, action over inaction, possibility over circumspection. He sucks in a shaky breath and steps forward. The mysterious tear stretches to accommodate him, as if beckoning him inside.

Theodore reaches for the tear with wide eyes and a thrashing heart. He steps forth and enters the transitory slit that's decanting his world into another.

III

With a buzz that sounds like the flapping wings of a million hummingbirds, Theodore is wrenched off his feet. In what is likely no more than a fugacious snap of a finger, but feels like a sprawling ocean of time, gravity attenuates, and then releases him entirely. He feels his insides begin to curl and twist as he is thrust forward by an unseen force. His limbs raise and hang in midair like those of an astronaut in space.

He is a minuscule object, neither flying nor falling, but simply watching as space and time unravels before him in an unrelenting wave of energy. Just when he feels as though his eyes might pop and his face might cave in under the pressure, he feels the soft tug of gravity again. The sensation of weight returns to his limbs—thousands of tiny beads of energy poke at his skin and then travel inward, infusing his bones and wrenching him downward.

The dizzying maelstrom of air surrounding him slows, pooling about him in a drowsy exhale. The fuzziness of his surroundings sharpens, blooming into reality; blobs of color solidify into people and based on his trajectory, Theodore is headed straight for one of them.

A lavishly dressed old woman is standing with her back to the portal through which Theodore is entering. She's wearing a black evening dress over which rests a prodigious pearl necklace. Her hand is cocked elegantly to the side and is tenuously balancing a cigarette; only, it's not the short cigarette

Theodore is accustomed to seeing. Instead, it is attached to a long holder, the end billowing smoke gently.

As Theodore is thrown into this mysterious dream world, he finds a footing, but too late. He stumbles, loses balance, and collides with the woman, nearly knocking the cigarette out of her gloved hand.

"My word!" the lady stammers in a thick British accent. As she turns to face him, Theodore expects to see a flustered old face, riddled with wrinkles and age spots, but instead, he comes face to beak with a raven. The old lady is wearing a party mask. In the shadows of the eye cutouts, he can see two beady lumps of coal staring at him in surprise, the whites of her eyes effulgent against the deep black of her mask.

Networks of red veins crawl their way to her irises, completing her minatory appearance. She looks like something out of a post-Edwardian nightmare. Theodore can smell the sweetness of gin and vermouth on her breath as she stares him down.

"Who are you child, and what in the name of Baphomet are you wearing?" She looks him up and down.

"I—uh..." Theodore searches for his tongue.

"I haven't the time for you and your nascent social graces, young one, my cigarette is burning right down to the filter as your words dither about in your mouth." A row of crooked, greasy teeth gleam as she talks. She takes a pull of her cigarette, chews on the smoke like a rabbit devouring its roughage, and then blows it out in his face. "There are unused accessories in the coat room. I suggest you equip yourself and move along."

The raven-woman nods to the foyer and turns away, patently uninterested in talking further with Theodore. Suffused with dubious wonder by what's happening to him, Theodore pivots to face the portal that somehow got him here, and finds it gone. There's nothing before him aside from a cushy, gaudily upholstered chair and a wooden table. Whatever it was that brought him here has vanished just as quickly as it came.

Theodore shakes his head, wondering if he is in a dream; wondering if the whole night was just a dream, but as he lingers at the spot where the portal dropped him off, he can hear a faint reflection of noise. He leans in closer, but the sound doesn't get any louder, as it's not so much coming from somewhere in the physical world, instead, it seems to be originating in his own head.

Concentrating, he can hear the scratch of a violin and the strum of a guitar. It's the same song that his record played when he put it in the gramophone. A voice starts crooning in a low but reverberating moan, as if it's coming from underwater. Theodore has trouble deciphering anything more, as the sound begins to attenuate into nothingness.

Am I dreaming? he thinks to himself. *I have to be dreaming.* He decides to take the raven-woman's advice and wanders down the extravagant hall to the coat room. Streaming from a nearby room is the din of live music—big band swing, by the sounds of it—and the cyclopean drone of dozens of voices.

He leans into the fusty old room, where he sees a plethora of vintage suitcoats lining both walls. These coats are analogous to the ones he saw people wearing at The Cat's Meow, only they aren't blatantly apocryphal like the posers' back in the real world, they seem somehow to be authentic. It reminds Theodore of the time his dad took him up to their creaky old attic and showed him his great-grandfather's war equipment. The authenticity of the items was apparent in the mere observation of their appearance.

He shoulders into the back of the room where there's a box brimming with various masks and accessories, but just before he grabs the ugly ghoul mask that sits atop the bunch, he feels a hard squeeze on his arm.

"What are you dithering about in the closet for, lad?" He turns to see a portly man in a red tailcoat and a pig mask staring him down. The man's eyes are piercing, bleak orbs. Bushy eyebrows encroach on the edges of the eyeholes as he frowns. "Why, didn't you hear? They are on the verge of announcing the next Shibboleth."

"Alright, just let me grab—"

"There's no time, Yank, lest you miss it," the pig-man says in crisp, eloquent English, yanking Theodore out of the closet. The two of them funnel into the neighboring room with a string of stragglers that are also rushing forth. Theodore begins to feel naked as he glances around to see that everyone else is equipped with a party mask.

A frightening fervency abounds amongst the gathering group. Theodore can sense this mounting energy, like he's tailing the charge of a horde of rabid animals that just caught the scent of a carcass. He looks around once more and sees a cat, a fox, a rabbit, and a hen, noting that within each veil gleams a pair of cold eyes and under those only covering half the face, a wide, covetous grin.

Opulent, archaic fashion suffuses the scene. He's in a hotel of some sort, this much he can tell. The group of stragglers march past a room with checkered tile and an elevator system whose cogs, levers, and brass remind him of the antiquity of the gramophone back at the bar. He thinks about Alice at The Cat's Meow and an inchoate sense of worry overtakes him. Theodore knows that she's as independent a girl as they come, and yet he never can help but feel concerned for her at all times.

The elevator room has a lift operator like they do in the old movies Theodore's watched; the ones who open the gate for guests and pull the enormous lever inside to move the contraption. Theodore does a double take as the crowd nudges forward. The operator isn't wearing a mask like everyone else, but he is sporting a crisp red and white suit. He's just standing there beside the elevator gate with his hands behind his back, watching the denizens push through the hall, like blood navigating an artery.

They dive into a narrow hallway where other stragglers lounge about. Men in rat masks wearing black and white-pinstripe suits sit with one leg crossed over the other, while ladies in flapper style dresses and mouse masks dance before them—or in some instances, on top of them.

Outliers in Theodore's crowd motion to the rats and mice, hoisting them from their plaid-backed chairs and remarking, "The Shibboleth!" and, "It's time, it's time!" Everybody here has three things Theodore finds himself lacking; a mask, a proper British accent, and a salacity to see what the new news is. Theodore is still reeling from the confusion of this place, which he thinks is bizarre enough to be a *Twilight Zone* spinoff.

The congested crowd pushes through the hallway, moving past a gold-plated sign that reads, *Regal Ballroom*. They fan out into an aurora of twinkling lights and glistening walls. The ceiling soars far over Theodore's head, laying anchor to several crystal chandeliers, which reflect light across the ballroom in a dizzying array of kaleidoscopic shapes. He has never in his life seen such decadence, such glamour.

On the bandstand is an orchestra replete with every traditional instrument Theodore knows of, and an early iteration of swing is the music of choice. Through the thick, smoke-laden air he can see a line of trumpeters wailing on their glittering brass horns, trombones extending and retracting in perfect tandem; clarinets, oboes, a sleek piano, and various other music makers clutter the grand stage; and they're all being played by musicians in tuxedos and rat guises.

Theodore begins to thread through the enormous crowd, passing a sea of fancy suits and dresses, observing that each face in this minatory masquerade is concealed. He passes a man in a bear mask who's cradling a cocktail in his hand. Underneath the bear's snout, his thin lips dance as he chats up a girl in a vibrant green sequin gown.

Over the growing swell of conversation, Theodore hears the man say, "Who will it be this month, Gracie? Another obsequious Labor sympathizer willing to give life and limb to the proletariat?" Gracie takes a pull from a thin cigarette and shakes her head.

"I heard talk it's one of the Andrysiak brothers; those land-snatching Polacks."

"The one prosperous family of Poles in the entire United Kingdom? Dare I say, the only two from that ramshackle country who have made anything of their migration? I call foul, dear Gracie. The Andrysiak's aren't opponents of enough clout to the success of the factories—the industrial or the textile industries—not yet. Sir Nithercott hasn't the time for such drivel."

As Theodore snakes through the crowd he begins to realize people are glaring at him, as if he was a bull trotting through a throng of bloodthirsty Matadors. He's young, he's American, and he's not wearing the proper attire. Feeling self-conscious and something worse—threatened—he flips up his hood, stalks to the back of the ballroom, and settles where the mass of people has thinned.

"Where is your concealment, young man?" the muffled voice of a woman next to him. He turns to see a short, fat woman in a chicken mask. Unlike many of the other masks in the ballroom, hers covers her entire face, her mouth inhumed under the swell of the chicken's beak.

"Oh, I um, I don't have one." Theodore shrugs. The short chicken-lady seems to withdraw immediately in response, cocking her head back and turning it sideways like a dog does when it hears the shake of a dry-food bag.

"You're a Yank?" she asks, and then shakes her head. "A Yank without a guise. If Sir Nithercott sees you, he won't be pleased. And he certainly won't trust you."

"Who's Sir Nithercott? I heard that name thrown around a minute ago," Theodore continues in a low voice, almost speaking to himself. "Come to think of it, where are we? This must be a dream."

For a terrifyingly tranquil moment, short chicken-lady doesn't respond. She just stares at him behind her mask, her consternation nearly palpable.

"How did you..." Her voice trails off as the crowd begins to chant and cheer. All masks turn forward, their wearers sharing a collective curiosity; some of them are leaning, stretching, and even shoving at each other to get a better view of the bandstand. The old swing song builds to a frightening crescendo, and just as the band reaches a fervent peak that nearly rattles the ballroom walls, someone strides onto the stage.

The figure is tall and lean; his gait, sprightly. He's in a black pinstripe tuxedo that compliments the band; the singular difference being his blood-red bow tie, which floats like an effulgent beacon before a sea of black suits. He stops just before the band, bows to them, and then bows to the raucous crowd.

Covering his face is a rat mask, the visage of which has a stark, twisted, somewhat melancholy look to it.

A realization dawns on Theodore, a stark remembrance, as if reliving a dream upon waking. The man in the rat mask, the crowd in vintage attire… this is the scene of the photo in The Cat's Meow. He jars his brain trying to recall the grainy old photo's caption. *Masquerade Ball at The King's Inn.* Well, the scene certainly fits that of an old-fashioned masquerade ball. Where is The King's Inn, and what has he gotten himself into?

"My dear and queer assemblage of peers; my ruthless Loyalists and venerable followers; thank you for joining me on yet another glorious Shibboleth. We have come far in our mighty conquest to root out the evil and the disingenuous; to subject England to the cleansing ablution of truth and justice; to weed out the naysayers, and those who would change the established economical system for which we have toiled, and even bled, for centuries."

Like a bishop at a holy ceremony, the man in the rat guise waves his arms emphatically as he talks. The crowd being his loyal subjugates, they probably leave his sermons as perpetuators of his teachings like theological deadheads after a Sunday liturgy. *But what is he teaching?* Theodore doesn't have a grip on the situation yet, but he is sure that he isn't a fan of this strange man, or the obsequious way the masqueraders seem to fawn over him.

"Come, friends and lovers. Let us dance together on this most resplendent of nights." The band strikes up an old waltz, to which the man in the rat guise begins swaying. He even holds up his arms and, much to Theodore's fascination and mounting horror, begins courting an invisible partner in time to the somber music. The crowd joins in, grabbing their partners and slow-dancing; a sea of ambiguous figures moving in tandem.

"One month, my lovers," he cries, while courting his invisible partner. "It has been one month of lobbying our voice and our vision to the masses; one month of nurtured progress and intrepid research. And this research has led to a name, or an alias rather—the alias of our next candidate. This most fortunate individual will show us tonight just where his loyalties lie. You, my lovers, know him as of now as little as you know the veiled dandy beside you.

"And I am oh so delighted to introduce him to you, my lovers." The man in the rat guise does a twirl and then motions to the side of the stage. "But first let us stand tall and proud for our venerable nation's history, for the salience of posterity and the propitiousness of our future generations, and for the moments that immortalize us." Two masked figures come forth at the man's tacit cue. They're carrying an ancient contraption in their hands— at least to Theodore it appears ancient—a folding camera, and a ponderous stand on which to prop it.

"Come, come, yes," the man announces over the crooning band instruments, herding the cameramen to the center of the stage. As they set up the device, Theodore glances over to the short chicken-lady. What he sees both bewilders and fascinates him. She's circling in a lazy waltz, her head leaning against the shoulder of another patron, a tall man in a double-breasted chalk-stripe suit. Covering his face is the drooping guise of a basset hound. The saturnine sag of the dog's cheeks complements the bizarre nature of the image.

Theodore knows these two are utter strangers to each other—their true identities concealed like everyone else's. But they're sharing a seemingly sincere and tender moment, appearing as a husband and wife would on their anniversary dance. Theodore chuckles to himself as he sees multiple examples of this throughout the room. It's fiercely peculiar seeing the innately human expressions of dancing and flirting blend with the static, expressionless features of the masks.

"Everyone, gather 'round," the man in the rat guise sneers. "Form up behind me, my lovers and friends." His voice has a scattered lilt every time he speaks. If this bizarre dream was a circus, and it certainly seems like one with the plethora of animal faces surrounding Theodore, the man on the stage would be the ringmaster, swinging his baton and imparting the upcoming events with a silvery enthusiasm.

Come one, come all. Step right up and enjoy the festivities. He imagines the man in the rat guise wearing a tawdry bronze tailcoat and gesticulating wildly as he introduces the next act. Theodore squeezes into the condensing crowd as the patrons swarm the ballroom in preparation for the photo. *This one's gonna blow your minds, folks; it's more audacious, more raucous and rowdier, and more bewildering than even the grace of the wondrous trapeze artists.* Theodore thinks to himself in a stereotypical circus announcer's voice.

He lingers at the rear of the pack, watching as the ringmaster gestures to the crowd, asking them to squeeze tighter.

Women and children first, as they say. It's time for the intrepid lion tamer! Don't worry, little ones, Leo the Lion won't eviscerate you, string you up by your innards, and devour you. He only does that if he's hungry. And Leo the Lion is a well-fed beast, you have the ringmaster's word.

"Please, my lovers, equip your most divine smiles; your dazzling cheek-to-cheek grins!" Theodore notes the glaring redundancy, considering that everyone in the room is adhering to the masquerade theme, and many of their disguises obscure the entire face.

"None of those coquettish smirks, my dears." He points a lanky, interminable arm toward a masked lady in the front of the crowd. "Smile large, like me!" The ringmaster raises his arms, his elbows flaring outward, and points between the rat's plump cheeks.

Theodore poses for the photo, his face pulling into a puzzled scowl. He's surrounded by a bunch of loonies. A vivid flash pulses through the room, followed by a crackle, as the arcane camera takes the photo which, paradoxically, Theodore has already seen.

"Marvelous! Stupendous!" cries the ringmaster. "One for the history books indeed, my lovers." Theodore looks back at the short chicken-lady to see that she is once again enveloped in the arms of her equivocal dance partner. They're not speaking, nor are they sharing bullet-fast glances at each other like most couples do on awkward first dates, they're simply turning to the undulating melody of the orchestra, as if there was nowhere else on the planet they'd rather be.

Perhaps, Theodore thinks, *these two wear the same masks to every Shibboleth and that's how they recognize each other. Maybe everybody at these strange events interacts in this way; closeness through distance; empathy through ambiguity.*

Whatever the case, Theodore feels he's had enough of his charade. He wants to return to Alice; to let her know he's all right. He wants to go back to his world. He turns and leaves the Regal Ballroom, finding himself in a decadent lounge. A sparse assortment of patrons dwell here and there throughout the room, and everyone that has a half mask has a cigarette dangling from their mouths. Tendrils of smoke swirl about the room, settling on the ceiling in an argent layer of opacity.

Theodore finds it odd that most of the patrons with half-masks are smoking cigarettes, but no one with a full-size mask has a smoke. Perhaps even sliding their masks off to take a drag reveals too much of their identity. Remaining anonymous looks like it's a top concern at the Shibboleth. Theodore wanders over to a grandiose lobby bar flush with ruddy velvet upholstery. He plops down before a bartender in a rat mask.

"Are you lost?" the man inquires in a sprightly English voice, while delicately rolling up his sleeves and dusting off his vest. He plants his hands wide on the bar and cocks his head to the side, sizing Theodore up with menacing, invasive eyes.

"No, I don't think so," Theodore stammers, combing his mind for something to order; a drink that wouldn't be a glaring anachronism in this odd English nightmare. "I'll have an Old Fashioned, barman."

"That'll be one rose noble, Yank," sneers the rat, possibly trying to throw Theodore off with an obsolete currency.

"Now, now Bertram. Level with the Yank or he'll do a runner," a spry voice grazes Theodore's ear. There's a youthful and more human quality to it than has ballasted any of the other masqueraders' tones this whole night.

He looks left to see a girl in a ceramic-white flapper dress sitting at the other end of the bar. She has one shapely leg crossed over the other and is slowly kicking it back and forth in a seductive affectation. Theodore follows the soft lines of her legs down to an opulent pair of heels that coruscate under the bar lights.

He looks at the gentle alabaster slopes of her shoulders, his eyes following through to a pronounced clavicle, and then down the mounds of her breasts. An aquiline mask covers her face, and he finds that the clandestine nature of the concealment magnifies his fascination with her. *What kind of face is hiding under there?*

He never finds himself instantly drawn to someone. Hell, he rarely finds himself interested in any woman, save maybe the classic elegance of Grace Kelly, or the raunchy teenage fantasy of Phoebe Cates exiting the pool in that quintessential dream sequence from *Fast Times at Ridgemont High*. But something about this girl pulls him in, pulls him in hard.

Silence frosts the atmosphere between them as Bertram considers the young Brit's suggestion. For a moment, the barman seems alarmed to see this mystery girl at his bar; as if this isn't a place she should be. Then he nods to her like a child submitting to his parent's instruction. "I'll take 50 pence."

Theodore's face twists in consternation as he wonders how on earth he got to England, and what 50 pence would equal in US currency. He dives into his back pocket and paws at his wallet, pausing briefly upon finding he doesn't have to dig around the curves of the cylinder record as he always does. That austere little item is a piece of his identity. He's in a ghastly foreign world and being without the record is like being a soldier on the battle march without gunpowder.

He exhumes a crisp ten-dollar bill and flattens it on the bar. Both the girl and Bertram stare at the ostentatiously modern bill, and as Bertram raises his head in sluggish wonder, the girl throws a few arcane coins on the counter, the tinny rattle of which seems to rouse Bertram from his stupor.

The girl in the hawk mask rises with swanlike grace and passes Theodore, patting him on the back as she goes. He leans in as she passes, lingering in her scent as it wafts over him in a fugacious hug of vanilla, and something else he can't define. Theodore watches her go, listless. Bertram tosses the cocktail across the bar, the amber liquid nearly sloshing out of the glass. He then grunts something inaudible and snatches the coins from the bar.

Theodore sips on his drink as he watches all the animals stalk and strut through the opulent lobby. People begin to filter in from the ballroom as the meeting with the ringmaster comes to a close. A man in a peacoat walks in cradling a gramophone. He places the device near the bar and sets it spinning to the tune of an old British dance song.

As the crowd thickens, Theodore takes a final swig of his drink and heads for the front door. Two doormen in suits and rat masks—apparently much of the ringmaster's staff is given this dress code—nod to Theodore, throwing open the prodigious double door for him.

"Will you be off before the Shibboleth starts, sir?" one of the rats asks in a cockney drawl. Theodore demurs, letting the door shut as he looks upon a new world. It's frigid. Snow is falling hard on a vast, arcane cobblestone street. Above, patches of milky defused light emanate from gas lamps, illuminating an impossibly senescent scene.

He's in some sort of town square, with a mostly barren park carved in the middle. Thousands of bare tree branches, like sharpened rapiers crossed in combat, loom directly ahead. Lining the square on each side is an eclectic assortment of buildings, some of which have tawdry old electrical signs that pulse across the winter night like distant strobe lights. And right in the heart of the square is a gargantuan pine tree, splashed with gaslight and adorned with a constellation of twinkling ornaments.

It looks like old London, but there's no way I'm actually in 1931 England as the photo back at the bar suggested...is there? Theodore steps onto the pavement and inhales deeply. It's just nice to be away from the stomach-turning oddity of the masquerade ball; although he wouldn't mind it if the British girl at the bar was still with him.

He clacks down the steps. At the foot of the stairway, a party-goer is taking a smoke break. A tall man in a russet overcoat, cradling a cigarette in his hands and taking short, anxious drags under his mask. A wolf. The man looks over. "Off so soon?" he asks Theodore, a menacing tinge in his voice. "You're not from around here, are you, laddie?"

"Uh, no." Theodore looks across the square in an attempt at nonchalance.

"Ah, a yank." The man takes another drag, sucking at the cigarette a little longer this time, like he's carefully crafting his next thought. "Well, if a touristy fancy has overtaken you, I'd take a stroll that way." He nods to the right. "When the architecture becomes more industrial, you know you're close to the docks, which have an intriguingly nostalgic feel to them. I hear there's all manner of things that happen near the docks at this hour." The man lingers a moment and then flicks his cigarette onto the sidewalk, stamping it out under his immaculate leather dress-ups. He walks back up the hotel, raps on the massive door. A brief and muddled verbal exchange ensues and the doors swing wide. The man in the wolf mask disappears inside without looking back.

Theodore sighs, pondering if the guy was just shooting the breeze or if he was trying, for whatever reason, to lead Theodore astray. He shrugs, beginning down the right side of the lane, whatever cardinal direction 'right' could be in this world. Before he's gone half a block, he comes upon a primly-dressed old couple, powerwalking up the sidewalk, vermilion spots glowing upon their cheeks. The old man is not so much ushering, but dragging, his wife up the street.

"If you insist on fumbling with that dress, Marcie, we'll miss the picture!" the old man rasps.

"Excuse me." Theodore holds his hands out before them. The old man pauses, the consternation on his face immediately apparent. His thin white mustache twitches, and his brow entrenches itself right above his eyes. He's looking Theodore up and down, confused by this young man's patently anachronistic clothes.

"What the date today?" Theodore asks, choosing to keep his hands visible to show he has no pernicious intent.

"Why it's December the 14th," replies the old man, remaining stiff as a paddle.

"December 14th?" Theodore repeats aloud, knowing full well that before he found the bizarre gramophone at the Cat's Meow it was mid-October. "And, I'm sorry, my mind is a little frazzled right now. What year is it?"

The look on the old man's countenance eases, a curious half-smile replacing the look of worry. "Are you quite alright, American child?"

Theodore feigns a chuckle, attempting to appear as unassuming as his puzzled faculties will allow him to. "I am. It's probably just an effect of the booze," he embellishes, attempting his best portrayal of an errant-eyed, doddering drunk; although he knows that he's never been much of an actor, something that is patently reinforced by the old man's quizzical look.

"It's the year 1931, dear child, and a year of great import, if I do say so myself. There are talks of a union of fascists burgeoning here in our grand nation," he scoffs, "if you can believe such a thing would ever gain footing on the British Isles...Why, Cab Calloway has released his new and utterly delectable track, *Minnie Moocher*... *City Lights* by Charlie Chaplin is premiering just down the street. In fact," the old man takes a fugacious glance at his pocket watch. "Marcie and I are running late for the picture. If you don't mind, young Yank, we will be on our way."

Perplexed, Theodore gives him a shallow nod. *1931? This must be a dream; some visceral, immaculately detailed dream*, he thinks as he watches the couple shuffle off, the man's coat tails licking at the wind. Everything in sight, down to the way the old man's coat flutters about, looks insanely real; more so than the content of any dream Theodore's ever had.

He continues down the murky, snow-swiped street, feeling the cold settle into his bones. Beyond the square is a peculiar mix of architecture; a smattering of gothic Victorian laced with industrial brick, and stick-style houses bespoke of an English city. Here and there, dangling under rain gutters and wrapped over casements like muted necklaces are festive garlands. Many of the doors around him are crested with wreaths and the lamp posts are snaked with ribbons, completing a true Dickension motif that doesn't fail to inject a bit of cheer into the moody aspect of the slumbering city.

He wanders through regal streets and corpuscular alleyways. The mingling of extravagant buildings and dark, dingy corners reminds him of New York, but this dream-like 1931 England, presumably London, has an altogether different look and feel. The older men passing by on the street are all furnished with a bowler or a fedora, the younger men donning flat caps and cutaway coats; vintage vests shining underneath.

A new scent pervades the frosty winter air. The putrid smell of garbage, rot, and perhaps feces, smacks Theodore right on the nose. It's so repulsive that his faculties beg him to turn on his heels and divert, but what his gazes catches on stays him. Through the silvery night, he sees a great body of water. It looks like it's splitting the city in half and has such breadth that Theodore can scarcely see the buildings on the other side gleaming meekly through a gossamer curtain of falling snow.

A string of saturnine boats is moored along the water's edge, along which hunks of debris—even murky and tattered habiliments—float along. Cresting the placid and poisoned river is a lurid bog, which doesn't comply with the breeze, but sits atop the water like a stoic, hulking miasma. Pinching his nose, Theodore walks along the riverside, noting that the architecture here is suffused with a more industrial look, with predominantly brick buildings lining the waterfront.

A cluster of old shipping crates sits beneath a streetlight just ahead. Tresses of rope snake about them, but the effete ribbons no longer secure the crates as was once intended. At night, this whole section of the city is like one big project held in stasis, abandoned. Theodore wonders what it will look like in the daytime.

Something shifts among the crates. Whatever it is, it's just beyond the light's paltry reach, so Theodore can't make out the shape, he can only divine the vagueness of the movement. He squints. A figure is crouching in the darkness, minatory and inscrutable. Theodore's breath escapes his lungs, and he freezes in place. All he can see is a dull, murky outline but he knows since he paused under the streetlight, the figure can see him plain as day.

"Death to draconian rule; prosperity to the state," a voice hisses. Theodore nearly leaps backward at the sound.

"Is it you?" the voice asks, its owner still smothered in darkness. "Are you Osprey?"

"Uh, no. I think you have the wrong guy," Theodore stammers. As he begins to back away, refusing to peel his eyes from the shadowy figure, Theodore detects a sudden mutation in the environment. His vision blurs, and the world begins to waver. Underneath the pallid gleam of the streetlight objects streak and sputter, like an oil painting under the callous lick of a candle.

Inexplicably, he hears the swell of music in his ear; the same scratch of the violin and the exact guitar that he heard upon entering this old English world. It's the same song, only it sounds like it's picking up at the last few bars this time, meandering through the final refrain. The violin plays a passage of high notes, soaring over the warbling accompaniment and then blending in with the chorus of instruments. Theodore's world, and the strange man within, fades away and turns to black.

IV

A vacuous nothingness swirls about, pulling and pressing on his body, tugging this way and that; a violent black encompasses his vision and stretches, stretches infinitely in every direction; a pinhole of white light; a mere bud that churns and flickers, and then surges forth in an effluence of brilliant energy. He feels himself move through this passage like a ghost through a wall. Slam! The oppressive world of vertiginous black yields, coming to an utter and abrupt standstill.

He's on his hands and knees, his senses overloaded. Everything is swooshing about him, like he's kneeling on a fixed platform while the world is fluttering about on loose hinges. Two bright lights, two garish, awfully bright lights appear before him. They're moving closer, closer, so close that they might just swallow him up. Something tickles his ear—an interminable blaring from behind those lights. At first, it's so distant he can barely discern the sound. And then this noise climbs a terrible crescendo as his senses steal some agency back from the void. The world seeps into the frame of his vision like ink on paper, and the lights move ever closer, surrounded by a blotted, mustard colored…something.

He looks down. Strips of white paint line the path underneath him all the way to a neon orange hand floating in the sky before him. Just above the hand is a blue sign that reads, Lexington Avenue. The realization of where he is hits him, and hard, but not as hard as the taxi cab that's about to. Just as the lights and the blaring of the horn almost encompass him, he tumbles back in one furious motion. The yellow cab peels by in front of him; a garbled phase spews through the open passenger window, "Watch where you're crawlin', you fuckin' moron!"

A lick of cool air kisses his face, a toe-curling crunching sound ensuing as the cab hurls past. With all the grace of a bodybuilder in pointe shoes, he paws at his face to feel nothing but damp skin. The mask. It must have slid off his face when he dodged the taxi. A quick hazy-eyed glance at the road, which is now a scattered sea of ceramic shards, confirms his assumption.

"Mommy, that guy just fell out of the sky!" a young voice teeming with excitement exclaims behind him. He stumbles backwards on jelly legs, making his way out of the busy midtown intersection. *Holy fuck, I was almost just killed. Like, one, maybe two seconds later and I would've been human roadkill for the city to scrape off the street.* He feels his heel connect with the bump of the curb. The sweet scent of churros baking at a nearby street vendor wafts into his nostrils.

"What are you talking about, Marissa? Men don't just fall from the sky. He just accidentally crossed at the wrong time and very nearly caused a dozen car pile-up, that's all," a hard-faced, industrious woman in a charcoal suit with her hair slicked back says to her daughter, whose hand she's gripping firmly at the crosswalk. Her daughter's little oval face and big, inquisitive eyes refuse to leave him for a second; the woman merely glances at Theodore and nods. "You okay, young man? Looks like you've had your first frightening encounter with New York traffic. The roads are a different breed of insanity here. Although, when we New Yorkers jaywalk, we tend to do it more often across streets than avenues. They're a lot narrower and usually one-way."

The feeling that his brain has just been pulverized in a Kitchen Aid and then thrown in a garbage baler keeps him from responding—from telling the lady that he, too, is from New York and understands street etiquette. Even if he wasn't experiencing shock-induced hyperventilation, it wouldn't do any good to explain his situation to her anyhow. What would he say? That he was just whisked away in time across some impossible temporal bridge, and then thrust back to the present in the same violent, and nearly, murderous, manner? Why did he beam back to 49th and Lexington, anyhow? Why wasn't he cozily dumped back in front of the gramophone?

The sun is only just coming up over the buildings, so it must be the next morning already. It looks like the time machine kept him in the past all through the night. That means the bar will be closed, and he should get past the inside door since he can't imagine Jersey Guy will be safeguarding the entrance with another riddle at six AM.

Theodore needs to retrieve his record. That's priority one. If anyone else, bar worker or patron, were to stumble upon it and activate the time warping mechanism, well...the rippling destruction of the chaos theory constituent known as the *"butterfly effect"* could ensue...or maybe something worse Theodore hasn't considered since until last night time travel seemed as plausible as young-Earth creationism theories.

Whatever the case, he needs to compose himself and get back to the Cat's Meow. Hopefully he can slip back in with the brick he and Alice used last night.

"No mommy, I really saw it! Promise!" Marissa continues, tugging against her mother's coiled hand and staring at Theodore with wonderment. "The sky opened up and he plopped right out of it. It was magic, mommy!"

"Yes, yes, and your lay-about father just scratched a winning six at the lotto and mommy doesn't have to cold call on Wall Street at the crack of dawn anymore." The neon orange hand of the traffic signal turns into a white crossing figure and the woman pulls little Marissa along, shooting a glance over at Theodore. "*This* is when you cross these kinds of streets."

Marissa keeps her eyes on the glassy-eyed magic man standing there stupidly at the curb until she's well across the other side; her mother yanking her along every step of the way. Theodore gives himself a hearty slap on the face, hoping to snap himself out of this zombie-like state, which nearly getting squashed by a taxi has thrust him into. He stumbles toward the crosswalk at 49th to make his way down to the Village. As logic seeps back into his mind, one question prevails: was the extraordinary experience last night real, or just a freakishly vivid dream?

With a blundered attempt at delicacy, Theodore retrieves the record from its clamped housing on the peculiar gramophone in The Cat's Meow. Rubbing his temples and trying to cope with the thrumming ache behind his eyes, which the mid-city walk didn't do much to mitigate, he rolls the unlabeled record over in his hand a few times. Like meeting a pen pal in person for the first time, it's remarkable finally knowing what was on that record after all these years—a quaint, somehow eerie, old-timey jazz song.

He looks about the backroom bar. The main lights are off, with just a tenuous set of secondary lights flickering above, telling Theodore that it's past closing time at The Cat's Meow. He's just thankful that the hippie owners of the bar aren't too keen on security beyond the extravagant lock and key system they've created. Otherwise, he'd have to have waited until business hours to slip in and retrieve the record. In that case, by the time he'd have gotten to it, who knows who else could have already accidentally activated the time travel mechanism?

The question currently tickling his mind is how—if last night really was a dream—is it possible that he ended up in the middle of the street near midtown this morning? Even the most exhaustive bout of sleep-walking couldn't transport him there by itself. He also doesn't recall having anything besides that one Old Fashioned here at the bar, and then that even Older-Fashioned back in 1931 England. That's not enough to inebriate him to the point of forgetting how he got home. Hell, maybe he never even went home last night. He had an unintentional sleepover on the busy thoroughfare, no biggie.

As he ambles out of the hidden bar, he mentally dissects each and every segment of the previous night. He starts with the droves of British folk, clandestinely veiled in masks, making up the body of what was, to Theodore, a bizarre and frightening phantasmagoria. And the ringmaster of said circus, with his profound public orator voice, and the eccentricities of his character that even now seem to have a lingering effect on Theodore. The term, "Shibboleth", which was mentioned multiple times and apparently was on the agenda for that evening in December of 1931, something he had never heard before that night. And the girl…

Oh, the girl! That mysterious and evocative girl of whom Theodore knows nothing, other than that she captivated him so. And why does she hold sway over his heart? Why, after all he had seen last night, everything he'd experienced—from the equivocal guests at the furtive masquerade to the flamboyant ringmaster's performance to wandering the streets of a bygone London—why was it she who held his heart captive? Was it the mystery enshrouding her, the ambiguity? Was it in the way the swift and delicate brush of her hand made his nerves sing, or was it the sonorous and sultry tone of her voice? The way she carried herself with the boldness and temerity of youth that was unlike anyone else at the hotel? Whatever the reason, her memory lounges in his mind like the warm, wet kiss of a lover lingers on the lips of a hopeless romantic—something he most certainly is not. Is he?

After the girl, he remembers the strange, murky, and utterly caustic channel of water that ran through the city. If that was London, and he's pretty certain it was, that body of water must have been the River Thames. What a confounding and fascinating experience to be on the edge of such a famed littoral landmark. And what a singularly terrifying experience to be solicited by a stranger in the shadows of the tenebrous riverside.

The entire ordeal of the previous night, Theodore thinks, as he opens the door to the bar and ascends the staircase—the early sun's light staining the barn-style entryway—*had to be something more than just a fever dream… or the result of a spiked drink at The Cat's Meow. It would have to be a hell of a drug to produce such a vivid experience, and I hardly drank at the bar,* *anyway.* Last night was visceral, and it made him feel utterly alive. Especially the laconic but memorable interaction with that girl.

Theodore leaves the hidden bar and catches a train to the Meatpacking District, where he shares his diminutive two-bedroom apartment with a loudmouth roommate named Henry James. The guy's parents chose to impart their love for the prominent writer into their only child, and Henry happens to talk just about as much as Mr. James wrote. *If only,* Theodore thinks, *the kid had even a jigger of the profundity and eloquence as the famous writer after whom he was named.*

The truth of the matter is that this loquacious roommate of his is actually his best friend—well, past tense would be more appropriate here—was his best friend. They met Freshman year of high school, where they developed something of an instant camaraderie. Or rather, the lonely and uncouth Henry attached himself to Theodore, who begrudgingly accepted him into his non-existent social circle. In the years since, Theodore found himself increasingly annoyed with Henry, though—as tends to happen with everyone in his life other than Alice.

As a result, Theodore's inadvertently reduced their friendship to nothing more than passing hellos and the inevitable awkward back-and-forth that ensues when they both wake up and go for the coffee maker at the same time. They work together too, Vanderbilt's Shipping and Distribution; both of them spending far too much of their lives in the pallet jack box, moving pieces for the dying railyard industry. Even there, Theodore keeps his interactions with Henry to a minimum. In truth, some part of Theodore feels terrible for the way he's treated his best friend since high school, a deep and salient part of him that he suppresses these days, but he's always had problems trusting people and has found it easier simply not to have them in his life in any meaningful way.

A second, more immobilizing wave of fatigue sets in by the time Theodore reaches the apartment. He trudges up the stairs and collapses into bed, but before submitting himself to the prying arms of sleep, he removes the cylinder record from his pocket and props it upon the counter. Staring at the item in a moment of reverential silence—realizing that this little device is somehow the intrinsic piece to last night's departure from reality—he notices his cell phone blinking behind it. Unlike the record, he forgets his phone every time he leaves.

He hits a button to illuminate the screen, which reveals a text from Alice. The time of receipt was last night, late.

Where did you go, Bear? I waited with Francis outside The Cat's Meow for at least a half-hour. I know that social situations aren't exactly your idea of a good time, but you have to admit that place was pretty cool.

P.S. You didn't have to split without letting your sister know.

P.P.S. Don't worry, I still love you. -A

Theodore groans at the idea of his sister leaving a bar with some hipster schmuck. Francis was probably the doorman, or the ginger-haired bicep she was dancing with when Theodore found the auxiliary bar and lost sight of her. With her text message elucidating that she left the bar with some random guy, he begins to worry about her all over again, even though he knows he shouldn't. Alice, in her trademark capricious way, has been training in martial arts—or was it kickboxing?—for some time now. And besides, she is the strongest person he's ever known, in the figurative sense, and with her socially adventurous nature, she's become more adept than most at sniffing out dangerous situations or individuals. He must keep reminding himself of that, even though he knows it won't quell his perennial concern for her wellbeing. He sends her a brief 'good morning' message and collapses into the sheets.

ACT II

I

The shingles on the roof shimmer under the callous summer sun. Over the lip of the rain gutter, Teddy can see the family's old toolshed—stark white and surprisingly small from up here. It's like he's gazing down on a big mouth, and the white shed is the lone, flat tooth. Molars, he thinks they're called; the ones that his mom says to brush extra-long, cause they're the ones that like to stay filthy.

He finds it funny that he's taking so much time to look at mundane things like the shingles and the shed, and the drainpipes glimmering with dew, but anything's better than the alternative. Up here in their safe haven, they can barely hear what's going on in the house. Last time, which probably wasn't even a month ago, the game of choice was counting the tree trunks surrounding their home. Sixty-seven. Sixty-seven majestic pines that normally loom way above him. Up here, he doesn't need to crane his neck to see the highest branches. He peers down on them like a god.

Alice is in a crumpled bunch just under the third-floor window awning. She's in the little nook that a couple years ago became her getaway. Under there she's safe. But Alice and Teddy can't fully escape the noises. They can still hear dad's drunken bellowing from up here; can still detect the guttural slur of his voice. It's amazing how quickly Teddy's dad becomes hoarse when he's drunk; amazing how he can't seem to hear himself anymore, can't hear how oafish he sounds.

Teddy can hear his mom, too. God, he hopes Alice can't hear her, but judging by the look on her face, Alice hears. Whenever he senses another moment building, Teddy carefully watches his father, eyeing just how much of that amber liquid he's consumed. If Teddy thinks his dad has gulped down too much, Teddy grabs his sister by the hand and yanks her out of the house. He sighs, staring at her little body, curled up on the floor. Every time they escape an episode, he wonders just how much her four-year-old mind can comprehend.

"Daddy's not hurting mommy," he says, as the argument inside snowballs into a confrontation. "They're just disagreeing. You know, like when I want to play with your green tank engine, what's his name again?"

"Percy." She sniffles.

"That's right. Like when I want to play with Percy, but you won't let me? And I make a big deal out of it and try to take him away. And then you start to cry, so I back off."

"Uh-huh," Alice says, her pudgy little hands pressing once more to her ears.

"Well, it's like that," Teddy says, and he pats Alice on the shoulder. Her hands break away from her little head and paw at his back, her arms coiling tightly about him in a fervid embrace. Meanwhile, the shouting gets louder. Teddy can tell from the way the sound travels—the way it reverberates off the walls—that mom and dad are in the kitchen. He hears a dull thud and a crash as he covers Alice's ears.

He pulls away just enough to give his sister a reassuring smile and sees two silken lines stream from her eyes to her cheeks. The sight of such an angelic face tainted with distress becomes too much for him to bare, and he feels the hot sting of tears begin to swell in his own eyes. He realizes that there's no way his manufactured smile—now mottled with fresh tears—is going to alleviate the little one's pain. But he's resigned to do what he always does when dad gets this way: keep on smiling; even if it's just for her.

"Teddy?" The diffident little girl stumbles over her thoughts. "Do you think mommy and daddy will ever get along?"

"Oh, they do, Alice. Daddy loves mommy, maybe not quite like he used to, but he does in his own way. He just has some…problems he needs to work on. But don't you forget, Alice, they both love you very much, and none of their problems has to do with you." As his words leave his mouth, Teddy is stolidly focused on one emotion: anger.

He doesn't care if what he says to Alice has an inkling of truth in it, he's eight years old now; old enough to formulate an educated opinion on his dad. The man is a monster. And he can't wait until he's old enough to leave this dreary place forever. He dreams of whisking his mother and sister away from that stumbling buffoon. It doesn't matter if his dad has never laid a hand on Alice or him; it doesn't change what the man will always be in Teddy's mind.

"Look Alice!" he exclaims, thrusting his still-shaking index finger downwards. "The sun's starting to set and look who's already decided to join us!" Down below, dozens of tiny effulgent dots begin to pulse on and off. Alice clambers over, and Teddy has to snatch the tail of her skirt to keep her from toppling over the side. He clamps down just enough to feel secure about his sister leaning over a twenty-five-foot drop but gives enough slack to allow her to see the green specks flash below.

"Fireflies!" Alice exclaims.

"Yep! Our friends are back." Teddy reels her back in. Alice smushes the teardrops from her eyes.

"Can we, Teddy? Oh can, can we, can we?" His sister's swift evolution from grief to excitement is precisely what Teddy was hoping for. Thank god for shiny flying bugs.

"Sure, sis." Teddy grabs his feet one by one, turning his scuffed and faded Chuck Taylors upside down to see if there's any remaining tread on either beaten sole. When he deems he has enough grip for a safe descent, he leans over the roof and flips onto the second-story landing.

"Catch me, Teddy!" the over-eager Alice insists.

"Hold on a second, sis." He's only pivoted half-way to face her when she dives forward, nearly throwing him off balance and over the edge when she collapses onto him. He drives his worn Chucks into the shingles until they bite and lowers his sister onto her feet.

"You gotta be more careful, Alice!" He ruffles her hair until it's a rakish and unkempt mess. "Don't jump until I say so, silly-head." She bats his hand away and attempts to reconcile the sandy-blonde clumps on her head.

"Teddy, don't touch!"

He crouches down before the drainpipe. Shakes it. It's as solid as the last time he checked it. Should hold. "Alright, remember this part, sis? You just make sure you have a grip, like this…and then you throw your body over." He lunges over the edge, his sneakers meeting the side of the house with a dissonant clack.

For a moment the two children stare at each other, her looking down upon him, and him up at her, praying that dad didn't hear the noise. The coast remains clear for a minute or two—no yawning of the old back door or thumping of footsteps—at which point Teddy signals to his sister to follow him down.

She performs admirably, wriggling her tiny frame onto the old pipe and shuffling down. Putting his sister into dangerous situations as such always makes Teddy's heart flutter with worry, but a more malign danger brews inside the house, making this a passable alternative.

When they reach ground, Alice doesn't hesitate to shove past him and begin dancing amongst what has now become a dizzying congregation of fireflies. Every so often as she twirls, she tries to cup one or two of them in her little hands, but each time they manage to climb in their errant and lazy fashion just out of her reach.

"C'mon, Teddy! Come dance with us all," she giggles. "Come dance the dance of light!" Teddy has always been captivated by how smart and creative his little sister continues to prove she is; only four years old and so inventive. He joins in the fun, running about with Alice through the garden under the coruscant glow of the dying sun.

For a while, he occasionally glances at the windows to see if his dad and mom are finished fighting, at which point he always worries dad might be looking for his next victim. Even though his dad has yet to bully him or Alice physically, Teddy's concern for his sister's safety is forever there. After a few minutes he manages to shelve the nastiness that's poisoning his young life, and revel in a moment of wondrous abandon with his favorite little companion.

II

Theodore awakens to a bilious flash of neon. He rubs his eyes, wipes a trail of crusted spittle from his chin, and sits up, groaning. As usual, he'd had his arms and legs folded over all night while sleeping in his diminutive twin-sized bed, and his joints are stiff as birch in the winter. He makes a meager attempt at stretching and then trundles out of bed.

Considering that he lives in the city, the caliber of apartment Theodore can afford means reaching anything he want takes just one lean in any direction. He droops forward and props his forearms on the casement. The neon sign of *The Mnemonic Tonic*—a slick, hipster bar just at the other end of the street— looms outside the window, the garish flash of which makes it once again the prime suspect in the case of 'what the hell woke Theodore this time?'

He must have slept clear through the day and at least partway into the night. It's raining heavily out there, and apparently no one wants to brave getting drenched, which renders the normally chaotic city into a shimmering ghost town. Yawning, Theodore reaches for his phone.

He squints under the effulgence off his cell phone's screen. It looks like Alice has responded to his earlier salutation.

"Well good morning to you, and good evening now. I'm sure you're sleeping off your big night. I assume you're living up to your name and hibernating over there. Anyway, I'm going out with Francis tonight. You know, the delectable bathtub gin-guy from the bar? Text me whenever your lazy butt wakes up or come visit me at Vincent's Vagaries tomorrow. Love you, Bear."

Theodore shivers at the thought of his sister going out with that cocktail-pushing Neanderthal. But Alice has always had an interesting taste in men, there's nothing he can do about it. Then again, would he ever really approve of any man she finds herself attracted to? Probably not. He shakes his head. His mind keeps fiercely shifting back to that old gramophone, and the fugacious, but mesmerizing adventure in antediluvian London. He grabs the cylinder record and heads for the door.

He stalks through the tiny apartment with the utmost care to be a ghost, hoping to avoid a derailing conversation with Henry. Every interaction with his garrulous roommate is like the reading of an unabridged Stephen King novel. Only Henry doesn't captivate his audience like the master of horror can.

He scoops up his house key from a narrow strip of wood that the landlord insisted was a kitchen counter, and heads for the door. A dull thud sounds from behind; Henry's bedroom door.

"Hey bro, I thought I heard some movement." A buoyant frizzy tangle of hair bounces into the living room. Henry's fiddling with his glasses as he walks, his thick hands thrusting them upon the bridge of his nose. Then he stands there, no longer squinting, just staring somewhat vapidly at Theodore.

"Hey man." Theodore angles his body toward the door.

"Somebody didn't come home last night." Henry props his hands on his hips, one of them quickly dipping below to pick a pesky wedgie. Theodore rolls his eyes at the insinuation of his comment.

"It's not like that. I just—"

"Oh my god, it's true. I know that look, Theo." Henry's shaking one stout finger at Theodore as he trundles over to the couch and plops down. "You... got laid, my dude."

"Your sagacity continues to astound me, Mr. Holmes," responds

Theodore. "But you're dead wrong. I was just…I was just…" Theodore can't think of a way to describe what actually happened to him last night, and even if he could, he knows he'd sound off his rocker. Either way, he doesn't want to get into that conversation with Henry right now.

"You were just…waist deep in poon, I get it. And hey! It's about time, my dear friend Theodore. I was actually starting to get a little worried there. How long's it been?"

"Listen man, I'd love to chat, but I actually have somewhere—"

"Two weeks after prom!" His pudgy finger is now attempting to poke the ceiling in a declaratory gesture of triumph. "That one girl that you were too afraid to ask out…Sally…Susie…"

"Agamemnon," Theodore's sardonic reply.

"Yeah, it was Susie." Henry James' social graces include disregarding the person with whom he's talking. "Man, that was a while ago. Good for you, bro, good for you. I was always pulling for you—even through this endless Age of Cessation." He chuckles, which comes out a cacophonous jumble of snorts. "So, what's her name?"

Theodore finds himself at his wits' end, and inexorably determined to visit that old gramophone again, as well as the crazy world to which it inexplicably led him. "Priam, King of Troy," he jibes as he turns and walks out the door.

The streetlights cast over the roads a vacillating swathe of colors, a pulsing preamble to the neon-drenched heart of the city. Theodore takes Gansevoort Street over to 8th Avenue, reflecting on just how empty the city is tonight, but all the better for it, in his opinion. In the middle of the street, steam leaks from the corners of a manhole cover, its tendrils billowing upward and uncurling into the night sky.

A young couple shuffles by, seeking shelter under the continuous weave of architecture looming overhead, pausing inside every entryway they can find to shake off like dogs. "Do you think my hair will stay?" the woman asks her companion while doing that technique Theodore has seen women do in old Hollywood movies; the one where they cup their hands and dab them against their hair, looking afraid to actually touch that perfect perm lest the world should end.

The diluvial downpour has already laid waste to your hair, lady, Theodore chuckles, *not much good a little petting's gonna do you at this point.*

Theodore edges into the part of town where the buildings wear their age with scorn. Argent stone conflates with sun-lashed brick in a tapestry of old-world character. The sturdy old materials don't shrug under their own weight. Their age becomes apparent in the finer details—the divots, the cracks, the lacerations that overlap each other through time, forming lines upon which he could scratch out a game of tic-tac-toe.

Theodore knows he's closing in on The Cat's Meow. He makes his way down the narrowing streets until he sees the saloon-style bar—the one that he originally confused The Cat's Meow with—looming on the corner. He makes a sharp left and he's up against the building. So close, and yet so far. He lets his fingers wander along the callous grooves in the brick wall as he ambles towards the bar's unassuming key.

For a moment his mind wanders, and he's no longer fingering the wall for the key to a bar but is investigating the murder scene of one Enoch Drebber—the victim in one of Sir Arthur Conan Doyle's most riveting tales.

As his fingers fumble over a brick that's too smooth to fit in with the callous bunch, his moment with the inimitable Holmes is over, but that's okay. Because he knows that soon he'll be in someone else's shoes—those of a clueless yank maundering about in the Queen's land.

He wanders to the back of the building and finds the slot, shoving the brick in and opening the industrial barn door with a less-than-sonorous screech. He descends the stairway that looks like it leads to a bomb shelter, and raps on the door. He waits, tapping his foot and autonomously fondling the phonograph cylinder in his hoodie pocket. Through the thick iron plates of the door, Theodore can already hear the rapturous music of the Jazz Age piping through—vivid, aural signposting of the world that lies ahead—or behind, really. And that girl. That mesmerizing bargirl.

The sliding door viewer barks open, revealing a small slice of a familiar face. It looks like Jersey Guy's working again tonight. Theodore unintentionally grimaces as he wonders to himself whether the password to get in will be the same as last night. Without Alice, he's screwed, should the little questionnaire be different tonight.

"Whaddaya know?" Jersey Guy chortles as he peers through the viewer. "A return customer. Say, where's that gal of yours?"

"Uh, she's not my gal," Theodore retorts. "She's my sister and she's not with me tonight."

"Ah that's too bad. She's a looker, that broad. A real looker." The doorman's faux accent feels like a canker sore on Theodore's mind; he can't stand the sound of the guy. "Well, I tell you what. I know you and all, so I'm inclined to give you a pass tonight, no questions." The doorman yanks the old steel partition open and greets Theodore with a handshake.

"My only caveat for your easy entrance is your sis's number." He smiles smugly, exacerbating the wryness of his features as he does so.

"Oh, uh, well…" Theodore hadn't expected this predicament. On the one hand, he knows he can't give this buffoon Alice's phone number, he just can't. On the other hand, he wants so desperately to be back in that other world, to see that girl again. Either way, he needs to act fast or Jersey Guy is going to get wise and give him the old heave-ho.

Theodore gives him Alice's number, in a sardonically slow fashion, but he modifies one number to throw the guy off. He feels no remorse in doing so, despite the resplendent smile that it carves onto the guy's face. Alice deserves better; Theodore knows that, and he also knows that she'd kill him if he gave away her number of his own whim. Despite being such a vivacious and outwardly social woman, he knows that below the surface Alice is quite discerning and protective of her heart. She guards it like a lowly squire would guard his king, and Theodore respects that.

"Enjoy your night, pal!" Jersey Guy says to his back as he advances into the room. Theodore can't be bothered with Jersey Guy now. Before the last syllable fumbles out of the pretentious gatekeeper's mouth, Theodore's already halfway into the bar immersing himself in the music of the roaring twenties, curls of cigarette smoke billowing about him.

He elbows his way through the crowd, taking note that the patrons are once again imitating the fashion of the period. But this time around, after being edified last night on what a genuine early-20th century party is like, The Cat's Meow jam feels like a dime-store Halloween version of the past. He glances at a girl who has taken over the dance floor, acrylic paint shining on her fingernails as she twirls about. The 1930s masquerade ball he visited last night felt so different, so authentic; not tacky and hyperbolized like this. *Still*, he thinks as he shuffles past the dance floor, *A for effort.*

He heads for the back left of the bar area and turns down the little hallway, hearing the crackling din of swing-era music attenuate as he ambles towards the little old bar in the back—the real Cat's Meow. Glancing left and right, he takes a gander at the wall of archaic bar photos. There's the photo of The Growler's Ball, with all the affluent-looking ladies and gentlemen doing the Charleston; there's The Cat's Meow receiving its first shipment, all the lovely gangster-types sneering at the camera, and then there's the equivocal image of the Masquerade Ball at The King's Inn; the photo that somehow captured the events that he experienced last night, including the image of Theodore himself, lurking towards the back of the ballroom.

Only, something in this photo is once again...off. As Theodore's eyes fervently trace the image, searching for his own figure among the masses, he sees an alteration—a disparity with the picture from the night before. Theodore remembers clear as day the image of himself lurking toward the back of the room and gazing forward as the masked crowd cheered. In this image, everything else appears as he remembers it. The enigmatic ringmaster posing in the foreground with his glass up high as the cameraman immortalizes his toast, and the legion of disguised followers joining him in celebration are identical. However, the Theodore in the image is somehow changed.

The Theodore in the photograph is not simply standing there staring forward. When the camera snapped this time, it caught his side profile as he was walking out of the room. Only, he's not merely walking out, he's being led by the hand by some woman. Theodore leans into the photo until the grains bulge in an ambiguous patchwork of chalky whites and inky blacks. The flapper dress, the long legs…the person holding Theodore's hand is the mysterious bar girl, the one with whom he is so captivated. Theodore shakes his head in disbelief. That wasn't what happened last night. He had interacted with the short lady in the chicken mask before deciding to leave the ballroom of his own accord. It was then that he ran into the girl at the lobby bar, after the image was taken.

So how, if the events transpired as he recalls them, can he be staring at what's happening in this image? Truthfully, no actualization of the events of last night make it any more believable—outside of the whole situation being some eerily tangible, freakishly corporeal dream. And Theodore still doesn't believe in time travel; he never was much of an H.G. Wells fan. He's heard science fiction nerds claim that certain places can serve as tears in the fabric of spacetime. Through this image, and with that ill-informed logic, he could be peering into another universe. *Whatever the case,* he thinks while glancing at the peculiar gramophone in the next room, *there's only one way to find out.*

He approaches the gramophone like a psychic would a haunted house. Theodore finds his finger yet again caressing the record in his hoodie pocket, as if the two pieces are admonishing him to reconcile them. They crave to be united like he craves to see that fascinating old world again.

Hands tremulous and diffident, he pulls the record out of his pocket, gingerly placing it inside its housing with a sonorous click. He lifts the old needle and moves it over the cylinder. But he hesitates before dipping it, much like a stultified writer hovers his pen over the page patiently waiting for the words to flow out of his mind and bleed into the ink.

A fear of the unknown is what's staying his hand, but it is the inexorable allure of the unknown that has brought him back here in the first place.

Intermittent, silvery tones blare from a trumpet in the other room; the muffled ruckus of the dancing crowd buzzes in his ear. He thinks of the mysterious bar girl and his decision is made.

Right as he moves to place the needle over the record, a hand claps thunderously on his back. Bathtub Gin Guy, aka Francis—though Theodore isn't ready to take him seriously enough yet to call him by his real name—is peering over his shoulder, his fire-tinted beard threatening to tickle Theodore's back.

"It's a crazy contraption, isn't it?" Theodore detects the odious waft of the man's creation on his breath. His mind immediately turns to Alice, who he knows left the bar with this loser last night. He wonders if they kissed, imagining his little sis letting that foul-smelling mouth touch her own. He cringes, and then, in seeing this lummox sans-arm candy, wonders just where Alice is tonight. Knowing her better than anyone, Theodore assumes the capricious girl is probably already investigating the next of Manhattan's best kept secrets.

"Yeah, it's really something." He lets go of the needle, instinctively wanting to snatch the record from its housing, but Bathtub Gin Guy's one step ahead of him. His puissant frame squeezes in next to Theodore.

"Yeah, I remember when I found this gem." He pats the machine as if it was his golden retriever returning a ball. "I won this bad boy at an auction in England a few years ago—"

"Wait, this gramophone is yours?" Theodore spits.

"Well it was. I sold it to Reggie when he opened The Cat's Meow. We're old buddies." He shrugs. "Although he clearly doesn't appreciate the antiquity or the sheer beauty of it, seeing as it's just gathering dust in this storage room. See that rusty old set of numbers there? I think that's the year it was made; although being engraved on a dial like that kinda makes it look like a time machine, eh? Hey!" Bathtub Gin Guy ululates, reaching for the machine.

"There's a record in it. Somebody has visited my little treasure after all."

"Oh. That's mine." Theodore's hand reaches in autonomous contest. "I was just—"

"Well let's fire the sucker up; see how she sounds!" The lummox wraps his fingers around the crank lever and begins spinning.

"Oh, um…" Suddenly inarticulate, Theodore fumbles for an excuse to keep the guy from playing his record. This is his little secret. Not to mention, he doesn't know if it's a dangerous one. "That record doesn't play; it's basically just an old family heirloom."

"She's got a bigger horn than most old sound systems," Bathtub Gin Guy exclaims over his winding hand. Apparently, he couldn't hear Theodore over his own captivating thoughts. "And a unique shape, too. So, I'm assuming she'll give quite a squall. Ah, there we go." The blundering behemoth spools the lever to the maximum of its revolutions, where it emits a ratcheting scream of remonstration.

Bathtub Gin Guy moves the needle over the cylinder as it begins to gyrate in its housing. "Dude, didn't you hear me? The record doesn't play," Theodore protests, feeling a rising panic.

"Chill out, man," his uncooperative new nuisance says while moving the needle up against the cylinder. "Let's at least test it out, eh?" Within seconds the horn blares into life, at first sputtering and choking, and doling out a cacophonous static. Bathtub Gin Guy lifts the needle, moving it ever so slightly along the cylinder until a more sonorous sound emits from the horn.

An inundating sense of nostalgia, somewhat euphoric and terrifying at once, hits Theodore as the first bar of music plays. The chilling opening notes seethe out of the violin; a forlorn and foreboding entrance.

"There we go!" Bathtub Gin Guy exalts. "Not too bad for a century-old device." But Theodore can barely hear him; his focus is elsewhere. He knows what's coming. He cringes expectantly as the band begins to weave its senescent melody through the horn. Bathtub Gin Guy's hands, which were triumphantly propped on his hips a moment ago, sag to his sides as he too begins to succumb to the otherworldly sensation.

The old bar swells and hiccups as two worlds conflate into one, Theodore and his oblivious companion standing at the precipice. "What? What's?" Bathtub Gin Guy struggles to find words as he and Theodore are yanked off their feet. Theodore watches his companion as the world around them is suffused with a boundless black. Golden strands of light gleam about them and disseminate into the ether.

Bathtub Gin Guy reels about, his temperance shattering as the world disappears around him. He's hollering and spewing syllables, but his cries aren't penetrating the void. A sobering pressure bears down on Theodore as the world begins to materialize around him. At first there's merely a glimmer of light piercing the stillness. As the light blossoms, a stealthy haunt of musical notes meanders into Theodore's ear.

He can hear the vocalist from his gramophone record, the words reverberating and crashing about as the foyer of the hotel trundles into view. Raven Woman—the same person that Theodore inadvertently landed on the first time around—is standing precisely in the same spot, her back unexpectantly facing him. This time though, he anticipates the collision, and as his feet touch down, he pivots and twirls about, landing directly in front of the old lady.

"Bah!" she vociferates, nearly flinging the cigarette out of her grasp in surprise. Holding his hands up in a gesture of apology, Theodore looks into her eyes and shudders. Those piercing, pernicious orbs are glaring back at him—he remembers them well from his first visit. "Sorry miss, I didn't see you there." He feigns a smile, glancing behind her at the portal through which he just dropped. Like a wall of liquid glass, the opening shimmers as it folds in on itself; effervescing and smoldering, and then disappearing into thin air. The song from the gramophone fades along with the portal, like the blaring radio of a car whizzing past on the highway. Theodore's only point of egress now gone, he turns to face an eerie hotel rampant with enigmatic and seedy characters, and thinks one thing to himself: *I'm back.*

III

"What on earth are you doing, you clumsy Yank?" Raven Woman spits, fawning over her nearly extinguished cigarette like a mother cradling her child. "Haven't you any manners, or don't they instruct you in the art of chivalry across the pond? You can't just go stumbling about like a pissed fool, colliding with everybody as if we're expendable as the swine with which you likely associate; we in this assembly are of an influential lot, and I have more clout residing in a single utterance than you will obtain in your entire life. Now, where is your doppelgänger?"

"My what?" Theodore stammers.

"Your doppelgänger, your cover, your mask? We're required to bring a blinder that suits our personalities, as a phoneme suits the word in which it's incorporated, Yank. It is a Shibboleth after all, no? These events don't sprout up like weeds; it takes the diligent, nuanced mind of Sir Nithercott himself to procure the list of traitors and prospects." *Traitors and prospects? A list?*

Theodore nods obsequiously and turns away. He needs to get a mask, and the fact that he nearly ran into Raven Woman again might signify something. If she was in the same spot as she was on the first night, he must have landed in 1931, London tonight at the same exact moment as he did yesterday. That means that if he's somehow traveling back in time to the date specified on the gramophone, events tonight might unfold in a similar manner. If that's the case, the other patron is going to pull him away from the coat closet before he's able to reach a mask.

He opens the closet's heavy wooden door just a slice, enough for his body to carve through while avoiding the salience of a creaky old door. He digs about in the bin of masks, or "doppelgängers," as Raven Woman calls them. They all seem hard and inflexible, not like the plastic masks of the 21st Century that Theodore is accustomed to.

He grabs the first mask that feels somewhat pliable—a soft-featured gazelle—and straps it onto his face. Out in the dazzling, Art Deco-inspired foyer, Theodore finds a splotch of red among a sea of black marble and coruscant chandeliers. A lanky man in a red tailcoat is chatting with two other patrons. Their backs are turned to Theodore, but the man in the red tailcoat is facing him squarely, and behind the pig mask covering his face are two beady eyes that aren't engaged with the people to whom he is talking, they're pinned on Theodore.

Hello you, Theodore thinks. *You probably don't remember me from last night, but I remember you. You're the man who pried me out of the closet to watch the ringmaster's show unfurl. Well, I got a mask this time.* If he doesn't approach Theodore tonight, though, perhaps not everything is going to unfold in just the same manner as the previous time like he thought. Hopefully that bargirl will be in her same spot. That's what really matters to Theodore.

He maunders down the hall and into the checkered-tile elevator room when it hits him; where's Bathtub Gin Guy? He made the trip from The Cat's Meow, Theodore's almost sure of that. He glances around fervently, but to no avail. All he sees is an antediluvian deluge of masked strangers crowding the halls of an old-fashioned hotel.

Feeling an acute pang of guilt, he entertains the thought that the guy didn't make it through. Theodore still doesn't know anything about this strange world he's found, let alone enough to know if these people might have a violent reaction upon discovering a patently anachronistic American figure strolling the halls. Theodore finds himself naturally inclined to dissolve at social gatherings, like a peel of wallpaper stoically observing the scene—almost from the outside looking in. Bathtub Gin Guy...a bit more obvious, probably. If he does happen to be wandering the halls with similar wonderment, Theodore hopes the dude's period-fitting clothes will help him blend in and avoid any trouble.

"I say, young man. Yes, you in that ghastly-looking attire." A husky British voice rouses Theodore from his reverie. This time he's being affronted by a man in a russet overcoat and a wolf mask discernible by its intimidating, open-jawed visage. If he remembers correctly, it's the same man who was taking a smoke break outside the building on night one. "Whence do you hail, and what brings you to our little gathering?"

Theodore searches for his tongue, his eyes darting back to the man in the pig mask, whose gaze still hasn't left him. "Well come now, lad, there's no need to be afraid. You're acting like a deer caught in the headlights, or a gazelle in the headlights, rather." He points to Theodore's mask, which suddenly starts to feel hot and itchy over his face. Theodore doesn't want to be bothered by random masqueraders; he wants to find that girl.

"Say, what do you think of that furtive Marxist movement, *The Pilfering Paupers?*" The man in the wolf mask inquires, clearly testing Theodore's legitimacy within this establishment. The fact that these masqueraders seem innately suspicious of him is getting old, and he doesn't have the faintest clue who The Pilfering Paupers are—although the name certainly sounds like a moniker suitable for this period. *Perhaps a gang of some sort?*

"I uh, I think that the people need change and they're promising to give it to them." Theodore knows little about post-war England, but he does know that the Labour Party was in contention with the conservatives for better work conditions. Who knows? Sometimes a shot fired in the dark hits its target.

The man in the wolf mask declines to reply for a minute, opting simply to stare at him with eyes that are softer than the other patrons, demure. "Right." His voice is terse, like a doctor doling out instructions to an intern. "Well, please enjoy the Shibboleth, Puddle Skipper."

Puddle Skipper? This gives Theodore pause. As children, he and Alice used to play in the rain, make a game of jumping about in puddles and dousing each other in splashes of mud. They called it, 'hopscotching the rain.' But there's no way this man from 1931 England who, in Theodore's time is long dead, knows of that silly little game.

Theodore remembers hearing that term before, but he can't pin down where. Perhaps it was in school. *Aha*! He manages to pluck the memory from its cozy sojourn within his subconscious. Not unlike the expression, "across the pond", a metaphor for Americans traveling across the Atlantic to England, Puddle Skipper was a prohibition-era term used specifically for younger people who made the journey. A Puddle Skipper was someone who would visit England in order to obtain real alcohol—anything other than the homemade liquor they forced themselves to choke down in America. *So,* Theodore postulates, *there's a deeper insinuation behind this man's choice of words than a mere reference to the childhood pastime of skipping puddles.* This moniker is, however, somewhat refreshing after being labelled the pejorative "Yank" by everyone else.

Having apparently passed the man in the wolf mask's equivocal test and free to continue his pursuit of that girl, Theodore angles toward the long hallway leading to the Regal Ballroom. "One more thing, Puddle Skipper. Have you ever seen an osprey take flight?" *Have you ever seen an osprey take flight?* This truly puzzles Theodore. He thinks hard about night one, recalling that shadowed figure he encountered at the wharf by the river. That man mentioned the word osprey as well. Could his and this man's affairs be somehow intertwined?

"No, should I have?" his response. The man in the wolf mask returns an icy stare and then breaks off into the crowd as a swell of masqueraders bustle in from some other room in this labyrinth of a building.

"It's time!" A woman in a leopard mask paws at Theodore, nearly sweeping him into the virulent tide of bodies.

"The announcement!" a voice inhumed amongst the masses declares.

"The Pre-Shibboleth Frivolities!" Theodore falls in line, feeling far less ostentatious than on night one when he was here sans-mask. In a series of events concordant to night one, the crowd funnels into a dim hallway, brushing past a swathe of masked female dancers shaking their bare bums and breasts before tuxedoed men sitting in plush, high backed chairs. *'Allo gents.* Theodore attempts his best cockney accent in his head. No good. He won't be blending in through his mastery of dialects anytime soon.

The Regal Ballroom sign glints as it whizzes past, and Theodore is once more in the midst of a raucous Jazz Age party. He weaves through the crowd; tufts of smoke billow and quiver about him, churning madly as dancers cut the air, and then evanescing into nothingness like steam off a cup of coffee. Feeling his heart race with excitement as the cornets and oboes clash on the bandstand, Theodore inhales deeply and takes the scene in.

"What are your dealings here, Yank?" a shrill, somewhat familiar voice pecks at Theodore's ear. The short, portly woman with the chicken mask is in roughly the same spot as she was on the previous night, strutting about the rear of the ballroom like a hen escaped from the coop only to be thwarted by the backyard fence. Theodore opens his mouth to respond but stifles himself upon realizing that she's not addressing him. She's talking to a broad-shouldered monolith in suspenders and a butter-colored shirt. *Bathtub Gin Guy! He did make the leap!*

Theodore moves to wave, but then realizes that he's wearing his 'doppelgänger' and his compadre won't recognize him. He chooses then to greet Alice's bar friend, but halts suddenly, his blood stanching in his veins. The guy's unhinged. His head's chirping back and forth like a startled animal and he's panting heavily.

"What's, what's going on? Where am I?" Theodore understands the consternation in Bathtub Gin Guy's voice, sympathizes as the guy tries to reconcile the logical part of his mind with the preternatural situation. The feeling's akin to severe jet lag coalescing with a heavy alcohol binge. He's simply failing at internalizing his confusion, something Theodore didn't have much trouble with.

Careful, man, Theodore thinks. *Careful, or you're going to get noticed.* And here, noticed isn't necessarily a good thing. Theodore knows that if the ballroom wasn't alive with the red-hot fervency of a '30s jazz party, the whole room would be staring at this mask-less American who's now flailing about like a fish that wriggled off the hook.

"What's your business here, young one?" Short Chicken Lady asks in a voice that's more interrogative than curious. "Are you one of the Brooklyn Chappies, or perhaps a member of another group of sympathizers? Who are you, and how did you get in here?" The tone of her voice escalates into a ragged shriek. "A non-believer!" The din of the dancehall isn't enough to overpower her vociferous outburst. The heads of several masqueraders nearby whirl around; a dancing couple beside the ululating woman stop mid-step and crane their necks as if an air raid siren had just blared. *Wrong decade for that comparison*, Theodore thinks to himself as he hurries to mollify the confused little woman.

"It's alright, it's alright," he declares, snatching Bathtub Gin Guy by the arm. His catatonic companion turns to him now, saying nothing but staring at Theodore with spellbound eyes, vapidly scratching his sideburns like an ape. "He's with me."

"And who might you be?" Short Chicken Lady inquires, having no way of knowing that Theodore talked with her last night, since technically, last night didn't happen—at least not from her perspective. But now isn't the time for Theodore to consider parallel universe theories, or causality loops, or any other pseudo-science that might explain this phantasmagoria.

"C'mon buddy, the bar's this way. Now, where did your doppelgänger go?" He turns to Short Chicken Lady, imagining the expression of dubiety that is likely making itself home under her mask. "He's just as excited as you for the Shibboleth, it's just that, well, my friend here is off his opiates again and he can never seem to form a coherent sentence during the withdrawals."

"I, what?" Bathtub Gin Guy stammers.

"Never mind all that, Jimmie, let's get you something to calm those nerves, eh?" He drags the lummox away from the Regal Ballroom just as the band begins to crescendo—a harbinger for the imminent appearance of the Ringmaster. Hands swatting at the mephitic, smoke-riddled air of the adjacent room, Theodore leads his confused companion towards the bar.

"Eugene, my love, when are we going to Italy?" purrs an imbibed woman in an off-green dress slumped over an informally dressed man at the bar. His hair is slicked back like in old black and white movies, and he has a cotton shirt on with the sleeves lackadaisically rolled to the elbow in lumped, uneven creases. One hand is tapping a cigarette into an ashtray, while the other is clamped around a large raincoat that covers his back.

"You promised me that after your next assignment—the very next one—we would scuttle over to Marche; to the Apennine Mountains, where that quaint little village awaits us. Remind me once more what it was called, love?"

"Montecassiano," he grunts in an arcane American accent.

"That's right! It sounds just as magical as the first time I heard it. Montecassiano, the little medieval village nestled away from the troubles and cares of the real world. You know, love, I hear the finest wine in all the world comes from central Italy. And they have this queer take on coffee that they call espresso. Now, that's a funny little moniker, isn't it? Lorraine told me they pour in these tiny little glasses only an ounce or two of coffee that is so concentrated Lorraine claims it has the consistency of mud. Wouldn't you want to try that, love?"

"Once we get there, doll. Once we get there." Her laconic companion sucks the butt of his cigarette while she leans closer, stroking his hair. *Where's the girl?* Theodore glances around the caliginous shadows of the lounge.

"You're Alice's brother, right?" Bathtub Gin Guy paws at him, darting glances about like a junkie surrounded by cops. "I recognized your voice." Theodore ponders the implications of telling him the truth; ponders what the consequences could be if this guy knew he was here, too.

After a long pause, "Yeah. It's me." He considers lifting the gazelle off his face a little but considers first the clandestine crowd about them. Dresses scintillating under old filament bulbs; tuxedos and suitcoats bouncing about the room; obscure animal faces hovering in the smoke. Through a soft undercurrent of chatter, heads tilt back in guttural laughter. Even the jovial affectations of this crowd seem sinister. He leaves his mask on.

"So, is this a dream? Did I drink too much? Sometimes when I drink too much of my still-booze, I pass out and my dreams are more…vivid, you know? But this…"

"Francis—is that what you go by?"

"Just don't call me Frank." Francis's eyes are still darting across the room in kinetic little bursts.

"Alright, Bathtub Gin Guy, look…" Just then, a light touch on the shoulder derails his thought.

"You blokes certainly aren't from around here." He turns to face the person he traveled over 80 years to see. Bargirl. She's just as alluring as last time, just as intoxicating. Her doppelgänger, the effigy of a fierce hawk, has a mesh that completely obscures her eyes. Her intent is swallowed by this enigmatic appearance, a flirtatious affectation espousing her every movement. Her slender arms are poised on her hips, her head cocked to the side.

"A gazelle? That's a curious doppelgänger you've got there. Rather docile for such an event, no?" Her voice is sonorous, with just a hint of something raspy, something edgy.

"Oh, I um, yeah. I just figured I'd switch it up, you know?" He can't believe how the words come out. There's a rattle to his voice that he's never experienced before, not even during the frequent interrogations in the principal's office in high school. Conversation never makes him nervous; bored would be a better adjective.

"Switch it up? That must be one of your Yank terms." The bar girl turns to Francis. "And whence do you boys hail?" Francis doesn't respond at first. He just stares at the hawk mask like a deer caught between two big white bulbs, his face sapped of color.

"Well I…"

"He's from New York, just like me," Theodore tags himself back into the conversation, knowing he's going to need to speak for his new traumatized buddy. *Ah hell, I just don't like it when she talks to another guy.* Theodore's accepted that he's no altruist. And besides, Francis has Alice. He can't take this girl, too.

"The Big Apple?" Her face curls into a smile. "I've always wanted to meet a dreamy American idealist. Those of us who call Sloane Square home can be so…bleak. We're in the throes of a minor socio-political crisis ourselves, and some of us make it out to be worse than it really is. The affluent people who call this patch of London home could never get through the disaster your kind are experiencing, couldn't acquiesce to waiting in bread lines for mere scraps of leaven and a meager dipping-broth, or take pride in accepting any old job that might provide heat for their families for just one night. Although, the two of you look like you've seldom missed a meal; especially you." She points to Francis; whose turgid lumps of arms are swelling out of the sleeves of his dress shirt.

"That's right. We've been in London for some time now. Managed to escape the worst of the Depression," Theodore lies right through his doppelgänger.

"Do I know you from somewhere, Yank?" The girl brushes her neck with a gloved hand.

"Uh, I don't think so." Could she, out of all these revelers, remember him from night one? No, that's not possible. According to the zany laws of time travel as Theodore knows them, on her timeline, last night didn't really happen. Theodore returning to this time and place is essentially overlapping his first visit, like white-out on a still-drying line of text. Her prim smile lingers on her face as she brushes past them to the bar and, patting her silvery swathe of hair, hails the barman, who is of course the same guy with the rat doppelgänger from night one. Bertram?

"What're ya drinkin', miss?"

"Bertram, dear, prepare something for my new friend here. He's got a case of the jitters, so make it puissant and punchy."

"Right miss." Bertram raises the large end of a jigger and waterfalls a clear liquid into it, disregarding the runoff that pools onto the brass table top. Theodore thinks of the Puddle-Skippers, a group to which he's pretending to belong, and understands why they come here. Bathtub Gin Guy has given him a taste of what the old makeshift stills must have produced, and it is repulsive. Plus, it seems likely that when alcohol was available in speakeasies the bartenders would probably ration it, stifling the flow on each pour as quickly as a stout kink in a water hose. *London is the place to drink in 1931*, Theodore ruminates.

Bertram commences shaking some sort of martini, garnishes the glass with an olive, and hands it to the girl, who in turns gives it to Francis. "Drink up, Yank; it'll squelch your jitters."

"This place is amazing, so lifelike." He swipes the cocktail from her hand. "Let's see if your gin holds a candle to mine." *Good, maybe he's adjusting*, Theodore thinks. The girl in the hawk mask struts away from the bar, but coyly tugs at Theodore's arm as she goes. They traipse into the ballroom, where the ringmaster himself is posing with the crowd for a photo op Theodore has already seen.

Snap goes the old tripod camera, an effulgent flash brightening all corners of the decadent ballroom. But Theodore doesn't care about the ringmaster right now. He doesn't care about the equivocal Shibboleth, or anyone else here. He's being led by hand by the wondrous Bargirl; the person with whom he has already fallen in love, despite having only seen half her face, and not knowing a thing about her. Her arm, a beautiful lissome form, moves before him, bending and straightening, and then bending again as she weaves through the crowd. Her grip on his hand is light, but obdurate, convincing him of her strong-willed nature. But where is she taking him? The thrill of danger courses through his veins as they cross the long, and now empty, corridor and pause before the elevator shaft.

"Ninth floor, please." As they wait for the operator to slide the gate open, she shoots Theodore just one glance, her lips folding into a half-smile. His knees become jelly. Where *is* she taking him? The operator enters the narrow and old-fashioned box, which Theodore thinks looks more like an old telephone booth than an elevator, and beckons them forward. Never once does the man scrub the manufactured smile from his face while he does so.

Somewhere in the corridors of the hotel a jaunty dance tune haunts the space, magnifying the hotel's unsettling, senescent vibe. The operator pulls a prodigious brass lever, and, after an intermission of cacophonous mechanical clunks, Theodore is on his way to the equivocal heights of the hotel. Having no idea what to expect gives him an unsavory twist in his stomach, but he's with Bargirl, and that makes things all right.

The elevator operator clasps his hands before his body and cozies up to the opposite wall of the elevator in an insouciant gesture. At first Theodore hardly thinks twice about the operator, but after a moment of averting his gaze toward the floor, something pokes at his peripherals; something garish and white. The man's still smiling. And it's not so much a harmless, how-do-you-do prim salutation, but more of a macabre, skin-stretching peel of a smile; the reckless grin of a madman. And, Theodore looks closer, he's wearing makeup. It's faint but bookending each corner of the operator's mouth is an arc of paint that looks like a hyperbolized, cartoonish smile; a delineation of his real smile, which is pried open wide enough to be creepy by itself. Beneath the corners of his mouth are two vertical lines, painted on, or perhaps scars, that remind Theodore of the flappable mouth on a ventriloquist's doll.

Refusing to look at the operator another second, Theodore fixes his eyes forward, watching as each floor rolls lazily by like the looping background image of a website. Pervaded with Victorian stylings and Romanesque pillars and arches, the hallways of the hotel are long, and every bit as opulent as the main floor. Each floor they pass is eerily deserted.

Theodore assumes that all the guests are in the Regal Ballroom enjoying the eccentric lunacy of the Ringmaster's show. But not the girl. She's taking

Theodore elsewhere in the hotel—to the quieter, emptier areas. He entertains another twist in his stomach as he considers the possible scenarios ahead; a spark of excitement igniting his mind into a frenzy. Fighting the inevitable smile, he tries to mimic the abstruse expression on the girl's face. He fails miserably.

The elevator rolls past the third floor. At the far end of the hall, a flourish of coattails in the hallway yanks Theodore from his reverie. Two men—no three men—are dragging something. He can't tell what, can only see enough to decipher the shape. Human. Before he's able to glean anything more from the situation, the lift has ambled past the third floor and the hallway has rolled out of sight.

He glances sharply at Bargirl with wide eyes, but she seems either not to notice, or not care. She slothfully turns her head to him and gives him a youthfully blithe smile. He wonders if she can see his jugular vein slamming in his throat.

When the trundling box of metal finally reaches its destination, the doors open six levels up from the mysterious third floor events. The operator tugs the gate open and, alongside another singularly treacherous flash of teeth, bids them adieu with a grand gesture of his arm. Theodore doesn't hesitate to fly the coop; this dangling two-ton metal trap feels like it might give at any moment. He has officially decided he doesn't like old fashioned elevators.

Bargirl takes the lead, once again pulling him by the hand, like a stoic young diver with a rare but impractical spelunking treasure with which she cannot part. His dealings with this girl have been cursory to say the least, and her ignorance, or indifference, to whatever was happening on the third floor with those men dragging what looked like a body sets off alarms in his mind.

Nevertheless, even if her method of communication has been less than verbal, there's a pulsating energy between them and Theodore feels truly desired by a girl for the first time in his life. It's a good feeling.

He lets her pick the pace as they walk the halls; a relaxed saunter through what feels like an interminable labyrinth of corridors. Having seen only the tiniest morsel of the building before, he hadn't realized the hotel was such an extensive feat of design and engineering. They pass a huge mahogany table, and upon it, a vase capped with a myriad of flowers. Every several strides, an arcane oil painting adds to the decadent, lavish look of the hotel. After passing a gloomy path that diverges from the main hall with a sign that reads, *Service Stairs*, Theodore and Bargirl waltz past a piece of art that strikes a familiar chord with him.

A largely monochrome scene with a cluster of soldiers in tall fur caps; a single soldier lying mortally wounded, or perhaps dead, on the ground; a concerned comrade is leaning over him, surrounded by a host of fellow soldiers drooping under an enervation so deftly brushed that Theodore believes no number of carefully-crafted war films could match the expressive content in this still frame. The saturnine expressions upon their faces yield more insight to the grim realities of war and instill in Theodore a sense of bereavement so puzzling to his faculties as to make him certain that he, too, knows and grieves for the still figure of the man prostrate on the gelid blanket of snow. The painting, while cinereous and bleak, is galvanized with emotional substance through these masterful adornments.

Attendance, Roll Call...he's certain the painting's title is something like that. He's uncertain, however, where he has seen it before or why the motifs of bleak socialism are giving him another sense of déjà vu. Was it something that the man in the shadows said last night, on the London docks just before Theodore was beamed back to his time? *"Death to draconian rule; prosperity to the state?"*

They pass multiple hotel rooms, maybe a dozen or so, before finally coming upon a door that only stands out in that it has no number, no designation whatsoever. The door carves a spot about midway down a long hall, hand-carved turquoise decals lining its elegant frame. This place is no mere stack of listless and interchangeable bedrooms as are so many modern hotels, but a hand-built haven of intricacy. Theodore wonders if the Ringmaster downstairs owns all of this, and if so, what does that guy *do* for a living?

His mind crests the surface of an ocean of possibilities for the Ringmaster's riches. In this arcane period where the law had as many gaps as a hillbilly's smile, the guy could be an illegal bookmaker—a race fixer like the various industrial-age mob leaders Theodore has read about. He could be a prevalent political figure, or perchance a prominent member of the gentry; back in Georgian-era England, the nobility nurtured many questionable friendships throughout its political struggles.

The girl's hand tightens over his. With her free hand, she nudges the door to what must be her private quarters and swoops inside, dragging the ever-willing but still-daydreaming Theodore in with her. The air is warmer in here, and utterly suffused with the same scent he found on the girl's neck. The whole room is a simulacrum of her cranked up to 11.

Theodore snickers at his little reference to '80s mockumentary *This is Spinal Tap*, and thinks of how odd it is that, in this world, the scene from the film that's running through his mind hasn't been made yet—hasn't even been conceptualized. He's watched it multiple times, knows it word for word. Like a wise old augur in a time when aphoristic narratives were the driving force of guidance for societies and when metaphor filled the epistemological gaps of man's relation to his world, Theodore has the gift of foresight. Whereas he has the privilege—or the burden—of knowing the course of events primed to take place from this moment on, these English chaps are dithering blithely about, ignorant of all the pain and all the joy that the 21st century will bring the world.

He ponders to himself, as the girl pulls him further into the room, about the amount of power that's in his hands should he stay in this time period. He could do a hell of a job in some cabinet or government position, knowing more or less the great blunders of history and how they came about. For the love of god, he could prevent World War II; could travel to America and wait at the grassy knoll for JFK's killer, dispatching him and forever changing the course of history.

If he could learn how to manipulate the gramophone to send him farther into the past, he could even wait in the balcony of Ford's Theatre, hiding amongst the box seats and biding his time for John Wilkes Booth to brandish the Dillinger from his bootstrap—or wherever he kept it. With this discovery, the door to a wealth of opportunities has been opened to him, for the first time in his mundane little life.

Theodore's mind maunders through the various scenarios of potential heroism, from squelching McCarthy's dissembled Communist inquisition—the Red Scare witch-hunt that stoked the budding flame of the Cold War—to the Munich Massacre in 1972, where a Palestinian extremist group abducted and killed a handful of Israeli athletes and coaches during the Olympics. He relishes the concept that he need only inform the relevant people of the who, what, when, where and why of each of history's famous catastrophes before they occur, and he'd be forever lauded for his miraculous foresight… or thrown in the Gulag, depending on what he said or did at what place and at what time. Altering the past could certainly result in a host of scenarios, both good and bad. Time manipulation is a remarkably powerful tool.

Reality, or this unreality that the gramophone has placed him in, floods back as he watches Bargirl crouch down and remove her heels. Her feet are nice, small and slender, with straight, round toes that go sequentially from longest to shortest at the pinkie. How is it that women seem to always have perfect feet? Theodore refuses to wear sandals or open-toed anything, because like most men he's seen, he has weird, scraggly toes that are unfit for exhibition at any time—except maybe at the beach. Growing up he always compared his own to Alice's. Like this girl, Alice has a graceful aesthetic to her feet; Theodore must have inherited his father's.

But he doesn't want to think about his family. He doesn't even want to think about Alice right now, a feeling that's foreign but welcome at this time. He wants to be in the here and now, with this girl, in this unlabeled, arbitrary hotel room.

"Are these your personal quarters?" his voice quivers like that of a nervous kid, which is odd because his vocal cords typically emit a lackadaisical, nothing-bothers-me drone. He glances around for emphasis when she doesn't respond.

The room is just a cut above unremarkable. To Theodore, it looks like yesteryear's version of a posh suite. An antiquated canopy bed is nestled against the left wall, gossamer curtains teasing down the sides of the frame. Pinstriped russet and gold wallpaper adorns the walls from the soft, tawny carpet to the low ceiling, and the only item that really stands out is a decadent ivory vanity that sits against the far wall. It's propped just under where a window used to be. The casement has been removed, or at least thoroughly painted over, with just a spectral outline—a subdued remnant —hinting at the sealed point of egress that once was there.

Why would someone paint over the window? For insulation purposes, perhaps? Theodore didn't pay much attention to where the room was situated as they approached it—his eyes were busy making fervent traces between the hallway paintings and the bar girl's sumptuous rear bouncing before him. Thinking about it now, it does make sense that this room has a wall facing the exterior; probably had quite the view of Sloane Square before the window was painted over. Maybe all the exterior windows were covered during the Great War to obscure the building during air raids? Even though it strikes him as odd, and makes the room feel more like a prison cell than a suite, Theodore chalks it up to the likelihood of the window getting sealed during one of the many phases of renovation. After all, this is likely a very old building, even for this time; could be 1800s easily.

Realizing this is the second time he's played Sherlock tonight, Theodore extinguishes his metaphorical pipe, removes his figurative deerstalker cap, and lays his investigatory spirit to rest. The girl in the hawk mask is waiting. For him. But to do what? She hasn't uttered a single word to him since they left Francis dazed by the bar. Is she waiting for him to storm over, hoist her onto his hips, and tear off her clothing like the Hollywood hunks in the trite sex scenes of so many crappy movies? He's no Hollywood hunk, although this is by no means his first 'intimate' occasion with a woman, either.

"So, what's your name, hawk girl?" He hates himself for the cheesy moniker he just gave her, but it sort-of just seeped out without his approval. She doesn't answer. She approaches him, her never-ending legs are shapely and toned; a nice curvature of muscle on her lower thighs pops beneath her dress when her legs straighten. Her calves have an immaculate grace as well. Suddenly, Theodore feels grossly inadequate. He straightens out his lumpy hoodie just in time for her to snatch him by it, her fingers digging into his chest and furthering his disheveled look.

Her hand clambers past his neck. With a deft swipe, she removes the gazelle from his face, deigning not to remove her own cover. This ignites something in Theodore. The people in this mysterious London cult seem to take secrecy and discretion so seriously that, sans mask, he feels as though he's just been stripped nude before a gaggle of nuns. Hell, nudity and prurience are probably a form of currency to these people. But keeping their identity concealed, that is essential. The girl's tenacity towards her own discretion retains the sexy, enigmatic quality that so viciously attracted Theodore to her in the first place. Not to mention, there's something a little kinky about the masquerade theme; hints of sado-masochistic motifs infusing the whole scenario.

Only able to take cues from the lower half of her face, Theodore assumes she likes what she sees. A smile washes over her, and she reaches behind him, brushing the door with her fingers. It acquiesces and slowly closes with a lengthy groan.

"You're...different, Yank," she says at long last. "I've wanted so long to meet an American, and until now I had not had the chance, so I haven't much to draw you against in my mind, but, you're somehow different." She paws at his hoodie once more. "This fabric, the design, well, it's certainly not chic, is it? I've heard stories about your kind from some of my mates around here, and I know Americans are more than a little uncouth in their nature and in their style, but I've never seen something with the peculiarity of this sweater in my life.

"And it's not merely that. You're face, your hair, your mannerisms… you're like a walking enigma that happened to enter my world."

"What...is your world exactly?" he inquires. "What is this place?"

"Why, this is The King's Inn, Yank." She chews her next thought like a tough piece of steak. "Naturally I was assuming that Father Reicart commissioned you; or perhaps Eunice Patterwal, They're our premier foreign emissaries, our diplomats, really." *God, she's speaking like someone with a job at the UN; an organization,* Theodore thinks, *that won't be created for another decade or so in this freakish other-world.* This is like being in a fictional alternate history story, but he's the author and the main character simultaneously. This latest thought excites him, giving just him enough bravado to make his move.

He pulls her close and wanders with his hand up her back, inhuming his fingers in her brilliant copse of hair. It's cashmere soft. He leans forward and draws his mouth to hers in a moment so passionate, so fervently charged, that he finds himself shaking. Her lips are nice, inviting. Theodore knows stereotypes only ever hold an inkling of veracity at best, and the one claiming the Brits to be stuffy, vapid creatures who are as intimate as driftwood, is proving to be false the more this girl dips her tongue into his mouth.

Kissing her isn't at all like kissing Molly-whatever-her-name-was in 6th grade. A kiss where, after missing the target a few times, Theodore landed a big wet smooch on her chin and called it quits. It's not a bit like Andrea Harper in 10th grade, who was more concerned with the flashing icons on her phone screen than the boy trying to smudge her lipstick; it isn't reminiscent of his most recent love interest, Sammy Goodwell, either, whose lip-locking was neither good nor well, nor any other positive adjective or adverb Theodore can muster. Kissing Bargirl is like putting his mouth to a peach wrapped in silk, or something of commensurate softness.

They stumble backwards against the bedpost, where Bargirl clutches at the drapes. Kissing a girl with a mask on is a singular experience, and so far, he's only stumbled once in an impromptu nose-to-beak collision with the hawk. He has to angle his face more to the right to connect properly with her mouth, but apparently, she wants the cover to remain at all costs; the only way in which she reminds Theodore of the freaks downstairs.

Bargirl is heaving a little now. Theodore himself feels a little like a poser-runner after the first couple miles of a marathon. He hasn't done this in a while and it's exhilarating. She pushes him away, deigning to uncover herself a little more; but she doesn't take her mask off, she reaches behind, arching her back and unbuttoning her dress. The shiny thing cascades like water off her ivory body.

Theodore takes a breath, takes her in. From the two prominent tendons in her neck, which reach up like a ladder to her elegant face; down to her small but audacious breasts, her nipples standing proud and erect on her chest; to the gracile stream of lines that trace her abdomen and gently widen at her hips; down to her shapely legs, one of which is posturing at him, attentive and intently crossed before the other in a provocative expression.

Every sense feels heightened. His thrumming heart the drumbeat of his desire, his rattling limbs a tambourine crash. He wonders if she's as nervous as he is. Her constant listless expression—an intimidatingly equable demeanor even while ass-naked in front of a total stranger—tells him she's not. But this is a mere confirmation of his earlier assumption of these people: as long as the mask stays on her face, she probably feels less exposed than he does even with all his clothes still adhered to his body.

He drops his pants, clumsily revealing the extent of his desire. He approaches the girl with a manufactured bravado, striding toward her like a soldier stepping up to a podium awash with camera flashes to receive his medal. The girl seems to notice his affectation, and giggles, which is actually a welcome response as far as Theodore is concerned—a real tension reliever.

In what must be the most transcendent moment of Theodore's life thus far, he envelops her with his arms, gently pawing about her tender form. She's soft, warm, and ethereal; he's afraid that she'll disappear if he squeezes too tightly. His hands meander down the supple, toned slope of her back, and then slide down the opal curves of her rear. He squeezes hard; she giggles under her mask.

She claws at his underwear; her fingers forming hooks and dragging his briefs down. He recoils briefly in an onslaught of embarrassment. Real intimate moments never play out like the perfectly choreographed, if prosaic, romance scenes in movies. They're punctuated with awkward silences and clumsy missteps.

She puts her lips around him. He quivers from his waist down, his head teetering back. He eases back against the bedframe, thinking with certainty that never in his wildest dreams could he have foreseen having a time-warping, mask-wearing sexual encounter with a stranger on the environs of an underground soirée held by the British elite. Life is a funny thing. He gently grabs her by the arms and hoists her upon the creaky old bed.

He goes down on her. She accepts him readily, wrapping her legs about his shoulders with a vehement squeeze. His hands explore her chest, gliding and squeezing, and then settling on her hips. An errant thought invades his mind, another troubled feeling about Francis, like a vague premonition of danger. But he pushes it out of the way. Now is most certainly not the time. Francis is probably settling in by now, mingling with the Shibboleth freaks.

Bargirl grasps his head, his hair scrunching between her splayed fingers in disheveled clumps. She arches her back and her fingers clamp down hard, almost to the point where he wonders if his scalp is going to peel right off under the pressure. Her sighing builds to a tremulous moan; her breathing hastens to a gallop; her body starts to quiver ever so slightly. Just as her pleasure reaches its zenith, he rises and enters her, in what is, for him, a surprisingly error-free motion. It's like their bodies were made for each other. He hasn't felt this kind of physical or emotional connection with a girl in his entire life. And he doesn't even know the beautiful enigma lying on the bed before him, not the color of her eyes, not even her name.

She grabs him by the hoodie and pulls him down, then clambers on top and begins thrusting. All he can see of her face is her delicate mouth, her pouting lips as she moans, but he wants to see more. He reaches up to swipe the mask from her face, but she intercepts him and redirects his hands to her chest. He desperately wants to see the woman beneath the mask, but he settles for merely watching what he can of her from below, her breasts shuddering on her ribcage as she moves above him.

He never thought intimacy with a stranger could be so good, and it's exquisite, but he's more focused—affixed, really—on her deliberate, coy nature. She's hard to describe and impossible to define. She's the twinge he gets in his stomach when he realizes that, at any moment, he might wake from an amazing dream; she's a real-life connotation to the word mystery, the eponym for the term beguiling; the effigy of intrigue.

And while he's fairly certain these trips to post-war England aren't mere dreams, he knows the journey tonight will be just as fleeting as a tenable dreamscape. Knowing this makes him grip her hips harder, driving his fingers into her flesh, as if holding onto her might somehow ebb the tide of reality. On night one, he was lifted back to the present day while exploring the River Thames. The sky over England was still dark when the gramophone brought him back, so it couldn't have been much later than four or five in the morning.

How many hours do I have left tonight before I'm magically whisked away? Two? Three?

Theodore rises, hands still locked on her hips, and hurls her flat against the bed, driving, driving, driving with his body, until the bedsheets and the drapes billow and twist about them like the tangled coat tails of a giant frock. His grunts evolve to meet her moans, and before long, the tingling heat of the climax builds, like an obdurate wave of pleasure that only makes their bodies drive and clash with greater force. He feels his toes curl and his pelvis jerk erratically. The sensation comes and goes far too quickly and he demurs a moment, lingering within the warm grasp of her body, his ratcheting breaths offset from the silken rise and fall of her chest. Finally, he rolls over on the archaic bedspread and stares up at the canopy. The drapes flutter and settle back against the mattress, relaxing in concomitance with the heaving bodies within.

He glances over with the timidity of a child. She's lying on her back silently, her mask still perched on her face. He wonders briefly if it's glued on there. From his experience, girls usually want to protract the emotional connection built during sex with cuddling or small talk. But this girl is cool as a cucumber and, so far, seems to have the emotional depth of one, as well. Helplessly, he deems to echo her monastic disposition. He has met his match, and will flounder in the sea of intrigue that encompasses this vexing girl until she decides to toss him a life jacket. And maybe that's what makes him all the more attracted to her; for once in his life, he's actually caring enough about a girl to pursue her emotional layers, and she's reciprocating just enough to keep him on her uneffusive tail.

He lies there, thinking about the myriad things that separate him from her, in spite of the intimacy they just shared; the space and time between their worlds. He thinks of how every second of the 80 plus year journey was worth it. He might just come back here every night for the rest of his life and enjoy this clandestine affair time and time again. *Then again, if the gramophone returns me to the same exact date every time, I'll continue to age and she won't. Eventually, I'll be too old to attract her, but cross that bridge, right?*

"So, yank," she says at last, rolling towards him and cradling her head in her hands. Her mask remains on her face, so all he can do is stare at her perfectly formed mouth moving above her elegantly carved chin. "You're from New York City. What is it like there?" She smiles as if imagining a world far from the one she's in, and he begins to wonder once again if she's mired here, tied to some obligation about which he knows nothing. He wonders if she's ever seen anything outside of London, hell, outside of Sloane Square.

"Well…" he demurs, knowing he'll sound more than a little cuckoo if he explains New York as it is in the 21st century to this pre-war brit. *Here goes.* "There's a veritable clusterfuck of bodies. Kind of like how it is here, only everybody's excessively rude, and everybody's always fronting."

"Fronting?" she asks, still gazing at him and smiling.

"Yeah, like everyone runs around as if they're chickens of the coop but on Adderall, clucking their beaks into their cellphones, acting like their so busy and they don't have time for anything because they have a lunch meeting after their morning briefing, and they didn't prep for either meeting enough because they have a big account with so-and-so and they had to make a new ten step plan to appease the shareholders—"

"Cellphones?" Bargirl casually reaches out and runs an ethereal hand through his hair, acting as if she actually knows him, as if they share anything more between them than just a couple fugacious and tender moments. "What's a cellphone?" He's caught off guard by her touch, but he finds a way to wrench himself from the ineluctable chasm of her charms.

"Uh, it's...well never mind that. It's just a thing we Yanks have, you know?" She chuckles, flicking the hood of his jacket.

"You sure are an anachronism, mister uh..."

"Just call me Mr. Gazelle," his enigmatic reply, referring to the guise he wore on the way to this ninth-floor haven; the guise he knows he'll have to don once more when he's faced with the inevitability of leaving her. "And you are?" To this she hesitates, mulls over a response as she shifts uncomfortably, exposing the silky slope of her left breast as the velvety bed sheet enveloping her tries and fails to find its grip.

"Why, you can call me Ms. Hawk, I suppose." She smiles and leans forward, her lips meeting his in one more beatific kiss. Theodore shakes his head, blissfully grasping at the concept that this girl is for real. It just seems too good to be true. He wishes he could spend eternity with her, or at least the next 80-something years watching history unfold by her side. "And what is it that you do, Ms. Hawk, how did you end up living in a suite at The King's Inn?"

After a moment that feels as wonderfully drawn out as the very time between their worlds, she leans over and delicately touches his cheek, and then the most peculiar thing happens. Her lips quiver and then stiffen; a gossamer thread containing a tidal wave of emotion. She bites down hard like someone does when they have so much to say but can't find the words. A shimmer beneath the mask—he thinks it's a tear, but can't be sure; she retracts too fast, hopping off the bed in a swift and lissome motion.

He watches with a vapid, jaws-agape expression as she scrambles across the room, wriggling into her clothes like it's the next morning and she's late for a meeting. Without uttering a single word, she slips her shoes on, pauses to assuage the raging tangles of hair hanging on her clavicle, and crosses to the door. She leaves without glancing back once.

Theodore idles on the bed for a moment, unsure of what to do; unsure if the girl is even coming back. It doesn't seem like it. He rolls out of bed and stretches. What a night. What a gloriously unexpected night. He doesn't know if he should feel put off by the girl's hasty exit, but the deft maneuver she just pulled is like leaving a beautiful sentence unpunctuated; it just feels wrong. He ambles over to the wall, thumbing the raised outline of the painted-over window frame. His eyes wander to the alabaster vanity; a single item resting upon the immaculate surface—an ornate pearl-handled hairbrush. Not one of the bristles is frayed or misshapen. *She keeps nice things, and keeps them well-maintained.* He knows he shouldn't pry, but he needs to know more about this girl, something, anything that might tell him about who she really is.

He opens one of the drawers. There's nothing inside except for a folded piece of paper. It's aged, jaundiced. Theodore sees his hand reach for the note as if it's acting on its own while his mind still grapples with the ludicrous and yet rapturous encounter that just took place. His other hand joins in and helps with the unfolding. It's a letter.

"On the morrow I must..." this is all the note says, as if it were hastily scrawled and then scrapped. But Theodore feels the sting of guilt for reading even these few words before carefully re-folding the missive and dropping it back in the drawer. Some light snooping doesn't feel like the worst thing in the world right now, but reading some else's personal correspondences is a step too far. He sits down in the plush, ivory-backed chair, idly rapping his fingers on the tabletop. Where *did* she go? He begins vacantly flicking the switch of a Deco desk lamp on/off, on/off, savoring the solid clunk of senescent machinery; and that's when the glint of metal awakens his eye.

Just to the right of the bed, inhumed in the darkness of a ventilation shaft, lies some vague object. Whatever it is, it's far enough back to escape the casual observer, but has a crepuscular glow under the light of the desk lamp that one would miss ninety-nine times out of a hundred were they not paying the utmost attention to such a negligible space. And—he rises and then sits again to confirm—sitting here at the vanity is the only angle in the room at which the object is viewable.

Whatever it is that the vent is hiding, it was probably left there intentionally, seeing as the vent's cover would obviously have kept the item from rolling in on its own. A tickle of curiosity plays Theodore's spine like a zither. Is it a secret trinket belonging to the girl? Did the previous resident leave it behind on purpose, to be found by a discerning viewer? He crosses to the vent, pries off the grate, and peers into the murky shaft. It's a relatively small, cylindrical item. He can't see more, as only one end is visible; the rest of it is hidden behind the corner where the shaft turns left. Either someone left the item there intending it never to be found, in which case they simply failed to shove it quite far enough back, or they placed it just so that the edge of the object would still be visible—meaning that someone wanted it to be found.

He reaches into the vent without hesitation, for once in his life actually giving thanks for his long, lanky arms. He grabs hold of the device and gently retrieves it, realizing instantly what he's holding—he's held something just like it many times before. It's a phonograph cylinder. An odd wave of nostalgia hits him as he pulls the record out, fondling its curves in a hand still rattling with excitement. It's nothing like the one that's currently playing in the gramophone back at The Cat's Meow. This one is of a different engineering; it's coated with metal and has a blank label. There is no worn-away raised text or eroded brand logos either. Nothing identifying it in the slightest.

The ambiguity of an unlabeled gramophone record; turning it over in the heel of his hand; wondering what pattern is inscribed within, and what that pattern would say when put to a record needle...these are all familiar to Theodore and, just like the record he and Alice found when they were children, he craves to hear what this one has to say. The other one opened a portal to a new—or rather old—world. Who knows what this one might do?

For this reason, and this reason alone, Theodore pockets the mysterious item. He knows that he might be stealing a piece of this girl's property, but if that's the case, he'll just put it to a gramophone tomorrow afternoon and then return it to the girl tomorrow night when he revisits her. She'll be none the wiser and ethical concerns are immaterial to him right now; curiosity has metastasized through his conscience.

Feeling a thief but exhilarated by the possibilities contained in the piece of history in his pocket, he dons the gazelle mask and slinks out of the room, taking one more look inside, as if this final look will avail something to him about who she is, and why he found her. Leaving with more questions than he arrived with, he closes the door firmly behind himself, glancing at the painting on the wall of the hardened soldiers in a ragged line.

The Roll Call, *yeah, that's what it's called.*

Having seen no sign of the girl after her expeditious exit nor that of any living soul, for that matter, he takes the elevator back down. He glances just once at the operator, whose haunting face twists into a smile. This time, his smile is more invasive, if that's possible; like an 'I know what you two were doing up there' sort of look. Theodore gives a slightly sardonic nod to the creep, with a half-raising of his eyebrow. Instinctively, he tightens his grip upon the cylinder in his pocket.

The elevator operator wrenches the gate open for Theodore, his immaculate white gloves positively scintillating under the harsh ceiling light. Only, they're not totally immaculate. As he rips the gate open, Theodore eyes specks of dark red on the fingers and palm of his right glove. Blood? Or has the elevator man been painting the hallways of the hotel in these late hours? He snakes through the gate before it's even half open, not relishing the propinquity a tiny elevator box creates between him and its eccentric—and according to the mysterious red droplets, potentially violent—operator. The hallways are far from abandoned now, but in comparison to how packed they were when he'd last seen them, it feels a little like New York City the afternoon of March 18th, when everyone's at home nursing their shamrock-shooter hangovers. Did he miss the memo while he was with Bargirl upstairs?

Strings of revelers thread through the lower level. Triumvirates gathered in different corners, drinks in hand, masks on faces, and Burberry suits, long coats, and scintillating dresses on beneath. *It's a stringent dress code*, thinks Theodore, pressing his mask further against his face as he crosses to the lobby, *and everybody follows it.* No sign of the girl at all down here. Perhaps she left the hotel, but to where? Judging by the appearance of that hotel room, Theodore gets the impression that it's her home up there; Rapunzel of the high tower…

There's someone else who's nowhere in sight: *Francis*. Now where could he have gone off to? Maybe, just maybe, he's off in some numberless guest room getting lucky with a jazz-age British girl, too. Maybe. Realizing that all the hotel has to offer him now is a bunch of nondescript old geezers in masks and posh habiliments, who cradle their spirits and cigars like precious infants, Theodore decides it's time to investigate the River Thames once more. After all, he can always visit the girl again with his secret formula for time travel, as long as he has that special cylinder record and gramophone at The Cat's Meow.

He leaves through the large front double-door which, just like on night one, is guarded by two sharp suits in masks that match the Ringmaster's creepy rodent visage back in the ballroom. He nods to the henchmen, who part the doors willingly, curtsying before him as he leaves. Déjà vu is an odd sensation, one that Theodore hasn't experienced many times in his life. It's odd because it hits all at once, like when he suddenly remembers a dream he had long ago but had forgotten; all his senses become inundated with the sights, smells, and sounds of the dream, as if he were experiencing it all over again in fast-forward.

The sensation always vanishes quickly, its fugacity a tease. And then he always spends the next few minutes trying to convince the sensation to return, but if it does at all, it fumbles back in some meretricious and forced way that has none of the marvelous sensory delights it did the first time. Theodore's had déjà vu more times on this one night than he has through his whole life, and this makes sense considering he's doing the impossible and not only treading the same steps he's trodden before, but the same sequence of events as well. If literally experiencing the same moment twice doesn't hurl a wave of déjà vu at him, he doesn't know what would.

The buildings of Sloane Square lie in a dense formation around the park; a checkerboard of lights play off each building. The temperature feels the same as on night one; the air has a concordant crisp scent, and an equally dense glittering wall of snow is falling from the dark London sky. The trees of the park, shucked of their foliage, sway before the lights the same way they did yesterday. Theodore heads down the street in the same direction as before, half expecting to see the couple he ran into the first time; the old man gnashing the cobblestone beneath him in his mad dash to the movies, his facile wife dragging behind. *What was her name, again? Marcie.* A warm pang of déjà vu settles in his stomach once more. *And what movie were they scrambling to make? City Lights with Charlie Chaplin. Bingo.*

Theodore knows he won't run into them, though. Because of that spectacularly unexpected sexual encounter with Bargirl, he was probably in the hotel longer tonight than last time, effectively skewing the two timeframes. Marcie and her impatient husband are probably already at the theatre, enjoying the vaudevillian gags of Mr. Chaplin. Although, it's hard to gauge just how long the events have taken tonight compared to night one, as everything is happening so quickly. He simply cannot declare with the certainty of his rational mind that he isn't moving through events quicker tonight than he did last night. Wandering through the same moment in history twice is like rewinding a movie and replaying a specific scene, only the scene unfolds differently based on what he does in it. He's the only real variable, like an actor saying: to hell with the script, we're gonna try the scene my way this time. He supposes, in this metaphor, God would be the director of the movie, shaking his head and rolling his eyes at the defiant thespian. He wonders if God's up there somewhere right now asking: what the hell do you think you're doing, mortal?

Having such a thorough reshoot tonight, including throwing in an unscripted sex scene, Theodore wonders if the mysterious figure at the Thames will still be there waiting for 'Osprey', whoever that is? He'll have to find out. He ambles away from Sloane Square, pulling his hoodie tighter against his body. It's cold and blustery out here, and it's making his mind dwell on how heavenly it felt to be in bed with the girl. Still, brisk weather notwithstanding, stalking the streets of Georgian England—that is, the time period during which George V reigned, and not the traditional Georgian England of the 18th century—provides more than a modicum of entertainment for him. Downtown, the buildings are an endless labyrinth of predominantly five-story buildings, an antediluvian curtain of old-world architecture. Closer towards the Thames, it transmogrifies into a dense weave of brick warehouses and beaten wharfs, the crisscrossing beams of old cranes looming eerily above like iron sentinels. He's close to the spot now.

Up ahead, a single streetlight carves a brilliant shaft of light; a cynosure on the murky docks. Underneath it is a lone figure clad in a long coat, a bowler cap, and a scarf covering the lower half of his face. He looks like a cross between a robber-bandit in an old western and an English gentleman. With the stench that pervades the air around the river, Theodore wishes he too had a scarf to cover his mouth; the mask he's wearing allows every putrid layer of the miasma inside.

"Osprey? Is that you?" the man whispers, as if anyone else were around to hear him.

"Uh, yeah." He goes along with it, wanting to see where this might lead.

"Blimey, you're late. I've been waiting here since the motor car replaced the hansom."

"Oh yeah, sorry about that. I got held up."

"Well I don't mind, you see? But the boss just may. He's been eager to meet you, and the operation's already under way."

"Well I'm here now, and I'm ready to meet him. Just, uh, lead the way, friend."

The figure under the streetlight does a half-turn, then looks back at Theodore, his coat tail dancing at his sides. "Why on earth are you wearing a party mask?"

IV

Theodore trails after the man in the bowler cap. He's keeping at least four or five paces back, although not because of a potent mixture of fear and uncertainty—things he's probably supposed to feel when following a stranger in a strange land. Now that they've interacted a little more, Theodore thinks the guy seems pretty innocuous. His voice has a silly lilt to it and, considering he was a dark figure lurking about the docks in a trench coat, with the physiognomy of a bandit with half his face covered, he has a friendly air about him. It's like when Theodore went to meet his distant cousin Arnold at JFK International last year. He had met Arnold probably once in his life before that, and he knew as much about Arnold as he did about the random dudes waiting in line for pizza at the airport Sbarro. But despite not knowing Arnold personally, he still felt like he could trust him, because he was family. While this guy's certainly not family, he has that same instantly familiar vibe.

Theodore dares a question, "So, what's your name, again, friend?" The guy whips around.

"You know quite well you're not advised to ask that, Yankee." His mouth looks funny, bobbing up and down behind the scarf. "None of us is. Call me by my alias, Peregrine, yeah? I'm Peregrine, you're Osprey." He points emphatically at himself and then Theodore. "And right now, Peregrine is more than a little concerned that Condor will be alarmed by our supposed absence at the brood."

Brood? As in, a brood of hens? Theodore's glad that Peregrine has turned his back and resumed walking because this is a laugh he can't stifle; their code names are chock-full of bird references.

"And what is it that you're wearing, Osprey?" Peregrine asks the river. "Not only do you find it necessary to wear a bloody gazelle mask to the brood, but that sweater. I guess that is of the drivel that passes for fashion in America these days. Although, our western emissaries have always been… eccentric." *Western emissaries? It only seems natural that they'd be spies of some sort, given all the aliases. What am I getting myself into?*

Peregrine continues to lead the way along the river redolent of toxins and refuse; the backdrop, a never-ending loop of factories and loading equipment. Taking a sharp left, Theodore and Peregrine walk a muddy lane wedged between groups of old brick factories, relics of a bygone industrial era. Although they still haunt the occasional street corner in Manhattan, they have started disappearing in Theodore's world. Seedy, grimy, insalubrious are the first words that come to his mind as his eyes dance about the dark, oppressing facades that now encompass him. Every so often, sallow rays of light throb from behind the tapestries of muck that once were windows. Viaducts loom above, linking two gargantuan factories with long, skeletal arms.

"You've been out of the game a while, Osprey," Peregrine says without looking back. "It'd serve you well to have a brief update on our doings here in London, no? You've been in the States conspiring with your ragtag group of rebels, doing…whatever it is you do to garner political support for our endeavors here. On this side of the pond, the Pilfering Paupers have expanded. We've linked arms with fellow fifth column organizations. You'd be agog at just how much support socialism has amassed here in the King's Land. Yes, along any row of houses in this venerable land there's bound to be at least one or two pea-soupers with Marxist theories swimming about in his head and that number is swelling. Violent upheaval is not the way; alas, it is at times expedient to striking fear in the hearts of the upper class.

"Furthermore, Lenin's philosophies on just how a civilization should bastardize socialism seem to be planting an insidious seed in the mindsets of a troubling number of chappies throughout London. Having an entire society that cannot see the difference between the working class truly owning the means of production and the one who is unwittingly transformed into a shivering dog obsequious to the hand that feeds it is something we Pauper's aim to prevent. Alas, the resistance is…firm. While we may have had success in softening the laymen to our cause, a victory accomplished upon the coat tails of the Labour Party, mind you, the monarchy and the societal elite have a fervent, uh, disdain for our cause, and a passionate indifference to our plight.

"Passionate indifference?" he continues, "an oxymoron, that is. Alas, dear Osprey, you, being a Yank and all, haven't a proper understanding of the ways of the aristocracy. High class snobbery aside, these sods truly have perfected the craft of cynicism; there is no matter too dull, no event too prosaic, for the conservative high society.

"You see, Osprey, when your impecuniosity is such that you cannot rub two shillings together, and you cannot reckon when or whence the next meal is coming, life has a certain danger to it—it develops a degree of excitement. We in the proletariat know how to throw a proper soiree; we dance, we sing, and we cheer, and we generally relish in the good moments when they spring up, because we have something to live for, something to fight for. The nobility, and the wealthy denizens of society that dangle from their silk pocket like an aureate timepiece, are so busy in life being well off that they've become indolent, bored. Cynicism is the only craft for them to perfect. Alas, I'm rambling.

"Much has happened since you left, and tonight, I'm introducing you to the leader of the new political party, the People's Party. Insipid name, no? Well, Sir Morrow isn't keen on having too strong a connection with any particular social group; our dealings be on the furtive side, as you can tell. The People's Party is an appropriate moniker for what we are trying to accomplish though. Classism has tainted what was once a proud nation; we aim to lessen the schism between the poor and the affluent."

This guy's in the Pilfering Paupers? Theodore recalls the man in the wolf mask mentioning the name. It looks like someone in high society might already be aware of the burgeoning movement.

"Sir Morrow was a member of parliament in York—refrain from bringing that up when you see him, he's still rather sore about the affair." When they're sufficiently inhumed among the factories and warehouses like a couple of ants rambling about in thick grass Peregrine leads Theodore up to an iron door. Partially rusted, unlabeled; the door's unremarkable in every way, and Theodore can guess why. Sir Morrow and these gangsters are having clandestine meetings, or 'broods,' and they want to keep it as low key as possible.

Peregrine curls his hand into a slack fist and raps out a string of binary messages on the door. After a moment, a sequence of metal sounds emanates— thick, auditory chunks of sound, like a series of bolts being thrown. Finally, a metallic spooling noise ensues. The heavy door eases, rather than swings, open. It's the kind of door he'd expect to see on a submarine, a hatch door, with the circular handle and everything, which explains the peculiarity of the unlocking sounds Theodore heard. Peregrine must take notice of his surprise, clapping him on the shoulder.

"While the architect and benefactors behind the Battersea Power Station are collectively eccentric and visionary people, it wasn't their idea to outfit the facility with these unique little touches. Many Londoners were concerned with the 1925 overhaul of the city's electrical systems. London went from smaller stations peppering the entire city, to just a couple of these prodigious hunks of brick and steel. The general public, imbeciles, if you ask me, have had their trousers in a twist over the potential for pollution and leakage from a 400-megawatt station. So the owners, in a deliciously sardonic gesture, outfitted the facility's exterior with waterway doors which seem ostensibly safer for the public. A bunch of pranksters, the lot of them.

"As you can clearly see," he gestures towards the curtain of bricks above, which makes up the completed portion of the power station. Above that is the skeleton of the unfinished upper structure, with two massive conical chimneys bookending what must be one of the largest standalone buildings in Europe. "It's unfinished as of yet. Both the substructure, and the upper levels. Fortunately for us, Sir Morrow is in good standing with a clever engineer who posed as an architect during the building of the substructure, and the bloke designed some key structural components for us to make our way around. I'll tell you one thing, Osprey, you may have seen a thing or two in your life— being in the line of work you are. I'm assuming you've experienced a trifle more than the average Yankee, but I guarantee you've never seen anything quite like the London underground."

A voice wafts out from the dim interior, "If you lot are pausing out there to hold a candlelight vigil for my patience, you're too late. That died soon after I opened the door for you, which was sometime before Queen Victoria taught half of England how to read."

"Ah, yes. Allow me to introduce our lowly doorman, Kestrel. I wonder just how long it will take for his sardonic waggery to reveal itself." Standing before the pulse and flicker of a series of industrial light fixtures is a figure dressed like Peregrine, only with a beige raincoat instead of a black overcoat, and almost two heads shorter than both Peregrine and Theodore. Kestrel, too, has a scarf covering the lower portion of his face.

Theodore wonders if any of these operatives know each other's identity. What with these guys and those secretive societal elites back at the hotel, his first impression of England is that nobody wants to know anybody else, or to be known by them; they all just maunder through lives peppered with hidden liaisons and furtive meetings.

"Well come on then, Osprey; it's time to introduce you to the big bloke." Kestrel's dialect is of a slightly less formal English than Peregrine's, but with the bowlers on both their heads—an accessory that once symbolized the English lower class—Theodore assumes they both belong to the rather exclusive Pilfering Paupers gang.

"Let's do it," he says, entering the cold, tenebrous atmosphere of the unfinished power station. Peregrine was waiting at the docks for some sort of operative from the U.S., so that's the man he'll have to pretend to be. Surrounded by brick walls strung with power cables and fuse boxes, they appear to be in one of the discreet service entrances. The walls climb high above to what will one day be a ceiling, but is currently a work in progress, with a tarp loosely fitted over the opening. The tarp flails madly in the wind, betraying fragments of the night sky above, and letting in torrents of snowfall when an especially violent gust disturbs it.

They're standing on a service walkway that hugs the walls of the narrow room. At the other end, a necklace of feeble lights leads down an iron stairway to another door. Peregrine seals the door behind and they walk down the stairs, hearing only the wuthering of the gale high above them.

"As I detailed before, there is an agent Sir Morrow enlisted to influence the development of the Battersea station, Hunter Marrs. The two of them together designed the substructure in secret to connect with the London Underground, or part of it anyhow—the damn thing is an interminable labyrinth. And this is the way in which we've been conducting business. Rather intriguing, is it not?"

Kestrel opens the door at the foot of the stairs and beckons Theodore down a long and unremarkable service tunnel. Pipes and electrical cords snake down the left wall, with the occasional vent hissing coils of steam.

"This is what the various fifth column groups are reduced to. Slinking about the vile corridors and putrid corners of the city. The game has changed since you left, Osprey; the liberals and conservatives are tightening their grip on the political scene, while the reformers are being snuffed left and right."

Theodore glances up at the flickering ceiling lights. The farther they go into the power station, the more the fixtures transmogrify into ineffective little boxes akin to the lights in a coal mine. They're taking to flickering more now, too.

"If the inconsistency of these lights is giving you a headache, just wait until you're thirty meters below ground," says Peregrine. "I swear the fixtures under the city spend more time off than on."

"I'm sure our Yankee friend is positively riveted by your relevant musings about electricity, Peregrine, but it might be apropos to brief him on what he's missed before we reach the brood," intercedes Kestrel. "Reformation for policies that would serve the proletariat is a dying thought in England. As are any other promising prospects for the abolishment of classism in our bleeding country. If you so much as mention the color red or the name Bolshevik in certain boroughs around London, you'll become tomorrow's food for the fish in the Thames. And that's if you're lucky, mind you. Now, we Paupers adhere to many of the tenets Marx, Lenin, and their ilk have outlined, but we believe that true change for the working class can arise without mass violence and carnage. The state can, we hope, be abolished swiftly and successfully sans threats of bloody uprisings and murderous coups, and without solipsistic party leaders who secretly aim for a large piece of the pie, as it were."

"With all the losses we've suffered of late I can't fathom they'd still be hungry," interjects Peregrine, referring to Kestrel's comment regarding the Thames. "Were you to comb the river, you'd find the Thames is three parts water, one part dead political dissidents."

"Well, that's just it," ventures Theodore. "Your hands aren't exactly clean of blood themselves, right?"

"Aye," Peregrine confirms. "But we are one of a small band of brigands who are willing to make the sacrifice for the greater good. If subversive tactics and the occasional skirmish is necessary to gain some purchase against the nobility, then so be it. The working class can raise its venerable voice against them when we've cleared enough ground for them to stand up as one."

"All the while, bands of rebels like us are denigrated in the daily mail and made to look like proper villains," adds Kestrel. "That is what makes us the unfortunate but requisite sacrificial lambs."

"Or the vanguards in the storming of the Bastille," shrugs Peregrine. "How I prefer to frame the situation. If those ninety-eight souls hadn't sacrificed themselves on obtaining the fortress in 1789, tyranny would have prevailed."

Opening a door at the hallway's end spills a narrow cynosure of light upon what looks like a huge bunker. The foundations of the station, largely unfinished, unfurl before Theodore, who marvels at the massive pillars that cut clean lines through crude-looking electrical conduits. He follows Kestrel down the stairs, breathless at the sheer breadth of the room.

"Our erstwhile parliamentarian of York has vested interests in London's evolving power infrastructure," expounds Peregrine, his voice churning out a succession of imitators that bounce about the vast concrete enclosure. "Without him, this station could not have left the inchoate stage of aspirations and blueprints. Hunter Marrs installed this crude connection with the London underground, or as we call it, The Involute Inn."

"Why do you call it that?"

"Tis nigh impossible for a single man to tread the entirety of the massive, complex, subterranean world of London. There are a great many tunnels, bunkers, and stations—abandoned places tailored for dealings not meant to be made under the sun. Our ancestors and contemporaries alike have used these catacombs for a variety of purposes; the tunnel system being used as a transitory space to suit each user's needs. We think the moniker fits."

"From drug peddlers to human smugglers, prisoners convicted by the monarchy of the highest of crimes, to some of the monarchs themselves, the bricks of these tunnels have presided over the most colorful pieces of England's human mosaic," Kestrel adds, opening a plain white door on the farthest corner of a plain concrete wall. "If the walls could talk, so they say, these would speak of the seedier side of life. And of the threat of possibility, as well. Only years ago, Bolshevik sympathizers roamed the tunnels, and just recently we've heard that the footsteps of a new wave of communist plotters. The British communists Peregrine alluded to earlier, they have been echoing about the tunnels. Their agenda is similar to ours, but the sods adhere a bit too much to Marxist philosophy for our liking." Theodore watches nervously as both bowler caps dart left to right every time they pass an auxiliary tunnel.

These men are clearly on high alert down here. Should he be, too?

A sampling of still, damp air that's been sealed in its subterranean lair seeps from the open door. The borderline-repugnant scent tickles Theodore's nostrils and makes him cringe. "Kind of like your grand mum's basement, no?" Kestrel knocks Theodore's shoulder. "Just wait until you get to the basement of The Involute Inn."

"That's where we're meeting Sir Morrow," interjects Peregrine. "In some of the deeper recesses. The scent down there will make you miss your grand mum's basement." Passing through the door is like crossing a threshold between the developed world and the crumbling bowels of Egypt's great pyramids. A trail of lights leads down a gently sloping cavern. In a crepuscular display of superposition, layers of rock and sediment pervade the walls of what looks like one giant excavation process.

They stalk the lengthy corridor until a monastic silence embraces them; the only sound being a slight hum from the overhead lights, and the occasional whistle of an air current escaping the depths. They arrive at a massive manmade structure; the brick hull of some sort of underground infrastructure. Along the worn brick façade, a simple railing leads down three steps to an unfinished doorway. Theodore notices a pressure budding in his ears.

"Everything from here to about 200 meters that direction is underneath the River Thames." Kestrel points past the doorway. *Egads*, thinks Theodore. Going from Manhattan to Jersey in the Holland Tunnel is enough to make him sweat. And that's a quick trip in a car through a tunnel with proper upkeep. This is all the synonyms of insane strung up in one giant run-on sentence. He reaches in his pocket and fondles the cylinder record he found in Bargirl's room. He misses her.

Kestrel and Peregrine filter into the doorway and pause, turning to Theodore under the strobe-like effect of the flickering lights. "It's a solid brick skeleton they built beneath meters of stone and solid earth," he grins. He must see Theodore's trepidation because he cheerily adds, "Nothing to fear, Osprey."

Taking a tremulous breath, Theodore joins his new comrades for a stroll underneath the river. *There's a first for everything.*

Down they go, with unsure footing and nothing to grab onto save the occasional gap between bricks where the mortar has receded. The last thing Theodore wants to find when wandering under thousands of tons of water is a fault in structural integrity; alas, some of the bricks do look rotted and friable. He opts to watch his feet and not the pulverulent cocoon about him as the group descends the narrow corridor.

"Over the last few years we've expanded our underground system. Tunnels about which only we know lead to the cellars of various buildings throughout London. Mainly pubs and cafes and what have you. This is but the newest leg in our vermicular lair."

"Why can't the fifth column groups just meet in nondescript locations around the city, instead of underneath it? Seems like an awful lot of work for nothing," Theodore asks.

"The enemies have ramped up their game, outsmarting or outgunning us at every turn," Peregrine explains.

"When we carry knives, they carry revolvers; when we kidnap one of their scouts, they take a Tommy Gun to one of our meetings; when they find we have an informant in their ranks, they throw him and his whole family in the river. This is the only way we can organize our new resistance against the emergent conservative aristocracy."

"To be honest, Osprey, shortly after you left the game everything crumbled. There was a man who came along years back who had the charisma, and the... what's that word you Yanks love to use?" Kestrel taps his chin as he thinks, his eyes scrunched in concentration.

"Moxie?" Peregrine offers.

"Right," Kestrel says, his face relaxing. "He had the moxie to change the political scene once and for all, but just when things appeared to be going our way..."

"We lost the lynchpin of our political game. This man was a respected laborer-turned-racketeer, and a powerful orator to boot, and if anyone could have instilled true change in Britain, it was him." Peregrine's tone takes a plaintive dive as he talks.

Kestrel reaches the bottom of the descent and turns about. "Sir Morrow sent the message about tonight's brood with merely two words: new lead."

"What does that mean, and what was this guy's name?"

Kestrel shrugs, "We'll leave the details of the current mission to Sir Morrow to explain. Even the Pilfering Paupers aren't fully up to speed just yet. Judging from Sir Morrow's message, we can only assume that the trail has warmed up a bit."

"So, there's a salient blue-collar man who showed promise in fighting the labor exploiters and he went missing?" To this, Peregrine and Kestrel give pause.

"Precisely," confirms Peregrine. The diminutive tunnel spills out into a wider space, replete with arched brick ceilings and a random assortment of old crates and long forgotten trinkets. They must be directly under the river now. Theodore takes a breath, closing his eyes for a moment against the garish pulse of the tunnel lights. In a matter of minutes, they went from what looked like the beginnings of an Egyptian tomb to a finished subterranean monastery. He gazes skyward, wondering just how old the infrastructure down here is.

"Alright, follow us closely Osprey, to the point where your toes are nipping at our heels. It gets a trifle labyrinthian here. You wander off too far, and you end up a heap of bones among the bricks," says Peregrine. *Gulp*, Theodore thinks, imagining the consequences of falling prey to the labyrinth's pernicious corridors.

Kestrel chimes in, "Like Fortunato himself, may he rest in peace behind the brick curtain." *A Poe reference? Gulp again.*

Like the clacking bills of a fleet of hungry ducks, their footfalls cascade off the corridor walls and down various chambers, fading off down avenues that lead God knows where.

"If you follow the lamps overhead, you'll find your way to sunlight sooner or later." Kestrel points to both sides. "Take any one of these abyssal paths and may the good lord save your soul."

"One of our mates got himself lost down here a couple years ago," Peregrine adds. "Although that was nearer another terminus point. Was that Lambeth or Southwark, Kestrel?"

"That's Southwark, mate."

"He's right lucky that's all he suffered from. Can you imagine eating human flesh, Osprey?" Kestrel inquires. "I hear that some of your compatriots are known for their proclivity to devour people. Somewhere in Appalachia…"

"Quit your teasing, Kestrel." Peregrine shakes his head. "I apologize for the insensitive bloke with whom I serve. His taste in humor is an acquired one, but perhaps you will grow accustomed."

"The Southwark tunnels aren't too far from where we are now," Kestrel continues. "If you amble down one of these alleys, you might just stumble upon his corpse," he says, in a sobering reference to the ally they lost in the tunnels.

Just then, a brief, sharp noise—like a whistle—cuts through the corridor. Theodore feels his blood stanch in his veins, alarmed by this less-than-sonorous intruding sound. Its origin is from the other end of a narrow passage ahead, at the end of which, a ribbon of light pokes through. Peregrine pinches his fingers to his mouth and returns the signal.

"Oy, thought you blokes would never make it!" A head pokes through at the other end, dressed up in a similar fashion to Peregrine and Kestrel, with a scarf strangling the lower half of his face and a bowler cap crown.

"I dallied and got a little turned about mate, what can I say?" Peregrine takes the fall for Theodore. They make their way through the narrow passage to find a large rectangular room with ceilings that even on stilts, a member of the *Sacramento Kings* couldn't reach. If the rest of the underground looked old, this is positively archaic, and the layout of the room is truly singular.

Adorning each wall are old brick doorways that lead down a separate path, but practically none of the doorways are even with the ground. Theodore actually has to hop down to reach the ground from the passage, and most of the other outlets are higher up along the walls. The entire room is like the backs of old industrial buildings Theodore's seen in Brooklyn. Those buildings that are so old, they have rust-chewed doors three feet off the ground that used to lead to a loading dock or a stairway, but now just serve as a bricked-up entrance to nothing. At one point in time, perhaps, the different passages around this room actually served a purpose. Now, they just stare down from the walls—some sealed up entirely, while others lead to a different pitch-black-somewhere.

"A very warm and gracious welcome to our newfangled friend," an equable voice resonates about the chamber. "I say, as warm and gracious as a welcome can indeed be in this oppressive, brick cocoon. It's a rather unfeeling place to have a business meeting, no?" Perched upon the makeshift throne of a dust-cradled ledge is a narrow-shouldered man with slicked back hair, and perhaps the most intense and piercing gaze Theodore has ever seen. A cop stash sits above a set of permanently pursed lips, while a pair of impossibly high cheekbones and an impossibly low brow press against his eyes like a vice. But the little eyes don't give up the squeeze without a fight; instead becoming all the wider; a frightening degree of cornea visible on the center of an oppressively pallor face.

"Osprey, meet Sir Desmond Morrow. Sir Desmond Morrow, meet our old acquaintance and new partner, Osprey." Still seated, Desmond Morrow raises a hand towards Theodore, his vacuous gaze haunting in the low light. Theodore approaches and shakes, taking note of the man's strong grip and calloused hand. He's wearing an immaculate beige pinstripe suit, the only imperfection a chalky patch of dust at the lower pant leg.

"A gazelle," he remarks, clinging onto Theodore's hand and yo-yoing it up and down in a slow handshake. "I was hoping for a lion. That's what this mission calls for, you see—a pack of fearless and powerful beasts. Nithercott has plenty of lions in his circus," Desmond Morrow says, in his creepy little parable. "Most of them guard the doors and survey the den, barring their teeth at anyone who might be deemed an intruder. But the biggest, most intimidating feral creatures at his disposal are the ones that roam the plains, sniffing out the gazelles and eliminating them en masse. Or snatching them by their necks and delivering them to Nithercott himself, at which point, you can bet they wish the lions had just finished them off in the plains."

Theodore recognizes the name. He was the ringmaster back at The King's Inn, celebrating the Shibboleth.

"Never mind." Desmond Morrow finally lets Theodore's hand go. "I suppose that's why I have gentlemen pugilists like Bill 'The Barron of Blood' Blake under my banner." He points to a short fortress of a young man leaning against the wall in an insouciant pose, a toothpick dangling from his mouth and his bulky arms crossed before him. His face is bruised and discolored, like the soft peach that fell from the highest branch. The knuckles of his oversized hands are swollen and red.

"Nevertheless, my associates provided me with your resumé, and the work you did with Robert La Follette back in America is inspiring. A shame your man wasn't made President. He's always looking out for the serfs with his anti-mogul policies and progressive views. How is old Fighting Bob these days?"

Fighting Bob? Robert La Follette? "Uh, he's doing well, I think. Still in politics, but I don't really talk to him all that much these days." *Was that the right answer?* His eyes glued to Theodore, Desmond Morrow's already impossibly low brow sinks.

"Naturally," he replies. "Onto a new chapter, eh? If the Americans aren't yet ready for a new treatment of the working bloke, perhaps we Brits are." An awkward pause ensues wherein Theodore swears Desmond Morrow is sizing him up. Perhaps he's not playing the role of this Osprey guy very convincingly. "Well, without further ado, allow me to introduce you to your new family, Osprey—the Pilfering Paupers." His arm sweeps left, where four additional men that could be clones of Peregrine and Kestrel stand, hands in their trouser pockets, scarves snuffing the bottom of their faces, and bowlers on their heads.

"The chap in the tan covert coat is Goshawk." Goshawk gives a subtle, two finger salute. "The chap in the grey ulster coat is Heron." Heron tips his bowler to Theodore. "The chap in the grey chesterfield is Sparrowhawk." Sparrowhawk gives Theodore a thumbs up. "And finally, in the black guard's coat is my right-hand man in this operation, Snake Eagle." Snake Eagle simply nods to Theodore.

"Nice to meet you all," says Theodore, nodding back at each of them.

"And if you're ever inclined to speak of me in a more…conspicuous location, refer to me as Condor," says Desmond Morrow, keeping up with the bird of prey theme.

"Now, thank you all for coming on such short notice. I know it is not always convenient to gather in such places as this—"

"Not to mention colder than a loo in an igloo," interjects Sparrowhawk.

"That, too." Morrow nods at him. "Alas, it is a necessary precaution these days. Now, let us get right down to business, because I'm sure your hearts are all thrumming with anticipation for details on the lead. Goshawk, we will deal with your progress on the Lambeth expansion after. And Heron, I am eager to pick your brain about your dealings in Hounslow; I hope to hear only good things about the Codsworths. That family has troubled me more than aided me. If Aldous hasn't managed to find a way to minimize the drinking at his tables, I'll see to it that the next thing he presides over is his family's funeral."

"It be a delicate situation with Aldous Codsworth, Sir Morrow," stumbles Heron. "He informed me yesterday that the men only want to gamble if they can drink. If you cut off the supply of booze, he claims he won't turn a profit, and will soon be out of business."

"Confound him and his profits!" erupts Morrow, slamming his fist on the stone. "Who's the generous man that bestowed upon him the capital to build his club in that migrant-infested slum? I am. If his factory workers, and his carpenters, and his grocers, and the rest of the sweat-soaked laborers with whom he wallows at week's end can't keep their mouths shut about my operations when they've got a pint of mild in their bellies, then they shan't be drinking where Nithercott's men might hear them. The man has eyes and ears all about the city, and he will vitiate our chance of progress with just the slightest cock-up." Morrow rubs his forehead furiously. "I fight for the proletariat, alas I do not make exceptions for loutish lay-abouts who contribute to no cause aside from submersing their bellies in rotgut until they become liabilities to our delicate dealings." Morrow breathes hard, sucking air in like a vacuum.

"I want you to return to Hounslow tomorrow, Heron," Morrow continues. "And press him hard. Use physical force if you have to, only not in front of the children. I know his family lives in that untenable cot above the club, and we don't want his little ones to see him beaten until he pisses blood, which I think is the extent at which the tenacious chap might comply. Make them think it was a drunkard, yes? A fractious sod who developed a fit over a loss at the tables and simply went berserk. The stubborn sod has had chance after chance to use his racket's earnings for good, such as acquisitioning a second home fit for a growing family. And yet he spends his capital on another gambling outfit in Southwark, and whores to entertain his burgeoning client list while his wife and daughters languish in that den above the hedonistic fools to whom he caters."

Heron nods obsequiously. "Aye, sir."

"We all must pay our dues to the cause of reform, not least the blokes for whom our battle is waged—the laborers themselves. If those poor chaps desire safer work conditions and legitimate pay, they simply must contribute and not wallow in states of drunken debauchery and derelict minds. Now," Morrow straightens his striped tie and clears his throat in two quick bursts. "Onto the real business, gentlemen."

"The new lead!" Goshawk gasps more than proclaims. "Could it be what we all believe it is?"

129

"That indeed. And yes, I should hope that what I impart tonight rekindles the moribund embers of our hearth. Long have we dithered in darkness, hoping for a sign, but clutching at shadows. We think we may have found him, gents." *If this guy's career as a politician doesn't work out, he could try his luck as a poet,* Theodore thinks to himself.

"Sir Alger Marley? How can that be?" Heron's voice thunders about the chamber. Theodore glances around, unsure about whom they're talking.

"We mustn't allow ourselves to become frazzled with excitement," Morrow says, his eyes sparkling with alacrity. "A lead is merely a lead. As most of you gents know, I have a wealth of connections across this city, some of whom I met in office, many of whom I met surreptitiously; in dingy back alleys where prying eyes daren't look, or huddled behind curtains of cigar smoke in gentlemen's parlors with other intrepid blokes sympathetic to the cause of the working man.

"After I had developed a cruel understanding of the ways in which London's political landscape operates, I knew this was the course to victory, as unscrupulous and meretricious as my methods have become in order to get us where we are now. The majority of my company since my temporary resignation from public service has been criminals, thieves, and gangs. And I say to you now, none of you Pilfering Paupers or even the Lambeth Guns, nor any other crime syndicate with whom I deal can come close to the duplicitous, conniving, backhanded ways of politicians."

"The Lambeth Guns," sneers Sparrowhawk, in a thick cockney accent. "You're still plotting with those gits? They've got their own cocks in their hands more than they do guns; I tell you that." A couple of snickers erupt amongst the men.

"Be that as it may, my dear Sparrowhawk, my operations are bigger than merely this. The aristocrats and the conservatives have eyes and ears everywhere, and if we hope to see a shred of change in the way the proletariat are treated this side of Scotland, we need as much help as we can muster. The cultist bastards at Sloane Square are hampering my plans at every move. But

Nithercott hasn't captured or killed me yet, that slimy little eel."

"Nithercott?" Theodore ejaculates. "You've mentioned that name a few times now; I know of a Nithercott." Everyone looks over at Theodore, even the nonchalant boxer over in the corner turns his head.

"Aye, boy, Alfred Nithercott, the unofficial king of Sloane Square. He owns The King's Inn, along with just about every other building that lines that sinister square. He's a corrupt sod, and he's managed to create a clandestine network of high society prats who all but equal him in perfidy. I say, they meet over that square and plot and scheme in secrecy. The government won't touch Nithercott, in fact, I've long believed he has the government and the royalty in his pocket, but he's a ghost. Anytime I come close to discovering a piece of evidence—when I get even the faintest whiff of scandal he slips through my fingers and unleashes his hellhounds to muck up all our plans. Then it's always one more iron door that closes between him and us, one more bar placed upon the windows of his pearly fortress." Where Theodore's question dampened Morrow's excitement, a rumbling anger boils now instead.

"Nithercott may have started out as a lowly entertainer," Morrow continues. "A three-copper charlatan who didn't know the difference between vaudeville and Shakespeare, but I know underneath the affectations, he's a racketeer, an extortionist, and a conman. *And* a failed impresario. The sod wanted to be the next Phineas Taylor Barnum, and I postulate he has taken stylistic cues for the macabre circus that is his masquerade ball from the tawdry cirque shows the world over. Alfred Nithercott is a dejected, talentless, and bitter actor who has turned his acrimony into something usable, a weapon against the common folk with whom he once belonged. Alas, he is merely one player in this vast political game.

"There's Randolph Hershel, the parliamentary succubus who's built his fortune selling contraband to the Americans. 'Hooch', I believe you yanks call it?" Morrow glances at Theodore, who shrugs and nods. "Oh, the Volstead Act…political sophistry at its finest. Restricting the production of booze has done nothing but turn honest men into crooks, and crooks into spurious, short-lived emperors," Morrow says, shaking his head.

"Although I must admit, the last decade, fecund a time as it was for breeding outlaws and mobsters, I watched the rise of none more closely than Al Capone. Now, that gentleman has a mind for business, and an eye for opportunity; *he* is one sharp outlaw." Morrow wags his finger at nobody in particular.

"It's an outright offense, it is, what they finally nabbed him for. Tax evasion? Imagine having a glorious seven-year reign over a crime empire that you built, just to have your legacy cut short for something as innocuous as tax fraud. It's an insult to the man's accomplishments—avaricious and evil though they might have been. I've long admired men with that kind of determination; long sought to be the king of my own institution, whether that means being revered or reviled."

The comment is met with an icy silence from the men, who seem to have an established etiquette with their bombastic leader.

"Alas, for the newcomer's sake," Morrow motions to Theodore. "I was detailing some of the political opponents in our game. After Randolph Hershel is Edith Kingsley. Yes, in case you had made the connection, Osprey, Edith Kingsley of the Kingsley clan, daughter of that erratic, kilt-wearing Scotsman who bore his way into the turbulent world of English politics through not charm nor wit, but a sharp discount on his 18-year single malt scotch. Apparently, you can buy an empire with 'hooch,' Kingsley ought to show the Yanks how to do it, and without all the illicit repercussions.

"Now, his daughter Edith sits upon the throne of Camden, sipping her whiskey and thrusting her Watch Dogs inside Westminster Abbey like a drunken businessman thrusts his cock up a whore's arse. Well, with perhaps a little more finesse than that."

"Watch Dogs?" Theodore asks.

"A clever little moniker for Kingsley's henchman. She handpicks these men in a particular fashion, as they need specific traits to carry out her bidding. Essentially, they serve as both the hired muscle for Kingsley's gang and the political emissaries that do her bidding wherever she needs them. Their faces must look trustworthy enough to be granted a position in Westminster Abbey—or they usually serve as clerks or scribes once inside— but forgettable enough that the members of Parliament don't dwell upon their existence after meeting them.

"Inside Westminster, Kingsley's Watch Dogs eavesdrop on everything the House of Commons whispers to the House of Lords, and whenever the Watch Dogs get a whiff of parliamentary reversals, upheavals, policy changes—you name it—Kingsley is the first to know. What she does with this information is dependent upon the political climate; on a typical day, she simply sells it to the highest bidder. Sir Alfred Nithercott and Randolph Hershel among them. And when her Watch Dogs aren't dotting the t's and crossing the i's on parliamentary parchment, they're serving Kingsley on the streets, assailing and murdering whomever she bids."

Morrow exhumes a pocket watch and shifts his upper body towards the radiant fingers of the nearest overhead light. "That, my new friend, will have to serve as a crude summary of recent events. For time is against us, and we must act now. You see, a dear associate and trusted confidant of mine from another fifth column group with whom I'm associated, let us refer to him as the Whistleblower, has left a little breadcrumb trail for me. This trail has led to none other than my old colleague, Alger Marley."

Another collective inhale at the sound of this mystery man's name. *For a lowly street gang, the Pilfering Paupers sure seem invested in this Morrow's cause. Could it be that they, too, are made up of higher stuff? Perhaps there are even some ex-politicians hiding under those scarves?*

"Um, I hate to be *that* guy," Theodore starts. "You know, the only guy who's missed the punchline of the joke and just stands around twiddling his thumbs and throwing an apocryphal chuckle here and there to fit in while the group just cackles like banshees...but I've been overseas for a while now and I'm not quite up to speed. What's so important about this Alger Marley guy and his nemesis, Mr. Nithercott?"

Morrow's eyes bore into Theodore's own, having refused, it seems, to pry themselves from his visage since he first stepped foot into the chamber. Hastily and with a labored intent on letting Theodore know just how taxing this inquiry is upon him and his sensitive schedule, he retrieves his pocket watch.

"We haven't the time to dally on the intricate details of the relationship between the two. Not on a night of such import as this. Alas, let a crude summation suffice for now. Sir Alfred Nithercott is a criminal foremost and a shrewd businessman second. Through political connections and dalliances with power, he and others, such as Kingsley, revitalized a bruised swathe of industry on the eastern bank of the Thames years ago. Nithercott himself came to own nigh all of them himself in recent years, accruing such capital that Parliament drew up a series of investigations into the conditions that might lead Nithercott to such compounded wealth; iron, timber, and coal are resources of salience and value, mind you, but those industries alone were insufficient in explaining the wealth Nithercott accumulated. Whereupon the government investigated, sources informed me of such villainous corruption and exploitation taking place within Nithercott's brick and iron empire that, rather than shut his operations down and toss him in the clank, the vitiated ranks of parliament cut deals with the sod.

"And I tell you, Yank, I've seen the insides of these chrysalises of corruption myself but once. The urban tales were true, child laborers of no more than five or six years of age; men and women slaving over smoldering foundries for sixteen hours per day; wages denied to honest workers, or in the best of scenarios divvied amongst dozens of workers and spread grossly thin...these corporations run by the big bloke himself were unfit for prison laborers, I say."

"And when the proletariat questioned their heinous work conditions, or if Nithercott sniffed even a whiff of strike, persons would disappear..." adds Sparrowhawk with venom in his voice. "Or family's lives would be threatened."

"Aye, and with the statesman in Nithercott's pocket, the proletariat had no place to turn," interjects Peregrine. "Until *he* came along, that is."

"Alger Marley," Morrow finishes the thought. "A laborer worthy of the sweat of his brow and of a brilliance I have yet to encounter since. The bloke was a lowly serf like the rest of the unfortunates in those factories, but he contained within him a spirit which glowed not with the feeble embers of his trodden fellow slaves, but with a conflagration that could have landed the intractable Icarus himself should he have gazed into it. Marley rose in the ranks swiftly, rallying many a man, woman, and child to his cause of social upheaval. He even came to be the proprietor of an industry along the Thames. Therein, he instated wages that far exceeded those of his frugal and vile adversaries by ten-fold, mindful policies and insurance umbrellas to protect his workers. He alone through appeal of character, strength of body and mind, and sheer longanimity paved the way for the dissolution of the crooked class system across England.

"When Marley at last felt he possessed the clout to take on Nithercott himself, he proposed to use his own growth of capital to sway the government into his favor and eradicate all possibility of exploited labor throughout the British Isles. As you can imagine, Yank, Nithercott understood the implications of letting Marley be, knew full well that ignoring him and his threats was, in effect, the gift of a rostrum upon which Marley could shout his new decrees. Marley was to expose to the public the myriad wrongdoings of his enemy, to remind the peoples of England that such labor practices were best left dead with the onset of the Industrial Revolution. On the seventeenth of October of the year nineteen twenty-four, on the eve of his planned communique to expose Nithercott, Marley vanished without a trace, never to be seen again as of yet," Morrow lets his words hang in the air, before he continues.

"Let that parcel of information hold you for now, Yank; we must act promptly, for the Whistleblower tells me that Marley may have been right under our noses this entire time. The years since Marley's disappearance has proven abundant of multiple supposed sightings, but as I've stated, it has all been naught but smoke and mirrors. Meanwhile, his own businesses are crumbling under the weight of his absence. His fire burns out and his grand plan to overthrow the tyrant falters with every passing day.

"Aye, so what clout does this *Whistleblower's* words possess?" Bill 'The Barron of Blood' Blake asks. "Why should we trust him? If this is one of your emissaries in Leicester or Camden, I'd put as much faith in him as I'd put in a flyweight challenging me to a bare-knuckle scrap," He raises his bruised moneymakers.

"And I'd put my entire pension on the flyweight knocking you out if you continue to stumble into the ring drunk as a mule." Morrow's auger-eyes narrow but continue to bore into Theodore as he speaks, his eyes never flitting to Bill Blake. Behind Morrow, Bill scoffs and rolls his eyes.

"Among the fusty old warehouses, those pulverulent brick fossils that blight our lovely Thames, is a senescent foundry," Morrow says, as if he was never interrupted. "Between Wandsworth and Hammersmith lie the bones of Doyle & Emerson Metalworks. Adjacent to the foundry, Doyle & Emerson owned a metallurgy machine. 'Puddling machines', they were called back then, prodigious reverberatory furnaces that yielded wrought iron during the early 19th century. A staple of English ingenuity, and currently, an impromptu prison for our erstwhile Labour Party reformer.

"Word is that the conservatives have held Alger Marley captive since his disappearance in 1924; that they've developed a sort of mobile circuit with which they transport him about in secrecy, bouncing him from place to place, ostensibly to keep people from growing wiser of his whereabouts. Although, why they've kept the poor bloke alive all these years just to shuffle him about is beyond me. The Whistleblower tells me that Marley's rotation has brought him back to the London proper for the time being, and that he is shackled up inside the remains of this puddling machine."

"A colorful anecdote for sure, but farfetched to say the least." Snake Eagle leans back and sighs, his hands inhumed within his pockets. "I've known you some time, Desmond, and I'd trust you with my life, so I'll place the same assurance on your inside man, whether I know him or his agenda."

"I trust you're all well-equipped, as usual?" Morrow glances about the old chamber. "If Marley is in fact imprisoned at Doyle & Emerson, he's bound to be guarded. We must strike now, before the sun rises."

The Pilfering Paupers collectively draw their revolvers from their coat pockets, and a cacophony of mechanical clicks resounds as they load their firearms. Morrow retrieves his own firearm from his suit jacket. If action video games have taught him anything about military grade firearms, Theodore knows an old Luger when he sees one. Morrow catches Theodore staring and gives him one of those sinister corner-of-the-mouth grins.

"While you were sucking at your Yank mum's tit, we were off fighting the Great War," Morrow's eyes flicker. "I cadged this beauty off the body of my first kill, some Jerry Lieutenant." He pats the pistol over the hammer as if it were a beloved pet. "Yes, I spent the spring of '17 wallowing in a quagmire of muck and human filth, under a constellation of bullets in what were the trenches of the Western Front.

"I led one of Britain's only real shock troop units. We were trained by the French Chasseurs—a handy batch of reconnaissance maestros—to pierce enemy lines in the trenches and disrupt the Huns' operations. Through what felt like a fortnight that April, I lay through a ceaseless rain in a dugout, observing this Lieutenant, merely waiting for a single opportunity to dispatch him furtively. The opportunity didn't show itself until the fourth morning of my stakeout, whereupon he chose a very inapposite time and place to take a piss. You can be sure that I dug my knife in the back of that Hun more than once. But I digress. You've brought a sidearm with you, Osprey, no?"

Theodore's eyes dart down, and he motions to the clump in his hoodie pocket. "Check," he says, hoping the bulging phonograph cylinder passes for a concealed weapon.

"Very good." Morrow motions to the men. "Come gents, our revenant leader awaits." The men begin to double check their pockets for spare shells and cigarettes, apparently the two necessities of invading enemy territory—

and Theodore begins to feel...a little strange.

Before he's had a chance to check his steepening pulse, the flickering overhead lights dissolve into an aureate necklace of diffused light. Between his ears, the pressure of a deep-sea dive seeps in, and a now-familiar old jazz tune swells through the vermicular tunnels. The sonorous trundle of a jazz orchestra waltz teases his ears, the chillingly senescent tune swallowing up the placid silence of the London underground. Theodore's headed home once more.

Please God, do not dump me in front of two-thousand pounds of swiftly rolling metal this time.

V

Endless dark capitulates to a yawning bead of light. Theodore knows he's about to be deposited back into his world, he feels the momentum of whatever's thrusting him there winding down. But he cannot raise his hands to protect his face; cannot tense a single muscle in his body to prepare for the impending impact. He must merely allow himself to catapult into God knows what. He hurls through the spreading light, realizing he can see more of the world this time and is more aware of his surroundings as he tumbles down than during the first re-entry. Maybe each time he returns, his body will adjust a little more to the rigorous demands of time travel.

He's almost there. He can feel the heat of the city caress his face and curl about his body. He catches the briefest glimpse of what's below—a manhole just off the curb spewing tendrils of steam, passersby hustle athwart the street, stopping occasionally to glance at…something, what is it? Whatever it is, he's headed right for it. Like a human asteroid inexorably careening towards Earth, he plummets downwards, thankfully plopping onto something soft and squishy. Upon landing, his head snaps back. The gazelle makes a swift escape off his face, and what sounds like a dinner plate meeting its fate at the callous hands of gravity and a hard surface, resounds from below. He's done it again.

"Ni ta ma de zai gan ma!" a shrill squall sounds somewhere above his head and off to the side. This irascible, foreign tongue barely registers with him, though. He's still acclimating to the effects of the time scrambler through which he was just thrust. He's also trying to divine the putrid smell that's currently invading his nose. Fish. Acrid, noxious, horrible fish. Theodore sits up, his fingers digging into the viscid scales of the massive tuna he's landed on. A curtain of astounded faces is drawn before him; puzzled onlookers gazing stupidly from the sidewalk at the young man who's apparently stumbled, leapt, or fallen right onto the fish stand.

"Mei zhang yan a, wang wo dong xi shang zhuang! What you doing, young man? That very expensive fish, cost more than all other combined!" The owner rounds the stand and begins tugging at Theodore's arm. She makes little progress with the leaden loser that's defiling her wares, though. With her diminutive frame, she might as well be trying to pry the quarter-ton tuna itself from the stand. Finally recovering from the shock of time travel, Theodore wrenches his hands up from the belly of the fish as if it were riddled with the black plague. He hates fish, can't stand the smell of it, the taste of it, the idea of it. As far as he's concerned the slimy little swimmers should be left to the sea, where they belong. He hobbles off the fish stand, gelid chips of ice sliding along his back.

The frustrated shop-keep approaches like a cantankerous gust of wind, throwing her fists in the air and hurling what must be a slew of curse words at him in Mandarin. He raises his hands in a conciliatory gesture, stumbling back into the crowd of spectators, the pungent stench emanating from his body and mingling with Chinatown's other less-than-savory scents. The fishy fragrance encapsulating him takes him back to the time Henry emptied out Theodore's brand-new bottle of *Hugo Boss* and replaced the contents with fish oil in a supremely clever and wickedly cruel April Fool's joke. Being drenched in the essence of his least favorite food type is about as funny now as it was then.

As Theodore steps out into the street to begin the trek back to The Cat's Meow, he sees a man with wavy brown hair in a glaucous sport coat shake his head and smile.

"Hey, lady," the businessman says to the saleswoman in a patronizing bark. "That Southern Blue Fin I was eyeing a minute ago that you said was $5,500, the one the kid was just dry-humping? I'll give you two-grand for it, final offer."

With all the delicacy and precision of a baby pawing at the mobile dangling above his crib, Theodore scoops the cylinder from its housing.

Damn, he thinks to himself, tossing the cylinder up and down and ruminating on his latest adventure, *just when the night was getting good.* He paws at the lump in his hoodie pocket. *The cylinder I found in Bargirl's room made the trip back with me.* He inhumes the cylinder he just retrieved into his other jacket pocket and lets his arms dangle awkwardly to the sides of the bulges.

It's peculiar how traveling 80 plus years through a bend in space-time amounts to a feeling as simple as an acute hangover. Or, perhaps, it's more akin to the preceding drunkenness; the effect of time travel on the body being like the angry cousin of over-imbibing. *Still, it's worth it for the experience;* Disney World *produces just as much nausea for its meretricious attempt at a journey to another world. This is the real thing*, he thinks, climbing the stairs out of the bar. And what a night it was.

He shuffles back home through a city that's only just opening its eyes to the shimmering brilliance of morning. He thinks about the inquisitive and intimidating man in the wolf mask—a person he's run into on both nights but about whom he knows nothing beyond the dude's choice of party accessories. And he thinks about the ringmaster, aka Alfred Nithercott, whom he didn't chance to see during last night's adventures. And he thinks about the girl; the way she held him, the way she kissed him, the way she embraced him in that divinely lavish hotel bed.

A thought strikes Theodore as he crosses the street, quickening his pace to avoid an overzealous yellow taxi. That man in the wolf mask egged him on, told him to head towards the river where he stumbled upon Peregrine and the Pilfering Paupers the first night. On night two, he once again pressed Theodore inquisitively. He seems somehow invested in Theodore, drawn to him in some enigmatic way. But one thing's for sure, Theodore doesn't like his vibe. Not one bit.

Only one thing is patently certain to Theodore: the people at The King's Inn's masquerade ball are a microcosm of a dangerous high-society, one intent on keeping the proletariat in their place. The man in the wolf mask is a part of that society, but if he was indeed encouraging Theodore to find the gang at the river, he could very well be a sympathizer for Desmond Morrow and the labour reformers. There is one way to procure a potential answer.

The internet is the great preserver of history. A digital heap of knowledge and all of history can all be accessed in one tidy keyword search. Using a couple quick inquiries on his roommate Henry James' laptop, Theodore will soon have the answer to what Morrow and the Paupers found in the decommissioned Doyle & Emerson Metalworks just after he was whisked away from their cause last night. The discovery of an ex-lower-class hero imprisoned in an abandoned factory on the River Thames was bound to have been featured in the newspaper that week.

Yawning, Theodore glances skyward as the morning sun begins to eclipse the lower tenements to the east. From having sex with a lovely stranger at a masquerade party to scouring the depths of the London underground with an eccentric economically motivated gang, he feels he ran around like a decapitated chicken on amphetamines last night. Time travel is doubtlessly an exhausting activity. After a quick nap, he'll do some research on whether they found Alger Marley at the old foundry that night.

He reaches the Meat Packing District just as the ankle-abusing cobblestoned streets begin to clack with foot traffic. He climbs the two-story stairwell to his diminutive unit that resides over an intersection which will, in just an hour or two, become a bedlam of noise and commotion. After last night, he's tired enough to sleep through the din, though.

Unfolding upon the plush bed that takes up the majority of his bedroom's paltry real estate, he paws at the cell phone that he always seems to forget. Flipping it open, he finds a message from one of the few people in the vacuous chamber of his contacts list. He chuckles to himself. Years ago, his little sis perfected the art of managing to be just invasive and just instructive enough in her texts to appease her motherly instincts, but not so much so that he could call her on it.

When their parents ceased to be a notable presence in their lives, Alice and Theodore both had the innate sense to take up their respective parent's roles. But where Alice is a diligent and calculated surrogate mom, Theodore is fatherly to Alice only so far as his diffident nature allows him to be. Which usually entails following after her in his bumbling manner, making sure the intrepid young lady doesn't get herself into any dangerous situations while she socializes with the slews of random guys. He knows how important her guidance is to his wellbeing, but how much does *she* really need *him*? *Not much*, he thinks, peering down at his phone. There's a new voicemail.

"Bear, I didn't hear back from you at all yesterday. Don't you read your texts anymore or have you decided that even that entails too much of a social life? Well, while you're hibernating as you very often do, I'm over here at Vincent's Vagaries slaving away. And by slaving away, I mean I'm slouched over the counter 90% of the time, wandering around the store, throwing my trusty duster over the same shelves until instead of being buried in dust, they show their nice peeling, decayed finishes in all their glory. I guess hobby and antique shops aren't all the rage anymore. Anyways, stop by the store if you're feeling inclined to save me from my fate—death from a slow but inexorable boredom."

Hobby and antique shop, Theodore thinks. *I have that old gramophone cylinder I found in Bargirl's room. Maybe Alice's shop has a gramophone that plays cylinders and not records. I'll have to pay her a visit after my nap. And if the return journey dumped me both in front of an oncoming taxi and on top of a cantankerous vendor's prized tuna, I can only hope Francis isn't floundering in the Hudson right now.*

ACT III

I

"Why do they call 'em steamers, Teddy?" Alice's little pointer finger thumps up and down on the grainy old image of a hulking, smoke-belching behemoth disembarking from Erie Station sometime after the Pan-American Exposition. Picture books with page after page of old-time locomotives always make Theodore smile. He isn't sure if little Alice really is captivated by them like he is, or if she's just playing along. Probably number two.

"Steam trains, silly." He tousles her gossamer curtain of hair until it's all clumped over her face. She swats him away. "Steamers are those big boats they used to cross the ocean on. Remember that one I told you about that sank like a million years ago?"

"The Tie-Tie..."

"Titanic, yup." Her eyes sparkle and expand until they look like they're about to burst.

"Did all those people dieded, Teddy?"

"Well, um..."

"Now Theodore, what have I told you about filling your sister's head with your scary stories?" his mother's voice sounds from the doorway, where she stands with her hands propped on her hips. Their mother Jenny is a gracious and strong woman, carrying with her but one tell of the domestic life in which she's mired; a voice that's permanently on the cusp of a rattle.

"Alice is too young to be learning about sinking ships, burning blimps and—"

"Airships," Theodore interjects, still looking at the picture book.

Jenny's hands drop from her hips, her head cocks to the side, and she lets out a quick sigh. A single sigh is how Theodore knows mom is a little irked; a sigh along with a cock of the head means she's irritated. All of the above combined with a raising of the eyebrows means she's borderline irate, and Theodore has gone too far with his smarminess. "Right, burning airships and world wars, and zombies and werewolves...you know that she's still impressionable, Theodore."

"Yes, mom." He thumbs to the next page and inhales sharply. This is one of his favorite historical photos. While the Pan-American Exposition in Buffalo, NY ushered in the 1900s with a brilliant showcase of technologies and commercial sophistication, this photo teases at life in Buffalo prior to that well-photographed and well-documented event. Thanks to the captions in the picture book, Theodore knows that during the 1800s Buffalo was the epicenter of the grain trade in America, with colossal storage elevators lining the waterfront at Lake Erie. He figures it's just a heap of retired, sun-beaten factories these days, a shadow of its former spectacle. But, his parents have never taken him that close to Niagara before.

In this grain-speckled black and white photo, a cyclopean grain elevator towers over the tracks of a rail yard. Theodore likes this one because in the foreground are several men standing atop the cars of a static train, wearing arcane suits and hats and the like. Ostensibly, they're just posing for the photo, but Theodore's always thought there was something other than the obvious with these men. It's like they're posturing; flaunting their property like gangsters or something. Cool. Theodore glances at the caption below: '1837 Charlie Dubner and The Daisy Nook Dudgeons, captured after the gang's acquisition of Buffalo's Third Ward rail industry.'

He glances up at the doorway and notices mom is gone. "So anyway, the Titanic sank like a million years ago, and most of the people on it died," he continues in a lower voice than before, which he thinks only adds to the drama of his little historical lesson. Alice watches him, wide-eyed, mouth agape. That twinkle is back in her eye; the wonder-filled kind of twinkle that says, "Tell me more, Teddy!" which makes him feel good, like he's all-knowing or something.

"Yeah," he nods. "They were stranded in the middle of the big, wide ocean. In freezing cold waters, too; colder than those ice chunks in the freezer that mom puts in your water glass. Some escaped on the lifeboats, but most of 'em sank with the ship."

"They dieded in the cold water?" she almost shrieks, but an excited smile tickles her face. Alice loves most stories, but for a young girl, she really loves the tragic ones or the action-packed ones or the scary ones; anything where someone has an adventure or when people die is what Theodore has found piques her interest the most. Mom seems to know this too and tries to steer him away from those kinds of "grown-up" stories whenever she's around.

Shifting in her little flower dress, Alice hunkers down closer to Theodore. She props her chin on her hands. *Now* she's ready for his story. He starts to go in depth with the sinking of the Titanic—as in depth as he can go seeing as he honestly doesn't know that much about the event and will have to fill in the knowledge gaps with stuff that sounds more or less accurate. But Alice doesn't need to know that; she can hang on his every word as far as he's concerned. As he fumbles about the description of the legendary ship's collision with the iceberg, he notices a rosy patch on her wrist.

"Oh, Alice." He shakes his head and runs his thumb over her arm. "You're scratching again." She sits up and shoves her little hand underneath her armpit, tenaciously guarding the telltale sign of her nervous habit. "Lemme see, Alice." She shakes her head. He straightens up and dons his best professional face. "Let Doctor Teddy see. He's good with booboos like that, remember?" She usually falls for the little affectation immediately, but this time she gives pause before giving up her hand. Maybe she's getting too old for the whole Doctor Teddy act. After all, she is four now.

He inhales sharply. It's worse this time than usual. Deeper. He can tell she scratched enough to have drawn blood. Did mom make dad mad again while Theodore was at school yesterday? Must've. "Did your mother see this, Alice?" He can hear the nervousness, and the rising tide of anger directed at his dad, in the lilt of his voice as he attempts to maintain the equable doctor façade. She nods her head.

"Mommy put a Batman on it."

"Oh, a Batman band aid? Those are the best ones. Batman really knows how to heal booboos 'cause he gets so many when he's out fighting the bad guys at night." She nods her head and sniffles just once.

There's a noise right after Alice's sniffle. It's muffled. Maybe coming from the kitchen. The murmur of a voice. And then a crash. *Not again, please god not again.* Mom's voice. It's loud and frantic again, shouting something inaudible at dad, who yells back even louder. Something else crashes and mom screams. Theodore looks at Alice, whose face puckers into a grimace. She begins to cry. He snatches her by the wrist and yanks her onto her feet.

With Alice in tow, he scrambles to the door. He's mad at himself—furious. He always catches their parents' fights right as they start, he's trained himself to do so in order to get Alice away fast. He leads her into the hallway while the clamor escalates. The vague desire to be bigger and stronger so he could make his dad stop floats just in range of his now-frazzled conscience. But he needs to get Alice out. Theodore doesn't know what he'd do with himself if he let his dad hurt Alice.

They make it to the bottom of the stairs. Mom and dad are definitely in the kitchen, which means the back door isn't an option. He needs to take Alice out the front door, but they'll have to take the main hallway and skirt right by the kitchen before he can get her to the front of the house and out the front door. He puts his hands squarely over her ears until they make it to the front door. He kicks it open wide like the cowboys do as they enter the saloon in those western movies he sometimes watches with dad.

I swear I'll never watch another movie with dad, not after the way he treats mom, Theodore thinks, fuming. But he knows that even though the pain and frustration that courses through him every time this happens is immense, somehow it dies off, with dad managing to smooth things over with presents or spontaneous trips to the lake. Theodore curses himself for not being able to hold onto the hatred he feels for his dad right now, but he never can. He can only hate this version of his dad, the one that rears its ugly head every so often. He knows that the father in the kitchen right now isn't himself, he's under the spell of the liquor cabinet's poisonous contents.

They're out on the porch now, and Theodore's surprised by how well he can still hear mom and dad. One time it got so bad that the neighbors called the cops on them, that's how mad dad can get. It's terrifying. He leads Alice down the steps and opens the little lattice door that leads to the crawlspace under the porch. There's a little storage area under the stairs that has enough headroom that Alice can almost stand down there. This spot has been a go-to for him and Alice for a while now. A little refuge from the storm inside the house.

Theodore lets Alice go first, watching as she shuffles under, barely needing to duck her head as she goes. He stoops over halfway and joins her underneath. Her face is puffy and red, but she's immediately relaxed upon entering. Something about the enclosed space feels comforting to her; hell, to him too. It feels just that much safer from their father's anger down here. Once she's squarely centered under the deck, she plops down and begins digging her fingers into the earth absentmindedly.

"Remember when we found that robin's nest, Alice?" He points to the dried-up remains of a bird's nest on a support beam right under the floorboards. She sniffles, rubs her red little nose, and nods; a smile brushes past her face. "And we helped the little chick—that's what you call baby birds, chicks—we helped the little chick back into the nest so its mom could feed it."

She nods again, her hands wandering deeper into the dirt as she stares up at the circular weave of dried-up sticks. Dad's still audible, but only slightly; his voice occasionally piercing through the wooden frame of the house.

Theodore can't hear mom anymore. Every few heartbeats, a soft thud makes him cringe, but he wrestles his face into a smile for Alice's sake.

He glances at her divagating hands as they paw about the soft earth that's now clumping up beneath her. What's that? A touch of color underneath her hand. She's uncovered the tip of…something…just the very corner, but she hasn't noticed yet, her little face still fixed on the old bird's nest. It has something printed on it…old lettering. *What is it?* Probably just an old newspaper ad that's yellowed with time.

He joins her little excavation project, scooping up chunks of earth until the item is fully visible.

"What did you find, Alice?" With the delicacy of a surgeon, he picks the old relic up and turns it over in his hand. It's a small, cylindrical object with something printed on it. But the words are illegible, scrubbed by the callous hand of time to the point where only one out of every few letters is visible against the object's sallow skin. Alice gasps and extends her arm in a 'lemme see' gesture. He lowers it and spins it a time or two for her enjoyment, then hands it over.

"Be careful, Alice!" He's beginning to feel like a stalwart paleontologist on a big dig. He's imagining the scene now, mopping his brow with a dirt-caked sleeve and squinting under the hot African sun; pulling the brim of his oversized green hat down closer over his eyes. Assistant Alice works to find the little treasures, but he's the one with the rock hammer, the one who gets to chisel the delicate objects out of their ochre prisons and be the first human to hold them. Having just safely extricated the tooth of a tyrannosaur from its ossified bedding, the fun part can begin: the part where he gets to examine the specimen. *It's in okay condition; chipped in a couple spots and more than a little decayed, but what can you expect from a millions-and-millions-of-years-old piece of calcium?*

"What is it, Teddy?" Alice breaks him from his reverie. He reviews the peculiar little thing again, but to no avail. Alice can't know that he has no gosh-dang clue what it is. He knows that normally at this time, a young boy would take the thing inside the house and ask his dad what it is, but now isn't a good time for that.

Theodore's stomach curls as he remembers the volatile condition his dad's in right now, and he feels like hurling when he thinks of his mother and the 'owies,' as Alice calls them, that will be on her for the foreseeable weeks. Approaching dad when he's had too much of what Alice calls the 'icky juice,' and what dad calls 'heaven in a dixie,' is bad; approaching him when he's had so much of it that he beats up on mom…that's downright stupid.

He eases the little cylinder back from Alice's hand, discovering that it has a lid on top. *It's just a container, the real discovery is on the inside!* He grasps it snugly but gently with his right hand and begins tugging with his left. At first it doesn't give, refuses to budge one bit. But applying the teensiest amount more pressure yields a cracking sound, affirming Theodore's suspicion that, whatever it is, it hasn't been opened in a very long time.

With more-than-mild resistance for a full two revolutions around the cylinder, the lid finally gives, popping right off like whatever's inside is eager to breathe fresh air again. But not a single genie pops out, nor a leprechaun dying to stretch its legs and say hello. He flips the thing and dumps out its contents; his alacrity melting away as a smaller, hollow, black cylinder plops out onto his hand. It's waxy and it's old and there's nothing intriguing about it at all.

"What is it, Teddy?" Alice rises to her feet.

"It's a uh…it's a manmade conch shell." She's puzzled. "See," he demonstrates. "If you put it up to your ear, you can hear sounds from…across the world." While all he can actually hear with the thing against his ear is a pitiful resemblance of seashell resonance, with the hollow shape picking up some of the ambient air sounds, Alice won't be able to tell the thing isn't magical. And she needs something magical in her little life.

"See?" He cups it over her ear and her eyes widen. "That little noise you hear is the waves crashing over the Cape of Good Hope in South Africa, or at least I think that's what it's called. Pretty cool, huh?"

She nods, but is too focused on the steady buzz of nothingness that he's now convinced her is the sound of Mother Nature transmitting from somewhere across the planet, to respond. To think that just a few years ago the same fib would've suckered him in too. But this wee little fib of his—the type of fib that even mom wouldn't mind Theodore making—has officially taken Alice's mind off of what's going on inside the house.

This can be their new go-to place for whenever dad has too much to drink; this little trinket, whatever it is, can be Alice's go-to distraction. She seems enamored with it. Even Theodore's intrigued by the mysterious little item, so much so that he's almost forgotten about the terrible, raging storm in the house he calls dad.

II

Theodore's standing in his shared kitchenette, stirring a dab of heavy cream into his extra strong coffee. He knew he needed it extra strong because if anyone wants to enter a conversation with the syllable-spewing, verbally vexing, vocal Tommy Gun that is Henry James, they'd best arm themselves, and arm themselves good. *Well, that and the fact that the quantum jump I experienced last night was almost as jarring as the first one. It's a leviathan of a headache swishing above a deeply set nausea that only a good, puissant cup of coffee will whisk away. Hopefully...*

First, he sips, then he stirs, then he sips again, stalling the necessary interaction as long as possible. If it wasn't for the fact that he's as tech-savvy as a retirement home's hippest old fart clacking away at a buckle-spring keyboard in the community tech center, he wouldn't need Henry to find the newspaper article detailing last night's events.

Interacting with Henry tends to be akin to plucking a molar sans anesthesia. Alas, he needs to get on the web. He's got to see if he can find anything out about Alfred Nithercott and Desmond Morrow, and the disappearance of that proletarian sympathizer, Alger Marley.

He crosses the apartment in about two broad steps and comes upon his roommate's door. Henry's far more technologically literate than Theodore. Seeing as the only gadget Theodore owns is a cellphone—and he hardly ever even touches it—he's not only going to need to borrow the guy's laptop, he's going to need a little help finding a search engine for archived English newspaper articles.

Theodore takes a deep breath. Why, when he's able to dive headlong into a clandestine masquerade ball replete with potentially psychotic British elites, and conquered claustrophobia to wander underneath the River Thames with a band of gangsters, is simple small talk with an old buddy so egregious? Maybe because he more or less cut Henry out of his life a couple years ago, like he does with everyone who tries to get too close. *Everyone besides Alice, that is*. And it's just painfully awkward between them now.

Knock-knock.

"Who's there?"

"It's your mother, Henry. I hope you're not be masturbating in there 'cause I'm coming in." He regretted it before it even came out of his mouth. He's never been good at jokes, conversation starters or, hardest of all, carrying out conversations.

"Oh! Just gimme like five more seconds, hang on. Oh man, it's really good this time. I went lefty today…" his roommate begins shaking the bed as he runs with Theodore's comment, slapping the walls for emphasis.

How long until the lease is up again? Theodore thinks.

"Okay!" Several heavy thuds as he moves across the room. The door squeals open and there's Henry, draped in an extra-large grey t-shirt promoting the alma mater of a college he didn't attend. He's sporting frizzy locks that look like they haven't been washed since the Mesozoic Era and, topping off the archetypal Henry James-look, he's in a pair of black, stretchy gym shorts that have spent less time in a gym than Hitler has spent in hell.

"So, I have to say man, I'm a little surprised. In all of our two years rooming together, I don't think you've ever actually knocked on my door." Henry brings his hand to his face in a pensive pose. "Yeah, no, this is it."

"I—" Theodore starts, but Henry shoves his chubby hand forward in a 'hang on' gesture.

"No, no, no. Just lemme soak this in, buddy." His patented smug, sardonic little grin graces his face, and that little twinkle in his eye appears: the one that means Henry's thinking right now about how he's probably the cleverest person on the planet. Behind him in mission control, upon the smorgasbord of tech which includes a Bluetooth keyboard, a dusty old mixer for prank calls he used to make, a vermicular weave of cords leading to different adapters and outlets, and a titanic desktop computer that Henry touts as superior because its water-cooled, whatever that means, is Henry's laptop. So close and yet so far.

"My roommate, Theodore, a dude you couldn't coax out of a burning building if it required a word or two with the firefighters, is actually soliciting at my doorstep. So, who died?" His face melts into a funereal stare.

"I'm just messing with you, buddy," he chuckles, slapping Theodore on the shoulder. "C'mon in. Chez moi, chez trois, or whatever." He kicks a couple pillows out of the way and waddles over to the AC unit, turning it down in an attempt to lessen the noise, but the sounds of the bustling intersection outside quickly take its place.

"Now, my dear friend Theo." Henry approaches and slaps both hands on Theodore's shoulders, and Theodore can feel his roommate's weight pool against his own wispy frame as Henry leans toward him. "What you came in here for…what you've been dying to tell me—and I can tell you're just dying to 'cause you always get that little sparkle in your eye, that little Theo glint that says, 'ooh Henry, I actually need your help with something for once'—is gonna have to wait."

He clacks his tongue and begins thumbing instructions out on the keyboard. "You know how we've both been having…well, let's just recognize the big, fat elephant in the bedroom—a dry spell."

It's hardly an elephant in the room if that's all you talk about, thinks Theodore.

"It's as simple as that." Henry's face is glued to the screen, but his hand shoots up in a 'that's all' gesture. "Regardless of how qualified us two bachelors are, we're just not landing any poon these days." *He used the word again. The antecedent Henry James is palming his face in heaven right now.*

"And I know, I know, there was that one girl at the one thing, and you like flirted for 20 minutes and finally touched her tit or whatever." He's referring to a girl Alice tried to hook Theodore up with at a cheese and wine social last year. Theodore's experience there was just about as dignified as faux-high society meet-ups can get. No "tit-touching" whatsoever. But Henry likes to hyperbolize past events, especially the ones involving women.

And it's not that Theodore was too scared to make a move on the girl or anything. They exchanged words over two glasses of some kind of red from some Napa vineyard, and as usual he just didn't feel a spark. The lack of chemistry did surprise him a little though, because if anyone knows him as well as he knows himself, it's Alice. Either she's simply not the best Cupid, or he's stupidly captious. It's probably the latter.

"But I think I may finally have you beat, buddy." He's opened a web browser now, and he's navigating through the pages of some archetypal dating website, aglow with the gleaming faces of many digital strangers who are somehow supposed to be seen as prospective connections.

Growing up watching movies like *Casablanca* has perhaps molded Theodore's vision of love, making him appreciate it for the beautifully reckless and helplessly tender thing it can be. Love is such a flawed, human sensation, and he's not about to hop on some machine and have it spawn countless thumbnails of what it thinks are good matches for him. Hell, if his sister can't find someone for him, why should he trust *Hewlett-Packard* to do so?

Two clicks and a page scroll later Henry shoots up, high-fiving the sky. Theodore doesn't get the excitement. All he can see on the screen is an open chat log with a girl named…Sexy Suz. Maybe this isn't a traditional online dating service? On one side of the log, Hardcore Henry has written:

'Yo Sexy Suz, Hardcore Henry here. Is your sexy ass in the 212?'
The bit with the area code is a nice touch, but what is Hardcore Henry

getting himself into? Is he really that desperate?

"Yeah baby, wanna have some fun?" is her cotton candy reply.

"I got a biter!" he exclaims, shoving his finger into the display. "I got a biter! Do you know what this means, pal?"

"You're on an escort website?"

"The lines of communication with the opposite sex have been reopened. Hardcore Henry is back on the map, baby!"

"Nice, man, I'm rooting for you!" Theodore feigns enthusiasm, but he has more pressing matters right now than to bother with his unfortunate and lonely roommate's quest for satisfaction. He needs to try and find out what happened, if anything, when Sir Desmond Morrow and the Pilfering Paupers investigated the disappearance of labour reformer, Alger Marley.

"Are these real girls though, Henry? Like, can you trust the site?"

"Yeah bro. If I go to her profile it has all kinds of photos of her doing everyday shit like hiking, shooting, fishing…must be a midwestern gal."

"Uh nice, let me know how that goes. But um, about why I came in here…I need to borrow your laptop for the afternoon."

Henry stands, clears his throat, and rubs his chin pensively. "No dice, boss. Little Zeus is out of thunderbolts." Now it's Theodore's turn to rub his chin ruminatively.

"He's what?"

"The laptop's fried, man. Battery's totally crapped on me. You're free to use Ares, though. He's got plenty of juice." He points to his desktop computer. Theodore sighs. He was really hoping on making this a private investigation, without his roommate mouth-breathing over his shoulder while he digs for articles.

"Oh, all right."

"What can I find for you, bro. If you need the URLs of some wicked hookup sites, you've come to the right man. Hey, did your sister say anything about me by the way?" Henry's always had a thing for Alice. Naturally, it's always driven Theodore mad.

"No, man, sorry. She's actually kind of seeing this one dude…" Theodore thinks of Bathtub Gin Guy, aka Francis. God, he hopes Francis made it back to the present okay. The last he saw of the guy was his stranded, catatonic form hovering at the lobby lounge, when Theodore chose to follow Bargirl around the hotel last night. *Francis probably fended for himself okay, though. Probably.*

"Anyway," Theodore continues, feeling a pang of anxiety creep in after realizing that his new buddy could be stuck 86 years in the past all because Theodore needed to pursue his own hormone-driven interests. He'll have to text Alice later and see if she can get a hold of Francis. "I just need to find a search engine for old newspaper articles; it's…for a project I'm working on."

Henry pushes his glasses further up the bridge of his nose and begins bludgeoning the keyboard once more. "And here I thought you wanted to borrow my laptop for a little VR porn." VR, virtual reality, the future love prospect for lonely, single men. "I mean, I've got the headset right there, and I just gotta say bro, it'll change the way you look at women." Theodore rolls his eyes.

"As nice an idea as it sounds to borrow my roommate's porn-enhancing equipment, I think I'll have to pass. In fact, I'm actually in a bit of a hurry man, sorry."

"All right, all right." Henry clacks a couple more commands into his keyboard. "Just thought I'd introduce you to something uniquely different. When you put that headset on…man, it's like you step into another world. It's unreal, dude. Video games just—*POW*—come alive." Theodore has no need for virtual reality. It'd be a meretricious and thoroughly dissatisfying experience after having literally stepped into another world like he has.

"So, this website here is basically a digital archive of western newspapers that goes back almost as far as the printing press. Whatever publication you're looking for—" Henry clicks his tongue and forms both of his hands into pistols, firing them off at the screen. "It'll be in there."

"Hey thanks, man. I really appreciate it." Theodore takes a seat at the helm of Ares and, fingers poised over the keyboard, hesitates. *It was the night of December 14th, 1931. I'll need to search for the following day to see if anything from the events was printed. I'm about to find out what, if anything, happened to the Pilfering Paupers and their leader that night—if they ever found that Marley guy. Or if Sir Desmond Morrow's whistleblower was blowing fewer whistles and more smoke up the asses of his trusting superior.*

He types in the date, followed by the words London and England, watching as an enumerated mess of relevant hits populate the screen. He scans the first couple pages, seeing the *Illustrated London News*, the *Hendon & Finchley Times*, the *Britannia and Eve*, and the *Illustrated Police News* pop up in little black and white blurbs. *Huh, the Illustrated Police News. That might be a good place to start*, Theodore thinks. *If you're probing for the activity of one gang surreptitiously rescuing a lower-class martyr from another gang then police news seems the most relevant. That's what these aristocratic freaks in Sloane Square are, just criminals hiding behind their masks and cocktail glasses.*

He clicks on the December 15th thumbnail and an entire newspaper issue loads in digital form before his eyes. And it looks nothing at all like the *New York Times*, or any other modern newspaper. Everything's large and animated; elephantine headings wedged between elephantine illustrations. And the illustrations aren't exactly solid attempts at realistic depictions of events, they're more representative of antediluvian cartoons or comic strips. Sensationalism is a word that comes to Theodore's mind when glancing at the old newspaper formatting.

On the front page is an illustration of a cloaked figure with a knife stalking a hapless woman down a murky alleyway. Theodore already knows it's a story about Jack the Ripper. He can recognize something as iconic as the preeminent London lady stalker almost as well as he can recognize the characters of *Full House,* not because *he* watched the show, but because it was Alice's go-to sitcom for most of her youth. Theodore, who was more of a *Frasier* guy, had decided that 80s shows were bad.

He shakes his head and sighs, looking at the cartoonish effigy of Jack the Ripper. *Conspiracy theories back when the story hadn't already been bludgeoned to death by them*, he thinks, clicking to the next page. Most of the stories read like *Penny Dreadfuls*, Victorian England's pulpy, sensational snippet stories that sold for a penny each. As far as Theodore is concerned they were more riveting than modern American comics and punched with more mystery-fueled clout than Batman or even Superman ever could. The illustrations add a layer of depth, visualizing the pivotal dramatic sequences in hasty ink scratches; the stories are short but impactful.

Theodore wonders if the ostensibly true events in the *Illustrated Police News* were fictitious, oriented more towards entertaining English constables in their off time rather than reporting actual events. And then he sees it. In the bottom right hand corner of *Law Courts and Weekly Records* is an article entitled, "Bullets, Blood, and Bodyparts: Ambush on Smuggler's Way."

In the early and rather gelid hours of December the 15th a succession of gunshots rang out over the river, and a smattering of blood coated the crumbling walls of Doyle & Emerson Metalworks, the long-retired and even longer-abandoned facility on Smuggler's Way in Wandsworth. While it is entirely impossible to determine just how long the firefight lasted, as it is improbable that anyone, private citizen or other, was in earshot of the nigh-forgotten vicinity in the cold embrace of winter's night, it is known that a confrontation between two gangs occurred. It is conjectured that fewer words were spoken than bullets flung, and it is known that a great deal of blood was indeed spilled within the decaying walls of the factory.

After a brief investigation by Commissioner Horwood, who was more than slightly irascible upon being awakened at 30 minutes after four in the morning, it was assessed that a rival gang baited, hooked, and clobbered the Pilfering Paupers with no fewer than 77 bullets. What was speculated, but not confirmed by Horwood's office, was that Sir Desmond Morrow—prominent labour reformer and founder of the People's Party—was the new head of the Pilfering Paupers. Along with several other persons of vastly inferior and infinitely more obscure positions in society, Sir Morrow's bullet-beleaguered body was identified by Commissioner Horwood himself at just after five o'clock in the morning. The perpetrators are still at large, although it is assumed that the Wandsworth massacre was the calamitous result of a territorial dispute between gangs...

Theodore stops reading; rubs his temples, which he's found to be throbbing upon finishing the story. It's a profound feeling for sure, but not one he can easily put thoughts, let alone words to: knowing that the gentlemen he just communed with last night, strangers as they may have been, were dead; mowed down like animals in an abattoir right after he left them.

And what's more, he could easily have been there with them. Had they bustled off to save their idol, Alger Marley, instead of chatting in the tunnels he could have died, too. Still squeezing his head, his nerves settling from a rolling boil to a simmer, rational thought ekes back into his brain.

While the *Illustrated Police News* surmised that the event had merely been a conflict between rival gangs, Theodore knows there's more to this story; and he knows that this shooting was somehow linked to that hotel. The King's Inn is the center of some corrupt elite dealings, he can just feel it. Behind closed doors, those masqueraders are concealing more than just their faces; their agendas are lingering flesh-deep, and somehow, they're influencing England in a big way through their furtive cocktail parties and 'Shibboleths.' And the ringmaster, Sir Alfred Nithercott, he's got to be the mastermind. Peregrine and Kestrel had told Theodore that Nithercott was a political opponent to Morrow, but there's a personal thread there, something deeper and Alger Marley is the crux of it.

Theodore leans back and rolls the cursor over to close the window, sighing. As he clicks, Henry slaps him on the back again, sending a little jolt through his arm and into his hand. He accidentally clicks on 'next page'.

"What *are* you into these days, bro?" Henry yammers over Theodore's shoulder, practically breathing into his ear. "I mean I assumed something odd, 'cause, ya know, it's you. I'd expected you to be researching quantum theory formulas, emailing correspondents in your illegal arms trafficking business…I dunno, something out there, ya know, and either incredibly boring or incredibly concerning, but…dusty, old newspaper articles?"

Theodore doesn't hear a word of Henry's verbal tirade; he doesn't even remind himself to breathe. He's just staring at the screen, his eyeballs piercing into the image of none other than Bathtub Gin Guy, aka Francis. The headache returns in all its pounding vengeance, and his chest struggles to rise, emitting a single gasp as he reads about a young man that was found floating in the Thames early in the morning of December the 15th.

The young man had no wallet or form of identification on his person, and had several injuries on his torso, arms, and head. The most brutal affliction is a missing left eye, which investigators deemed to have been extracted just hours prior to the finding of the body by a local merchant.

"Buddy? Hey, Theo, you look like you've seen a ghost man," Henry's voice squirms slowly into Theodore's ears, like the siren of a distant police car as it barrels down the road towards him. "It's like you've never seen an obit. I mean, granted, that crime-scene pic is particularly gruesome, but it's not like you knew the dude. He died in 1931, man. Doesn't really look like a dude from the '30s though. That shirt and whatnot. Whaddaya call that again, an ana-anach?"

"Anachronism," Theodore's flat response. "Uh, listen man, thanks for letting me borrow you're uh…your thing here…" A now speechless Theodore fumbles over the words. He swivels in the chair and stands. Henry's staring at him, bug-eyed, like he's locking eyes with a ghost. Theodore needs to go back, he just needs to. He's got to right his terrible, terrible wrong and save Francis *tonight*. Right now, he needs to find out what's recorded on the gramophone cylinder he found in Bargirl's room. For a reason he can't grasp, he feels like she may be in some sort of trouble as well.

Between the Pilfering Paupers being gunned down in cold blood, Francis's battered body washing ashore in the Thames, and Sir Alfred Nithercott's suspicious masquerade party at his hotel, there's got to be an intersection.

Which means Theodore, however unwittingly, stepped into some truly dangerous shit when he first traveled back in time. He might need a wingman if he's to go back again. Insufferable as he might be, Henry is the closest thing Theodore has to an actual friend besides Alice, and Theodore's not even about to think about bringing her back with him, it's too dangerous.

"I've, uh, I've gotta go take care of something right now, but I'll be back tonight…there's something I need to show you."

"Oh, I see, Bear. You've not only stopped responding to my texts, but you've stopped eating, too?" Alice's eyes are daggers, piercing into Theodore like no one else's can. Even from across the dusty, oversized antique workbench that her boss repurposed into a front counter, he feels like her expression alone could leap out of her and gobble him up. He looks down at the table. "You're paler than usual and those dark circles are back under your eyes. Missing sleep too, I see."

Her face rises, like an inflating balloon, from one that's nothing but concern for her older brother into an expression that's somewhere between funereal and coy. Getting better.

"Could a woman, perhaps, be to blame for the latter, Bear?" Her hands fall onto her hips and she smiles out of just one corner of her mouth. Theodore's mind shakes last night's events about like a mental paint-mixer, Bargirl making up most of the images that dart across his mind; her angelic face, her divine body, the fugacious but exquisite time they shared between the sheets…

"You have no idea.," his dry response. Then, as a sullen and terrible reminder of what he's done, Francis' face floats before his eyes. He alone got that guy brutally murdered—the sobering reality of which is killing him—and he needs to go back, see if he can fix it, scrub the event from ever happening. He fondles the gramophone cylinder in his hoodie pocket, his skin starting to itch underneath it.

"So, um, listen Alice, I kind of need to borrow an old gramophone machine if you guys've got one here. Like the really old ones that play wax cylinders and not turntable records." Alice's smile falters but doesn't quite fade. Yet. Her curiosity in his ambiguity is piqued beyond the point where concern over what the hell he might be up to could reclaim a hold of her mind.

"Like the one we found under our porch? The one that you carry with you literally everywhere and is probably in your pocket right now?" An incriminating finger points to his belly, at an incriminating protrusion in his pocket. "Are you gonna finally figure out what's on that thing? God, so many memories associated with it…"

Uh-huh, and I'm making some new ones with it now, too, Theodore thinks. "Yeah, like that…but not exactly." He turns; begins ambling down one of the myriad shelves covered with a tarpaulin of dust. There's a beautiful antique telescope at the end of one aisle. A delicate, skeleton of brass, it looms in his periphery; a forgotten sentinel from a forgotten world. Its lens, like a great big eye points to another aisle, as if saying, *down here, Theodore! It's down here*!

"Did I tell you that I'm dabbling in fine art again? Thought I might as well see if I still have that uncanny ability to transform a blank canvas like I could when we were teenagers. And Vincent let me set up an easel in the stock room for slower business days. In other words, I'm honing my magic hands each and every shift…Bear?"

"Oh. Fancy." He puts his skills of concision and disinterest to work, even knowing they won't slow Alice's verbal tide.

"So, what exactly do you need such a thoroughly obsolete, utterly abandoned piece of technology for?" Alice's voice drifts closely behind. She knows Theodore well, so she's giving him just enough space so as not to make him feel suffocated, but not so much space that she'll lose him amidst the sea of bobbles and trinkets before her interrogation is over. "I mean, I've gotta say Bear, this is some unprecedented territory we're entering here. Can't think of the last time you showed up at my shop unannounced."

To Theodore, Alice's mind is like a disassembled clock, the hour and minute hands, and all the cogs and springs laid bare. He knows the inner workings well enough to be sure she's not going to stop pestering him about his dealings unless he really puts his foot down. And he wants her to stop pestering him, because he really can't stand looking his sis in the face right now. Every time he does, he just thinks of Francis, and the fact that just two nights ago, Francis and Alice were together, an incipient romance blooming between them. Just as she starts dating a guy, Theodore goes and inadvertently gets him killed. He needs to fix this.

"Alice!" He stamps his foot for emphasis. "Now is really not the time...I have something I need to do, and if you have one of those antique record players that takes cylinders, I really need to borrow it for the afternoon." She stops mid-step, sizing him up and down with wide eyes and an expression that speaks volumes. She's surprised at the outburst since Theodore practically never raises his voice, and he can tell she's visibly concerned for her big brother. She is biting her bottom lip, and he can practically hear her mind whirring as she stares at him. There's something underneath her gaze too; a simmering understanding that he's neck-deep into something unique.

"In front of display case four on the old mahogany table," her flat response, chased by a guiding finger that's pointing toward the window. He rushes down the aisle, takes a right, and beelines for the last window display on the left. Just in front of the display sits a device considerably smaller and more pragmatic-looking than the time machine back at The Cat's Meow. In a style that reminds Theodore of signage for the 1890s World's Fair, the words *Tellyson & Co* are printed on the box.

Taking great care with the old relic, Theodore lifts it off the table and holds it before himself. *This'll do*, he thinks.

"Alright, Bear, since you're being so tenaciously secretive, you can borrow that for the day. But it had better be here by tomorrow morning or else my boss is gonna kill me. And be careful with it! That's an antique phonograph machine from—" She pulls at the tag and winces, "1903. So, it's probably ready to crumble at any minute. Speaking of which!" Alice jogs down the aisle and into the backroom, where Theodore can hear her clanking and thudding about, until she returns with a little tin can. "Lubrication. You're gonna want to oil this sucker up before you even think of using it. Get all the joints and the cylinder housing coated before you put the record in. Those are my conditions, okay?" Her hands are back on her hips.

Theodore nods.

Pulling the door to his room shut tight, Theodore throws aside a model train to clear space on his meager bedroom table. He sets the old relic down and begins lubricating it with the utmost care, anxiety over touching it in just the wrong way budding, like a demolition specialist dismantling a bomb amongst a maelstrom of bodies sweeping through Times Square. He retrieves the cylinder he found at The King's Inn and uncaps it, letting the record fall gently into his hand. Something slips out from inside the hollow record, an old and friable slip of paper wrapped around the interior of the cylinder.

He sets the slip of paper down and eases the record onto the housing, hovering the needle above it but waiting to spool up the gears. He takes the paper into his hands, forcing with his thumbs and forefingers each tenacious corner to flatten; something the little note fights hard against after having adopted the shape of the record that housed it for almost a century. Written upon the paper in brilliant cursive is a missive that's still legible, barely.

If you are reading this then there is hope. If you are reading this then, perhaps, she can be saved. My name is Alger Marley, and by the time you find this, future explorer, I will be long gone, for my fate is already sealed. But there is still time. With the device you have already discovered, temporal constraint has ceased to be an issue. My story is unusual to say the least, and to anyone besides you, I would sound a raving lunatic. I beseech you: insert the record into a phonograph machine and I will bring to light the many burning mysteries in your mind.

Feeling his heart gyrating in his chest, Theodore kisses the record with the needle. A chorus of bleeps and scratches ensues. A man's voice trundles in. The audio quality is abysmal. It sounds like an old-time radio broadcast... very old-time. Through a thick static that hugs onto every word the man says, Theodore can hear an unbridled and desperate yearning in the man's nasally voice. It's coming through in erratic grunts and whispers, like a child mumbling into the phone under the bedsheets after lights out.

III

I am a man of sound mind; a man of dignity and largesse; a man who looks at the people—and no I do not mean the draconian, labor-exploiting, parliamentary succubus that is the upper class—and refuses to accept the current state of things. With unemployment at 9 percent and rising like the price of petrol, I cannot sit idly by.

I hold the door to the Alabaster Café for a downtrodden old woman in a battered long coat, who shuffles right through, giving me a look a lamb might give in passing to a lion. I pay no mind, however, as I can't expect the proletariat to busy themselves with courtesy for a man who dresses as if he's above them. Whether she knows it or not, I serve this downtrodden woman; and I serve her humble but vital family; and her blighted but promising community.

My cabinet has been working around the clock this week, I reassure myself as I enter the café. Like the dewy petrichor that wanders from the ground after a heavy rain and rifles your nostrils, the smell of coffee in the morning has always been of a great comfort to me. The line at the Alabaster Café is long today, mirroring the bustle outside. The Strand is a veritable mess of people, hopefully many of whom will be present at my symposium today. Alfred Nithercott is the object of my vitriol. A myopic mogul with morals as straight as a coat hanger, he is, and his hands inhumed deeply within the pockets of the upper class. He is the leader of the new political scheme, the Patriciate Party, and he's gunning for me and all those who oppose the upper class's societal infringements.

He'll be pushing increased labor and decreased wages, more openly and boldly now than he would have dreamed of doing prior to winning over much of parliament. Meanwhile, I'll be fighting for the proletariat and the bourgeois alike; any who haven't a silver spoon in their mouths and silk tissue wiping their arses; those who weren't given an auspicious start and want merely to be able to feed their families. Those are the people for whom I fight. And I've come far in my mission. As a member of the lower class for much of my life, as I do here as a factory owner myself in 1924, I speak for the unspoken. I concede, such a duty sounds a trifle more poetic than it is. It's a gritty process, reformation is. The political scene of London being so thoroughly tainted and twisted does not help matters either. And with Alfred Nithercott, this venomous asp of a man, slithering out from his den of corruption once more, I cannot sit idly by.

I glance left, squinting through the condensation-caked, rain-spattered window of the Alabaster Cafe. No sign of him yet, or any of his emissaries for that matter. I've been following Sir Alfred Nithercott on and off for years now, putting a team of my most trusted subordinates on reconnaissance missions into the world that he now owns. Sloane Square is his miniature kingdom, and the wealthy elite that pervades it, his noblemen. The lower-class citizens of London, the poor chaps who actually make this cyclopean engine of a city run, are his serfs.

As for how Alfred Nithercott fits in to this political gumbo? To put it crudely, Alfred Nithercott has the political clout of a statesman and the anonymity of a saboteur; he has his shared interests with many corrupt individuals of the policy-crafting kind, and the lot of them are profiting wildly from free or nigh-free labour. Their serfs procuring for them such profits that they deign to live as lords, kings with ill-gotten crowns adorning their skulls and ill-gotten habiliments enswathing them all winter long as the proletarians huddle closer together to share blankets. All manner of affluent men and women flock to Sir Nithercott. It makes me cringe, putting the title before Nithercott's name, seeing as he did nothing to deserve the distinction of 'sir' aside from having money and an endless perfidiousness.

Precisely three years ago this month, September of 1923, a host of wealthy persons appeared as if sprouting from the very soil of Black Heath, London, and York; sirs and madams of ostensibly no honorable background or pedigree, but with the crucial allegiance to the blackguard Nithercott, owning vast stretches of land across England. He builds his empire swiftly, the only requisite for membership being sworn deference to him and sworn reticence over the doings of his cult.

Whereupon I discovered the furtive dealings of this sprouting criminal enterprise, I found it imperative to recruit the aid of someone simultaneously wise in politics, but with a blighted political record—someone who wouldn't draw attention to themselves as my agent of subterfuge, as whatever attention they have received has damaged their credibility.

Desmond Morrow became my companion in this game of shadows. His time serving as a member of Parliament of York, where the continent's eye was drawn not only to multiple dalliances with married women, but to the policies he attempted to instate that led nigh to a collapse of York's economy, shed doubt among the people as to whether or not he could lead in office again. Morrow's political career is a jigsaw puzzle whose pieces simply weren't fashioned to fit together. Thus, nobody is following his political agenda now, making him a prime candidate for my anti-Conservative agenda.

Aye, but my mission is one of greater import than merely associating with fallen rulers-turned saboteurs. This ecosystem has become more than partisan contention and fierce economic divide. The Conservative Party has chosen a sadistic and corrupt man to spearhead their funding, and I need to uncover 'Sir' Nithercott's wretchedness in order to show London the true substance of him, which lingers beneath the lavish costume parties he throws and the apocryphal community fundraisers he hosts.

Alas, I am here at the Alabaster Café to meet with Desmond and detail tonight's mission: tailing Alfred Nithercott once more to catch him in the act of recruiting yet another politician to his crooked cause and retrieving proof of said affairs. It will be a risky endeavor, but one of worth if we are to reform England's political landscape and redistribute her wealth in a way that benefits all.

I reach the counter, which wraps around the shop in a U shape, such as one you'd see at an Irish pub, and remove the bowler from my head. Dangling over the bar on my right is an American couple—tourists no doubt—who are engaged in an imprudent and absorbed session of affection. *We Brits scoff at this sort of thing*, I think to myself as I watch the woman's long blonde hair bounce while she laughs, her teeth of a gleaming white that mirrors the tile backsplash of the bar. *Alas, the Yanks…well, they're a different breed.*

To my left is an assortment of glassy-eyed blokes in suits and suit coats, some of them staring at their copy of the *Daily Herald*, others just staring into their steaming mugs of tea, pensively prepping themselves for the lengthy day ahead. These gents don't realize how fortune has struck them; to have a job at all in this economy is worth at least two hips, if not a hooray. I can guarantee as I look them up and down, that these men of the bourgeois have a home to return to at the end of the day, a good woman waiting in that home, and the prospect of a decent future glaring them right in the face. All they need to do is look up from their steaming mugs of English Breakfast and rejoice over the simple blessed fact that they are not of the lower class. The Alabaster Café isn't of a propriety fitting for the proletariat and I can guarantee at a glance that these men, from the tidiness of their suits and the well-trimmed hedges upon their faces, to the suppleness and daintiness of their hands, are above the meager means of the proletariat.

Looming past the far end of the bar, like a pallid phantom casting a shadowy pall over the room, is my one-time political leper turned ally and valuable asset, Desmond Morrow. He's white as chalk, thin, but not to the point of emaciation. It looks like the bugger is still eating his morning toast and biscuits, and upon his face that impenetrable, unnerving, piercing gaze. He's staring at me with such emblazoned determination I'm rather surprised I hadn't noticed him before. I pull the chain of my pocket watch. Three after seven. As always, the hands of time strive to nip at his heels, the punctual sod.

I approach him, at which point he relocates to a pair of barstools at the most isolated section of the bar. We clap each other on the shoulder, but no formal greeting is spoken between us. We're both too aware of the fact that, in London proper, and even greater London, nowhere is fully safe from the prying eyes and ears of Nithercott's agents. His gaze darts to two men in suitcoats across the bar, and the expression that falls upon his face is one I'm familiar with: he's pondering the likelihood that these gents are tailing us.

As they wolf down their apricot-lathered, burnt slices of toast and laugh between sips of tea, I know that they may well be spies for the master of ceremonies himself regardless of their insouciant and disinterested airs. The thought makes me hunch in my chair, to the point where I'd almost pass for Quasimodo himself, were I not wearing a neatly pressed Chesterfield overcoat.

"Marley," Morrow husks, his eyes darting about and then settling on my face. "It's been some time, mate."

"That it has, Desmond, that it has." I smack my lips together, realizing I had jumped out of the order line when I located Desmond. They feel like two strips of sandpaper. Some tea would be nice. He raises his own mug and takes a hearty sip, his expression stoic and unrelenting.

"I have developed some…connections as you requested. It wasn't easy, nor was it glamorous, but," he sighs an interminable sigh. "I have met with the new head of the Pilfering Paupers. Those ill-mannered, rabble rousing street-types may now be our best bet in terms of security. I've given them their instructions for tonight. I've also implied the life expectancy of dealing with Nithercott and his men, should there be any…unforeseen circumstances. I've given them a quarter compensation, promising that you will cough up the remaining funds after the job is done."

My mind flashes to my adopted father. A striking fear paints my conscience as I consider what might happen to him were harm to befall me tonight. I am dreadfully worried, which is a silly thing. For if everything goes according to plan tonight, Nithercott and his cohorts will be none the wiser of our presence.

"Well done, Desmond." My hand lunges into my coat pocket, fishes about, and produces a thick wad of bills. "Here, for your progress so far, as promised." He nods, still unsmiling, and snatches the money, padding it into a neat lump and inhuming it in his suit-vest with such celerity it's like watching a magician displaying a vanishing trick.

"Now," I continue. "My inside source informed me that Nithercott carries out these business deals himself, in person, with three of his most trusted men at his side. They will be armed, although the highly sensitive and surreptitious nature of this dealing will prevent them from twirling their munitions out in the open like batons in a bloody circus." It's true, I have a man on the inside—a double agent, if you will, who's been a pivotal piece in my plot against Nithercott all along the way. My adopted father, who has a tenured profession as both one of London's premier architects as well as a tactical advisor during The Great War, became Nithercott's personal attaché. He even designed The King's Inn, Nithercott's luxury hotel and headquarters for all things clandestine and wicked.

But my father, regardless of his professional relationship with Nithercott, must remain ever cautious and ever circumspect in his mission. Any time he relays information to me, he's risking his own life, and I remind myself of that fact day and night. If that madman ever discovered the true nature of his treasured architect and councilman, he'd flay my father alive and murder the next five of his personal associates out of sheer paranoia.

"Nithercott will be meeting with his new client in the Moorgate district at Moorgate and Telegraph Street. We will wait in my town car, observing from across the road. Your Paupers will be doing the majority of the work. I'll brief them on that prior to the operation. Did you find a man with swift fingers?" Morrow nods his head, dabbing at the gathering beads of sweat on his forehead with a kerchief.

"Bloody fine work, mate. Now, your swift-fingered Pauper will wait for my signal down Great Bell Alley just off Moorgate. Upon receiving my signal, a discreet tip of my hat, which will indicate to him that the exchange is complete, he'll approach Nithercott's client. But not Nithercott himself! This is crucial Desmond: Your man must approach Nithercott's client and not Nithercott nor his own men. Nithercott and his men will be wearing their trademark rat masks as a precaution. I know this because whenever he conducts a business deal in public, he conceals his identity in the name of his best friend, ambiguity.

"So, tell your man once and tell him again to tail the other party, and not those with faces of vermin. That is imperative. As soon as Nithercott and his men are out of sight, your man will jam a pistol into the client's side and instruct him to acquiesce calmly into the back seat of my town car, at which point we will obtain the official document of partnership signed by both Alfred Nithercott and his *new client*. This document, as well as any needing coercion of our new abductee, shall be our ticket to the full public exposure of the slithering asp and all of his wrongdoings. A signal that he and the other vitiated parliamentarians are to play *our* game now or else we'll blow the lid off the entire operation!"

Morrow nods his head, his beady eyes darting about. "Shall we go over the plan once more?" I ask.

Rain thrashes against the window in a cantankerous deluge. The caliginous night sky reflects the city lights in a milk-white haze. Down at the end of Moorgate, the light from a single oil lamp stretches its paltry arms into the darkness enshrouding it. I'm hunched in the backseat of my town car, Desmond is lying in the front passenger seat, twitching nervously; one of his Paupers is in the driver's seat, tapping his fingers and chewing on a now-eviscerated toothpick. He's been gnawing at it since we shut off the engine. Gnawing at it and staring off into the distance, waiting for the furtive meeting to begin. I forgot the bloke's name already, something Hanley.

"Hanley, make sure you're crouched low enough that they won't see you. It's imperative Nithercott thinks he's not being observed during the interaction. I gaze down Great Bell Alley, where I can barely discern the outline of a trench coat bobbing about like a specter in the tenebrous dark. Desmond's other man is in position. I lower the brim of my bowler cap, listening to the interminable tick of Desmond's pocket watch. His beady eyes pierce the timepiece, while his hand rattles as if the car were moving down a dirt road.

"Midnight," he sputters, glancing about.

"Check your pistols, mates," I whisper, withdrawing my Webley & Scott revolver and methodically checking each cylinder. Hanley brandishes a Kerr's Patent revolver, an antique sidearm used by cavalrymen in the Confederate Army during the American Civil War. "Really now, mate? That archaic paperweight is what you've brought?"

Desmond turns and shrugs. "The Pilfering Paupers are a trifle sentimental about the past."

"Shh," Hanley interjects. "Down at the end of Moorgate." I squint past the coruscant diamonds of rain glittering on the windscreen. Four figures in long coats materialize out of the dreary night, creeping up the street like raccoons prowling for their banquet of refuse. As they approach, I discern the haunting, floating visages of four rats. A tall and lanky figure strides in front of the others; confidence and determination dominating each step he takes. Crowning his head is a top hat, and underneath his notched-lapel, mid-length coat are the zebra whites of a pinstripe suit. This figure is surely 'Sir' Nithercott himself.

Approaching from the opposite direction, boots clacking sonorously upon the pavement, is a single figure in a generic mask, toting a briefcase. The two parties meet not 20 meters from my town car, where they perfunctorily shake hands. I notice that one of Nithercott's accomplices holds a single umbrella over Nithercott's head, while he and the other two grunts are pummeled by ineluctable torrents of rain.

Some brief, muffled words are shared and then Nithercott's carefully played affectations of formal composure fall faster than the slivers of rain around him. He grasps the shoulders of his new associate and draws him in, throwing one arm about him and making a graceful arc in front with the others. I scoff audibly inside the car; he's a dejected stage and silent film actor, but he'll stop at nothing to display to his associates just how much of the expressionist's heart beats within him.

Over the knuckles of rain that rap about the town car I hear him say something about "the zenith of business ventures," and "a world of possibilities." His new associate plays along, a mere puppet in his game now. I can almost see gossamer strands of string attach to his arms and back as he consigns himself to the masked madman.

The thought of this new associate of his, surely just another sod emerging from a family line of pampered pedigree and artificial wealth, who cadged their coin off the backs of child laborers and indigent working-class families, repulses me. I'd bet my last sovereign he's just another affluent lad with inherited wealth, having no toil or talent to show for it. Parliamentary title or not, he's an asp maundering about the tall grass like the lot of them. Alas, he joins Nithercott's army, the ranks of which are suffused with disinterested, unimaginative, egocentric sycophants who own prodigious swathes of land this country through, and esteemed rank in society to boot. It makes my hand curl into a fist just thinking about it all.

And yet the conservatives claim that we labour reformers are communist sympathizers. That has long been their modus operandi against me and my allies. This is why I must catch Nithercott's new associate and expose the signed partnership forms. So that I might show Britain that it isn't the clandestine communist, or the slovenly socialist that is the greatest threat to our nation, but it is the very seed of evil, long since planted in our own soil, allowed to swell up from its fecund earthly prison, spreading its roots throughout and growing in the dark, transmogrifying like some wicked fungi until it has all but enshrouded our nation under its umbrella of deceit. This! This is Nithercott and his army of unscrupulous elites! He and his followers will take over England if they're able, buying off politicians, buying lands and tawdry material possessions while the rest of the nation suffers, languishing in squalid homes untenable even for the rats that scamper about them.

My mind fumes and fumes, as yet before me unfurls an incriminating scenario with the most dangerous man to England since Napoleon. I must stay focused. I give myself a spry little slap on the face, to which Desmond turns about, his dour eyes telling me not to make any sudden movements for fear of Nithercott seeing us. I watch on as the deal comes to an abrupt end with the switching of two briefcases, another handshake in which Nithercott draws his new ally into his arms once more, and pecks him on the cheek, the plump rodent snout engaging in a brief dalliance with the man's nose.

Without uttering another word, the two parties separate, Nithercott's right hand man sedulously clutching to the idea that he might keep even a single raindrop off his master. As soon as Nithercott's group takes a turn, scampering off like a pack of elated rodents coveting a single crust of bread, I glance over to the alley, my teeth rattling in nervous anticipation.

I tip my hat—the signal for Desmond's pauper to approach the newly distinguished servant. He complies, disinterring himself from the shadows of the alley and cutting across the street. In a coruscant flash of metal, he brandishes his pistol and jabs it into the man's side. The unassuming bloke is able to emit a single grunt before the pauper throws a gloved hand over his mouth.

"Good on you!" I grunt. Desmond just licks his lips and dabs another fleck of sweat off his head, his eyes boring through the glass of the town car's windscreen. I thrust my hat as low on my head as it will go, reach over with a trepid hand, and throw the door open.

"Bring him in, bring him in!" my voice rattles. "With haste, old chap, before anyone sees us." The Pauper thrusts our new captive inside so that his elbow teases my own. I can smell the ripe rust of a cigarette on his breath, can see the terror in his eyes as they dart about the car. He's in over his head with this 'Sir' Nithercott character, and he's only just now realizing it. The poor sod.

As soon as the pauper is in the car, he and Desmond make our message even clearer by foisting the tips of their pistols in the man's face. "Who, who are you? What's happening?!" he stammers. I shake my head.

"I'm sorry, chap, really I am. My apologies for the less-than prim greeting from my associate; my apologies for that whiz bang in your side a moment ago; my apologies for the whiz-bangs in your face right now. This isn't how I prefer to do my business, but your new partner has forced my hand." I shoot a glance to the driver. "Let's get that petrol spinning, mate. Take us to Battersea." I return my focus to Nithercott's associate.

"Now I want to assure one thing, chap, no harm shall befall you under our watch. While two of the blokes in this car are members of a rabble-rousing street gang, the one beside you with the antique pistol tickling your cheekbone, and the bloke behind the wheel, not a one of us is in the business of bringing physical pain to anyone, regardless of associations."

I feel the wheels begin trundling over the cobblestone street as the town car lurches into motion. "No harm whatsoever. All I ask is first and foremost that you sever your ties with Sir Alfred Nithercott now and forever. Secondly, that you hand over that briefcase to me right now without questions." The rain drums with a maddening precision on the town car as it builds speed down Moorgate Street. Nithercott's new associate complies, stifling a sob and thrusting the sopping wet briefcase into my hands. Just as the car is about to pass the street Nithercott and his henchmen turned down, I unsnap the buckles on the case and, not unlike a child feverishly unwrapping his birthday present, I swipe it open. My heart sinks. Staring back at me is not the legal document I've been yearning to get my hands on—it's no piece of evidence against Nithercott whatsoever. Staring back at me is a single handwritten note, upon which are four sardonic words penned in immaculate cursive: *I've got you now.*

I'm not sure which I hear first, the jarring eruption of a Thompson submachine gun as it rips into the tires of my town car, or the bone-chilling cackles of the madman pulling the trigger. The car lurches side-to-side intractably, Desmond ululating over the frenzied din of gunfire. A moment later, all goes black.

The next thing I recall is watching fuzzily as the rain pockmarks the cobblestones, which are near to my cheeks now, and feeling a tremendous pain violating my head and my back. I'm lying on my stomach in the middle of the street. I must have been thrown onto the ground face-first because my cheek is ablaze with a bludgeoning ache. I look up, desultorily gazing into the night sky. As the rain cascades into view it scintillates a golden white, and an immense heat blooms from somewhere off to my right. I lift my head enough to shift my gaze. My town car is a heap of rubble, a massive, overturned metal conflagration, casting a flickering framework of light upon the surrounding buildings.

"Not so fast!" I hear suddenly, as something wallops me from behind, driving me back down and pinning me to the stones. An acerbic flash of pain emanates from my lower back, and that's when I realize that I must have severed one or two of my lower vertebrae in the crash. My vision warbles in and out of focus, like a turntable trying to eke a song out of a warped record. Cogent thought pokes at my mind, trying its best to slip in, but a great buzzing deftly sweeps it out each time. Two figures loom above me, two quavering shadows haunt the stones beside me. The gas lamp at the street corner is a paltry simmer in comparison to the mechanical bonfire beside me.

A third figure hustles over from somewhere down the street, thrusting out words in short bursts, thoroughly out of breath. "We've lost the other one, sir. He must have dashed from the vehicle before it erupted."

"De-Desmond," I grunt, looking up. Tall, lanky, terrifying, Nithercott stands over me with the rat mask shielding his face. The smoking barrel of his Thompson sub-machine gun rests insouciantly on his shoulder.

"Morrow?" Nithercott sneers. "He got away, did he? He got away? Bwahahaha!" he cackles, and his dejected henchman seems to shrink deeper within his own skin. Nithercott checks the cheese-wheel magazine of his Thompson and reaches into his coat, where I can see at least two more magazines attached to his belt. He slams a fresh one into the gun and I can hear his doomed henchman begin to howl in fear.

"Now, I thought I provided you with the simplest of instructions, a directive that a child playing hide and bloody seek could follow," his voice is a high-pitched squeal, that of a weasel's or some other slippery, slimy vermin. "I wanted you to chase down the others and deal with them; I wanted no loose ends." He points the gun at his henchman, who rips the mask off his own face and raises his hands defensively. His jejune face, soaked in rain and perhaps tears, disguises the rugged, calculating disposition of the thug that he must surely be.

"Look at me, sir! It's me, Alton. I've been nothing but loyal to you for years, and I've never let you down," the young man bargains. "Now, if you'll grant me an audience for but one second, I'll tell you my plan—"

Nithercott leaps forward twice, twirling upon the slick cobblestone and swooping down upon his henchman like he's Von Rothbart in *Swan Lake*, the smoking barrel of his automatic weapon symbolic of his pernicious intent.

The henchman takes a step back, holding up his arms in a meager defense. I watch on, incapacitated by the pain in my back, my head still reeling from the collision. The flames engulfing my town car crackle and sputter to my right, flinging a smattering of embers against my cheek.

"If I'll grant you an audience?" Nithercott croaks. "When I was auditioning for roles at the *Royal Theatre*—showering the people of London with my smarmy wit and refined nuance few actors possess—did they grant me their audience?" Nithercott's voice rises to a shrieking hysteria, his lips quivering beneath his half-mask.

"When the arts fell into an existential quagmire brought on by the funding of a world war in which England had no stake, and I alone procured the funds to revitalize the dying industry, did the producers grant me an audience when I told them I deserved a mere supporting role in their first reprisal? That if they shan't make me a Romeo or a Hamlet, they owed me as much as a Tybalt or a Claudius? Nay! The unimaginative, myopic lot has failed me time and time again, giving me the courtesy they'd give a common sewer rat if it pawed at their elitist heels. Well, the sewer rat is back, and he's prepared to scuttle right through the foundations of the vitiated liberal system that he helped build!

"The world is a crooked, wicked, twisted place, Alton, and I shouldn't like you going through life assuming otherwise!" He raises the submachine gun, and before Alton has another opportunity to protest, Nithercott pulls the trigger. Alton's arms instinctively rise like a matador shielding himself from the charge of a baleful bull. Pockets of furious light erupt from the nozzle; the bullets chew through their target, shredding Alton's hands and driving further until his torso is a vitiated mess of crimson streaks. Alton falls limply to the ground as I let out a helpless whimper. It's all I can do in my state of profound injury.

Nithercott leaps upon Alton, kicking and driving his heels into the lifeless body, cackling to himself all the while. "One fewer mouth to feed, no?" he yells back at his remaining associates; whose obsequious and fervent nods are the only movements their paralyzed bodies permit.

"There you see chaps, I've created an extemporaneous piece of modern art. It just requires a few bullets and a good body. It's a delightful thing, really," he says with a pair of cold, hungry eyes gleaming under his mask. "You never know exactly where the bullets will land, or how the blood will flow from the puckering wounds." He gazes down and stares at his thoroughly dead associate, lost in some murderous reverie.

"Sir, we mustn't linger," the more intrepid of them grunts. "The coppers are surely on their way!" Nithercott ignores this.

"And you!" His head darts over to me like some carnivorous animal watching as its injured prey tries to find its legs to flee. "Oh, you must see the rest of my handiwork." My eyes flutter as he dances over to me. I'm beginning to lose consciousness. "Oh no, no, no, Alger, you cannot slip away into careless slumber, not before you appreciate my centerpiece!" He cups my face and slaps my cheek over and over, then nods to his men. They hurry over and scoop me up, hoisting me up onto their shoulders, my feet dangling beneath me, my head a searing mess of inchoate thoughts. As my weight shifts from the prostrate lump in which I found myself to that of a wounded soldier, I hear a hollow pop; a sound unlike those of the cracks and snaps of the giant fire before me. No. This emanated from my own body—my lower back. Judging by the curls of throbbing pain just below my waist, it's either a spinal fracture or a slipped lower vertebra.

I let out a single, ravaged moan as Nithercott's men drag me towards the flaming pyre of my town car, Nithercott leading the way in some macabre, gleeful prance. The heat is staggering, and I begin to bless the cool shards of rain that continue pelting me from above. "Look at it!" he exclaims. "Look at my handiwork, Marley. I knew you'd appreciate it." Through arms of smoke and tongues of orange flame, I see the smoldering remains of the driver, Hanley.

Nithercott grabs my face with both his hands and yanks me forward until all the pain in my tormented back is supplanted by a horrific and pervasive burning in my face. I'm so close to the flaming wreck now that if I had longer hair, or perhaps a loose upper garment, I too, would be ablaze.

"What do you think of it, Marley?" Nithercott cackles beside me. "I think all proletariat sympathizers look better in this light." My stomach turns as I'm forced to watch as layers of skin peel from Hanley's face and ooze onto the car seat. I didn't know the man at all, but I do know he was one of Desmond's closest associates. I'm sure he had a family. As for Desmond, I can only hope and pray that he's the one who escaped; the one Nithercott had his man hunt down after the crash. I glance into the backseat, my face as hot as a combustion engine.

A large, glistening lump is melting on the backseat. It's impossible to tell if it's made up of one or two bodies after the deleterious effects of the fire. Could Nithercott really have let his new partner perish in the fire as collateral damage? Set him up as bait in this scheme, and then just callously left him there to die with the Paupers? The unfortunate bloke with the dummy briefcase isn't observable anywhere around the wreck, so I must assume that the madman simply left him in there to burn with the others. I wonder, as I stare at the mess of deteriorating bodies, if this poor sod knew he would go down with the enemy, or if Nithercott assured him he'd retrieve him from wreck before setting it ablaze?

"This, my friend, is what becomes of those who threaten me." Nithercott brings his face to mine, a pallid, jagged chin jutting out beneath the mask and a pair of cold, beady eyes gleaming through the cutouts. He erupts in a maniacal cackle once more. "But you, my pesky proletarian rival, this flaming heap is not what shall become of you." His mouth coils into a feverish smile. The solitary thought that's permeating my mind right now is not of the despair of dejection, of coming so close to obtaining hard evidence of this man's criminality and then losing it all; it is not of the pain in my head or that in my broken body; no, it is the thought of my adopted father. I hope to god that he's alright, and that he will look after himself now that I no longer can. "Oh no, I've got plans for you, Marley." He bounces away and motions to his henchmen, just as I hear the tender wail of a police car in the distance. "Let's move, gents!"

IV

Theodore unclasps his tangled hands, little alabaster buds slowly disappearing from his knuckles. He's been gripping his hands together tensely through the entire audio recording, and he's not sure, but it feels like he's been holding his breath the whole time too. He lets it out in one shaky sigh as Alger Marley finishes his message. The constant scratch of the primitive recording equipment lends a contextual layer of eeriness to the message. Frequent fits of static swallow entire syllables of Marley's speech, muddling words and gargling phrases in a verbal cocktail, but the immediacy of his voice and the desperate nature of his message remain fully intact through the distractions.

I am confined to the technologies of my time and though I wish I could inform you to my heart's content, this record has a limited capacity, so please excuse this crude summation, future explorer. My grandfather, Walter Marley, was a man of extensive knowledge and intractable imagination. You may have read that he was the inventor of the first moving-pictures device, and while the veracity of this should alight the faces of historians, it is of no consequence to you. My grandfather took me in at a very young age after my parents were killed in an accident. He raised me in Oldham, in the very warehouse where he conducted his experiments and conjured up his greater findings. This moving-pictures machine that he created was surely a startling product born out of years of diligent work in an age where still images were the only known and trusted commodity. But it was a mere guise over another, concurrent invention; his true magnum opus.

As you, future explorer, have surely divined, Walter Marley invented a time machine. I shan't begin to feign any real scientific knowledge, as my mind hasn't the capacity for such things, therefore I won't trouble you with details about the device that even I, his grandson, do not fully understand. Suffice it to say that the machine he developed uses highly specific frequencies to alter the very fabric of time and space. The massive, handcrafted horn of his phonograph—or as he called it, Sonophone*—only produces these frequencies when certain songs are played through it. Alas, I can tell you firsthand that these songs are very few and very far between.*

You see, even though I became a successful and driven man of industry, every night of my career I was trying a new record on the Sonophone, waiting for the day that I might find the right frequency and unshackle myself from the linear constraints of our world. For I had a personal motivation to travel back in time, an edacious need to return to the past. I was most desirous of an opportunity to go back to the moment my grandfather died, and intervene in whatever way I might in the unjust and atrocious event. Allow me a moment to elaborate.

After he adopted me, from when I was an infant of three years to a sprightly young lad of seven, my grandfather was slaving over his best and brightest, and no doubt most challenging, creation. My grandfather was a man of illimitable genius and boundless curiosity. Therefore, while most of us would be thrilled with producing the world's first moving-pictures device, my grandfather merely deigned to tinker with it when he wasn't bent determinedly over his time device.

Imagine that, future explorer! Having in your workshop one of the single greatest inventions of the modern age and having the creative liberty to choose to work on something even greater. Imagine standing at the foot of the mountain of creation; the height of its cyclopean peaks and the breadth of its mammoth slopes unfurling before you, stealing your breath and arresting your vision...that was my grandfather. I remember watching him in his workshop all those years, myself without any comprehension of what he was accomplishing, nor how he was accomplishing it. I only retain the feeling, like a pulsing beacon in my head, of understanding that the things on which he was laboring were of great importance to him, and of great mystery to me...

Now those felicitous years are nothing but worn memories, faded, like a gravestone rubbed slick by years of relentless rain.

Alas, on the night when both his time-distortion device and his moving-pictures machine had been perfected, my grandfather plucked me out of my bed and thrust the both of us on the late train, taking his greatest invention in tow, concealing it under the blueprints of the moving pictures device in case we were accosted by the corporate mercenaries he swore were on our heels. Our destination was London, where he hoped to premier his time machine to the masses. Unfortunately, word had spread like a cancer throughout Oldham about my grandfather's miraculous creation.

Over the years, baleful figures would lurk outside the windows of his shop and peer in. Alas, as you might have deduced, a batch of unsavory characters was waiting for my grandfather on the train that night, preparing to pounce upon their prey and steal the invention—to some lucrative end I have no doubt. I disembarked at the London stop that night, but my grandfather did not.

Theodore startles, *What is that?* he thinks, as he hears within the recording, what sounds like an old wooden chair creaking. Theodore can picture Marley pivoting on his seat. Then, the rumbling thunder of distant footsteps spears through the static. The chair creaks once more.

I am recording this message from the very bowels of my confinement within The King's Inn. There is too much activity about me; someone's stirring beyond my chamber door. Alas, let me say this: I cannot, without the swift and thorough reprehension of my conscience, say what I am desperately imploring you to do is a task that will be safe for you. In a sense, I am throwing you into a pit of vipers and asking you to crawl; I cannot tell you with any certainty that there is no risk on your part, in fact, I am asking you to risk your own life to erase my failures. Alas, you have made it this far. Perhaps you are willing to take one step further.

There is a person of great import to me, future explorer, and one I should like to see suffer a much better fate than the one for which I am destined. She is an angel I've met during my wretched sojourn at The King's Inn and a person wholly too good for this world in which she's found herself. By the time you are listening to this I will have long since stashed another recording, one further detailing my predicament and how it mingles with hers. If you, future explorer, are so inclined as to save my friend, then you will need to first find the other record. For I have spent the few years Vivianne and I have been trapped in The King's Inn together monitoring Nithercott assiduously, and I have learned much about his daily routine in doing so. This second recording will have inscribed on its very grooves instructions on how you might both escape with your lives. Come back to The King's Inn and take the lift to the top floor. Take a right upon leaving the lift. Down that hall you will find Nithercott's penthouse—his monogram is upon the door. Beyond the girl, I have an ally within this hellish prison. He happens to be a close associate of Nithercott's, and he alone has a spare key to Nithercott's suite. I will instruct him to hand it over to you, but only when the two of you are away from the watching eyes of the aristocracy. For the safety of all souls involved, it is imperative that my ally's ties to me remain unknown to those tyrants and their bloodhounds.

You must find my ally, future explorer. He will aid you in ways only he can—and you must find the second dead drop, the surreptitious spot in which it resides. I am low on time and I cannot risk having his men apprehend this record and thus discover the location of the next one, so I will merely say that I hid it right under his nose.

Allow me to close with these few remaining words. You see, I came to realize that, in my lifetime at least, I would not likely find the exact right frequency for the Sonophone. For this reason, I welded the dial of the destination input to December 14th, 1931, and chose to make and stash these recordings, even knowing the overwhelming odds stacked against me. I know the scant probability of someone finding a record with the proper frequency, as well as stumbling upon the Sonophone itself so as to open the connection to my world. Pairing this with the likelihood of this person making it alive to the dead drops where my recordings are hidden, my chances are slim to none that anyone will come to my Vivianne's aid. Still, perhaps these facts illuminate the true desperation of my situation; I am grasping at straws, and though it is likely I am merely sharing a monologue with myself just now, I must try. With the Sonophone, there is always hope.

There's a short pause, where little explosions of static pop and fizzle, like the sound a dry twig makes when it's thrown over a campfire. *Please, future explorer, you must save—*

The recording comes to an abrupt end. Theodore exhales. His mind is a pinwheel in a maelstrom; his fingernails anxiously digging into his knees. Even with this deluge of information, from the Master of Ceremony's abduction of this ex-labour hero and Desmond Morrow's narrow escape at the feet of the madman himself, to the halt of the proletariat uprising in post-war London, all Theodore can focus on is the bargirl. *Is she the young friend of this Alger Marley guy? It's hard to say.*

Even though he did find the audio recording in her chamber, it was left there many years prior to Theodore's arrival, so it's possible that an entirely different family used to live in the room Bargirl occupied. Either way, his heart is now ablaze with the flame of concern for the girl. *It certainly seemed like she was being held captive in that hotel room,* he thinks. He rises upon rickety legs, double checks that the space-time distorting gramophone is still in his pocket and leaves the room. He stops in front of Henry James' door, with the mental gale of all that he's just learned still swirling about in his mind, floating and twisting and twirling just out of reach of his conscience;

he can't take it all in, not just yet. He knows the incredible risk he's subjecting his friend to, but he'll need all the help he can get if he's to try and rescue Francis. And asking Alice for assistance is out of the question. Theodore would never, ever let his baby sister go back in time with him. As much of an intrepid adventurer as Alice is, he'd never forgive himself were something to happen to her.

Theodore clears his throat and chuckles to himself, realizing how insane Henry's about to think he is. Knock, knock.

"So, lemme get this straight." Henry James skips a few paces ahead of Theodore and turns, nearly waddling backwards into an unsuspecting street vendor. A worn man with thick glasses and a salt-and-pepper beard glances up from behind a curtain of steam to give Henry a disapproving look, but Henry doesn't take heed. He slides his glasses up the bridge of his nose and continues to maunder about the sidewalk in front of Theodore. They're coming upon the intersection of Barrow and Bedford in the Village. Not too far from The Cat's Meow.

"You've somehow, uh, stumbled upon this old record player—"

"Phonograph machine," Theodore interjects. "The difference is actually pretty important here."

"Right, this old phonograph machine. And the thing doesn't just churn out tunes our grandparents would've slow danced to, it zaps you back in time—"

"When you play specific recordings that emit just the right frequency, the phonograph machine kind of...distorts the space-time continuum, I guess, and opens up a portal to the past, if you will."

"And so, it catapults you back to the past, but only to a very specific date and time—"

"And location, yeah," Theodore shrugs, amazed that Henry's maintained his backwards gait this long without tripping.

"And it takes you to this hotel in London, on December 14th, 1931, where you're thrust headlong into this Illuminati masquerade ball."

"I never said Illuminati, although I think that would make sense too…" Theodore wraps his hoodie around himself tighter, feeling the gelid fingers of a mid-October breeze sift through the street and into his hoodie. Vehicle traffic is sparser in the West Village than other neighborhoods, but as bikes and cars trundle down the street, they hover their hands over the horn, scowling at Henry as he backsteps into the Village's clustered intersections. Theodore offers his hand in conciliatory gestures to the drivers, but honestly, he understands his friend's tunnel-vision interest in his story. If he were Henry, he'd think he was out of his mind too.

"And it's chock-full of these British snobs who are illegally profiting off the backs of the lower class; a gentry-turned-nobility situation. And these snobbish cocks are out to keep the middle and lower classes in their place, while making themselves all the wealthier in the process?"

Theodore nods, with a shrug thrown in for emphatic ambiguity.

"Sounds kind of like politics in America today." Henry brings the tips of his fingers together as if he were deliberating over some diabolical plot like a villain in a Bond movie. "So anyway, we can throw into this whole, uh, royal clusterfuck this heroic laborer guy. A dude who was loved by the working man, had this X-factor about him that drew people to his cause—but he disappeared almost a century ago without a trace." Theodore nods again.

"And so, you've traveled back twice now. The second time you stumbled upon this gangster near the river who mistook you for someone else?"

"Yes, an associate of his; someone code-named Osprey."

"And you went with him all the way underground to meet with another lower-class icon who was searching for the first lower-class icon, the dude who vanished like smoke into thin air." Henry James snaps his fingers, his curly hair bobbing up and down on his head.

"Desmond Morrow."

"So, this Morrow dude wants to revitalize the labor movement, and feels he needs the vanished dude around in order to do it. But to top it all off you're saying that the second time you were zapped back, one of Alice's friends, some dude named Francis, accidentally took the tumble with you. And you've discovered now that he was killed and left for dead in the river later that night, probably sometime before you came back to the present."

"Right, and that's priority one: saving Francis."

"So, he's the proud owner of the Sonophone? He's the dude that led you back in time?"

"He's the sole proprietor of the old device, yes," Theodore says in his snarky, verbose manner. "But he had left it in the old section of the bar to gather dust; dust and maybe the occasional mildly curious crowd who would stoop over it and wonder just what the hell it was. I just happened to play my own record, you know, the one Alice and I've had since we were kids. And the thing came alive."

"Wicked," Henry says, and Theodore watches as his companion's brows furrow, his expression pinching as if he'd just bitten into a hunk of salt lick. "Say, this Francis guy…He wouldn't happen to have heaps of fiery hair and veiny muscles that look like they're hewn from marble, would he? And is he perhaps into the art of distilling?"

Theodore's eyes widen and he finds himself nodding fervently. "Yeah, how did you—"

"I knew the mangled face in that crummy black and white photo reminded me of someone! That's the asshat who used to torture me back in Junior High. I ran into him last year at a dive bar. Sucked since I was hitting on this hot chick—real close to bagging her actually—when he pounced on me and gave me a noogie until I thought my brain would slop out onto the floor. Total cock blocker, that dude."

A few blocks into the Village, after Theodore and Henry are comfortably nestled within the antediluvian maze of neglected buildings surrounding The Cat's Meow, Theodore takes Henry left down the alley beside the massive brick building that houses the old speakeasy. He leads Henry down to the worn print sign of 'Harold's Antiques,' where he locates and retrieves the discordant brick from its crumbling housing in what has now become an increasingly perfunctory exercise.

"What's that for?" Henry pokes a finger at the spot that normally houses the dummy brick.

"You'll see…" They walk around the back of the building to the rustic barn entrance, but before Theodore shoves the brick into its makeshift keyhole, Henry paws at his shoulder.

"Dude, I've known you…how many years now?"

Theodore considers. "Many."

"And I've always thought of you as a friend, even with all your antisocial tendencies and your weird, little eccentricities." Henry wipes a loose frizzy strand of hair from his face. It bounces upward and then, like a slinky slung over a tree branch, bounces right back down in front of his eyes. "And I know I'm not perfect, fuck I mean, far from it. All I do when I'm not at work is sit around trying to find women online, and when that leads to a dead end, I just settle right down in front of some hi-def German porn; so I've got my shit too—but I gotta say, dude, you're freaking me out a little. Like, I get that you found this modern speakeasy-style bar, and that it has a very unique entry ritual," he points to the brick. "But as for the whole time-traveling, evil British cult party thing…like, are you on shrooms, man? 'Cause if so, I'd like some. Like, those are some wicked shrooms, dude," Henry chuckles, and for the first time since he's known Henry, Theodore detects a nervous undercurrent in his laugh.

"I know it sounds really…out there, and I know I haven't always been the easiest person to call a friend, but you just have to trust me, Henry. I mean, I'm not stupid, but I don't have one ounce of creativity in my body. That's why I move freight for a living. Do you think I'd be able to conjure up something like this? And for what purpose, just to get you to go to the bar with me?"

Theodore realizes as soon as the words escape his tactless mouth just how callous they sounded. The frail bulwark that's holding Henry's expression together, his pursed lips, quiver a little, and he sniffles, his eyes darting to the ground. "Well, I mean, I might have been hoping that maybe you'd want to go to the bar with me, just to hang. Even if it meant creating an elaborate story behind why, and even if I'm boring and for some reason you decided you didn't like me anymore.

"I mean, I get it dude, being social is tough, I suck at it. That's why I'm basically just one big, fat yammer box—because I get nervous too," Henry chuckles again, reflectively gazing at the ground. "It's weird how something as simple as asking someone to get a beer can be so terrifying. Knowing that you don't have much to say, and every prolonged sip the two of you take will be bookended by awkward silence. So, I thought that you whipped up this whole crazy story to distract me from the fact that you might actually want to hang out. But now I'm starting to think you're serious about it all."

Theodore pats Henry on the shoulder. "Listen man, I didn't mean it that way, okay? I do like being your friend, and...maybe the reason why I'm always shut up in my room, leaving you out there by yourself, is because I'm the one who's not an interesting person. And maybe I hate rejection, you know? Maybe I figured that if we got close like we were as high schoolers you'd realize how little I'd changed. And you'd go off and find more interesting friends. People like Alice..." This time, Theodore's voice is the one that rattles. "But now really isn't the time to prattle about all that, okay? I know I sound like a raving lunatic, but you just have to trust me. What I'm about to show you is gonna rattle your mind, and royally fuck with your perception of time and space." With a short clack followed by a sound like a coffee mug sliding across a marble countertop, Theodore shoves the brick in its housing. "It's going to make your extravagant virtual-reality headset back at the apartment feel like a tawdry little eight-bit adventure game."

Henry gives a slight nod to show that he's somewhat satisfied with Theodore's response. However, his furrowed brow tells Theodore that he's still as puzzled as a baby being handed a screwdriver and told to build his own crib. The old relic of a door screeches open, and Theodore leads his usually-gregarious, currently-diffident friend down the musty old stairway. He looks at Henry, whose face is a spectral wash of white under the garish Edison lamp that dangles above. Theodore raps on the door.

Metal screeches upon metal as the sliding door viewer opens, and Jersey Guy, who apparently has no other occupation, vocation, or duty in this life but to dole out riddles at The Cat's Meow, greets them with a wink.

"Hiya, fellas," his apocryphal Jersey accent releases the words in a perfunctory fashion until he realizes with whom he's speaking, and then it changes considerably. "'Ey it's you! The dude with the smokin' sister. How's it hangin', fella?"

"Uh, yeah,um—"

Jersey Guy steamrolls over the first few syllables of Theodore's response, divagating into a clumsy line of questioning about Alice, if Theodore happens to know if anything happened to her phone because she hasn't responded, et cetera, et cetera. Knowing full well that he gave the guy the wrong number last night, Theodore plays dumb, gearing himself up for his entry riddle, which will surely be some obscure and thoroughly unanswerable question about some prohibition-era gangster. Where's Alice when he needs her?

"Alright fellas, you know the drill. Well, maybe not you, tubby," he nods through the door viewer at Henry, whose brow digs down over his eyes like a furious gopher burrowing into the dirt. *What a douche,* Theodore thinks, shaking his head. "Here it is: well-known prohibition hitman and thug, Bugsy Siegel, had connections with various mobs and criminal rackets through the '20s. Which of these other mobsters was he a close ally to, Al Capone or Lucky Luciano?"

Theodore feels the smoldering heat of frustration settle on the crest of his cheeks as he realizes, unsurprisingly, he's stumped. It's a 50/50 chance, and an uninformed guess is his only recourse. But he needs to get into the bar, Francis' life is depending upon him getting inside. Why didn't he consider brushing up on his knowledge of that one particular decade before coming back? He knew that Jersey Guy wouldn't pull any punches for him.

"It's a trick question. Siegel was involved with Luciano's gang in the '20s, potentially being recruited by Luciano to kill some big-name gang bosses for him, but he was chummy with Capone when they were kids," Henry says with an equable tinge of confidence in his voice, like he knows he's the shit. Right now, as long as Theodore's concerned, Henry is the shit. Theodore wrangles his face into an equally nonchalant stare, but it fights back hard, his jaw feeling deeply inclined to fall to the floor over his roommate's apparent grasp of random trivia.

Jersey Guy considers for a moment, and then begins slamming bolts on the other end of the archaic door. "That's one for smokin'-sister, one for tubby, and zero for you, smokin'-sister guy," he says as he wrenches the ponderous door open. "You surround yourself with good company, pal."

Within the aureate-kissed, marble-white walls of The Cat's Meow, a swell of bodies oozes back and forth to the lackadaisical croon of trumpets. Theodore recognizes the tune; he may not be the world's leading expert on gangsters, but he happens to know a thing or two about the music they danced to. And this particular tune is appositely titled *Speakeasy*, performed by Clarence Williams and His Orchestra. A stratosphere of cigarette smoke curls above the dancing mass, and in almost everyone's hand is a colorful cocktail bespoken of olden times. Theodore inhales. He's back.

"Cool place, man," Henry examines the crowd and steps towards the dance floor, his hands on his hips and his turgid belly giving the crowd a subtle salutation of skin. He glances down at his slightly-too-short t-shirt. "But I can't help feeling that were slightly underdressed, bro."

Theodore pats him on the shoulder and begins steering him around the dancers. "That won't matter in a minute. We won't really be mingling with these swaying anachronisms." Henry nods as Theodore leads him through a thick flock of dance floor outliers; some of whom are so comfortable in displaying their affection that their tongues are spending less time in their own mouths than in those of their mates.

These lip-locked couples, whose interminable kissing sessions are punctuated only by long drags of their Lucky Strikes, are particularly difficult to navigate around, but Theodore trudges on. The rest of the outlying group is composed of the sad saps—dudes who either have no date or no dance moves, and no other recourse but to hang on the sidelines trying to look cool in their pinstripe vests and spectator shoes.

"Look at this freaking bar, bro," Henry stammers, as he and Theodore sidle between lines of raucous patrons fumbling on the barstools. Behind this group is an assembly line of lips insouciantly plucking at stout cigars and slender cigarettes in the long holders belonging to the '20s. Those that aren't smoking swish their Whiskey Sours and Old Fashioneds, ruddy ribbons of cherry colliding with ice glaciers in their little glasses, as they exchange words over subjects Theodore frankly couldn't care less about. Edison lights bloom overhead, their brass shades capturing tangles of smoke and throwing a misty gloom over the bar.

With all the excitement, Theodore has practically to drag Henry into the unassuming little hall to the left that leads to the original Cat's Meow.

"You said you were having trouble believing my story," Theodore says, pawing at the wall underneath each framed picture. "I don't blame you, buddy, but wait until you see this…"

At the end of the hall, the second to last picture on the right is the inexplicable, impossible yet somehow extant photograph. Even before Theodore arrives at the image, his heart plummets into a chaotic thrum. This happened the last two times he gazed stupidly at it; although, life is all about perspective, and in a sense, he's never actually looked at the photograph. In a way, he's seeing it for the first time right here, right now, because each time he goes back he's altering the past, and thus altering the way in which the photo turns up the next time he sees it.

"Here's something that's going to bring you some peace of mind in knowing that your roommate's not a fucking lunatic," he says, turning before the image. "Or, it'll give you an early coronary from how much it shocks you…it sort of did that to me the first time I saw it."

Henry shrugs. Theodore can tell that his comments are mostly reflecting off Henry's forehead by the vapid expression beneath it. As Henry approaches the picture, he continues to watch Theodore, his eyes initially conveying a message of which words would fall far short; a message of concern for his friend. But he finally leans in and adjusts his glasses.

"Masquerade Ball – December 14th, 1931," he reads. "Alright, what am I looking at here, a swanky old dance party where our great grandparents learned to do the Charleston together?" Henry scans the image over, a painfully bored glare on his face until he sees it. Theodore can detect the very moment when Henry's very world is turned upside down.

"Huh?" Henry squints and presses his bifocals further into the bridge of his nose, until the lenses are almost kissing his eyeballs. "That's…that's you and me." Theodore leans in beside his friend, his eyes falling precisely upon the spot where he stood, 86 years in the past. He's there at the back of the Regal Ballroom, he and Henry both. They're standing closely side by side, Theodore in the hoodie that he'd wear more than his own skin if he could, with his now customary gazelle mask over his face; Henry's in his undersized t shirt, wearing the visage of a hippopotamus with a gaping maw. The only thing that catches Theodore off guard is the two matching long coats draped over the both of them. These must be items they're going to acquire at some early point in the night, for what reason Theodore cannot yet say.

And there's someone else close beside them. Theodore squints. Some tall masquerader is leaning into Theodore's ear. He just can't quite make out from the angle the man's leaning what type of animal he's wearing on his face. *Shit*, Theodore thinks, *that kind of intel is important when you're in a pit of vipers. Could this masquerader be the person Marley mentioned in the recording? The ally he had within the walls of The King's Inn? Or is it one of the crooked aristocrats eyeing the suspicious young* yanks?

Not knowing whether this mysterious figure, who's clearly whispering something to Theodore in the picture, is a friendly or baleful presence,

Theodore shakes his head in defeat. One thing is certain.

"No Francis," he mutters. Henry, who's clearly in a state of mild shock, doesn't respond. He's busy scratching his head and muttering under his breath a string of inaudible expletives. "That means we're going to have to save him after the picture is taken. God, I hope it's not going to be too late."

"I literally have no memory of this," Henry says at last. "Did we go to some massive, vintage masquerade ball, and I was just too cross-faded to remember?"

"Normally, that guess would be spot-on man, but this is not a 'normal' situation. You just have to trust that what you see in the picture is an event that occurred 86 years ago, and you were there. You just don't have a memory of it, because the 'you' in the timeline of our lives hasn't been there yet."

This explanation, a paltry attempt to tame the reckless thoughts that are surely assaulting Henry's conscience, is all that Theodore can think to offer up—even he doesn't really understand the logistics of it all. But burning at the fore of his mind, like a pair of inconsolable torches of salience, are the faces of Francis and Bargirl. Vivianne. They must be saved, and fate has made it so that he and Henry are the only ones that can do it.

"You, uh, you all right man?" He places a tentative hand on Henry's shoulder.

"I'm not gonna lie, this picture has me a little out of sorts," Henry's voice seems distant, ebbing out from some deep recess of his body. "I feel a little like the dog that just got run over by the mailman."

"Well, pooch, hold onto something." Theodore glances over at the Sonophone in the other room, its glistening brass skeleton beckoning him to draw nearer. "Because your world is about to be turned upside down."

"This is it?" Henry trundles into the old bar. He stops in front of the Sonophone in some curious coalescence of veneration and disbelief. "This is the time machine?" His hands extend forth, and then recoil out of uncertainty, and then his elbows cradle against his sides while his fingers tickle at the air, like an impecunious child coveting a shiny toy through a window display.

"This is it," Theodore says, reaching into his hoodie pocket and fondling the archaic little gem. Before he's able to yank the record from his pocket something deep within Theodore bubbles to the surface; an emotion. It's something like concern, but concern alone doesn't really complete the picture…compassion. And this throws Theodore.

There's only one person in the world besides his mother that Theodore has ever really cared for, and that's Alice. Feeling genuinely concerned for anyone else is, frankly, a rather foreign feeling. As befuddling as his roommate can be, as frustratingly crass and boorish as Henry is, standing with the guy before the Sonophone—like two fools standing on the precipice of converging worlds—Theodore feels…close to Henry.

"Listen, man…" he fumbles his words like a distracted wide receiver fumbling a catch. "You know just about everything that I do about this… place we're headed to; I don't need to recite the events, but I do need to revive the notion that it's dangerous in there." Henry looks over, but only briefly, before resuming his dumb glare on the intricate craftsmanship of the device. "I can't let you go with me unless I'm certain you know the potential consequences. We will be in a hotel surrounded by a ton of corrupt people— people capable of gruesome murder, as we've seen with Francis."

Henry picks absently at a rogue chunk of a particularly friable snack on his chin. "Yeah, yeah, I gotcha dude. Enough with all the melodrama. I get that it's dangerous and all that, but if what you're telling me is true—if this really is a musical time machine—how can I not go back with you, perils and all? I mean, I work for Vanderbilt's Shipping and Distribution," he says with a sardonic bob of the head. "My day job consists of loading and unloading freight Theo, super exciting as you well know. At night I come home and look for women online. And I do it online because when I go on a date in real life, girls just beeline right back to the front door as soon as they see me."

Theodore can see the welling tears. He's taken aback by how candid his friend is being with him tonight, but he certainly feels closer to Henry than he has in forever. A pressure builds inside of him, and Theodore knows he's been taking Henry for granted all these years.

"Hey man, I get you," he replies. "We have the same dead-end job, so I know exactly how invigorating it can be." Theodore shakes his head, considering how much of his life he's wasting lifting things up, hauling them from one spot and putting them down in another; which is, boiled down to its basic and pathetic essence, exactly what his job is. The one conceivably interesting aspect of moving freight is when he gets to operate the pallet jack. And he knows there aren't that many women out there thrusting themselves at scrawny guys like Theodore who exploit heavy machinery for the lifting they'd rather not do. He entertains a curious thought. Maybe that's why he's so enamored with Bargirl.

She's literally from another time, and through this temporal curtain that separates their worlds, she's far enough removed to see Theodore for who he really is, and not the way the girls in his world view him. She doesn't have the context of modern culture to judge him for any number of things; how skinny he is, how boring and awkward he knows he can be. *For how blah I am*, he thinks to himself, using a term that girls today fling like biscuits in a bakery.

Everything about Theodore fascinates Bargirl. He can sense it when he's with her. And all the minutiae of her being, every little aspect of her fascinates him in return. Any awkwardness between them, he thinks, is due to the rather bizarre and unprecedented situation they've found themselves in, and not to any fault in his own character, as he knows has been the case with modern girls.

To her, he's a unique specimen, a young Yank from New York, a different breed of human than the posh folk in Sloane Square she's grown up around. To him, she's a living, breathing exposition of a life gone by. The world has long since moved on, but there she is, this shimmering panopticon through which he gets to experience history and its denizens, not to mention the sheer bliss of acceptance.

"Well," Henry James says at last, breaking Theodore from his reverie. "I know you've been on this theme park ride twice, but I have yet to take a spin! Fire her up, son!" Theodore complies, brandishing the record from his pocket, while a thread of tingles attacks his hands and disseminates up his arms, leaving a trail of goose pimples in its wake. Henry watches with glib fascination as Theodore settles the record into its housing. Theodore shoots a cautious glance down the hall behind to make sure no curious bar goers are in eyesight. The coast is clear. Theodore nods to the side of the device.

"Crank that lever until it won't crank anymore," he commands, remembering how Francis had done so the previous night, and how it seemed to give them more time in the past than when Theodore first journeyed back and hadn't cranked the lever all the way. Henry reaches his hand out and clears his throat as if preparing to tell the brass piece of antiquity before him that he's not going to hurt it. At first, he clutches the lever with all the timidity of a junior forensic analyst scooping up their first piece of evidence, but within a rotation or two, he's showing a robust confidence in his movements.

"I'm not sure how this works exactly," Theodore says. "But the lever unwinds slowly on its own while the song plays; when it's done unwinding the cylinder stops turning and the song ends. Time in the present seems to move way slower when we go back though, as if the song itself plays out in super slo-mo, but as soon as the song's over in this world we're zapped back to the present day. So according to this logic, we don't want to waste any time after the record starts rolling. That way we're not sent back here too soon."

Before long, a hearty mechanical clunk signifies the last repetition, and the moment Henry's done winding, Theodore places the needle over the record. With his body stooped just in front of the Sonophone's elegant horn, Henry flinches under the onslaught of static that begins to erupt from it.

"Here we go," Theodore exclaims.

"Shit man, I'm about to go back in time!" sputters Henry, throwing his arm around Theodore. "And with my bro from another hoe!" Theodore eye-rolls at this, both at the simple gratuity of Henry's mind, and at the unwarranted physical contact, which always makes him cringe a little. But his friend's foibles are beginning to grow on him. A sense of camaraderie briefly envelops him, like he has someone he can really trust alongside him as he dives once more into the unknown.

The inimical scratch of the violin escapes the speaker as the song's ominous intro begins to play. Theodore feels Henry's grip on his shoulder bite down like a vice. He watches as the deep black of nothingness begins to perforate the old brick walls of the bar behind the Sonophone. It's like he's holding up a bullet-riddled photograph of the bar before a gaping black hole.

"Oh, one more thing," Theodore says with a wry smile. "This might feel a little weird."

V

"Why, hello there, young man," Raven Woman says, nodding to Theodore. There's more honey and less menace in her voice this time than on his encounters with her on nights one and two. But having become adjusted to the rather jarring experience of time travel on the third go around, he's managed to avoid slamming into her upon entry, so she has no reason to be disgruntled with him just now.

"Whence do you hail, and where is your doppelgänger?" Her voice thins out into a shrill caw as she enquires about his mask. Underneath her own cover are those beady onyx eyes that Theodore believes he'll remember the rest of his life. He makes the mistake of establishing eye contact for a moment, which fires up his synapses and sends an army of tingles down his spine. Her sable eyes cunningly observe his every move.

Without responding, he raises his hand to his head in a clumsy and vain attempt to mollify the hammer that's pounding away at his skull. Aside from avoiding the loss of all motor control and tumbling into Raven Woman on his way into 1931 London, it turns out that Theodore has every other acute symptom of time travel: a jarring headache, a turbulent swell of bile threatening to rise and jettison from his mouth—and give Raven Woman a reason to show her erratically truculent side to Theodore—as well as a pair of treacherously unstable legs swaying beneath him.

"You don't look so well, young man," she spits, curling her thin lips around a cigarette and letting out a parenthetical puff. "Perhaps you'd like a barbiturate to settle those nerves, or a good long drag from an opium pipe. That'll smooth out the creases. I can have Wendell fetch you some before the Shibboleth begins." Her head darts in every direction like a discontented owl upon its perch.

"Oh, *Wendell*?" Her voice pierces every corner of the ornate foyer. Theodore looks about nervously at the multitude of animal faces now glaring at him. This isn't what he wants; drawing attention to himself is the last thing he needs.

He bends forward, feeling unstable and unsure, like a drunkard does after stumbling out of a pub, jerking over and gauging whether he's going to spew or if he's okay to stumble on home. The polished checkered floor spins into a constellation of blacks and whites. He glances up at Raven Woman, watches the smoke from her cigarette waft and curl, and then dissipate against the elaborate crown molding of the lobby ceilings.

"That insufferable little cur," she mutters under her breath. "One of the most important nights of my year and he deigns to wander away. Wendell couldn't fetch me a pail of water if I told him where the faucet was, what makes me think I can count on him for my medicine?"

"It's…it's all right," Theodore manages. He looks around the foyer and, much to his relief, all of the opulently dressed guests have returned to their own conversations. Glancing from mask to mask across the foyer, Theodore notices a man lurking in a darkened corner alone. He has on a golden vest over a white button-up and slick black dress pants beneath. Covering his face is the mask of a wolf. Suddenly a warning light in Theodore's head goes off, like a distress signal piercing a thick fog in the night. The man in the wolf mask Theodore ran into on the first two nights seemed somehow to be following him, glued to his trail like an edacious canine to a girl in a red hood.

On night one, from the front steps of The King's Inn the mysterious man subtly pointed Theodore in the direction of the River Thames—and thus in the direction of the ambush awaiting the Pilfering Paupers. On night two, the man in the wolf mask was even more bold, directly questioning Theodore about the Pilfering Paupers, as if he somehow figured Theodore was a member of the group. And now, he's just staring with an icy equanimity, arms crossed, watching Theodore's every move.

Theodore averts his gaze from his observer, feeling the liquid slam of his jugular start to equalize as his body adjusts to its new setting. He knows he's going to need to keep tabs on that man; the one person of all these aristocrats who seems to understand the uniqueness of an American interloper wandering in his midst. Theodore looks around the foyer, stumbling away from Raven Woman. Something's amiss though…something's not quite right. The man in the pig mask isn't here. Each of the other nights he was right here in the foyer, and he was watching Theodore, albeit in a less overt manner than the man in the wolf mask. Where could *he* be?

"Suit yourself, Yank," he hears Raven Woman squawk over his shoulder. "I do hope you find your doppelgänger." *Doppelgänger*. His synapses fire off once again. *Henry*! Theodore begins frantically threading through the foyer crowd, who are growing increasingly aware of this young, oddly-dressed Yank who really should find his doppelgänger. *Not until I find Henry and make sure he made it through okay. He can't end up just like Francis; there's no way I'm gonna let this evil hotel swallow up him up, too.*

Theodore dashes down a hall leading away from the foyer, one he hasn't taken yet, gravely aware of the man in the wolf mask, whose gaze is still piercing Theodore from the shadowy corner of the room. He stumbles down the hall, the diaphanous glow of a series of Art Deco lamps lighting his way. Here and there about the corridor are pockets of partygoers, sipping their cocktails and throwing their heads back in casual laughter. Hanging, as if caught below the stale ceiling of cigarette smoke, a mixture of floral scents attacks Theodore's nose. The women about him reek of rose, lily, and jasmine, and the men, with their slicked back hair and crooked mouths smiling under thin mustaches, the leathery scent of patchouli and some other archaic fragrance Theodore can't define.

He picks up the pace, from a calm trot to an arrhythmic jog. He doesn't want to attract too much attention to himself, especially since he hasn't grabbed a doppelgänger yet, but he knows that every second he doesn't find Henry is one more second that an unsavory reveler might. And that could mean he'll be coming back tomorrow night to save two of his friends. His slow gallop leads him down a right turn in the opulent hallway, which unfurls into a beatific sight. A room grander than any Theodore has laid eyes on, save the Regal Ballroom on the other side of the hotel, or perhaps old pictures of St. Petersburg's Winter Palace that he's seen in history books. Austere marble walls, like shimmering sheets of emerald, gleam before him.

Bookending each side of the lengthy expanse are phone booths with ornately carved wooden partitions to separate them; cresting each partition is a figure of Dionysus, the Greek god associated with gluttony and hedonism. In one hand he holds a kantharos, presumably brimming with wine, and in the other, a dangle of grapes. Upon his face is a salubrious smile, punctuated by two fat cheeks, beneath vermicular tangles of hair. The symbolism isn't lost on Theodore, even in his haste to find his friend. He ducks in and out of each phone booth, just in case Henry happened to drop down in one upon his arrival. No luck. Only velvety cushioned pews and old rotary phones staring back at him. If he weren't in such a panic, Theodore would stop and admire the phone booths; the size and accommodations of which are more like narrow train cars than the diminutive vertical cells to which he's accustomed.

Towards the end of the line of booths, on the left, Theodore throws open the only closed door among the stalls and hurls himself into the enclosure, fully aware that he has no idea what he might find within. The door clicks shut. This booth is darker than the others. A suit jacket is slung over the light fixture, a murky effluence of green splashing over the stall. A tenebrous shape moves in the shadows and a man is standing with his back to Theodore, swaying back and forth slightly and grunting lowly. He cocks his head back to acknowledge his voyeur, and Theodore sees rows of uneven teeth barring down hard in an overbite, the muscles of his jaw fluttering through pockets of tension. Under a mask with tall rabbit ears, a rapacious and wicked smile.

Theodore gets a glimpse of a fierce, aquiline nose and a pair of cold, glimmering eyes before the man turns away again. Both his hands are gripping something in front of him. After a moment, they move clumsily away to paw at the walls of the booth. Something stirs beneath the man, and from zipper-level in front of him a face peers at Theodore: a woman with a tiger mask. Her mouth is agape and glistening with saliva, a strand of spit dangling from her chin to her clavicle. Theodore's stomach plummets to his feet as he realizes the situation he's just stumbled into. He begins fumbling for the doorknob.

"Sorry," he spouts. "Really, sorry." Ignoring Theodore's platitude, the rabbit smiles a haughty smile once more, grasps the tiger's head, and resumes thrusting. Theodore finally finds the knob and gingerly closes the door behind him.

"Henry!" he says somewhere between a whisper and a shout, hoping to god that he doesn't barge in on any other revelers in the midst of their hedonistic pleasures. He stumbles past the phone booths to the swelling sound of music. Down another corridor and he's standing in a cyclopean atrium-turned-dancehall. It's longer but much narrower than the Regal Ballroom, and the ceiling extends far above in the form of a series of skylights. Pillars line both sides of the expansive room, and on the right side are the floral-clad balconies of the hotel's myriad guest rooms stretching towards the ceiling. Streams of multi-colored ribbons cascade down from above, where throngs of revelers peer over their balconies; masks glinting and gleaming in the artificial light. Theodore feels his budding panic bloom. The onlookers are staring down at the dance floor, glaring at the only guest without a mask. He starts to feel like he's on display, an injured rabbit dragging itself along the forest floor with a group of pernicious hawks eyeing their prey from upon the tree branches.

In a modest bandstand to the right, four figures sway to and fro, a stream of plaintive notes flowing from their instruments. The crowd is mellow, somber, but as the song winds down the band flows into a frolic of upbeat melodies. The group is incandescent in the low light, dancing to the up-tempo melody, and ironically chipper vocals, of *My Melancholy Baby* by the Charleston Chasers. Theodore may not be up to speed with all the gangsters of the prohibition era, but he's fluent in the language of jazz-age music. And the Charleston Chasers, with their roster of impressive musicians like Jimmy Dorsey, Benny Goodman, and Glen Miller, is among his favorites.

The masqueraders seem to concur. They're jeering and laughing and swinging, all except for one pair in the far corner: a man and a woman who are treating the song like a slow-dance, drifting along and whispering into each other's ears. Theodore narrows his eyes and leans forward for a better scout, although without need: the man in the slow dance is also missing a doppelgänger. Henry.

He makes for it across the dancehall, somewhere between a mad dash and a casual stroll so as not to attract too much attention to himself. He weaves past young women in loose, ornamented dresses, and young men in sharp suits. Each pair of eyes behind every mask seems to follow him as he goes. The smell of champagne wafts into his nostrils and, like every other part of the hotel, the air is thick with smoke. Suddenly, his eyes fixed on Henry, a memory taunts his mind and slows his gait.

For a fluttering moment, he's back at high school in upstate New York. He's at the winter formal, without a date, of course, and he's hugging the shadows, never daring to creep out too far into the light of the dance floor. His eyes are stinging. His cheeks are ruddy and hot to the touch. Embarrassment isn't just a feeling for Theodore; he's always worn it as a physical feature, a facial expression. First, it's the stone that swells in his stomach. Then, a great heat that travels up his spine and settles on his face. Then his vision softens, and his eyes start to drown under the sting of embarrassed tears.

He's tenaciously avoiding looking over to half-court, where Brie is slow-dancing to some trite and shitty 80s tune. She's holding onto Jake, who's a whole head or two taller than Theodore, and twice as thick with muscle. Jake's smiling vapidly at Brie and she's aptly returning the gesture. *Well, your longtime crush has stood you up at the dance, Theodore,* he thinks to himself, rolling his eyes and nervously twiddling his thumbs. *What else is new?*

"Brie Connelly," a voice erupts in Theodore's left ear. Caught off guard, Theodore jumps. He wipes his eyes and puts his hands on his hips in what is his best insouciant look. Some short, tubby dude is standing next to him with a bowl of nachos in his hand.

"Tough break, bro." The guy's hand goes searching for the cheesiest chips on top, brings four to his mouth at once, and then it moves to pat Theodore on the back. He jumps forward like he's just been tasered. *If this dude wants to have the appearance and demeanor of a slob at winter formal, that's his call, but I'm not gonna be caught dateless, and with a smelly patch of nacho cheese on my back.*

"How do you know she stood me up?" Theodore asks, pawing at his back for any extra greasy residue that might be lingering on it. He hates when things are untidy or disheveled, but nothing is worse than greasy or slimy. "You don't know who I am, and I don't know who you are."

"Name's Henry." The guy flicks his cheese-strewn fingers over the words 'Quid Pro Quo, Bitches' on his crew neck in a fruitless attempt to dab away the mess, then extends his hand to Theodore. "Henry James." Theodore contemplates shooing this Henry guy away. He's never been good at making friends and right now is not exactly the most opportune time for him emotionally. But the outstretched hand remains, as does the vapid but inviting smile on Henry's face, and Theodore is, after all, alone at the dance.

"Like the author," Theodore says. He scoops Henry's hand up in a solid shake, shuddering under the viscid squelch of the cheesy palm.

"So everyone tells me." Henry James shrugs. "Literature isn't exactly in my wheelhouse." A sly grin plays on Henry's face; his thick eyebrows bow upwards towards his hairline, and for a second under the scant lighting of the dance hall, Theodore thinks he looks like a young, plump Jack Nicholson. *Here's Johnny!* Theodore, reminded of the climactic scene in Kubrick's *The Shining*, chuckles to himself.

"At least," Henry continues, "literature that extends beyond the riveting discourse I find in my dad's Playboys, if you get me." He nudges Theodore, who feigns a smile, but continues glaring at Brie. "Those big, juicy words and the soft, voluptuous phrases in those magazines, man…" Henry James makes a motion with his hands like he's honking two big clown horns. But then he seems to realize that his new friend, although Theodore is feeling more like a hostage right now, couldn't care less. He looks back to the dance floor.

"You wanna know how I knew that girl stood you up?" Henry asks, Theodore noting a more somber tone in the ungenteel jokester's voice. "Because I've been there, bro. More times than one. One quick look at the expression on your face as you slow danced with the shadows, never once taking your eyes off her? It's all I needed. Well that, and also, she's Brie *fucking* Connelly: rated most infectious new smile by the school board, and most motor-boatable tits by all the freshies. Hell, I even hear Zach Bruebank and some other seniors making comments about her around the water fountains and lockers, and you know seniors. Besides the occasional freshman hazing, they don't usually give one rat's ass about us newbies. So, for Zach Bruebank and his cronies to be drooling over her, you know she's hot stuff, man. Question is, what made a loser like you think you had a shot with her?"

Theodore's eyes end their dalliance with Brie Connelly's curves to shoot a 'don't mess with me right now' kind of look at this uncouth jerk, but the expression on Henry James' face softens his assault. Henry breaks down into a fit of laughter, nearly spilling his overflowing tub of nachos in the process. He throws a meaty arm over Theodore's shoulder, as if to let him know he's just messing. And Theodore does something for the first time in god only knows how long; he erupts in a fit of real laughter.

"Henry!" Theodore gasps. "Thank god you're all right!" Henry glances at Theodore, then back at the lavishly dressed lady with whom he's waltzing, then back at Theodore again. His expression is like that of someone who's just been jerked awake from a beatific dream and doesn't want to accept the inevitability of reality. For a flash, he looks like he hardly recognizes Theodore.

"Excuse me, my darling…what was your name, again?" Henry asks the lady in what is, to Theodore, a patently manufactured voice of elegance. She shifts in her jade dress and from under her mountain lion mask, says,

"You can call me Jersey Doll. To match that heavenly accent of yours, young man." She emits a muffled giggle.

"Well, actually I hail from the Big Apple, New York City, my darling Jersey Doll, but I shan't hold it against you, and I do appreciate the sentiment." Gingerly, Henry raises her gloved hand and kisses it. She cackles viciously, and he joins her, cocking his head back and letting out his version of a proper gentleman's laugh, trailing off into an exasperated, "Ooh dearie, dear, you are just so charming, Jersey Doll."

Gag, Theodore thinks, but he really doesn't have time for Henry's antics. Or rather, Francis doesn't have time for Henry's antics, regardless of how singular it is to travel back in time and regardless of how dazed Henry must be by the entire ordeal.

"Henry!" Theodore butts in, his panic rapidly unbuttoning his composure. Jersey Doll shoots a glance to Theodore, whose sensation of being utterly naked in a public setting comes rushing back; they need to grab some masks, and fast.

"What's wrong, Yank?" Jersey Doll asks, her voice muddled with impatience and surprise. "We should all be eschewing our anxiety and raising the banners of celebration on this of all nights, I say, for Shibboleths only come around every so often."

"That's exactly it," says Theodore, trying to calm himself and thus perhaps not alarm Henry's new friend, or anyone else that might be watching the queer trio. He glances back, and through the throng of reveling dancers, he thinks—but isn't sure—that he spies the man in the wolf mask leaning with his arms crossed against a banister. As the bodies in the foreground fly between them, he loses sight of his stalker, and then when he catches a glimpse of the banister again, the man is gone.

"That's exactly it," he repeats, turning back to Henry. "We can't attend the Shibboleth without our doppelgängers, Lester." *Really, Lester?* Theodore doesn't know if using Henry's real name around these people could have malign consequences, but somehow using an alias seems safer. *Even one as silly as Lester. Where did that come from?*

Henry glances over with an abstruse look on his face. "Yes, young Lester," Jersey Doll looks Henry up and down. "Your friend is correct. You simply mustn't be here without that most important accessory. Come to think of it, on whose sponsorship are the two of you here?"

"Sorry, Mrs. Jersey Doll, I just need to borrow my friend for one minute." Theodore pulls Henry away, trying to keep his cool and mitigate any unnecessary suspicion that must be mounting behind the lion's mask. *Great,* he thinks to himself, *we already have an officious Jersey Guy back home. The last thing we need is an officious Jersey Doll here in this setting.*

"Oh, well, I was hoping you'd show me how to do the Charleston." She snatches Henry's arm like a protective mother keeping her young son from stepping into the street. "I've long desired to see a true American dance the Charleston." Jersey Doll clasps both hands over her heart and begins to sway. She's clearly quite enamored with Henry. But to Theodore, everyone here is inimical, and none of them can be trusted no matter how harmless they attempt to appear. It's a lair of vipers, and Theodore and Henry are the mice.

"Allow me but a moment, dear, to field some questions from my assistant. He really can be quite the…how should I put it? Worrywart." Henry bows ridiculously to her and succumbs to the digging of Theodore's fingers into his skin. When they gain some distance from Jersey Doll, weaving through the vermicular gaps between the bodies on the dancefloor, Theodore yanks him aside to a quieter corner.

"Thank god I found you!" Theodore stammers, feeling the prickling fingers of anxiety fading.

"Dude, you don't cock block a brother like that! I was laying my intricate web of charm over that hot British chick, and I was just about to snag her number when you came in with all the delicacy of a jackhammer and shattered my chances of getting to know what was surely a refined and classy chick."

"Her number? Henry, I know this must be a lot to take in. It certainly was for me the first time around, still is, but we didn't just take the express-gramophone to London. We traveled in time, dude. We're in 1931. If you asked her for her number, she'd give you some arcane landline whose circuits would probably malfunction and catch fire if you tried dialing it on your cell phone…although I've forgotten mine each time I've come back so I couldn't test that theory if I wanted to. Henry, give me your cell phone."

Henry's face wilts into a pensive, jaw-agape droop, his eyes ambling from the dancefloor to the Juliet balconies above. He seems only now to be realizing where he is; the impossibility of the journey he just took. "I know," Theodore concedes. "It's pretty crazy, but it's 100% real."

"It is crazy, man. Balls-to-the-wall crazy. Are you sure that gramo-thingy isn't just some freakishly advanced VR program, and we aren't just in some nostalgia simulator or something?"

"You mean like the virtual reality headset in your room? No. Francis and I came here last night. I came back and somehow, he stayed in this world. He was trapped. VR systems don't literally suck you into the worlds they show you, do they?"

"None that I know of…God this really is nuts." Henry gives a gentle slap to both his cheeks as if to rouse himself from the opulent reverie that envelops him.

"It is nuts, but being a…different tangent of real life, it's also very dangerous. Remember everything I told you before we took the leap? These people are part of some surreptitious cult, and they killed Francis."

Henry plops the backs of his wrists onto his waist, an unconscious body-language declaration that he's comfortably surveilling the area. He's coming to terms with the odd reality of where he is. "Huh, so this is what it's like to be in a world before you were born."

"I know it's a lot to take in, but Francis' life kind of depends on us right now. We've got to move. Just keep in mind, we need masks on our faces at all times to help us blend in better, and everyone is a potential threat. Especially this dude wearing a wolf mask. He's been sniffing at my trail each time I've come back, and he seems to know something about the true nature of my being here."

"Gotcha, dude. This is a video game in which we have only one life and the enemies are real."

Theodore leads Henry back into the telephone center on their way to the foyer. "So, can I borrow your phone really quick?" Henry nods and brandishes his flip phone. "Like I said, I left my phone back in my apartment on nights one and two, so I've never been able to test this." Theodore snaps the phone open and dials Alice's number. He doesn't expect anything to happen, being that they're in a time long before modern urban infrastructure and cell towers, but it's worth a try.

At first, there's nothing. The vacuous silence of space, an aural representation of the ether that separates him from his own world, from Alice. "Nothing," he confirms. "No, wait! I'm getting something!" It fades in slowly at first, and garbled, like portable speakers playing from the bottom of a well. Music.

"How is this possible?" he asks, wrenching the phone from his face to hear the distant music disappear. "It's not coming from in the hotel." He places the receiver back on his ear and the fantastical melody returns. "It's coming from within your phone. Or at least, from the frequencies your phone is picking up from…our world?"

"What is it, bro?" Henry leans in, but the sound is too faint to discern. "Where are my earbuds when I need them?"

"Hang on a second and I'll let you hear it. It's music, but almost inaudible, and it's going really slowly, like if you were to put a track into one of your editing programs and reduce the playback speed. I'm trying to figure out… yep! It's the song from my gramophone record, the one that's playing in the machine right now. How is it transmitting across this much spacetime?"

Henry's hand hovers before Theodore. "How do you know it's that song, if it's playing super slowly?"

Theodore hands the phone to him, expounding. "I don't know if you heard it when we first landed in this time-world, but the record that initiates the time travel sequence plays out for a short while as we enter, almost like a prelude to our journey."

"Yeah, I did hear that. I just remember being too physically fucked up at the time to really take note. Like if my worst hangover in senior year had a baby with the inner ear infection I got in junior year."

"Right, well it starts at normal tempo, but then as it fades out, it slows down immensely. And just before it fades, it sounds exactly like this. It's so stagnant that it kind of sounds like a great long blare from a war horn."

Henry listens intently. "Like the horn of Heimdall blasting through the fields of Folkvang!" Another nerdy reference of Henry's that Theodore just doesn't get. "What are those great big crackles layered over the music? Man, that must be static. You can actually hear the static of the record piping through," Henry shakes his head dubiously. "I'm listening to ambient track noises slowed down by the spacetime continuum to the point where they sound like gunshots resounding through a tin can. Man, past-me would've thought I'd taken up dropping acid."

"Well, technically, future you," Theodore posits, taking back the phone. "Hey, the vocals just started. Even through the slowing of the track, I can tell that's a voice. Do you think we can use the progression of the song as some sort of marker for how long we've been back here, for how long we have left before we're transported back to the future? I know that the end of the song pipes in through invisible speakers in the air just before the night ends…"

Henry shrugs, looking back at the vibrant horde of masked revelers scuttling about the dance floor.

"Dude, this can count as your birthday *and* Christmas present to me; it's so cool. You bringing me here is so much better than that nearly dead fichus plant you got me for my birthday last year, and it's in a whole 'nother ballpark from the pat on the back you gave me for Christmas."

"Yeah…I've never been the best gift-giver," concedes Theodore. "Sorry, Henry. Man, Christmas was a new low for me wasn't it?"

"No, no, no!" Henry slaps his hands upon Theodore's shoulders and gives him a light shake. "This really trumps everything I've experienced, bro; I feel alive! Fuck Vanderbilt's Shipping and Distribution and my cul-de-sac of misery there, I'm gonna find a way to bring this experience to the masses, *and* make a massive profit in doing so. You have officially redeemed yourself for the way you've let our friendship slide over the years."

Theodore would feel the heft of guilt in his stomach right now were it not for the ineluctable, crushing anxiety that's currently bearing down on him. "You're welcome, Henry. But remember, we can't lose sight of why we're really here. This place is no theme park." He shrugs after considering his own words. "Well, it's kind of a Jurassic Park-style theme park in that the entire exhibit is really just one big T-Rex coming for you. The Sonophone back in The Cat's Meow is no toy, okay? And we're only going to come back here as many times as we need to in order to save them."

"Them? You mean him," says Henry. "Wait, there's someone else we're saving here isn't there?" *Damn it,* Theodore. *Henry wasn't supposed to know about Vivianne, at least not yet. Tonight, we're just here for Francis. I was going to come back for her next time, after I'd heard Marley's other recording. If I tell Henry about Vivianne, he'll insist on coming back with me tomorrow. I can't keep endangering my friends' lives.*

"Uh, I meant to say him. My bad."

"Oh no you didn't. I may not be Hercule Pirate—"

"I think you mean Poirot," Theodore interjects.

"I may not be Hercule Parrot, but I can always tell when you're lying to me, bro."

Theodore sighs. "Alright, I met this girl here on night one. She's... amazing. She's the daring and singular Eve; she's the beautiful, inimitable Aphrodite; she's the pure and holy Madonna; she's...unlike anyone I've met in our world."

"Dude," Henry patronizingly pats Theodore on the back. "I hate to break it to you, but whoever this girl is, I don't think she's Madonna. I'm pretty sure Madonna wasn't born yet. Remember, this is 1931."

"I didn't mean the pop singer. Uh, never mind. Can we move? We need to find Francis before it's too late."

"Yeah, yeah, but you gotta divulge on the way there, man. Who is this girl? Can I meet her?" Retracing his steps back to the foyer, Theodore makes sure to choose his words carefully.

"No, you cannot meet her tonight. She's my problem, dude, and I didn't really want anybody else to know about her. Not yet, anyway. Suffice it to say that I met her here on night one, and I fell in love instantly, and I think she's in danger."

"What do you mean?"

"Well, it just seems like she's being kept here as a prisoner or something. But she seems used to it, almost like it's the only life she's ever known. She doesn't fit in with everyone else at The King's Inn. She lacks their sinister nature; I can feel it."

"Well, I'll be damned. You always act like you're different from the rest of us Joes, Theo. I don't mean to sound like a dick, but I mean, you hardly show any interest in the ladies; you keep everyone at an arms distance, like you're above it all. For a while I was kind of under the impression that you're asexual, or an alien, or both," Henry chuckles. "But in the end, you are human! You're motivated by your pecker just like the rest of us."

"It's not like that, man, not exactly." Theodore hasn't chased girls back in his world because he's never found one interesting or intellectually-challenging enough for him. Alice is the only girl Theodore's ever really cared for back home. She's sharp as a tack, and charismatic, and mysterious. Vivianne is the only other girl who's ever come close to matching Alice, perhaps even surpassing her in that x-factor way.

Henry's beaming. "Theo's finally back on the dating wagon! This is big, bro, truly exciting." Theodore groans. Having reached the foyer, they begin weaving through a restive crowd, dozens of masqueraders galvanized by a seething current of anticipation. These people are ready for a Shibboleth. Carefully ducking past Raven Woman—who's too busy scolding her servant, Wendell, to notice the pair of Yanks drifting by—Theodore pulls Henry into the coat closet where a pile of doppelgängers is waiting for them.

"Ooh, I haven't been yanked inside a closet like this since seven-minutes-of-heaven with Bethany!" teases Henry.

"Shut up and grab a mask," Theodore finds his gazelle atop the bunch just waiting for him like the first two nights, and places it on his face. He looks up to see Henry's black hair snaking out from behind the visage of a hippopotamus.

"Does this mask make me look fat?" Henry jests, his voice obscured under a layer of porcelain.

"No, but it makes you nearly inaudible. You should wear masks more often." Theodore chuckles, nudging Henry on the shoulder. Henry laughs his nasally laugh and then points over Theodore's shoulder.

"Bro, if we really want to blend in with this crowd, we should probably don the appropriate habiliments, should we not?" Theodore's eyes follow Henry's finger to the racks of overcoats and accessories that line the closet walls. Among an array of outerwear that would make the offerings of a department store look lacking are the two identical, oversized coats that Theodore spotted himself and Henry wearing in the impossible photo at the bar.

"How do you know the word 'habiliments', let alone the proper way to use it? I mean, no offense."

"None taken," Henry shrugs. "I think I read it in the big book of Edgar

Allan Poe my dad used to have lying around...*The Man Around Town* or something along those lines. He was always into that morose, gothic crap, my dad."

"*The Man of the Crowd*," Theodore corrects. "Not bad, Henry."

"Hey, I may act like an idiot, but it doesn't mean I don't know a guitar from a shamisen," Henry waltzes past Theodore, throwing on the prodigious Chesterfield coat.

"You're a little more cultured than I thought," Theodore concedes, snatching its mate from beside Henry's on the rack. "And more resourceful, too. Having all these extra party accessories at hand is awesome." He slides the Chesterfield on, aware that his coat is sagging down even farther than Henry's; on himself, it's like a nine-foot curtain in an eight-foot-tall room.

"All right," he says, "we have donned our doppelgängers and covered up our modern *habiliments*; we are ready to get this 1931 secret society party started. Let's go save our friend."

"Francis?" says Henry. "I mean, I went to junior high with him, but he was kind of one of those hipster dudes who also thought he was a jock...I wouldn't exactly call him a friend." Theodore cocks his head at Henry in disbelief at the implications of Henry showing more concern for the fact that he has a sketchy history with the guy and less concern for the fact that Francis—regardless of whether he was a jerk in school—is in grave danger and needs their help. Something in the eyes glaring at him from behind the gazelle mask must make Henry's stomach turn. He throws his pudgy hands up. "Not that I'm saying we shouldn't save the dude or anything. Poser-jock-with-a-beard doesn't deserve the fate he received last night. Geez, quit looking at me that way. You look like you just took a mammoth bite out of a lemon with my face carved into it."

"Well, I just want to make sure we're on the same page before we wedge our heads back into the jaws of the lion. I think I know where Francis might be in this labyrinth of a hotel; the question is not how do we find him, it's what do we do once we *have* found him, and no doubt under the close scrutiny of his soon-to-be murderers?"

"I'm with you every step of the way, whatever happens, bro," Henry nods. "No matter how many foppish old British dandies we have to slug in the face in order to save him. And hey," Henry stops in front of the closet door and adjusts his mask. "Were just spending a night at The King's Inn, not walking the one ring all the way to Mount Doom."

J.R.R. Tolkien. Finally, a reference I understand, thinks Theodore. With that, Henry opens the door, cocks his chin up, props his arm perpendicular to his shoulder as if he's linking arms with a date, and stalks out into the foyer with a confidence Theodore knows he himself can't muster.

Bringing Henry along on this venture has deepened their friendship beyond the 'hello, please don't bug me' phase Theodore forced it into years ago. All it took to rediscover his old companion was an impossible sojourn in 1930s England. *Man, have I really shut myself away from others that badly?* he wonders.

Either way, he's finding Henry to be full of delightful surprises, replete with qualities Theodore himself could never possess; unflinching courage, youthful nonchalance. If Theodore could only have a kernel of such qualities… and he may need more than a kernel to save Francis and get everyone through the night alive. Suddenly, Theodore feels nothing but gratitude, realizing that there's no way he could have done this without his friend at his side.

"Hey man," he says, ducking out of the coat closet and catching up with Henry. "We may not be walking all the way to Mount Doom, but I'd be honored if you would be my Sam." Henry pauses, briefly lowers his chin and his unlinked arm, but says nothing. Behind the hippopotamus, Theodore swears he can see the shimmer of a tear.

"Dude," Henry whispers. "That was too fucking cheesy, even for me." He sniffles under the mask. "Now, I'm acting like I know exactly what I'm doing here so nobody gets suspicious, but I don't have an iota of an inkling of where we're going. You lead, Theo!" He cocks his head back up and stalks forth once more, nodding at the little throngs of people he passes by. A man in a mauve suit, with one hand grasping his overalls and the other cradling a cigar that he's carefully dipping under his bobcat mask, nods to Henry, apparently none the wiser about the anachronistic young man in the oversized Chesterfield.

As he passes the man, Theodore attempts to mimic Henry's bravado. He cocks his head up and thrusts his arm out like a cocktail waiter missing his tray. Even though he's copying Henry to the tee, his act seems to appear fabricated. The man merely stares at him as he walks by, with gelid little eyes that linger upon him, as if he's peering right into Theodore's soul. But just as he's about to break away from his group and approach Theodore and Henry, the gin-swilling penguin next to him threads her arm under his and begins nibbling on his ear, unconsciously throwing the bobcat off their scent.

Without glancing back at Theodore, as if that would shatter whatever dignified and salient persona Henry's taken on, he whispers, "So, what is your lead, anyway? How do you know where Francis is in this maze of a hotel, and where everybody's face is concealed, no less?"

"I have less to go off of than I'd like. Last night, when I was in the elevator heading upstairs, I saw something." Theodore grimaces just thinking of the terror and suffering Francis went through last night, thinking of what he put Francis through while his own Lothario-blinders were on. If he hadn't been so damn distracted by Bargirl, he wouldn't have left the poor guy to fend for himself in this foreign and hostile place.

"What'd you see, dude, a fuckin' unicorn, a leprechaun jerking off at the end of the rainbow? After traveling through time like that, I'd believe anything."

"No, none of that, at least not yet. But in the elevator, I had a good view of the some of the hallways and some of the rooms. You'll see in a minute; the elevators in this hotel are centrally located, and you can see down many of the corridors as you're going up, kind of like at the massive airport Hiltons, you know? So, at the end of the third-floor hall, I saw some commotion."

"Commotion?" asks Henry, looking agog at the polished black and white checkered tiles that are now beneath his feet. "Wow, this has gotta be the poshest hotel I've ever been in." He glances up at the old-fashioned elevators in the middle of the room. He gulps. "We're using those rickety old things?"

"It's okay, man. Those rickety old things aren't nearly as rickety or old as they seem, remember? If we were to see equipment like that in our world, we'd rightly assume that they're broken-down, dinosaur-age relics. But in this world, this is state of the art, high tech stuff. This is the electric car of its day, the smart watch."

"I mean, I guess I'll take your word for it. But this thing looks fit to be our coffin." Henry approaches the nearest terminal and extends a trepidatious arm, like he's about to shake hands with a grizzly.

Theodore watches as a murder of crows scuds across the lift room. Women all dressed in black, gossiping and giggling to each other as they drift by, leaving behind them an effluence of gin and perfume. Other revelers drift in and out of the room, men and women lazily strolling throughout the hotel, waiting for the Shibboleth to commence. Theodore hears the murky squall of a muted trumpet echoing down the corridors from what is likely yet another dance hall or rumpus room.

As soon as the ambling crowd has thinned, Theodore approaches the elevator and pushes the hailing button, hoping that the ghoulish operator from last night won't be there to greet them when the gate screeches open. "Well, like it or not, Henry, we've got to get upstairs to save Alice's friend; we've already dawdled too much, and we don't have time to look for a stairway in this labyrinth." Henry shrugs and then nods in compliance.

"Yeah, I remember seeing his face in that newspaper article you pulled up online...or what was left of his face, anyway," Henry says with a saturnine gloom to his voice.

The elevator trundles down and screeches to a halt. Theodore feels his pulse quicken as he watches a white glove speckled with red draw the iron gate back. His eyes wander up the lanky arm while his mind admonishes that they stop. He doesn't want to see the ghoul staring down at him. He desperately begins to wish he and Henry had chosen to search for a staircase, but his eyes are on a pursuit of their own. They scroll farther upwards until they collide with an avaricious pair of eyes. It's the same creep from last night. Henry seems to devour this unsettling vibe instantly; he jolts upright like an inquisitive diver grazing the tentacles of a jellyfish.

"Going up, gents?" The operator's maniacal smile protracts outward until his cheeks bulge. Ragged tufts of hair spill out from under his cap, and the harlequin smile that's painted on his face is deformed, mutated by perspiration and perhaps a careless swipe or two of the hand. From the corners of his mouth down to his chin are the faint scar lines that Theodore spied the previous night. *How would someone acquire such a peculiar pair of scars?* Theodore shudders as potential answers begin to pour into his brain.

Henry shoots him a sideways glance, his expression screaming, 'fuck no, we're not going up. Not as long as going up means standing in an enclosed space with you.' Theodore whole-heartedly agrees, but Francis' life is at stake. He has to find whatever dormant courage resides within him—he needs to find it and grab hold with all he's got.

"Why yes, we are, Jarvis. How kind of you to ask," Theodore produces a smile that doesn't come close to matching the alacrity in the operator's infrangible grin, but he figures it's convincing enough to get him through the threshold. He steps into the cage, refusing to hide the pearly whites under his half-mask until he's turned to face Henry, who's still lingering outside the elevator and eyeing the strange creature within.

"Let's see where this amusement ride takes us, Lester," he revives the alias he gave Henry when he was attempting to pry him away from Jersey Doll earlier. He gives a brief c'mon nod to Henry that he hopes the operator doesn't see.

"Right," Henry stammers, clenching and unclenching his sudorific palms at his sides. Theodore can't help but notice that only moments before, Henry was cool as a cucumber, stalking about the hotel like a peacock amongst pigeons. Now he's the catatonic, tongue-tied bozo and Theodore must take charge. *This apocryphal outpouring of confidence…well, it doesn't feel too bad,* he thinks. *Even if I am forcing it. Now, get inside the freaking elevator, Henry!*

As if he somehow read Theodore's mind, or simply the exigence in his wide-eyed stare, Henry stumbles onto the lift, cramming himself against the corner farthest from Jarvis and grasping the handrail behind him with white-knuckle intensity.

"Right," Henry repeats. "Up is…where we're going."

Jarvis sneers, jerking forward and glaring at the two of them. "And to which floor might I take you, young gents?"

"3rd floor, Jarvis, and make it snappy," Theodore commands. "We two have much business in The King's Inn tonight."

"Much business? On the 3rd floor?" Jarvis asks, sliding the gate shut and cranking the large brass operating lever. "You, young gents, must be important guests of Sir Nithercott's." The lift lurches into life; Henry grips the handrail even tighter and whimpers like a beaten dog. Jarvis seems not to notice, though. He cones his hand over his ear and starts swaying. "Ahhh, the music choices on Shibboleth nights are always superlative. Dum, dee dum, dee duh duh dee dum…"

"Why, yes. Yes, it is," says Theodore, his perception of the elevator operator turning from one of disgust and revulsion to one of sympathy. The man seems like a quarantined fool, locked away from the rest of the world and only allowed to watch the frivolities from the openings in his metallic cage.

"How, um, how did you get those scars, Jarvis?" Theodore hears the words pour from his mouth before realizing that he even wanted to ask. He then shoots Henry a glance, his eyes asking, 'am I prying to much?' Henry shakes his head slowly in a 'what the hell are you doing, Theo?' kind of way. Jarvis stops swaying and considers the question, looking at Theodore, then at Henry, and back at Theodore, rubbing his hands together nervously.

"You mean these scars?" He touches his face, caressing the old wounds with his thumb and pointer finger. "Well, I…I…it was an accident—in a factory. Years ago." He knows that Jarvis is lying, desperately refusing to admit what truly happened to his face. Jarvis keeps rubbing at the scars, his nails beginning to bite; harder and harder he presses, until he's frantically digging into his skin. "Yes! That's it! That's all it was!" he cackles. Henry whimpers once more, shriveling farther into his corner. Theodore's heart tumbles down into his stomach; a metallic taste settles under his tongue; the unfailing early sign of a panic attack. He needs to get off this elevator, and now.

"Ah, floor three, the gentlemen's stop," Jarvis' tone shifts in a heartbeat. He reaches a blood-dappled glove out and cranks the lever, leaving a gossamer sprinkle of red on the knob as he lets go. The errant train of Theodore's thought realigns on the track of his mind and he peers through the gate to see if what he saw last night will repeat itself tonight. *Am I too late?*

A crippling sense of déjà vu hits him as he peers down the corridor to see three shadowy figures sneaking across it. One of them is leading the pack while each of the other two is dragging something ponderous behind himself. Theodore can't discern much through the screen-door effect of the gate through which he's peering, but it looks like the events of the previous night are unfolding tonight in the same manner and thank god that they are. He feels it in his gut that one of those objects being dragged down the hall is Francis.

Jarvis stirs to open the gate, but Theodore can't be bothered with that now. He has one singular goal on his mind now and they need to move, no time for Jarvis or his eccentricities. Theodore rakes the gate open in a clamor, jumping out and leaving Henry to stare once more into the twisted, blood-smeared face of the operator.

"Uh, thanks Jarvis," says Henry, his voice rattling like a baby's toy. "You must excuse my friend. He, uh, he really needs to use the loo."

"Not to worry, young gents," Jarvis chuckles, and insouciantly straightens out his suit jacket as if he hadn't just become a psychotic mess a moment before. "Enjoy your stay at The King's Inn. Going down!" He closes the gate slowly, swaying once more to the far-off music and retracting back into his curious, lonely world. Theodore grabs Henry by the collar of his Chesterfield and yanks him forth.

"That's them! Those are the guys I saw last night! They've got Francis, I know it!" The figures slink slowly away past a turn in the hall.

"Oh shit," Henry's eyes widen behind the hippo mask. "You weren't kidding. Let's get him back, bro!" They rush down to the end of the hall and peer down cautiously. Theodore eyes the two bodies being dragged. Both their faces are concealed under canvas sacks, leaving Theodore with nothing to go off of save their attire. The one up front he doesn't recognize, perhaps just some poor fool who somehow got on the wrong side of an argument with these murderous thugs, but the one in the rear he recognizes in a heartbeat. Suspenders slung over a white shirt with the sleeves rolled up over a pair of burly arms, dress pants on beneath, and just a few strands of ginger-colored beard hair sticking out from under the canvas sack.

Theodore feels his chest tighten. He looks down to see his hands already clamped into fists. "That's him," he says flatly. "That's Francis in the back." He hasn't felt this kind of rage since he was a child. Back when he lived with his parents, when his father would succumb to the inexorable madness that booze brought upon him, pummeling Theodore's mother indiscriminately in front of both him and Alice. The pain and anger he felt for the unwarranted and undeserved injustices to his mother, which didn't come close to the disgust roiling in his belly over the fact that little, pure Alice had to bear witness to the brutality. Just like Theodore's mom and his little sister back then, Francis doesn't deserve this. He has nothing to do with these people and their twisted ways. It isn't right. And it's Theodore's fault.

"Alright, Theo, let's think of something," Henry whispers. "There's gotta be something we can do. Someone who can help us here. We're no superheroes...right, buddy?" Theodore doesn't respond—he barely hears Henry's trepidatious statements. He's caught in his own world now, reliving baleful old memories in his mind. All he's thinking of is helpless little Alice crying at the sight of their mom struggling at the hands of a monster. The monster within their dad.

"How dare you?!" he shrieks, dashing forth and raising his tremulous fists. He's caught them off guard. Startled, they turn about. Theodore's running headlong towards the man dragging Francis, and in the mad, swirling haze of hallway lamps he sees the two heavy lifters are wearing rat masks, and the man leading the group has the visage of a sow. *The man in the pig mask from the foyer! He's in on all this?* Somewhere behind, as if coming from miles away, he hears Henry yell something about regretting being his wingman. Then, a cascade of footfalls from behind as Henry follows after him into the fray.

The man holding Francis around the shoulders drops him just in time to brace himself against Theodore's charge. But he struggles to find the right footing and Theodore slams into him full force. He's sturdier than he looks, though, and even without his feet firmly planted, the impact Theodore feels upon throwing his shoulder into the man is jarring. They topple over each other onto the ground. The henchman grasps Theodore by the shoulders, trying in a desultory attempt to wrench him off. But Theodore is tenacious, and Francis needs him. He can't let him down; he won't let him down. He throws his fist down upon the man's mask, cracking the porcelain shell and revealing the slit of an awestruck face. The henchman howls and thrusts his ponderous arms upwards, but the collision must have knocked the wind out of him because his struggling limbs fail to produce enough force to push his assailant off.

"You," the man in the pig mask ejaculates to his other henchman. "Take the little one; he is of the utmost importance to our master." His henchman fervently nods and resumes dragging the first body off, *where*? Theodore can't tell; he doesn't have time. He realizes that Francis' body is limp; he's not moving a muscle. *Is he already dead? Please, god no.* Theodore's fury takes hold of him, and he throws his fist down upon the henchman's face again, and again, and again, until a warm, damp wetness cakes his hands.

"You sick motherfuckers!" he hears himself shout. Henry dashes past him, flailing his arms and screaming like a banshee. He collides with the man in the pig mask, but his combatant proves ready for the confrontation. Widening his stance and bracing for impact, the man turns his shoulder, and with a great heave, throws Henry towards the wall in one swift deflection. Henry hits headfirst, his mask flying off his face, and tumbles to the carpet in a daze. The man in the pig mask grabs Theodore by the shoulder. His hand clamps down like a vice, tossing Theodore off the henchman. Theodore falls backwards and rolls onto his back, panting heavily. As the adrenaline surge wanes, his vision begins to oscillate between thickening darkness and dizzying streams of light. An inchoate blob moves before his face, close enough that he can smell the man's fetid breath. He forces his eyes shut and tries to slow his breathing. He wrenches them back open to see the pig staring him in the face, an ominous smile curling below the mask. The man's eyes carry a venomous intent as he whispers to Theodore,

"I say, the little fifth columnist has friends, does he? How quaint." *Fifth columnist? Is he talking about the other guy they just dragged off?* Sneering, the man pins Theodore's arms down. A squall rages inside his head, keeping him from any form of retaliation. He turns to see Henry trying to stand upright, but sliding to the floor over and over, a crimson trail oozing from his friend's nose.

"Theo, I gotcha buddy," Henry mumbles, deliriously rising and throwing a punch at the air and falling on his face.

"When are you meddlesome yanks going to learn that we do things differently here in the Kingsland. And if you interfere in our affairs, a thing for which your kind has a nagging proclivity, there can be real consequences." His grip tightens over Theodore's arms; the man is remarkably strong, and Theodore knows Henry is incapacitated, tapped out of the fight. He is on his own and everyone's fate rests in his hands now. Francis' fate, Henry's fate… Vivianne's fate…

This can't be it! I've got to do something...for her! Theodore lifts both his legs, tucking his knees to his chest. Before the man in the pig mask can even react, he kicks with a furious vigor, his feet connecting solidly with his assailant's solar plexus. He flies backwards, colliding with one of the hallway's many ornate credenzas. Clashing with his scattered senses, Theodore clambers to his feet. But for a portly man, Francis' captor is agile and alert, jumping to his feet and throwing an arm at Theodore. Theodore dodges down and left, hurling himself at his enemy's torso with everything he's got. But the sheer mass of the man is too great, *Christ, he's huge*, and the impact is as effective as a waif tossing herself against a fractious bull. The man grabs him by the throat, flings him against the wall, and coils his fingers around Theodore's windpipe. Theodore brings his arms up, feverishly trying to pry the man's hands from his airways.

"Hen-Hen-Henry," Theodore pleads, as all feeling in his limbs reduces to a placid numbness. Henry grumbles down below, still too fazed by the head-on collision to come to Theodore's aid. Tunnel vision overtakes Theodore's eyes in vicious black swirls, as a constellation of golden stars darts about from the opposite wall down to the carpeted floor. His arms become a pair of dead eels, curling back down to his sides where they begin to twitch about and then merely dangle. He's lost all control of his body. A gelid ghost pervades his body, ice prickling at his throat. *This is it. I'm so sorry, Henry. I'm so sorry, Francis. And I'll never see Alice again. I'll die here in 1931, leaving no trace of my fate to be found back in my world. She'll be all alone...*

Before the hands of a moribund blackness take him away, he feels something to the side; steps thundering down the hallway. He feels a cool swathe of air kiss his face. Something slams into his assailant with such force that he's knocked swiftly away from Theodore. An inexorable gust of air floods into Theodore's lungs, brilliantly painful and exhilarating all at once. He collapses to the floor, his back flopping against the wall. He clutches his throat and coughs up a hard wad of phlegm onto the maroon carpet. Peering upwards, he sees a tangle of two bodies; now smashing into the credenza, now rolling around the floor. They trundle over Henry, who's become lucid enough to crawl out of the way and over to Theodore.

"Are you, are you all right, Theo?" Henry sputters. Theodore merely nods, unwilling and unable to procure the words to respond just yet. Over to the right, it looks like one of the combatants has overpowered the other. He's climbed on top of him and is striking him relentlessly. It's unclear which one is winning the fight, with the man on top's back facing them. He just hopes that it's their savior and not the man in the pig mask.

Theodore's equilibrium is still battered, but his faculties have returned to him enough to move. He snakes over to Francis, who has failed to move a muscle since they found him. *Please, don't be dead, guy. Please God, don't let it be too late!* His fingers curl over the burlap sack, yanking it off to reveal Francis' face, swollen and bruised, but with both his eyes intact unlike in the newspaper image. Henry peers over Theodore's shoulder.

"That's good, right? He's not as pulverized as he was in the picture, maybe they knocked him out, but we got to them before they could finish him."

"Francis," Theodore croaks, slapping his face and peeling his eyes open with trembling fingers. They fold loosely shut as soon as Theodore lets go of them. "C'mon Francis, wake up!" He glances over to the peripheral struggle.

The man on top pauses the thrusting of his fists to brandish an item, a lick of silver shining at its tip. His opponent emits a wretched cry as the final strike falls. Then, all goes silent. The victor sighs, relaxing his shoulders and rising slowly. Theodore and Henry gasp, both unsure whether it was their rescuer or their assailant who survived. In tandem, they throw their arms protectively around Francis, as if they could do a thing against this person fresh and ready for a fight, let alone in the discombobulated state they're in. After the victor has risen, his eyes remain on the pulpy mess of the body beneath him. With a monastic discipline to his movements, the man turns to reveal the face not of a pig, but a wolf.

"It's you," says Theodore, softly enough that his words barely squeeze past his teeth. "All along it's been you. Since night one when you steered me over to the River Thames, to last night when you called me a…a puddle skipper and insinuated that I might know the Pilfering Paupers? All the way to tonight, when you were following me through the hotel like you were onto me. Maybe the only reveler in The King's Inn who was…I thought you were evil, sir, just like the rest of them. This whole time I thought you out to get me. Just, just waiting for your moment to strike." Theodore clutches his throat, realizing that the vocal tirade he just unleashed wasn't the best idea after having been throttled nearly to death.

"If I may," Henry says, thumbing one nostril shut and snorting a curd of blood out of the other. "I mean, I wasn't here on nights one or two Theo, but it looks like this dude just Linked our Zelda. He Mario'd our Peach, man." Still clutching his throat, Theodore shoots Henry a warning glance. "He saved our asses, Theo." Henry translates.

The man nods slowly, his eyes soft and dignified, untainted by the impurities of greed and wealth-mongering that his fellow masqueraders wear under their brows as casually as the jewelry that glitters upon their wrists.

"This is true," says the man, stoutly refusing to take his eyes off Theodore's own. "I have been watching over you with a vigilant and ever-concerned eye. I know, future explorer, that you have many questions, and little reason to trust anyone here, alas, I implore you; you must come with me. It is not safe here, and there is much I must tell you. You have made it this far, and I feel your interest in our affairs warrants you to go further."

"Future explorer…" Theodore utters aloud, although fully meaning only to trace the words across the blackboard of his mind. *That's precisely what Alger Marley called me in his recording. This must be his agent on the inside that he was talking about. There's something about this guy's voice. He even talks like Marley, as if they were best buddies or something.*

A rejuvenating warmth flows into Theodore's torso and up his neck. He knows that it's not just he and Henry against the whole of The King's Inn now. "Yes," he says with alacrity. "Yes, we will come with you."

The man in the wolf mask nods. His gaze finally ambles away from

Theodore over to Henry. "Reacquire your mask, young one. On the nights of the Shibboleth, these floors have ears and these halls have eyes. We are not safe. Far from it, and the more we dither, the less safe we shall be." Henry obeys the austere man's orders, shuffling over to the credenza and donning the hippopotamus once again. The man in the wolf mask stalks down to the turn in the hall leading to the elevator and peers down, silent. Then, he stares down the protracted expanse of the hall in which they are, as if he's drawing a bead through his mask on some invisible target.

"Right," the wolf grunts to himself, returning to Theodore's side and helping him to his feet. Gently, he lifts Theodore's chin and examines below. "How is your throat, can you breathe? Are your airways swollen and impaired in any way? You've taken quite the hammering to your larynx, future explorer—"

"I'm fine, just a little…shaken up. It's him I'm concerned about." He points down to the cadaver-like, supine body of Francis. "Please god tell me he's not dead."

"I'm fine, by the way," Henry spouts sarcastically, with a shrug and a nonchalant wave of the hand. "This nose of mine that just made jelly against the wall back there is okay. No need to inspect me at all Mr. Wolf. Nope, Henry James is as tough as nails. Who cares if the head-on trauma is causing some wicked hemorrhaging in his brain right now?"

Much to Henry's chagrin, the man in the wolf mask ignores him entirely, kneeling swiftly before Francis. "Dude," says Theodore to Henry, "you're breathing and vertical, just like me. Francis looks like he's in a coma, or dead. Don't you give a shit?" The man in the wolf mask brandishes his knife, swipes the fresh pearls of blood off the blade and holds it in front of Francis' nose, watching as little humid clouds gather and dissipate on the shaft.

"Your friend is alive," the man says dryly, pocketing his blade and retrieving from his inner vest pocket a glass vial no larger than an eye dropper. "The two of you are very fortunate. Any longer and Harold would have begun the true interrogation process. Your young friend would have had his kneecaps shattered by a hammer for information they assumed he possessed. Then, Harold would have brought him before Nithercott himself, who surely would have used his trademark method of correction on the poor sod: eye gouging." Henry remains surprisingly silent, but Theodore knows that his best friend is just like him, entertaining visions of that horrendous image of Francis in the paper right now. Sweeping tributaries of shivers wend down Theodore's back when he imagines the living hell through which he nearly put Francis. The man in the wolf mask pops off a Lilliputian cork and dabs the vial against Francis' nose.

No shudders, no twitches, no sputtering or choking, Francis merely bolts upright like the man in the wolf mask just shoved a cattle prod where the sun doesn't shine.

"Jesus, fuck!" Henry sputters, leaping back.

"Get away from me! Stay back!" Francis shrieks, his forehead caked with sweat, his temples mapped with throbbing veins, and his chest heaving erratically under his shirt. With one brusque swish of his arm, the man in the wolf mask covers his mouth.

"Shh, shh, shh," he grunts. "Remove your masks, young men, so that he might look upon a comforting and familiar sight in this nightmarish world in which he's awoken. You see these lads, here? They're your friends, young one. You're safe now; all is well. Shh, shh." Francis' eyes make a frazzled dance between Theodore and Henry, and for a moment at least, Theodore's certain Francis doesn't recognize him. It's a bucket of gelid water seeing Alice's new friend beaten, disoriented and terrified, but Theodore feels positively buoyant in knowing that the guy's alive. Beneath the man in the wolf mask's hand, the interminable shrieks subside into staggered murmurs.

Henry points at him with a quaking hand. "He's trying to say something."

The man nods and whispers, "When I remove my hand from your mouth, you shall be composed and quiet, young one, eh?" Francis gives a fervent nod, and as soon as his lips are free, he blurts out,

"Ted! Alice's brother, oh man!" He lunges at Theodore and embraces him, his hefty frame nearly knocking Theodore right off his knees.

"It's Theodore—you can call me Theodore, but yeah, it's me!" He pats Francis' sweat-sopped back, feeling him dissolve into a fit of convulsions as he begins to weep in Theodore's arms.

"Christ on a fucking cracker, am I glad to see you, man," Francis spouts. "I don't know what happened. One second you and I were checking out that old gramophone I bought, and the next I was…lifted off my feet and dropped here." Francis pulls away, his eyes wandering to the ceiling as his mind gropes for a solid recollection of recent events. "You were here, too, Ted. And we wandered around until we stopped at bar…and then you went off with some girl and left me to nurse my drink…"

Theodore feels the ruddy sting of embarrassment form upon his cheeks, wishing he could just slip his face back into the mask. "Yeah, I did and I'm so sorry, man. But we're here now, and we're not leaving your side until we're out of here!" Francis glances at Henry, who nods, squeegeeing a fresh blot of blood from his nose with the back of his hand and then extending the contaminated limb forth in his usual, uncouth fashion. Francis accepts it gladly, clasping Henry's hand in his own strong grip. The inner germaphobe in Theodore eyerolls, but he ignores that side of himself, understanding that Francis couldn't care less right now about such a thing as a bloody handshake. He's just been beamed back in time, assaulted by strangers, and violently awoken all in—skewed time frame aside—the span of one night.

"Hey, I know you, too, buddy," says Francis, squinting and tossing the matted drapes of his hair back. "You went to *Booker T. Washington*, yeah? A grade behind me? I ran into you at the bar last year."

"Bingo, bro," Henry says with a bite of acrimony. "I'm the dude you noogied at the bar last year in front of a very promising dating prospect, as well as the dude you chucked into the nearly-full trash bin at lunch to impress Vanessa Cordray, with your jock muscles and do-anything, fuck-wad attitude."

Francis' brow furrows. "Right…sorry 'bout all that."

"It was enchilada day…" Henry pours salt on the old wound.

"Well, I think it goes without saying that this petty, old dudgeon of yours can wait, Henry. I mean, considering what Francis has just been through?"

"Quite right," interrupts the man in the wolf mask. "In fact, any and all verbal divagations must wait. We are not safe here, none of us. Your mate is lucid and will not need require dragging like these two bodies will. Young one," he points to Henry. "I ask that you temporarily shelve this juvenile squabble and help the boy to his feet. You will assist him down the hall—I am under the assumption, lad, that though you're alive and breathing, you must be rather knackered from what you've experienced?"

Francis' face pinches into a battered scrunch of determination as he attempts to stand, but vertigo sets in before he gets higher than a catcher's squat, and he tumbles back to the floor. "Alas, there is my answer."

"No, no, it's cool," says Henry sardonically, donning his mask again and pulling Francis to his feet. "I mean, you and me knew each other, like, half our lifetimes ago. I'm sure you're not the total douche you were back then."

"Alright, I'm willing to be patient so that we can get out of whatever hellish situation we're in, but I have questions. Lots of questions." Francis raises a tentative hand to a purpling bruise above his eye. "Ow! Confused doesn't even begin to describe it. I'm like a fuckin' goldfish flopping on a living room sofa here. This place doesn't make any sense. I've gotta be in some sort of dream…a really, *really* immersive dream. Yep, that's it. I'm having one of those ungodly hangover sleep-ins where my dreams are always either way vivid or way demented."

He glances at everyone around him, then up and down the hallway like he's trying to find some obscure telltale sign that might confirm he's in a dream. "This hangover-dream must be particularly acute because it's been equal parts vivid and demented so far…Man, looks like I'm gonna be tweaking my artisanal gin recipe again; no more of those cheap domestic botanicals, this shit is *fucked*."

"Yes, I am sure you all have many questions; you most of all, future explorer," the man in the wolf mask dips his head to Theodore. "And they will be answered shortly and sufficiently I assure you. Now, future explorer, the man with the rat doppelgänger, scoop up his wrists. I'll take Harold. You two, make for the end of the hall; the last door on the left, yes? Quickly now."

Henry and Francis nod in tandem, beginning to limp down the corridor like two drunkards in a three-legged race. "Shall we, future explorer?" the man asks, snatching up the pig-masked murderer by the wrists as casually as a farmer snatches up a chicken by the talons to toss it in the coop. Theodore doesn't budge. The last thing he wants to do right now is face the pulverized reality of his barbarous rage that lies unmoving on the floor. "Well?" the man barks impatiently. Theodore approaches the body, waves of trepidation coursing from his chest up through his shoulders like ice and then down into his fingertips; a dull thump, thump, thump cautioning him, reminding him of the last time he had lost his mind in a fit of intractable rage.

He was standing in the living room of his house in the country. His hands were contracted into tight, tremulous rocks of fury. They were bloody. Someone was outstretched beneath him; imploring hands like tenuous shields hovering over a crimson-soaked face.

"Young one!" the man in the wolf mask snaps Theodore from his reverie. "We must flee now!"

"R-right," Theodore gulps hard, interring the hazy memory back into the recesses of his mind. "Right. I've got this." He makes the mistake of looking down at the contorted body before him; the shirt's ruffles lapping up ropes of blood; an unhinged jaw protruding from a clumpy mass that once was a face; uprooted teeth and sundered bits of mask scattered about the head. Theodore massages his hand pensively. The whole appendage, from his swollen, blood-smattered knuckles up through his forearm is radiating with pain.

"I-I've killed him."

"That may be the case future explorer, but it is imperative that you keep things in perspective, eh? I know these men personally, and I can guarantee that they are pernicious, hateful, dangerous chaps. They kill before their morning tea and, were it not for you and your mate over there, they would surely have tortured and killed your captive friend. Now, pull the body with all of your might, future explorer!"

The last thing Theodore pictured himself doing tonight was dragging a man he'd just killed with his bare fists down the hall. And doing it alongside the man in the wolf mask of all people. Hell, the fact that he just pummeled this stranger to death hasn't sunk in yet, but taking the man by his limply abiding wrists takes a mental fortitude he didn't know he had. His hands feel cold already, at least, a little colder than he imagines they'd be if his heart was still squeezing blood into them. He inhales sharply, thinking of anything else; pleasant things; Vivianne's soft touch and her breath on his neck, and pulls hard.

"Right, now reach into my trouser pocket and retrieve my keys, young one," the man in the wolf mask commands of Henry, who props Francis next to the door at the end of the corridor and rushes over to the new leader of the pack's side. One silvery cascade of jingles later and Henry brandishes a comically large key ring from the man's pocket. Whoever the guy is, he must hold a rather salient position at the hotel to have a master key for what looks like every room.

"It's that one, there! The scraggly little one is the key to the broom cupboard." Battling his own nerves, Henry fumbles the circus-size key ring between his hands for what is likely only a few seconds, though it feels like an hour, protracted by the grisly fact that all the while Theodore is shaking hands with a dead man. A man he just killed. Theodore refuses to look down at the medley of flesh beneath him; he stares at Henry as blood pumps through his ears like thunder. Finally, Henry snatches the proper key up and opens the janitor's closet. He then hustles over and helps their newfound ally and Theodore to drag the bodies within while Francis hobbles through the threshold. They snap the light on and briskly shut the door. Theodore, Henry, and their savior all take a collective sigh. Francis merely stares at them all from under the garish overhead light, clearly still a little dazed.

"If you don't mind, young one," the man says, his hands delicately cupping Francis' face and turning it about. "I should like to have a look at that eye of yours…splendid! Your forehead wound had me a trifle concerned, but the swelling hasn't encroached upon your eye and that's a right good thing! The other bruises coloring your face just now are all parenthetical issues; applying some ice should do the trick once you're back in your time."

"Back in your time?" Theodore repeats, wondering how much this stranger knows about their situation. "What do you mean by that, sir?"

"Well then. Now that we are all safe and secure, at least for the moment, eh, I believe introductions are at hand. Under ordinary circumstances, I should never like to give out any personal information, here, at one of Nithercott's masquerade parties. But these circumstances in which we find ourselves are far from ordinary, wouldn't you say, future explorer?"

"You're a friend of Alger Marley's, aren't you?" asks Theodore.

Deferring the question to the silence about them, the man reaches up and removes his mask to reveal a face much older than Theodore had anticipated. Like little fissures on a porcelain vase, wrinkles adorn the man's face. Tangled wisps of white hair delineate the sides of his head, the top of which is barren as a cue ball. A narrow, twist of beard juts out from his chin, completing a look that Theodore would call a 20th century politician spliced with a mad scientist. Underneath his strong brow is a pair of hard, determined eyes that catch the light like fire on a field of heather.

"I shouldn't like to give you my full name, as this could cause a ripple that might endanger all of our lives, and those of others as well. No, in these circumstances, the less you know of someone the better. I will provide you with a moniker of mine from long ago; a name I haven't used since the turn of the century. You can call me Watters. I am Alger Marley's father."

A puzzled silence falls over the tiny facilities room.

"You're his father?" Theodore stammers. "Marley mentioned in his recording that he had an ally on the inside…"

"Allow me to clarify, I am his adoptive father. Alas, the lack of shared blood between speaks nothing of the bond that I had to Alger. He was my boy, through and through, and I raised him the best that I could, given the circumstances."

"Circumstances?"

Watters retrieves a pocket watch. After a brief glance, his face turns into a dour pinch. "There is an exigence in this situation of which we cannot be remiss. We have little time for idle chatter. But I will tell you what is pertinent for you to know now, and you must let that suffice, eh?"

Theodore and Henry give a fervent nod yes.

"I know not what Alger divulged to you on the recording he left, nor do I know precisely where the next record is located. That is information for you and you alone, future explorer. But I know he provided you with a snippet of the scenario in which he found himself. He told you about his grandfather Walter Marley, and his invention?"

"Yes, and the fact that he never saw his grandfather again after that train ride to London…"

"Alas, no, he did not. I, too, was on the overnight-to-London. Although at the time, I did not know either Alger or Walter Marley personally. I had vocational ties with a government agency that had caught a whiff of Marley's exceptional invention. This agency placed me on that train with the two. You see, many eyes were upon this man and his rumored creation, and not all of them friendly. I spoke with grandfather Marley for but a moment, on the lounge car of the train. After my arrival, I became aware of a particularly brutal batch of sods called the London Bilge Rats, a vicious gang that had got wind of Marley's invention. They, too, were on the train, waiting for the right moment to pounce on him in his compartment.

"After my brief discourse with Marley in the train's lounge, I headed for his compartment, hoping to speak with him privately in his quarters about the danger he was in. But the Bilge Rats were already in his compartment, and whereupon I entered, they assaulted me, bloodied me up right good in an attempt to find the Sonophone. I, being the scrupulous fellow that I am and believing in the good such a device could bring the world in the proper hands refused to aid them in their evil quest. At the time, I hadn't a clue that the trunk carrying the Sonophone was actually in the hands of young Alger at the front of the train, but even if I had known I wouldn't have squealed to those wankers, I tell you!"

Theodore, Henry, and Francis bolt upright at the outburst, watching as Watters' face turns a murky aubergine. "I apologize, young ones. It isn't wise for me to raise my voice now, but even after all these years have passed, the memories burn." He clears his throat and adjusts his tie as he finds a little composure. "They tortured me within a bloody inch of my life. I slipped out of consciousness there in Marley's sleeper car, losing sight of my mission and the fate of the old man, the boy, and the Sonophone. I later awoke in the London General, a well-swathed mummy, bandaged and suffering from a collection of lacerations and broken limbs; a pain greater than any I'd known before."

"How did help find you in Marley's compartment before you bled out?" Theodore asks.

"Alger was a brave young bloke, sagacious and resourceful as they come. You see, I had shared a row of seats in coach with a sweet lass and her daughter. I chose to sit beside them with the hopes that we might appear as a family, to throw the Bilge Rats off my scent. Fate had it that the lady had been an army nurse. Whereupon Alger ventured to his grandfather's cabin, with the lights of London just beginning to scintillate in the distance, he found my battered, unconscious body instead of his grandfather. He did the only thing a youthful sprig might; he approached the only lady on the train that reminded him of his own late mother. The lass found me just in time, providing the necessary life sustaining care right before I slipped away for good."

"When I awoke in the hospital in Wandsworth, Little Alger was there, along with the nurse; both of their faces awash with the glow of surprise and concern. Surprise that I hadn't hopped the twig from the series of internal injuries; surprise that I might actually make it..." Watters pauses, an abstruse smile painted upon his face. "Christ in heaven, for the life of me I can't remember the name of that army nurse. And why should I?" he grunts sardonically. "She only saved my life, the angel. Was she Cora, or Nora...? Ah well, what does it matter now?

"Naturally, until the pain subsided, and my strength returned, I concerned myself not with Walter or his device. But the moment I was a trifle more lucid I inquired with young Alger, who had lingered beside me in my convalescence for days like a pup with no owner. He informed me that Walter never got off the train.

"I knew all too well the fate Alger's grandfather had suffered, and as I recovered, I took the boy under my wing. He cared for me, tended to me, fed me and washed my wounds until they were but scars. As a form of recompense, I taught him how to think for himself, how to fend for himself. I showed him what it was to be a man; what it was to fight for the good in this world. He became a son to me."

"We learned through Marley's recording how he ended up here, but how did you get thrown into this whirlwind of chaos?" Theodore inquires, leading up to the only real question he finds himself wanting to ask. "And...how are you guys connected to Vivianne?"

Watters' face lights up, his eyes like two torches set in a cold skull. "I thought you'd never inquire, future explorer."

"You can call me Theodore, by the way."

"The name with which you can—refer to me—with is...Henry." Barely making it through the treacherous waters of formal speaking, Henry holds out his hand for a shake. Theodore eye-rolls. "I'm Theodore's friend. Best friend, actually, and I work freight at Vanderbilt's Shipping and Distribution back in New York, and this is my first time coming here, and I know I might not look like much, but I promise you, Mr. Watters, sir, that I can be really useful when put to the task, just try me; Theodore will back me up on that, just tell him Theo—"

"Alright, alright Henry, ease up?" Theodore says.

"Hi, my name's Francis and I still don't know what the fuck's going on here." Francis extends his hand, his lips finally pulling into a slight smile at the corners.

"Yes, yes, you really are a fish out of water, young one; alas, you should be supplicating, to whatever god you Yanks pray to in the future, that you're not a bloated corpse in the Thames even as we speak. That being said, I should have ample time to bring you up to speed while Theodore searches for Alger's last recording on his own. But we shall go over all the logistics in a moment. Just now, it seems curiosity has got the better of me, and I must know! From what year do you gents hail?"

"We gents hail from the year 2016," Henry asserts. "The year of our lord, bless-ed be his name."

"Henry you're not even religious, and that doesn't make sense, anyway. Can you try to be normal in front of strangers for once? This is why I don't take you anywhere back home." Theodore realizes that his little lectures to Henry, of which there have been many through the years, always have such a callous bite to them that they veer off the cloistered path of lecture and go on a full diatribe safari. "But, you're still the Sam to my Frodo, bro. Wouldn't have it any other way." He nudges Henry on the shoulder. Henry's response is austere, attempting to ignore Theodore as if he's pouting, but at the mention of the brotherhood they're beginning to redevelop, his lips go into autopilot, and pucker into a furtive smile.

"2016…well I'll be damned," says Watters, shaking his head. "Are the automobiles slicing through the air like buzzards with motor engines, and do they run on the thoughts and dreams of suburban families, who haven't the woes of vicious social class schisms?"

"Well, uh," Theodore clambers through his mental library for tender euphemisms, or at least tenuous synonyms, for what he thinks the world has become since Watters' time. "It's not as different as you'd probably think or hope it'd be. I mean, we have cars that run on electricity, which is cool, but even in 2016 our tires are still firmly grounded." Theodore thoughtfully considers how much to disclose to Watters. Time is ticking both in the present-past and the present-future.

"Scientists have just about eradicated some diseases that are really brutal in your time," Francis chimes in. "Measles, mumps, typhus, polio." Francis ticks them off on his blood-spattered fingers.

"The class divide is still a thing—maybe even worse in our time," Theodore muses. Watters' face falls slightly at hearing this. Henry sees the shift in excitement and reaches into his pocket.

"And, we carry our telephones in our pockets, now!" Henry extracts his flip-phone, brandishing the device and handing it to Watters. He receives the phone with trepidatious curiosity, much like the characters in a Lovecraft-ian story.

"Honestly, Marley's Sonophone is far superior to anything that the world has seen since, technologically speaking of course," Theodore adds, but Watters isn't paying much attention, his focus solely on the little silver square in his hand.

"Mine's not as swanky or decked out as other peoples' from my time are 'cause I'm not exactly swimming in cash," says Henry, bashfully eyeing the flip phone. "We call these bricks nowadays."

"Never be ashamed of your modest earnings, young one. For in this community you have seen what avarice can do when it overtakes a person's soul...what an eccentric little thing this is," Watters exclaims. "Might I operate it somehow, just to get a taste of tomorrow?"

"Unfortunately, the whole time-traveling thing seems to disable our modern tech," says Theodore, grabbing the phone and snapping it open. He remembers the eerie sound it emitted earlier. He thrusts it onto his ear. Through the layer of static, an elongated note tickles his ear. It's more organic sounding than the transmogrified, time-warped instruments in the background. The vocalist is slowly churning out some unintelligible phrase, but the fact that he hears a vocalist at all means the record has run through a significant portion of its length already. They're running out of time!

"So, anyway, how is that Vivianne girl connected?" he inquires, his voice lathered in a newfound fervency.

"Yes, of course, time escapes us. Young Vivianne, why she is the darling lass tethered to this wicked corner of the world; another shard in the mosaic of collateral damage Nithercott is cobbling together. Alas, what a dazzling shard, no?" Watters' eyes become daggers, piercing the bulwark of Theodore's mind. "You have come this far for her sake, I imagine, eh?"

"Uh, yeah. I first came back here by accident two nights ago, and that's when I came upon her at the lounge bar, completely by chance. There was something about her that struck me. She was…different from everyone else here. I knew I needed to discover more about her. So, I came back again last night, Francis here in tow, and found her again. That's when I happened upon Marley's first dead drop, which informed me that she was in danger. And here we are on night three."

"Yes, Vivianne is a captivating young lady," Watters concurs. "You see, Alger was wrongly imprisoned here at The King's Inn when he poked his nose too far into Nithercott's business. When he eavesdropped on some of Nithercott's former associates, he uncovered precisely what their aim was: to build a clandestine community of upper-class citizens; aristocrats, nobles, and gentry who might use their newfound clout for wicked and lucrative ends. Being the founder of this cult, Nithercott naturally grew concerned about the implications of this greenhorn labour racketeer snooping about. He caught and imprisoned my poor lad within these very walls. Soon thereafter, Alger found Vivianne, developing a brilliant rapport with her here in the hotel. Even taking her in as a sort of daughter figure for the few years he was here…"

"Whatever happened to Marley? The Pilfering Paupers are under the impression that he vanished from The King's Inn, potentially being dragged out to be killed. But they had a whistleblower within that claimed otherwise. I think it was a young American guy who goes by the alias of Osprey. He claimed Nithercott had been moving Marley about between various undisclosed locations. The Paupers trust in this whistleblower so much that they're banking on finding him at an abandoned factory near the Thames. But it's a trap, and Nithercott has an ambush prepared there just for them. Being from the future, we have the hindsight to say that they were in fact ambushed tonight, and we absolutely need to prevent that from happening before we're sent back to the future."

"Yes," Watters says at long last. "Condor is nigh to falling into the trap once and for all. This whistleblower of whom you speak is a bloke that I've been tracking for months now. He resides within this hotel somewhere, but he's slippery as an eel and resourceful, too. He's evaded my pursuit, the conniving bastard. As for that Osprey fellow of whom you speak, he is not the whistleblower, and has nary been in this hotel. Until this night, that is."

"What do you mean?" asks Theodore.

"Alas, our time is spent. The Pre-Shibboleth Frivolities are nigh commencing, and I must show my face, lest Nithercott grow suspicious. You," he says, aiming an aging but puissant hand at Francis. "Your face is a roiled wreck that would surely bring attention to us, and by now, word might have spread amongst the revelers regarding your description and the fact that you should currently be in Harold's custody. Even with a doppelgänger covering your face, your safety cannot be guaranteed.

"Take the key to my private quarters, it is the only place you will be completely secure. It is room 0739 on the south nook of the seventh floor. You will find a change of clothes in my wardrobe that shan't be a perfect fit; alas, look at these two. They could make bedsheets out of the Chesterfields upon them. Theodore, you and Henry will join me at the Frivolities, after which, the three of us shall wait for you in my quarters while you scour Nithercott's penthouse for the last dead drop. I know not the extent of Alger's plan, but I do know that he believed in the off chance a future explorer might follow his temporal breadcrumb trail. And he worked tirelessly to concoct a ploy with which he might save Vivianne, his love for her was such. In the end, he kept me in the dark, deeming the less I knew of his plot, the safer I might be. He has proven correct on all fronts thus far."

The room is somber, and Watters hands Henry back his phone before he straightens. Time is of the essence.

The Regal Ballroom is alive. Draped in party-favor decadence, clad in crimson and golden strands of confetti, and festooned in the spirit of vivacity and mirth; a living, breathing panopticon of excess. Theodore can feel the very pulse of this hivemind collective, and it disturbs him. It makes him want to eschew the mask and flee for the farthest corner of London until the night comes to a close and he finds himself back in a world that makes sense to him. But if there's one positive thing mingling with murderers has done, it has brought him and Henry closer together; shown them inner strength and resolve they didn't know they had.

Nithercott is on the stage, flourishing, feeding off the frenzied crowd like a succubus dining on a lonely man's desire. The arcane folding camera is centerstage; the crowd contracting eagerly to fit into the frame. Theodore can see Short Chicken Lady and her prim partner throwing elbows at other revelers as they attempt to get as close as possible to the Master of Ceremonies.

"Shining satin shit-balls, this is one crazy place," Henry stammers as he witnesses the Regal Ballroom for the first time. "Man, what a trip it'd be to actually live this time period, to hold off going back to our time for a while. I mean these stuffy, old doilies really know how to party."

Theodore shakes his head. "Don't you remember what we just went through? These people are nutcases and murderers, Henry."

"Nutcases and murderers or not, they're more alive than New Yorkers in the 21st century. I feel more alive here than I have in forever, like I've found a place where my flaws don't matter, where nobody will notice my shortcomings, you know?"

"Unfortunately, yes, I do know what you mean. But we have to remember that this is no video game, Henry. Everything here has a real consequence."

"Quite true," Watters says. "While I cannot speak for the rest of London, I can say with surety that these masqueraders are not your friends." As Watters speaks, the sprightly effluence from the bandstand dies down, the cameraman taking his spot and beginning to corral the revelers into position.

Theodore whispers over the attenuating murmurs of the crowd, "Watters, I need to know: what did happen to Marley?"

"Alas, I cannot say. My beloved son was taken from me one day, taken by the deadliest of Nithercott's henchmen. Ostensibly to be killed. Late in the year 19 and 27 Alger came to me, a paranoid specter of his former self. He confided in me that his time was nigh, that it wasn't long before they threw him in a town car and painted some desolate field with his brains. But I know in my heart that he is out there...somewhere. My Alger is the most resourceful bloke I know, and he would have fought tooth and nail for his life, especially knowing that Vivianne remained in this depraved institution. Yes, he is out there somewhere."

"Just not where Condor and the Pilfering Paupers think he is," adds Theodore.

"Where no one thinks he is, Theodore. And mayhap, should I be fortunate enough, I might see him again one day. Although I have no evidence to corroborate this instinct. Mayhap I should accept the probability that he is gone...Vivianne is not, however, and I'll be damned if I let his last wish go unfulfilled." The crowd before them raises their glasses to the heavens, a volcanic uproar shattering the momentary stillness of the ballroom. The camera flashes.

"It is time. Henry, you will accompany me to my quarters where we will rendezvous with Francis and fill in the holes of his knowledge. Theodore, you must go now to Nithercott's penthouse while you still might. Prior to every Shibboleth, Nithercott takes to his room to prepare. But he will be fettered down by his hosting duties for now, and you shall be undisturbed if you abscond quickly."

Watters retrieves his ponderous keychain and plucks a large brass key from the middle of the cluster. "His room is 0929; you cannot miss it."

"All right." Theodore accepts the key and pockets it before any of the myriad curious eyes might wander over to the furtive exchange at the back of the ballroom. Everyone's ensnared by the pull of the party, though, and the entire room is back to its kinetic mayhem, the orchestra included. Theodore's mind is abuzz with more questions for Watters, including how the guy happens to own all these master keys to the hotel. But time is not on his side. He knows it's now or never. Time to pay Jarvis another visit.

VI

Stalking the oaky, wainscoting-lined hallway of the 9th floor, Theodore is inhumed in thought once again. He's paying no mind to the priceless works of art peering down at him from the walls, nor the grandly detailed, divinely opulent hotel he's exploring. The only time he hoists his head up from gazing at the carpet is to throw a perfunctory glance at the room numbers trundling by his vision. 0926. 0927. He might as well be crossing the River Styx on a tightrope. He can't stop turning the previous conflict over and over in his mind.

He killed a man down there—killed him with his bare hands. And what really claws at his soul, the cause of this moral schism he finds widening within his heart, is not knowing whether the guy he pummeled was an evil murderer or a Sunday school teacher. These possibilities didn't matter to Theodore while he was wailing away at the man. His mind had gone blank as a fresh page atop a typewriter.

He begins to wonder, not for the first time, if he's got a little of his father in him. His dad had a good side; even perhaps a demure and gentle side not entirely unlike Theodore himself. But as soon as his old man reached for that mahogany liquor cabinet in his study…

By the time he was six, Theodore had trained his ear to detect the sound of the antique shutter door on that cabinet. He had memorized the squawk of antediluvian wood scraping its hinges. Those sounds meant it was time to snatch Alice up and get her away immediately.

Sometimes, though, he and Alice would be upstairs playing, or watching the tv with the volume up too high, and Theodore would miss his only fugacious clue, subtle as it was, that a storm was on the horizon. He still kicks himself for the few times he didn't stand with his ear glued to his upstairs bedroom door, tirelessly listening for the cue while Alice played with his old picture books.

0928. But no, he refuses to believe that any of his dad's deleterious habits or wicked nature carried over to him. He has only ever snapped when he was protecting someone else. Instances where losing himself was the only recourse to preventing harm to somebody else. With that kind of situation foisted upon them, any sensible, good-hearted person would do the same.

0929. Here it is. Nithercott's penthouse. Plopped right in the middle of a short corridor is a doorway with decals bespoke of majesty and decadence. An array of aureate vignettes, like lightning captured and stricken upon the wall, twists and splays about the molding overhead. Frugal and precise Art Deco lines delineate the door frame, and a rigorously polished placard with the four numbers 0929 splashes Theodore's reflection back at him. The vision of himself he spies in it appears older, more mature and wearier than he remembered himself being. A swell of anxiety, like a hot, sticky fever, overtakes him as he realizes that Nithercott might come strolling down the hall at any minute. In his existential reverie, Theodore wasn't exactly power walking through the halls like he should have been. How much time has he eaten up? Before he even commands it to do so, his hand is dredging the bottom of his pocket, sweat caking his palm.

Bowing to the demand of a burgeoning paranoia, he cranes his head down both sides of the hallway, but ever since he got off the elevator, the 9th floor has been as abandoned as an almshouse in an affluent neighborhood. It remains completely still. He wrenches the key out and slides it into the lock with a resounding clunk. He opens the door.

Crushed red velvet bleeds down the walls and over the upholstery. Lights adorned with thick sconces haunt the walls, leaking a murky fog throughout the prodigious room. Lining the walls and suffusing the space between them are legions of trinkets, gadgets, and stage props; a vast and laudable assortment of theatrical motifs. Tall glass cases displaying the more precious items in Nithercott's collection bookend the primary assembly of objects that partitions the room right down the middle. At the very back is a raised landing that yields to glamorous floor-to-ceiling windows overlooking the city. On the left-most corner of the landing is Nithercott's personal desk. Upon it is the only light in the room desirous of a lampshade, giving the desk a sallow glow against a sea of red.

Nithercott's penthouse has a sweet, musky scent to it, as if everything is doused in one of those archaic bottled perfumes; the ones that have squeezable atomizers and always smell more like liquor than fragrances. Nithercott's room is different from the rest of the hotel; a microcosm made up of the man's eccentricities, and Theodore found that passing the threshold from the hallway to here is almost as bizarre a change as that of traveling between centuries.

The room pulses with a veiled energy; the various stage props glaring at Theodore from the dark recesses. The atmosphere in the penthouse is ineffably disturbing. Words like eerie and unsettling falling miserably short of doing the job. He has the sudden urge to turn tail and run. He wants nothing more than to quickly find Marley's last dead drop and get out before the fusty old costumes come to life, or the walls start to bleed, or some masked lunatic jumps out from behind the knickknacks to carve a new smile into Theodore's face.

He begins tiptoeing about the room, inspecting the books and the innumerable crannies between shelves, underneath old bar carts, and inside glass display cases. *I hid it right under his nose,* Theodore repeats the enigmatic clue Marley gave to him. The record is not going to be easy to find, or else Nithercott would've long since had it. Theodore glances inside a priceless Ming Dynasty dish, peers into a pulverulent Byzantine mug, and does a double take at a senescent scroll to see if the cylindrical record is wedged inside. The shape of the latter matches, but no such luck.

In the middle of the room, he comes upon a giant, stitched bear, probably a costume from some arcane play. Theodore pauses to examine it. Maybe this is what Marley meant by claiming that he hid the record right under Nithercott's nose. Stirring up a maelstrom of dust, he cocks the bear's head back, prying open the gap where the wearer could stick their head out for a fresh breath. Nothing inside but musty smells and dust bunnies. Theodore knocks the bear's head back on its shoulders and moves on. Perusing the shelves that cut the diameter of the penthouse, he comes upon a tiny curtained room off to the left side of the penthouse. He pulls the cushy blue velvet curtains aside.

He's peering into a room barely wide enough for a grown man to spread his arms across and touch the sides. Friable, red brick lines the room, an assortment of theater props pervading the awkward space. Up above, a pair of stage lights spew garish streams of golden light down upon a three-step platform not unlike one Theodore would expect to see an elephant balancing on at the circus. Propped just in front of the platform is an antique mannequin which, in this hellish situation, wouldn't normally stop Theodore dead in his tracks, but...there's something off about the look of it. It's too *lifelike*. Theodore steps into the room, the stage lights belching a curtain of heat onto his shoulders.

Department store mannequins have always made Theodore shudder. Unlike most other young boys, he had never been one to linger about the lingerie section while his mom shopped the discount bins, simply because the negligee-clad, plastic pseudo-humans staring down at him with their listless eyes and alien faces turned his stomach inside out. But this is no department store mannequin. She's outfitted as much as any human woman might be. She's sporting an arcane polka-dotted blue summer dress with a lengthy gash in the shoulder, and a pair of raven-black evening shoes. Upon her face, melting like ice cream under the heat of the stage lights, are two painted-on eyes, tawdry red lipstick covering the thinly carved mouth, and dabs of rouge on her cheeks. Who would take the time to layer a mannequin in more makeup than Theodore's seen on most actresses? Was it Nithercott? For what purpose? Then Theodore sees it smattered upon her summer dress.

The name 'Ms. Osgood' is scribbled in red on her chest in violent streaks. The red is tinged a muddy brown, as if made not of paint, but of blood. Cascading down her shoulders is a golden wig…only…it's plastered on in thick, haphazard clumps. And, while Theodore doesn't exactly do wardrobe design for Hollywood or anything, he's pretty sure he can tell the difference between a standard wig and a full head of real human hair. The blonde strands on the mannequin's head are simply lacking the buoyancy of a wig. Theodore reaches out with a shaking hand to feel the hair. Nervously, he tries to swallow but realizes that his throat is dry as a strip of jerky. *This is human hair all right.*

Just then something tickles his ear. Slow, languorous thumps on the other side of the wall. Someone's walking down the hallway. He leaps from the stage room as the footsteps trace the wall towards the front door. His heartbeat thrums its gushing rhythm between his ears. *Where to hide? Where to hide?* Panic takes over and he begins to seize up, freezing like a deer in front of a semi. The footsteps pause before the front door. *He's here! I've taken too long!* Theodore turns and ducks behind a clothes rack just in front of Nithercott's desk.

He grasps an old dressing gown with one hand and a thick white robe with another and squeezes himself between the two, trying to immerse himself as much as he can within the ocean of old theater costumes. The thought hits him that the coat he's got on his body is so big it alone could almost fully conceal him if draped properly. Frantically fumbling out of the sleeves, he wrenches the oversized Chesterfield from his shoulders and drapes it over his head. Just as he finishes adjusting within the wardrobe rack, the front door creaks open; a golden ribbon of hallway light floods in. For a terrifying moment, the silhouette of a tall, gaunt figure haunts the threshold. Nithercott slides into the room, shutting the door and bending forward to examine the lock, tilting his head side to side like some feral creature evaluating the quality of a carcass it's found.

I forgot to lock the door behind myself! He's onto me already! Nithercott stands with the grandiose motion of an impresario after the curtain-close bow. The globule eyes of the rat mask pan over Theodore as Nithercott gives the room a slow scan. He sniffs the air and, apparently satisfied with whatever he does or doesn't smell, reaches up and removes his doppelgänger. Theodore's blood stanches in his veins at the unnerving visage that blemishes the softness of the low light ambience. Pale, jagged cheeks loom over the coiled asp of a mouth. Beady, fiercely intelligent eyes pierce the very space they survey. Nithercott sighs, reaches up, and peels back the slick, onyx curtain of hair that had fallen over his forehead upon removing his mask. On his cheek a soft, indelible mound of scar tissue lingers from some recent injury.

He floats through the room, towards the clothing rack in which Theodore's hiding. Theodore sucks in a breath and holds it; holds it as long as he can while Nithercott approaches and stalks past him. Theodore smells the inimical man's sweat mingled with the floral notes of his cologne as he passes, sees the shimmering, sudorific beads upon his forehead that dapple his makeup. Nithercott pauses just before his desk, placing his mask upon a nail in the wall. Theodore hears the protesting moan of a loose floorboard beneath Nithercott's foot – four floorboards from the wall just under the mask—the rat's protuberant nose practically hovering over the melodious board. As Nithercott steps away, Theodore notices the floorboard wiggle. *I hid it right under his nose.* Could that be it? Could the record be hidden under that loose floorboard?

Nithercott stalks past Theodore once more in his languorous, calculated fashion. Theodore holds his breath again, feeling like he might faint were the thrashing of his jugular in his throat not keeping him lucid. He watches as this curiously evil man waves the velvet curtains aside and disappears into the room with the mannequin. Realizing his chance to retrieve the record and flee before Nithercott finds him and does god-knows-what to him, Theodore begins pushing with both hands against the layers of dress that enswathe him. Slowly, gently, silently, he steps out from the rack, hurls his coat back on and ducks down towards the floorboard, his hands greased with sweat. He pulls, lightly at first to see if the board decides to talk again and then a little harder when it doesn't.

"Hello, my dear," the deranged lilt of an austere voice sounds behind him. He gasps, craning his neck and expecting to see Nithercott's mad grin beaming down upon him. Nothing but the ruddy glow of the lamplight kissing his forehead, however. Apparently, Nithercott's still in the other room. *Whom could he be talking to in there, the mannequin? Himself?* Theodore resumes his excavation, pulling until the floorboard jiggles out of the relenting grasp of its housing. He uncovers a slim, tenebrous cavern, too dark to see anything within. Wishing he had his cellphone to illuminate the crevice, Theodore reaches and paws about. Nothing. Nothing but the gossamer threads of cobwebs and dust covering the foundation beneath.

Panic grips Theodore, its icy fingers making him shake like a palm tree in a hurricane. Nithercott might peer out from behind the curtains at any moment; Theodore certainly cannot linger here. He leans forward, fully on his knees and elbows now, and dips his arm deep within the crevice. Left, nothing. Forward, nothing. Towards himself, nothing. He thrusts his arm to the right, so deep now that if he were to pucker his lips, he'd kiss the floor. Something's there. Something solid and cylindrical. He tries to hook a finger around it, but it's just barely too far away to get a grip, and in his eagerness, he applies too much pressure. The item rolls lazily away, just out of his reach. *Fuck!*

Without knowing whether it's Marley's recording he's risking his neck trying to retrieve, or the boxed set of Anne Boleyn's knitting needles that accidentally got boarded up in construction, he glances about, fervently searching for some object that might help him snatch the damn thing up. With

Nithercott's muffled voice still emanating from the other room—entertaining an animated conversation with himself or with no one—Theodore returns to the shelves as light-footed as he can manage. A blade from Cornwall, whose plaque states it may have been the very sword of Arthurian legend, *Excalibur*, stares down at Theodore from the wall. It'd be a viable option to knock the item forward were it not for the glass case enshrouding it.

He moves along the far wall, crouched like a Special Forces operative on a reconnaissance mission. An eclectic tapestry of trinkets and treasures gleam down from the wall, pristinely preserved Samurai swords, a hunk of wood on another hunk of wood whose plaque states that it's a piece of debris from the civil war battle known as *Pickett's Charge*, and a host of old pistols from the flintlock days to the Colts, Remingtons, and Derringer pocket pistols of the 1800s. Beside these is a grisly assortment of medieval torture devices; iron-clad, rusty, jagged, formidable. Among the instruments of pain is a pair of tongue pincers, the kind Theodore read about in school which the torturer would get blazing hot and then put to the tongue of the poor bloke accused of treason or blasphemy, and pull until he had no more tongue with which to blaspheme.

Theodore has no idea if these relics of Nithercott's are authentic or not. Although he can't imagine the guy would collect a small warehouse's worth of replicas. His stomach twists at the thought of even touching a device that, perhaps, many centuries ago was used to rip out someone's tongue. Even with all this temporal padding in between that time and Theodore now, it just feels wrong to his maudlin sensibilities…but he needs to find the record, and he needs to find it fast. If the item under the floorboards happens to be something else, he's back at square one. Only now, Nithercott's in the penthouse with him.

He inhales sharply and reaches for the pincers with fingers that prove to be just as hesitant as the rest of him, spidering onto the handle but refusing to grab hold. Then, he thinks of Vivianne and Alger Marley and all they've been through, of Henry and Francis and everything to which he's subjecting them, and of Alice, whose smile he hopes he hasn't looked upon for the last time. He's not falling prey to Nithercott or his masqueraders; not now, not ever. He yanks the pincers from their housing, but he does not consider the heft of a medieval torture device when he does so. Within one beat of his heart, the pincers plummet, nearly clattering to the countertop in what would be the last careless move of his life.

All those years throwing a football around with his dad—the one activity the two of them ever did that he could actually count as bonding—pay off and his snappy reflexes react before his mind does. The tip of the pincers grazes the countertop, but luckily for Theodore, Nithercott doesn't seem to hear the whisper of iron on wood. He draws a rattled breath and slinks back over to the pried-up floorboard. He knows that the mystery item, whatever it may be, is just far enough away to require that he holds the pincers as far back on the handles as he can manage. With the rusty old torture device already becoming a boulder in his hand after holding it for mere seconds, he knows this won't exactly be a stroll through the park. *Or a journey across almost a century of space time,* Theodore snickers silently.

He grips the pincers with both hands, thanking the good lord, or fate, or whatever the fuck, for seeing to it that he be cursed with an unusually petite bone structure, and pulls them wide enough to clasp around the sides of a phonograph cylinder. Luckily, he's had plenty of experience handling those in his life, so he's certain he can estimate their diameter within a few millimeters or so. With the timidity of a demolitions expert clipping wires on a bleeping IED, he dips the pincers into the gap between floorboards.

It's a precarious balancing act from here. If he pushes the pincers in too far too fast, the item will roll away, lost to him forever. If he fails to properly grasp the damn thing on the first clamp, he's shit out of luck as well. *And damn, from this leverage, these aren't pincers but metric-ton meat hooks*, he thinks, the burn in his arms now penetrating his shoulders. *There it is!* He can feel the hook shape of the pincers tap the item, but at this confounded angle, trying to stabilize the tool enough to snatch the thing is like trying to hold a lightning rod during the strike.

Come on! He's going to leave that little room any minute now; he's going to stroll out expecting to amble down to the Shibboleth, and he's going to find you on his way out, flailing at the floorboards with his goddamn antiques. Then it'll be your hair adorning a mannequin in his penthouse of horrors. Letting a deep breath fortify him, Theodore closes his eyes, steadies his arms, and dips in once more. No rolling, no bobbing against the top, this time the item slots right into the welcoming arms of the torture device. He had guessed the dimensions perfectly. *Easy does it, Theodore.*

He retracts, feeling the end of the tongue pincers begin to dip and sway, teetering like a racehorse on Quaaludes, but he manages to pull the item clear out with no clamorous event. It's an arcane, cylindrical container; lemon-rind yellow, and lacking any label or identifying marker whatsoever. It's got to be Marley's recording. *That's a hell of an inventive dead drop location,* Theodore thinks, releasing the breath he had fettered inside his diaphragm for far too long.

He unclamps the cylinder and slides it into the inside pocket of his Chesterfield with no time to verify that the unlabeled container even has anything in it. He needs to get out, and now. He rises, coming face to face with Nithercott's doppelgänger hanging on the wall. *Right under his nose, indeed, Mr. Marley.* He begins zigzagging through the death maze of antiques. It's a death maze because if one elbow dips too far out, if one long, intractable sleeve of his coat happens to brush against a table, he's dead. But, even with the risk, he pauses in front of Nithercott's little side room before absconding. Theodore's always been a curious one. That's partially why he's in this logic-bending, mind-fucking situation to begin with. But he has what he came for; he just *must* know what the madman is doing in there.

He shuffles across the floor and sidles against the wall, peering past the velvet threshold while staying just far enough from the doorway that his face will still be drenched in shadow. Nithercott's atop the little podium making grand, swooshing gestures with his arms, his lips peeling apart and stolidly shutting over and over, as if he's memorizing a series of lines.

"No, no, no, my sweet, you must watch me!" Nithercott leans forward and snatches Ms. Osgood the Mannequin, propping her against the wall so that her porcelain eyes are fixed upon him at the podium. "Keep your pretty blue eyes upon my face, dear. You mustn't focus on anyone else, lest I become envious of you, and resentful of the freedoms with which I have bestowed you. And you know how envious I can become." Nithercott's voice rises, and Theodore finds himself wincing at every disturbing syllable coming out of the guy's mouth. Who is this Ms. Osgood, and why the fuck is Nithercott talking to her like she's alive? Was there a Ms. Osgood in real life, and if so, is that her actual dress? Her real *hair*?

"C'est bon, mon petit bouton d'or." Nithercott flashes Ms. Osgood his jagged smile. "I apologize if I raised my voice, my sweet. Alas, you know the passionate man that I am, and, sometimes it gets the better of me. Now, time is short, and I must rehearse the Shibboleth in full at least once before I perform it for my colleagues and compatriots." Theodore finds himself gripping the velvet partition with white-knuckle intensity, his heart a pounding premonition in his chest. Nithercott clears his throat.

"Ladies and gentlemen, friends and colleagues, lovers and loyalists, I gather you here tonight on this, the most special of nights, to engage with me in an enquiry, an enquiry into the state of our affairs. For there are those who would see our great plan crumble into dust, and my faithful servants have teased one of these pernicious traitors from the shadows—oh, my sweet!" Nithercott exclaims, swooping down the podium once more and scooping up his mannequin. "What on earth has happened to your dress?" With a temperate sweep of his hand, far gentler a motion than Theodore would expect from a murderous thug, Nithercott takes the shoulder of her summer dress into his hand, examining the tatter that Theodore himself had noticed; a tatter that looks like it's been there for years.

"Oh no, this simply will not do. We will have to sew this up at once, my sweet. I am so sorry; I have been utterly remiss of your needs, my bouton d'or. And what have we here?" Nithercott examines the faded red streaks spelling out the mannequin's name on her chest. "No, no, no, we cannot have your good name sullied by fools. If you are to be present at the Shibboleth, we must address your appearance, my sweet." Nithercott dips a gloved hand into his suitcoat. Theodore gulps at the coruscant glare of a pocketknife.

With a shaking hand, Nithercott raises the knife toward his face. "This just won't do at all, my sweet." In one conservative motion, he thrusts the knife to his cheek, moaning lightly as he digs in. He pulls the glove off his left hand and dips his pointer finger into the wound. "No, this just won't do!" Nithercott ululates, pressing the finger against the mannequin's dress and coloring in the 'Ms.' portion of her name with fresh, sanguine strokes. He lifts the knife and carves a little deeper, this time howling a little under the self-inflicted torture.

Theodore looks away as Nithercott jams his finger into the fleshy maw upon his cheek. He just can't look at the ghastly sight any longer. He stares stoically down at the floor, feeling beads of sweat gather on his forehead, and writhing a little every time he hears Nithercott's throaty growl. A morbid curiosity tackles his senses and, just like when he and Alice would watch horror movies as kids, he finds he can't look away through the gruesome part. He lifts his head to see Nithercott's tenacious finger prodding through the oozing caldera of skin upon his cheek. Theodore feels his toes curl. His teeth grind furiously. His hand clutches the bit of curtain bunched within it tighter. Nithercott finishes painting through the letters 'Osg' when Theodore's tensing body gets the better of him. His hand squeezes too firmly on the curtain, undoing the braided golden sash tethering it to the wall. The blue curtain cascades down like a wall of water, rippling back and forth and then hanging limp across the doorway. Theodore freezes, an agonizing silence emanating from the stage room.

He hears the clack of a footstep resound from within, then another. *Nithercott's stepping off the podium; he can't find me!* Theodore lurches backward, ducking into the wardrobe rack and throwing the old theater gowns about himself again. He sinks into the inviting billows of the Chesterfield once more and peers out from behind the mesh of an old bonnet, trying to tame the uncontrollable spasms of air his lungs are forcing in and out, in and out. A languorous, spindly hand reaches out from behind the curtain and grasps it where Theodore's own hand was but moments ago. Nithercott's aquiline nose ekes out, followed by his harsh, angular face. Unkempt streaks of hair bob down over his forehead as he scans the penthouse for an intruder. His eyes carry in them a glint as he glances to and fro, looking like some wild and voracious zoo animal whose enclosure door was just opened for the first time.

He steps out, treading throughout the room, floorboards whining underneath him. All is silent and still, and as Nithercott maunders closer to the clothes rack, Theodore squeezes tighter on the handle of the pincers he's still holding. Bad comes to worse, he's swinging this hefty tool right in Nithercott's face and making a break for the door. Theodore's eyes wander to the spot where Nithercott will be in only moments—the open space just in front of Theodore. His heart sinks at what he finds…dear lord, he's a goner, an absolute goner. The lone plank is just lying there idly, quaintly, so readily observable right on top of the others. In his haste, he forgot to put the fucking floorboard back!

"Hello?" Nithercott's villainous timber haunts the space. "Have I a visitor in my midst?" Slowly, carefully, Nithercott stalks the space. Then his eyes lock upon a set of antique dressing gowns across the room from Theodore. Like it or not, Theodore is officially playing a macabre game of hide and seek with a murderer, and he's left one ponderous breadcrumb for his pursuer to find. Nithercott dances over to the gowns, gently dipping his arms down the middle and then wrenching the gowns apart with a furious flailing of his hands. A posh suede gown goes drifting to the floor with its hanger clattering in tow. "Have I a curious enquirer in my quarters?" Nithercott moves closer to Theodore again, to the giant bear costume in the middle of the penthouse. "Come out, come out, wherever you are." He curls his bony fingers about the tufts of fur on the bear's arms and throws the entire costume aside. "Aha!" he cries, and then falls silent upon finding nothing but another fusty shelf glaring back at him.

Then, he slowly cranes his neck, turning his head towards one of the few unsearched places big enough to hide a grown man: Theodore's clothing rack. Nithercott snarls a preemptive victory snarl, his eyes dead set on the rack of clothes. Theodore ekes out a whimper, he can't contain it. Feeling his heart rise into his esophagus, and the tingling warmth of anticipation sweep over his face, he tenses his arm, preparing for the inevitable confrontation.

He only hopes that in the low light, he can get the jump on the lunatic and land one good hit. If he doesn't use the advantage of surprise that he hopes he still has—if he doesn't manage to whack Nithercott right in the face as he's throwing the clothes aside—it's not just Theodore who will suffer for it. Henry and Francis are with Watters, so they should be safe until they're warped back to the present, but Vivianne…she'll be forever locked away in Nithercott's tower, another prisoner in his hotel of horrors. Theodore can't let that happen.

Nithercott pauses right in front of the rack—his shoes clacking only inches away from the glaring piece of evidence behind him—leaning in until his face is but a few inches away from Theodore's. With his free hand, Theodore covers his mouth. All that's separating them is the gossamer thread of the old bonnet, and the room's scant lighting which has Theodore enshrouded in darkness. He can feel Nithercott's damp, hot breath kiss his chin; can smell the sweet tang of liquor on his breath; can see the gash on his cheek spilling little red pinstripes that gather on his jowl and drip to the floor. *It's coming. He's raising his hands. He's got me,* Theodore thinks, poising for the strike. Nithercott clutches the dresses on either side of Theodore and inhales. Theodore closes his eyes.

"What's that, dear?" Nithercott cocks his head, lowering his hands. "The Shibboleth is about to begin? Well, my love, the event surely cannot commence without the Master of Ceremonies present, but yes, as usual, you are right. I mustn't keep my compatriots waiting." Nithercott spins about. He doesn't have to peer down in the shadows to find the upended floorboard as his dress shoe slips right into the opening. He squeals, tumbling to his knees. He flicks the loosened dangle of hair at his widow's peak back and sucks in a long, emphatic breath. Exhuming his foot from the baseboards, he squats down and scoops up the plank. Theodore's quivering violently now and soon he'll shake himself right out of the rack. He was so close!

Barely able to steady his nerves enough to keep his eyes on the figure haunting the room before him, he watches as Nithercott rises slowly, his face panning the entire room as he pins the floorboard against his chest. His visage is far less whimsical now. Like a gambler who only just learned the table stakes, any hint of playfulness he'd had during the hunt is crowded out by a seething rage. His teeth are barred; the freshly dug scallops of flesh on his cheek are dancing, leaking crimson tendrils from his jowl down to his lapels now. He's wielding the piece of flooring like a war hammer as his gaze clambers across the penthouse.

Theodore's legs feel like saplings in a storm. He's going to faint, he's sure he's going to faint. He's never been so frightened in his life. As if sensing Theodore's anguish, Nithercott moves toward the clothing rack again, raising the makeshift weapon in his fervent grasp. He's prepping to swipe the clothes right off the rack, he cocks his arm high. Theodore wrenches the pincers out and presses them into the costumes on his right, ready to strike. A single tear courses down his cheek and stings his lips. Nithercott grimaces and moves to knock the rack right over when his head pivots to the side.

"Yes, yes, I know, my sweet. It is beyond time and you hate when I keep my contemporaries waiting." His shoulders relax, the floorboard lowering and dangling at his side. He turns about. "There is just one thing I must—yes, I am coming, I am coming!" The figure slinks away from the clothing rack at the behest of his loved one, the floorboard clattering to the ground to meet its mates.

Gradually, Theodore steadies his breath, feeling warmth begin to rush through his limbs, a map of tingles forming along his back. But he can't untense his arm; can't lower his guard for one second in this wicked man's presence. Maybe it's all pretense, and Nithercott is just playing with him. Has he known Theodore's been here the whole time? Surely, he at least knew someone had broken in once he saw the flooring had been tampered with? Either way, Theodore can not make a peep until Nithercott's gone off to the Shibboleth.

"Thank you for the very pertinent reminder, my bouton d'or," he says to the lifeless prop in the other room, briskly walking over to his doppelgänger and slipping it onto his face, letting out a little hiss as the mask touches his wound. He then steps up to his desk and rounds it, snatching an overcoat from the back of his chair. He strides past Theodore, blood seeping out from under his mask and leaving a trail of red dots behind him. Without looking back, or saying another word to Ms. Osgood, Nithercott swings the door open, and exits. Theodore waits until the footfalls dissipate. He unclamps his hand from his mouth and bends over in an unassuageable fit of sobs.

VII

The corridor lights are lower down here; everything has a more clustered, intimate feel. Theodore, Henry, and Francis are following Watters down to the Shibboleth, something Francis feels, still being rattled by his near-death experience, is unnecessary and even reckless. Up in Watters' quarters on the seventh floor, his exact words were, "That's as good an idea as arming yourself with a salad fork and lifting the tail of a sleeping lion to take his temperature. It's just buying trouble where there doesn't have to be any."

Theodore noticed Henry didn't give a word of protest to the proposition. Perhaps he's hoping to bump into Jersey Doll again, but Theodore assumes his compliance means that Henry's curiosity—like his own—has trumped his many concerns about staying in the hotel one minute longer than necessary. They've taken a series of long passages past the Regal Ballroom, Theodore noticing the stark change in ambiance as they've gone along. Watters did warn them that things were going to get weird the deeper into the establishment they went, and that the private room reserved for the Shibboleth was in the very bowels of The King's Inn. Theodore thought he was ready for whatever he'd encounter, especially after having watched Nithercott conversing with a mannequin like it was his girlfriend, just before carving into his own face with a pocketknife. But the reality of the situation is a little stranger than these last three nights have prepared him for; who knows what's next?

They come to an unassuming wall in the middle of a stretch of hallway. Now and again, a few masqueraders amble up and down the lane, arms intertwined, and eyes locked upon each other; spirits in their glasses and avarice in their eyes. Watters stops. Theodore and the others follow suit, glancing dumbly at each other and then expectantly at him. After the thinning throngs of revelers disappear into the myriad rooms or around the corners on either side of the corridor, Watters ushers Theodore forth. He hovers his hand over what looks like a painted-over panel; a slightly raised little square in the wall that Theodore would've easily walked past a hundred times without a second glance, and raps his knuckles in a tight, rhythmic pattern over the panel. Henry looks over at Theodore, who looks at Francis, who just stares back through his gorilla mask above a snazzy—if somewhat tight—pinstripe suit with which Watters supplied him in his room.

A moment later, the response to Watters' call emanates from somewhere above; a muted knuckle-rap followed by a sharp screech and low, trundling groan. There's a solid thud behind the wall and Watters pushes upon the square, revealing a compartment with a wooden bucket on a pulley system.

"A dumbwaiter in the middle of the hallway, how eccentric is that?" says Francis. Watters' hand fishes around in the bucket, retrieving nothing but a small golden key. He flings the mini door shut, raps out the same code to return the bucket, and motions to Theodore. Their dress shoes and loafers squeal across the lacquered floor as they pass by several unlabeled doors until Watters pauses once more before a painted-over entryway. There's no doorknob, just a camouflaged notch at waist height that Theodore discerns merely from the gold glint it gives off under the hallway light. He has to bend over and almost touch his toes in order to confirm what the little anomaly in the wall is. A keyhole.

"So," Henry starts. "I'll ask the obvious question that's on all of our minds. What the fuck is a dumbwaiter doing in the middle of this random hall, and how do you know about it? Oh yeah," he continues sardonically, "this whole place is a maze of mind-fuckery, and you're leading us through some secret, elaborate entrance to the Shibboleth." Watters slots the key into the hole, shooting glances up and down the hall.

"I've wondered for the past years precisely how young Vivianne's saviors would look, how they'd speak, should Marley's impossible plan ever come to fruition of course. I knew you'd hail from the future, and thus your fashion would be nothing if not alien to me, and your mannerisms anachronistic. I knew not from which nation you'd hail, but I always assumed your prosody and your lexicon would be delightfully strange to me. I wasn't mistaken, especially with you, young Henry."

"Well, first off pal, we from the future don't use such fancy terms as pros-prosody? Or lexicon, whatever that is—at least, those of us less pretentious than my pal, Theo, here. And we definitely don't say we *hail* from anywhere. We say we're from New York. You old Brits have a way of making simple sentences into highfalutin tongue-twisters a skilled auctioneer couldn't work his way through. I mean, no offense."

Watters chuckles, pops open the door, and ushers them into a small Parisian lounge. The room is picturesque, pristinely white and ornate in its decorations, as if it had been hooked by a crane, lifted straight off the Seine, and plopped right here in busy London. There's only one jarringly discordant element in the room: a London phonebooth along the middle of the back wall. Two revelers sit on the left side, pressed snugly together and heavily petting each other to the sonorous swoon of an accordion on a gramophone. They don't appear even slightly miffed that their secret little grotto has been invaded by four outsiders, choosing instead not to miss a beat with their amorous display.

Watters leads the group over to the phonebooth, patently disregarding the two lovers on the sidelines. Theodore and Francis comply, eager to get on to the night's main event. But Henry lingers back, slowly plodding over toward the revelers. Theodore watches over his shoulder as they take note of Henry's voyeurism. The woman, wearing a peacock mask and a white deco flapper dress, pulls gingerly away from the man and, watching Henry with an edacious look, slowly drops both shoulders of her dress to reveal her voluptuous breasts. The man cranes his neck, looking up at Henry and nodding vapidly in his aardvark mask. He extends a gloved hand and beckons Henry closer. Feeling the rosebud of a blush blooming under his mask, Theodore hurries over to Henry's side and yanks him by the arm, but to no avail. Henry is already subscribed to the likelihood of groping a girl's chest for the first time in years.

"C'mon, man. We can't screw around right now," Theodore whispers. Henry responds with some sort of avaricious gargling noise. "These people are trying to suck you into their crazy world, but you have to remember why we're here, man. You're still my Sam, right? I can't lose you to the sirens of Mordor, bro."

"Yeah, but even Sam wanted some every now and again," Henry's brain stammers on autopilot, and he shuffles closer to them. "Given the circumstances, I'll forgive the canonical blender you just pureed your mythoi in."

"Come and sit with us, big boy," the peacock's saccharine voice.

"Have a little fun," says the aardvark, gesticulating an invitation with his arms. "On this of all nights."

"Guys, we've got a little situation," Theodore says into the phonebooth. Watters cradles the receiver under his chin and shoots a glance over at Henry. He hangs the phone up.

"Francis," he commands. The two of them hurry over and enswathe Henry, wrenching him away from the open arms of the revelers.

"No, let him *play*," whines the peacock. "Three is a savory number."

"Perhaps another time," Watters barks at them, tugging at the incorrigible Henry. They pull Henry right into the phonebooth, where he finally manages to wriggle free.

"Okay, okay! Get your paws off me you gorilla!" Henry spits at Francis. "First you ruin junior high for me with your douche-baggery. Then you have to spoil what was looking to be my first really juicy sexual encounter in…

well, way too long."

"C'mon, man," says Theodore. "You weren't actually about to strip out of your Chesterfield and join them, were you? I know you pretty well and even that is beyond you."

"I mean, I was gonna watch for a while, maybe give some audience requests. Did you see the way that chick was looking at me, Theo? I've never had someone look at me that way." He leans back out of the phonebooth and waves at the peacock. She giggles, waves back, and then resumes smooching and cuddling the aardvark.

"Not to mention those first-class jugs, man."

"Yeah, I get it, dude," Francis says, giving Henry a series of conciliatory pats on the back. He's so burly, though, that his pats are hard enough to look like he thought Henry was choking on an almond. "But none of these shows of affection are real. It's like one massive closet, and we're just watching people file into it for their no-strings-attached seven minutes of heaven." To this, Henry merely shrugs.

"I don't need genuine shows of affection, Franny," his fractious response. "Not when partial nudity and potential heavy petting is involved."

"Gonna have to wait," Theodore interrupts. He crosses his lips with his forefinger and points to Watters, who lifts the receiver and clacks a few digits into the rotary dial. There's a brief pause during which Theodore can discern the mumbles of a nasally voice on the other end, and then Watters says in a stately voice rather than the expected whisper, "While frequently attributed to Lord Byron, *The Vampyre* was in fact penned by his doctor, John William Polidori, during the year without a summer." Another pause, during which Theodore hears the mysterious correspondent ask another riddle.

"Man, what exclusive club are we trying to get into, The Cat's Meow?" Henry teases, jabbing Francis with his elbow. Being the almost-too-nice guy that he is, Francis fakes a chuckle at his new patently unfunny friend.

"During the time he was housebound at the villa on Lake Geneva, Polidori was accompanied by Claire Clairmont, as well as Mary and Percy

Shelley." After another pause Theodore hears the handset on the other end click as Watters' correspondent hangs up. A shrill, metallic noise emanates from the other side of the telephone and Theodore only now realizes that the back of the phonebooth isn't encased in windows like the other walls, it's some sort of trap door that the phonebooth was built into. The metallic sound was that of someone sliding open a little grate on the wall. Watters replaces the handset onto its hook and then scoops up a key from within the newly furnished cubby. He then retrieves a locked phonebook from under the telephone and slots the key in.

"Okay, maybe this is a *little* more sophisticated than the entrance to The Cat's Meow," concedes Henry, in wide-eyed-wonder.

Watters thumbs through the phonebook, mumbling to himself, "The code is located between pages 317 and 323; which correspond with the days of a very salient year for Nithercott; the day he won over the nobility, and the day he and his benefactors founded the Patriciate Party. The pages betwixt read as an acrostic puzzle, with the ascending digits of the first phone number upon each page making up the code."

Francis tosses his ginger hair back, raising a single dubious eyebrow at Theodore, who bounces the same expression over to Henry, who picks his nose and flicks the gooey plunder at the window of the phonebooth. He then smiles at Theodore and shrugs. Watters dials in the secret code on the telephone. Theodore hears a click and a slide from above. He peers outside the phonebooth to see a ceiling tile peel away, a wooden handle dangling on a cord uncoils like an asp and makes its way down just before Theodore's face.

"Pull down, young Theodore," Watters instructs. Theodore obeys, watching dumbfounded as the wall to the back of the phonebooth gives way, taking the telephone with it. Tenebrous shadows meet them at the opening, bleeding into a steep set of stairs that leads down at least one flight. Theodore can see past the doorway at the bottom a hallway replete with revelers. The sweet, eerie clamor of a clarinet meets Theodore's ear.

"Hurry, gents," says Watters, ushering them into the darkness of the passage. "Before the door closes. That's right, Francis, in you go. After you Henry, just make your way into the passage and walk with authority. Theodore, I am right behind you, good sir."

"What an ordeal to get here," Henry's voice bounces off the narrow cloister of walls as he fumbles through the clandestine stairwell. "Anyway, this Shibboleth business must be some pretty top-level exclusive shit if the key to this section of the hotel it's in wasn't on your massive loop you've got there. You had to go through the motions like any other schmo."

"You're very perceptive, Henry. Only Alfred Nithercott holds the master keys beyond this section. Nevertheless, the somewhat excessive layers of security involving the hidden dumbwaiter and the phonebooth, while intended to minimize the number of revelers that gain access to the Shibboleth to only the most devoted of his followers, is more for show than anything else. It is merely another eccentricity of Nithercott's, for dramatic purposes rather than legitimate crowd-vetting. Were he to decide he wanted only certain individuals in his community to attend, he'd see to it, and sure as you were born some sixty years from now, you wouldn't be gaining access even with my assistance.

"While he doesn't intend to estrange the less sagacious of his people from his flock by truly excluding them from the Shibboleths, he wants those who crack the code of the hotel to experience true, unadulterated hedonistic bliss on the other side. Consider it all for the twisted symbolism which it represents: those who prove they have the wit and assiduity necessary to pass his little test shall get their foot in the door of his secret labyrinth, as well as get their names on his shortlist of allies. It is the first real step to becoming one of the many agents who do his bidding about the United Kingdom; a rather coveted position amongst his followers, I do say. And now you may understand this, the rather surreptitious reason to attend one of his Shibboleths."

Watters pauses, poking his pointer finger at Theodore and the others for emphasis before they pass through the threshold. "A word of caution to you all. Once we are inside, do not stray from under my bastion; do not speak a word to anyone besides me. Each of you is well aware now of the macabre nature of the activities that occur within the hotel, but going forward, the gloves truly are off and no punches shall be pulled. I cannot stress this enough." In pervasive silence, they follow Watters into the underground section of the hotel.

Warm hues bounce across a hall dressed in party favors and balloons. Sparkling dresses and sharp, jet-black suits swim about the space. Masqueraders line the way, some lying about in cushy chairs and sofas, others dancing in tight-knit groups to an old jazz tune spinning on a gramophone. *One of those dreamy waltzes by Artie Shaw?* Theoodore mulls, listening to the clarinet-driven song. As Watters leads them further down the hall, Theodore hears Henry utter, "What the fuck?" When his eyes catch what Henry's already seen farther down the hall, he has to fight to keep himself from asking the same question. He imagines Henry's expression under his mask, his jaw dropping all the way to the floor and being too entranced even to bother picking it back up.

A mosaic of moon-white skin paints the hall. Men and women openly engaging in a host of sexual activities. On the wall to the right are a licentious pair of masqueraders with only their masks on. The man pushes the woman up against the wall and begins furiously thrusting his pelvis against her, rapaciously grasping her throat and squeezing. To the left is a masquerader propped upon a credenza, her shapely legs parted wide. Under the black netting of her dress Theodore can see a party mask bobbing up and down. Collections of sexually inclined masqueraders are disseminated through the rest of the hall, some of them casually flirting in the shadows, others ripping their mates' opulent outfits apart and digging edaciously into each other's flesh; more still are standing in the corridor and merely watching the salacious sequences unfold before them, cocktails and cigars in hand.

Theodore, Henry, and Francis tail Watters through the scene, trying to keep their composure and refrain from showcasing their surprise at the massive English orgy through which they're treading. The ecstatic caws and fervid grunts of the revelers is enough to make Theodore's stomach turn, and he finds himself burying his hands in his pockets and narrowing his frame to squeeze through the crowd without coming into contact with any wandering body parts. He passes under a monolith of a man wearing a three-piece plaid suit and an eagle mask, who peers slowly down at him, raising his gin and tonic to Theodore in a silent toast. Theodore averts his eyes and focuses on Watters ahead of him, the wolf mask weaving through the throngs like a pack animal on the hunt.

A hand clutches his sleeve and tugs hard three times. Theodore turns to find the hippopotamus' face glaring at him. "That chick is giving you the 'fuck me' look, bro," says Henry. Amongst a set of lounge chairs to the right is a cockatiel in an emerald evening dress. She follows Theodore with her eyes as he passes, the forefinger of one hand playing with the lip of her garter, her other hand buried underneath a cloche hat that's propped on her lap. He can't exactly see what's going on under the hat, but the arch in her back and the quiver in her arms is enough to clue him in. Before he's able to meld into the crowd and out of her line of sight, she bounces to her feet, dances over and begins walking alongside him, slipping a breast out from under the loose neckline of her dress. She snatches his hand out of his pocket and places it on the warm mound of flesh.

"It's okay, handsome. On this of all nights, we hold nothing back. Unleash your heart's desire, uncage the animal within; the doppelgänger that you must normally hide away." She drags his finger over the bump of her nipple.

Theodore feels a galvanized current of excitement shoot down his spine. He's never done anything like this before. It's so wrong, and it goes against the catechisms of morality his overdeveloped logical mind has taught him…and yet it feels so right in the undercurrent of his scrupulous side, the adventurous part of Theodore that's swelling to the surface with every second his hand spends upon this stranger's chest. A little fun wouldn't harm anyone. He rubs her chest, hearing Henry shouting in the background, "Get some, dude!"

She leans in for a kiss. Before her lips meet his, her cockatiel mask dissolves, and in its place is the visage of a hawk. *Vivianne*. He shakes his head and looks back to see the cockatiel once again. His mind is merely playing tricks on him, but it's reminding him of one important thing. He recoils from this solicitous stranger, feeling the sting of guilt upon his cheeks. He's not here to fulfill some bizarre sexual fantasy. Vivianne is the reason he's here; he cannot forget that.

The cockatiel pouts and flies away, landing in the welcoming arms of some other masquerader. "Theo, you got to second base in a matter of like, two seconds. That's gotta be a world record. Why'd you stop?"

"The mission, dude. We have to focus on the mission," he stammers, catching up with Watters while shaking off the jitters. "And we still have to get to the waterfront to warn the Pilfering Paupers of the ambush," he adds in a whisper. "We're running out of night here."

"Right, right, duty calls and all that. But can't we just stay in paradise for this one night?" Henry extends a hand to a topless reveler who's spinning pirouettes towards him. She pauses her twirling, taking his hand in hers and spins into his arms in a close tango. "I mean, if this isn't heaven, I don't need to know what heaven is."

"Come, gentlemen," Watters beckons them forth. "We are nearly there." They course through a maze of dusky, grand hallways. Sweeping through a firelit parlor where, in one of the darkened corners, Theodore swears he can see one naked man atop another. As if heeding some tacit call, men and women from around the room flock to the corner, strip down, and join them in one writhing heap of bodily desire.

Theodore and the others shuffle into a smoking lounge where the less overtly avaricious of the Patriciate Party dwell. On one side of the room, masqueraders huddle over decks of cards and cubes of dice. Beside them is a group of intrepid revelers playing five-finger-fillet under candlelight. Threaded through the rest of the room are batches of people engaged in simple conversation; a jarring contrast to all they've just witnessed.

Passing through, Theodore hears talk of politics, of state matters, of parliamentary concerns, and strings of casual banter between old acquaintances. In the far corner of the smoker's lounge, a raucous bare-knuckle boxing match is in session; swarms of revelers throwing cash and coin at their projected winners.

"Twenty-five quid on the indigent!" a voice pierces through the din.

"Nay! Thirty guineas on the dock worker!" another man spits.

"Eyes front, gentlemen," Watters reminds them, picking the pace up to a heavy trod. They carry on through the lounge and then some rather desolate and listless hallways.

"Watters, sir, I've been meaning to ask you to clarify a couple more things," Theodore says.

"Well, now would be the time to do so, young one. There are but a few more turns and we'll have arrived."

"Well, how did Vivianne come to know Nithercott? How did she end up a prisoner in his world?"

"A prisoner? Alas, that is a complicated question, Theodore. You see, many years ago she was an orphan child, living on the streets, lurking in the alleys behind affluent households, dining on the scraps discarded by the wealthy. He found her in that lonesome world and took her in, the exact reason for which I know not. But my theory through the years I've known the man is that Vivianne is the one piece of humanity left in him. She represents the trodden flower of his kind heart, for there was once some kindness and mirth in him, before this madness…He wrenched her from that world and put a roof over her head. And while some part of me holds that he covets her in his way, he has never once laid a finger on her, to my knowledge.

"And yet his love for her has proven to be overzealous, and through the years, his paranoid nature got the better of him. He disallowed her to leave his property or to see the young blokes that desired to court her. Perhaps his avarice this sheltered lifestyle he has foisted upon her is favorable to the hunger and destitution she would have faced on the streets. Perhaps it is not. Alas, Alger spent a great deal of time with the young lass while he lived within these walls, and this elaborate rescue plan of his was born of his ardent belief that the girl deserves a real life, a second chance. And with Alger, I fully concur."

"It seems like you don't really know her that well yourself, Watters. How can that be, after all these years?"

"My dear boy, I will state it again: these walls have eyes, eyes from which you are seldom shielded. The most substantive thing you will learn of anyone here is their favorite color; mayhap, should you be so lucky, the level of wellness to which they prefer their meats cooked. It is a superficial life in these walls, and rarely do any true kinships blossom. That is why Alger and Vivianne's connection is truly singular. Clearly, he allowed himself to become too familiar with Nithercott's youthful treasure, and he suffered the consequences before long…

"Besides, I've always known my part in this furtive game is supplementary. Were I to develop too close a bond with Vivianne as did Alger, I would not be here today to provide this crucial assistance to you all. I watch and I wait, and that is my duty in life."

"So then, how do you know so much about the hotel? It seems you know every nook and cranny, all the ins and outs."

"Why, I am the architect of The King's Inn. I designed this edifice. There are passages and hidden grottos in the hotel of which only I know, to this day. Places more secret than this section we are in now."

"With all these hidden elements, why can't the girl get away? Why couldn't Marley?"

"Nithercott's guard is a sedulous lot; ever vigilant and observant they are. Each possible exit is held under his watchful gaze, or that of one of his many henchmen. Alas, Alger has tried to save the girl on multiple occasions and the outcome has been horrendous to say the least. I will save that part of the story for him to tell. I'm sure he will detail his tribulations to you in the grooves of that record you now possess."

"So, there's a good chance we'll end up like this Marley dude if we try to save her…great," moans Henry. "I should've followed my heart and stayed with that nudist colony back there."

"Nay, young Henry. Alger spent his remaining months here plotting your escape. If all goes according to plan, you will leave the building unscathed and with the girl in tow."

"What's the deal with the barman and the doorman; everybody wearing rat masks? And what's with the lift operator and the scars on his face?"

"Nithercott's henchmen all wear the mask of their leader for two reasons: one a pragmatic purpose and one a symbolic representation. They wear his mask for quick and easy identification amongst them, but also for the underlying symbolism in such an action. The donning of his doppelgänger showcases their fealty and it exemplifies their true role as extensions of his spirit; like lesser objects of his nature. As for the scars you discerned upon their faces…Nithercott disfigures all his henchmen in this way as a sort of ritualistic assimilation. They must undergo the physical agony of having their faces carved by his acrimonious hand to prove themselves worthy. Did you notice, young Theodore, anything peculiar about the design of the scars?"

"Well, yeah, I thought they were curiously shaped like the flapping mouth of a ventriloquist's dummy."

"Capitol, young Theodore! All of his servants have these same scars upon their face for that very purpose: to show that they are but mouthpieces; silent and watchful bodies through which his actions will speak."

"Boy, Theo," says Henry, "you've really dropped me into a carnival of California King-sized crazy. Is there anyone here that's not a total freak? No offense, wolf dude."

"All right, to the next piece of confusion," glosses Theodore. "Who is Ms. Osgood?"

This inquiry seems to stanch the very flow of thoughts to Watters' brain. He hesitates before replying, "How…how do you know about *her*, future explorer?"

"Oh, uh, it was just something I discovered in his penthouse," Theodore's laconic reply.

"Ms. Annabelle Osgood was a young actress with whom Nithercott was smitten many years ago. I believe they met during work on the same production…I cannot for the life of me remember the name of it…Ah, but she was a comely and sprightly blonde; certainly, one of the most beautiful lasses upon which my lowly eyes ever found themselves. I believe they nurtured a dalliance for a little while—a doomed little thing it was, though, and it did not end well."

A maelstrom of thoughts batters Theodore's brain with this new morsel of information. Was that really her hair and her dress up there? Did she threaten to leave him, and he refused to let her go, finally killing her and then creating a shoddy effigy of her through which she could live on…in some capacity? Most importantly, Theodore acknowledges the fact that the woman's description matches that of Vivianne's. He wonders if he's finally found the crux of Nithercott's interest in Bargirl. Is the man holding her captive and pretending she's the woman that broke his heart? Is he hesitant to ask for her hand, lest she refuse, causing him to spiral into a madness and murder her?

"Did Nithercott kill Annabelle Osgood, Mr. Watters?"

"Oh no, dear boy! The girl was taken by pneumonia. And it's a damn shame, too. She was a bona fide talent, that one, and might have made it to Broadway as she aspired to do were fate not to intervene. The one peculiar item regarding her death was the mystery surrounding her interment."

"What do you mean?"

"Days after they buried the girl, a morning constable found her gravesite desecrated. Whereupon he opened the casket, much to his horror, he found her long blonde locks torn right off her skull."

And you'll never believe where those long blonde locks have ended up… thinks Theodore, feeling a map of goosebumps forming under his chesterfield. "One more question, Watters. When we saved Francis from that Harold guy in the pig mask and his henchmen, there was one other prisoner they were dragging with them. Who was he?"

A gelid silence pervades the hall while Watters gauges a response. He replies simply, "I think you shall see soon enough, young Theodore." They take one final bend in the labyrinth until they come to a narrow stretch of hall lined with rich, sanguine velvet, aureate crowned doors lining the hall on either side. In the murky corridor's end is one final pair of lustful, libido-crazed masqueraders. The man is leaning against the wall, craning his neck as if he were under the stars gazing at Orion's Belt. There's a woman in front of him, glaring starry-eyed up at him and unbuttoning the front of his dress pants below. Her curious hand dips in and combs through his trousers, pulling his desire right out from his beltline and stroking it in the low light. Theodore looks away, realizing this is probably the fifth time he's had to avert his gaze since arriving at this section of the hotel. He curses under his breath when he realizes he must approach the action in order to get to the Shibboleth.

They follow Watters about halfway down the lane, pausing before an A-Frame sign festooned with art deco letters and comical swooshes of color bespoke of a pre-World War II-era advertisement.

Tonight, we dine, we drink, and we dance, and we revel in all that makes this night special. Welcome to the Shibboleth.

The door to which the A-Frame is adjacent is crested with a golden placard.

The Treasure Trove

As Theodore and the others gather around Watters, he detects a trickle of music from within. Eager, oh so eager to discover at last the true nature of this 'Shibboleth' he's now heard so much about, he presses his ear to the wall. Cheering, clapping, a host of furtive festivities lie just beyond the door.

"Gentlemen, we have arrived. I cannot prepare you with saccharine words and trite expressions for what you are about to witness. It will be unlike anything to which the three of you have been exposed. Now, you will enter with me confidently and surely. You will walk with me and stand beside me as still as lake water in wintertime. You will not utter a word to anyone. Is that clear?"

Theodore and Francis nod.

"Crystal," says Henry, peering over to the lovers down the hall and openly shuddering at the sight of a certain buoyant body part he'd rather not be witness to. "Man, this is left field. Ever since we stepped out of that stairwell, I've felt like I've been watching a kinky vintage porno with my VR goggles on."

"With what style of goggles on, dear boy?" Watters asks.

"Never mind him," Theodore butts in. "We're ready for the Shibboleth."

Watters stops just before opening the door. "Oh, and whatever you see inside, refrain from making a single surprised peep or horrified gasp, lest you attract unnecessary attention to yourselves. As far as any of these pernicious, champagne-mongering, game-hunting, blood-coveting, wretched revelers are concerned, you have precisely as much reason and right to be here as they." He opens the door.

The hallway's crimson velvet bleeds right into the darkened walls of the Treasure Trove. The humble space within reminds Theodore of an old French cabaret: cigarette smoke churning about the room, the sweet scent of liquor conflating with a cornucopia of fragrances, indolent bodies oozing into chairs and sofas, with a sprinkling of revelers leaning against the walls about the sides. The lighting is scant, with splashes of golden hues thrown from a couple ornate Victorian sconces, illuminating the chillingly macabre grin upon the face of every reveler within. Theodore and the others follow Watters in, huddling next to him against the back wall.

He realizes with a burgeoning horror how the muted energy of the room contradicts the true nature of the Shibboleth. The action is up front and center, on a cozy Vaudevillian stage. Glowing in the beam of a single stage light, like an edacious lion poised over its prey under the burning light of the full moon, is Alfred Nithercott. His back is to them, but Theodore knows what he's doing. He hears Francis gasp when he too realizes what the Shibboleth really is. Watters glances over in an equable attempt to remind Francis to remain calm.

Fettered to a chair in front of Nithercott is the figure of a young man, enervated and broken. His face is a purple twilight of inchoate flesh. Underlying the tortured flesh are the pieces of an expression, but Theodore finds himself forcing his eyes shut before he's able to cobble the pieces together in his mind. He tries fruitlessly to slow his panicked breathing. Regardless of how sick these people are, of how deplorable their intents and their actions, he didn't expect to see them gathered before anything like this, the barbaric torture of a helpless man. Watching them, they're like a crowd of curious serfs in medieval times lining the town square, casually observing the harrowing acts of a public interrogation as if it were a game. They're all just lounging around, nonchalantly composed, as if they're viewing a forgettable cast of stand-ins performing Hamlet.

The prisoner's injuries on his face are too swollen, too unripe, to have only just been inflicted. This must be Harold the Pig's other captive that he was dragging along with Francis.

"I will ask you once more, young man," Nithercott hisses, leaning over the unfortunate prisoner with the blade of his small knife—the one with which Theodore is now intimately familiar—shimmering in his hand. "Who sent you forth to my little kingdom with the intent of subversion? Was it the Clapham Chappies? The Pilfering Paupers? The Lambeth Guns? The Hounslow Hounds? Some wretchedly desperate fifth column group that needs yet another catechist to show them their place in the scheme of things…" He rips a line of tape off the captive's lips, a rope of blood erupting from his mouth and further painting the spackled mess of red upon Nithercott's suit.

"Like…like I said before," the man sputters in an American accent. "You and your crooked cronies can kiss my stubborn Yankee ass! I'm not spilling the beans, no matter how hard you press me."

"Tis a shame, young man," Nithercott says, taking long strides behind his victim and nodding to one of his henchmen, who traipses over to the corner of the little room and dips a record onto a gramophone. "Tis a real shame, for things needed not go this way. You may very well have slinked back into the shadows like the indigent little cur you are, and my whistleblower would inevitably have fallen off your scent. All he has given me in his investigation is a codename. They call you Osprey, no?"

Osprey? Theodore nearly spurts the words right out loud. *The Pilfering Paupers' American correspondent? The guy the gang has mistaken me for on both nights one and two? No wonder he was unable to make their Battersea meeting.*

A flurry of trumpet notes erupts from the old speaker, followed by a brisk old British dance band melody; clarinets, oboes, trombones, muted horns; the pleasant effluence discordant to the exquisite horrors Theodore knows are to come. He shoots a glance over to Watters, his eyes admonishing that the old wolf understands his discomfort. Watters gives a slow nod and nothing more.

Up on the little platform, Nithercott begins twirling stage left and stage right, up and down and all about Osprey. The psychopath is humming along to the music, taking an invisible dance partner in his hands and nimbly, gracefully charting a course about the stage with her. As the band heightens to a crescendo, Nithercott waltzes back to center stage and does a quick pirouette, the coruscant blade of his knife flying through the air and slashing Osprey across his pulverized face. Osprey howls, writhing under his constraints; the chair fervently shaking beneath him. The torpid crowd oohs and aahs, perking up in their seats ever so slightly.

"For whom do you work, Osprey? Tell me and your suffering shall cease."

"Fuck you and your English nobility!" his defiant retort.

Nithercott continues prancing about the stage, apparently unaffected by the invective the bound man just flung at him. On the contrary, Theodore thinks Nithercott's hoping the poor guy will hold out as long as he can. That would give his audience the proper bloody show that they've waited months for, and frankly, at this point Theodore thinks Nithercott just likes pain; whether it's inflicted upon somebody else or even himself, he simply enjoys it.

"Duh-du-du-duh-duh," the villain's voice pervades the room as he hums along to the instrumental piece. He waltzes in front of Osprey and rips open a gap in his cotton undershirt. He shuffles away with his imaginary dance partner, circling Osprey and feigning a stab at his stomach that procures an excited gasp from the audience. Osprey slams his eyes shut and grimaces, preparing for what looks to be his death. When Nithercott resumes his dance, Osprey opens his eyes and releases a blood-curdling squall. The horrific mind games his captor is playing with him are too much to bear; they'd be too much for any man to bear. Theodore looks wide-eyed over at Henry and Francis, who return his horrified glare in tandem. He can see the shine of a tear in Francis' eye.

Threading through the room and dipping in front of every other table is a tuxedoed man in a rat mask. The tunnel vision these horrors have given him almost kept Theodore from even noticing the server, like a shadow passing by him in an old house that he'd swear was a specter. The server approaches the back wall, graceful and silent. He stops just before Theodore, blocking his view of the stage and fugaciously breaking his macabre reverie.

"A drink with which to enjoy the show, sir?" the man inquires in a flat and formal tone bespoke of an old butler. Theodore's tongue is a piece of lead in his mouth and it doesn't allow him a response. "I have a tantalizing French 75 which is, perhaps, not quite as gelid as a proper gentleman like you would prefer, as I've been making my rounds with it, but it is crafted with the finest of champagnes from France. If the gentleman is interested in something with a little more bite, I have here a delectable cocktail, the nimblest brandy with a blot of fresh clementine and a sugar rim—one of my finer embellishments; I'm quite positive it will soon catch on with the public."

"If you'll direct your attention to the middle of the tray, I have swirled up a Bee's Knees, *tres magnifique*, and perhaps more suited to the refined tastes of an American." Theodore, still unable to let a well-formed syllable, let alone a word, past his teeth, simply shakes his head at the server.

"Very well, sir." A small bow and the rat scurries away. The onlookers collectively cheer once more, some rising from their chairs and giving a standing ovation at the macabre act, others still lounging back and casually kissing their cigarette butts as if they were at a moving picture show. After surveilling the crowd, Theodore realizes the reason for the uproar; it looks like Nithercott has slashed the poor man across the other cheek and the congregation of baying animals can't get enough of it. Osprey is moaning and jerking in his restraints, causing it now to lift fully from the ground and hobble stage right a few inches.

It's sickening to see that his howls of anguish are met in volume and ferocity by the crowd's own excited wailing. Theodore's stomach tightens. He doesn't know how much more of this he can take.

"What say you, interloper?" Nithercott asks in his insincere, saccharine voice. "Will you confess to your misdeeds and provide your new family with names; the names of those who duped you and carelessly left you in this mess in which you find yourself?"

"I...I say it would be real swell if you untied me and let me put my hands around your throat, Alfred." The crowd gasps at the audacity of the prisoner. While the beatific charms of the jazz song continue in the background, Nithercott pauses, slapping the blade of his knife into the meat of his palm over and over like a teacher does a ruler when lecturing an intractable student.

"Very well..." he purrs at last, motioning to one of his henchmen just offstage. The man sweeps onto the scene, brandishing what looks to be a common dinner spoon and handing it to the interrogator. "You leave me no choice." He places his foot on the chair between Osprey's legs and, spoon in hand, readjusts his mask. He peels off his suit, then, button by button, undoes his silk vest, Osprey wriggling and moaning underneath. Once Nithercott has stripped down to his less constrictive cotton dress shirt, he hovers the dinner spoon over Osprey's face.

"What the fuck is he gonna do with that spoon?" Henry whispers the question to which Theodore would really rather not know the answer. The crowd hangs in utter suspense, their tightly coiled breaths resound through the now monastic silence of the room as the vinyl jockey swaps records on the turntable. Another discordantly joyful tune bellows from the gramophone horn as Nithercott lowers the spoon's tip against the bridge of Osprey's nose. He dips it gingerly against the tear duct of his left eye.

"Jesus Christ," Theodore hears himself say feebly, as if his own voice is coming from another room.

"What—what are you gonna? Please, God no!" Osprey's utterance falls short as Nithercott thrusts the tip of the spoon into the soft jelly of his eye. Theodore doubles over, sealing his eyes tight and fighting the ineluctable urge to vomit right here and now. He's forced to listen to the shrieks; shrieks he knows he'll never get out of his head until the day he dies. They come in desperate, staggered torrents that so effectively convey the young man's suffering. It's as if Theodore's on the very stage with him. The audience rises, clapping and cheering over the ripples of music and the thunder of Osprey's cries. Even Watters joins in with applause beside Theodore in an ostensible display of approval he must conduct in order to continue playing his hand.

With his jaw clenched and a spill of white bleeding across his knuckles under the furious squeeze of his hands, Theodore dares a peek. Onstage, Nithercott's bobbing up and down with his entire body, his elbow cranking hard and unevenly. A few masqueraders up front are actually egging him on, punching the air with their fists and yelling, mists of spittle ejecting from their mouths.

"Come now," sneers Nithercott. "Only your pesky little optic nerve remains and then it's all over. You've done so well, young man." Osprey merely howls in response, seemingly no longer registering Nithercott's voice or anything other than the searing pain emanating from his skull. Determined he's seen more than enough, and certain that if he stays one second longer, he'll spew all over the Treasure Trove, Theodore turns and stumbles out of the room. He storms into the velvet hall and throws his fist against the opposite wall, a gale of frustration tossing within him and then rising, escaping his body as one long, full throated yell. He turns to see Watters with his hands on his hips staring at him with a curious look in his eyes. Francis and Henry trundle out of the room behind him like two catatonic nuns walking out of a Tarantino movie.

"Steady, young Theodore, steady," cautions Watters, pressing his arm on Theodore's shoulder with an effect like ballast on a rocking ship. "Is everybody all right?" Nobody responds. "I feel an apology is necessary on my part," he continues, "for no one can truly be prepared for such a sight, and mayhap you three needed not see this; alas, I thought it of great import for you to witness the depth of horrors with which you are dealing. This is what they do to those that oppose them." Behind him, Osprey's muted screams continue. Every cheer, every round of applause from the audience, sends a shockwave of firing nerves down Theodore's back.

"We have to save him, we have to!" He moves for the door, but Watters stays him with a strong hand.

"No! There is nothing we can do for Osprey now. Not unless we would like to be up on stage with him." Theodore staggers away and down the hall, anywhere the barbarous interrogation can't reach his ears. The others slowly follow him down the hallway to an isolated corner.

"I very nearly was," Francis says, his voice thin, frail under the weight of the realization.

"Yes, I understand this must be particularly difficult for you, young Francis."

Theodore recalls the old newspaper clipping, seeing Francis' battered face with a darkened cavity where his eye had been. The conjured image is enough to topple the last remaining piece of Theodore's composure. He props his hands on his knees and releases a stinging soup of bile.

"There, there, young one," Watters pats him on the back. "Don't mind the mess; they'll simply assume one of their revelers let the vodka get the better of him."

"We were so close!" exclaims Theodore. "When I jumped the guy who was dragging Francis, Harold instructed the one dragging Osprey to move on. We could have saved both…if it's too late tonight, we'll save him tomorrow when we come back for Vivianne." Feeling this newfound resolve take hold, Theodore straightens up and wipes his mouth. Osprey is suffering in there tonight, there's no way around that. But coming back tomorrow night will erase the torture as easily as an eraser scrubs words off a chalkboard. He can set things right.

Francis shakes his head gravely. "Man, 1930s London is a tremendously fucked up place to be. I mean, I've seen some dark shit in 21st century America. I was living on the streets for a while before I found my niche as a liquor supplier, so I've seen some shit. But from Pinemist Bay, Oregon to Portland, Maine, I've never seen such bloodlust or depravity."

"Wow, the walking paragon for hipsters everywhere *and* living on the streets to boot?" snarls Henry. "Are you sure you don't mean Portland, *Oregon*?"

"Really, Henry?" scolds Theodore. "After all we've been through tonight—after everything we've seen—you can't get past the junior high bullying thing? Your phone, please."

"Whoa, whoa, I was only trying to lighten the tone, bro. We're like a band of brothers after all we've experienced tonight, right Bathtub Gin Guy?" Henry snaps his phone open and hands it over.

"Well, you could start by learning my name, Tubby," Francis retorts, a smile forming on his mouth and his hands quivering on his hips. Theodore blocks out the ensuing background banter and listens intently to the eerie song playing over the wavelengths of time. The segment with just strings has kicked in; the finale of the song is imminent.

"All right, we have to go," Theodores asserts. "We still have to warn the Pilfering Paupers of their danger and the night is wearing thin. The song is almost done spinning on the Sonophone back home."

"Yes, it is time," confirms Watters, patting an anemic-looking Henry on the back.

"One more thing before we go, though," Theodore says. "This is little more than a hunch, but I feel I have to tell you about that record that's playing on the Sonophone; the catalyst for the time machine. That record somehow wound up buried under the front porch of my family home in New York. My sister and I found it many years ago…Something in me, like some weird inner voice, is telling me I need to let you know which record it is, so you can plant it there for me to find. One final dead drop in this crazy series of events."

"A very astute observation, my seasoned future explorer. What is the name?"

"*A Waltz on the Veranda of Evermore* by Donald Mattley and His Orchestra."

"Oh," Watters says with an air of some affectation on which Theodore can't put his finger. "You mean, this record?" He pulls a cylinder out of his inner vest pocket with a cocky grin on his face.

"That's…that's it? That's my record? You have it already?" Theodore leans in, examining the item from all angles. It has the same yellow hue as the cylinder he dug up under the porch, the cylinder he's carried with him every day of life since, but this one's in mint condition, replete with a crisp label and an old black and white image of the band to boot. "It's the weirdest thing to see my little keepsake in such lustrous shape."

"Not to mention," adds Francis, "the fact that it's essentially extant in two places at once right now."

"I hate this spacetime shit," declares Henry, curiously glancing over Watters' shoulder. "Screws with my mind like a chick who gives you a come-hither look at a bar and then shoos you away like a pesky gnat."

"Can I hold it?" Theodore asks, his open palm extending forth.

"Nay, I'd rather you not," Watters says flatly. "I know little of this temporal jigsaw puzzle in which we find ourselves. But I shouldn't want to tamper with the delicacy of a causality loop. Your obtaining this device in two different timelines may just unravel everything we've worked towards, or worse."

"Well, let's leave it at that, then," says Theodore. "But, how did you find my record without my help?"

"You'll recall how I told you young Alger was reticent toward me in regard to his escape plan for the girl? Well, just before he approached me on that day," Watters pauses, looks to the floor, and shakes his head. "Until I die, I'll never forget the severity of his countenance that day. Alas, he told me that it was only a matter of time before they did away with him, and that he had still one more task for me. He left me with his grandfather's Sonophone and told me to obtain as many wax records as I could get my hands on, never to stop looking for them until I had found one with the right frequency for time distortion.

"Whereupon I asked him how I should know I've found the correct frequency, he merely told me that he welded the destination dial to a specific date and time which was, to us back then, years into the future. He went on to say that the machine only works in a reverse temporal direction, and that, according to his grandfather's notes, should a future date be chosen with the proper frequency in play, one would know by the machine's singular attempts to catapult him through time. The Sonophone's horn would spew waves of fragmented light before the traveler; ripples, like a rush of wind over a still pond, would permeate the air just before him.

"For the last few years Alger has been gone I have searched surreptitiously and tirelessly for phonograph records—any and all I might get my hands on. Only less than a year ago did I finally obtain the proper record." Watters stares with wonder at the simple device. "Little did I know just how much of his scheme was left to chance and little did I know just how pivotal my part would be in the execution of his plan. It is by the grace of God himself that you lads are here. We mustn't fail now."

"Okay," Theodore says at last. "You need this one last piece of the puzzle, though Watters, or everything may still be undone. I need to give you my address in the future so that future me—"

"Or past you, depending on how you look at it," adds Henry. Theodore rolls his eyes.

"Can find that record right there. If you can leave here and make the journey to New York without raising suspicion, then do so yourself. If not, then send someone you trust more dearly than anyone else, to do so. In some seventy years, I will be living on 745 Tempus Lane, Halifax, New York, in a big old colonial with a deep porch. You'll need to bury the record right under the stairs, pretty deep too, since any number of things could exhume it through the years; animals, rain, flashfloods…"

"It will be done, young Theodore."

"Oh, and Francis, you told me that you're the one who bought the Sonophone from some auction before supplying it to The Cat's Meow. What was the name of the auction?"

"Uh…it was a benefactor's auction for the London Society of History and Humanities. They were selling a portion of their museum displays. I bought the thing just thinking it was a really cool-looking old piece; I had no idea the hidden nature of the purchase I was making. And at the price point, neither did they," he chuckles.

"Okay. So, Watters, you'll have to donate the Sonophone to them, and hopefully they'll keep it in the museum display until Francis buys it from them at the auction in the future."

"It shall be done," he replies, sighing. "Well, lads, this is it. You must move on lest the night close before you complete your task. I shall say goodbye for now, and I look forward to seeing you again tomorrow night. Although…while every moment we've shared tonight will be burned into your memories, I will have no recollection of it myself. You will be rewriting history, as it were. Keep on the lookout for me, boys, as I will be looking out for you."

"Thank you, Watters, for everything you've done. For Vivianne and for us." Theodore says, giving the old man a surprise hug that he certainly wasn't expecting. Watters hesitates, and then squeezes back tightly, as if he had long missed a kind and simple gesture from another human. He pats Theodore on the back.

"There is some good left in this baleful, old world," Watters says. "All I needed to do was look to the future to find it."

"Dude, this is beyond creepy," whispers Francis. He and Henry are stalking the dock of the River Thames just behind Theodore. "This is Ridley's Scott's *Alien* being the first R-rated movie you've ever seen at the tender age of eight, eerie. Just fucking unsettling, dude."

The murky river, which spends the day churning and frothing under legions of steamboats, is now an indolent curtain of little waves that barely peak before disseminating silently in the dim void between docks. All about Theodore the air is a thick and caliginous blanket, punctured only by the occasional overhead lanterns which only escalate the eeriness of the river at night. This being Theodore's third visit does little to quell the vibe that sends shivers down his back.

Francis continues his descriptive tirade of the experience, making voluble Theodore's own thoughts. "I feel like, at any moment, from behind any one of these ratty, old barrels or those sketchy, crumbling containers, Jack the Ripper is going to stalk out and slit our throats. Or Spring-Heeled Jack might bounce down from the rooftops and steal one of us away into the murk...or any other British urban legend with the name Jack, because come to think of it there were a few of those..."

"Jack the Ripper wasn't an urban legend, bro," corrects Henry. "That guy was legit."

"Legitimately fucked up," Francis retorts, snorting. "And able to eviscerate us before we'd even notice he was on our tail."

"It's a profoundly unsettling place to be, I'll give you that," Theodore says over his shoulder. "But you don't have to worry about Jack the Ripper. Whitechapel was that guy's district of choice, and he preyed on the opposite sex. Not to mention, that was still forty some odd years ago even from this date."

"The really scary thing about this place is actually the smell, dude," Henry posits, taking in a deep sniff for emphasis. His face puckers like he's just chugged sour milk. "It's rancid out here. Like one nose-shriveling blend of human waste, mold, rotting equipment, horse shite," he spits the expletive in his best Cockney accent. "And something I can't put my finger on. Something...ripe. Like a grocery bag you forgot under your sink, only to find it a few months later with a family of maggots making their home in a mushy apple."

"So, basically your armpits after a good, long jog, right?" teases Francis. Henry shoots him a glare that says, "Buddy, I'm getting over the fact that you made Junior High hell for me, but one more comment and the two of us are through as soon as we're back in our world." Theodore knows, however, that Henry is pretty good at letting insults molt right off himself like a snake shedding its unnecessary cargo, and the guy's been the butt of jokes so much by now, he always bounces back quickly. This becomes evident as Henry's face untwists itself.

"I triple-lather my Speed Stick prior to my track meets, thank you very much, Francine," Henry replies. "But if you're feeling particularly intrepid tonight go ahead and take a whiff." He thrusts his arm skyward. "My pits got pretty moist wandering around that stuffy hotel in this heavy-ass coat. See for yourself, my dude." He begins bouncing toward Francis, his shoes playing short musical clacks against the blighted boardwalk as he clops along. Across the way, a ghostly contrail of clacks bounces between the solitary gloom of brick buildings.

"How are you guys able to josh each other after what we've just witnessed?" expostulates Theodore. "A man was just tortured, possibly to death, at the hotel, and you're teasing each other like a couple of nimrods on a casual hike."

After a ruminative pause, Henry says, "I mean, what happened back there was terrible, Theo, unthinkably terrible. But I think this whole experience is like one big sensory overload and I'm just fighting to stay in the driver's seat, you know? Besides, as they say, if you don't laugh you cry, man."

Henry's response has an oddly agreeable resonance with Theodore. He remembers the cumbersome sensory experience night one forced upon his own psyche. "Anyways, to me, the really creepy thing about these docks is the silence. It's positively suffocating. I bet if someone simply *thought* too loudly on the Chelsea Docks over there, we'd hear it."

They come upon the tall lantern casting a cone of light over the decrepit collection of shipping crates with which Theodore's now familiar. This is where Peregrine was waiting for him on nights one and two. And yet, peering through the gloom, Theodore can't see anyone at all. Are they really that late? It's certainly plausible that, with everything they did tonight involving Watters, he's more than a little behind schedule.

"Shit!" Theodore's hands find his hips as he pivots this way and that, craning his neck as he glares into the dark recesses of the shipping yard. He ambles over to the edge of the lantern's influence, peering over the crates. "Peregrine, you there?" Nothing but the rhythmic whisper of the water down below, and the bugle of a freight liner off in the distance.

"What are you looking for? Who's Peregrine?" Francis asks.

"He's one of the Pilfering Paupers, and the dude who's met me precisely here the first two nights. We must be behind schedule tonight, but I know the way to their secret meeting spot. Hopefully, they're down there now and we aren't too late to save them. Hurry up guys, follow me."

He leads them down the docks until they're in the thick of the industrial forest; factories and warehouses lining the waterfront as far as the eye can see. "Okay, just to the left here is the factory that hides their secret entrance. Now, if we do happen to find the gang, let me do the talking, guys, okay?" He barely begins powerwalking down the lane before jerking his body around once more. "That's double for you, Henry."

Halfway down the side of the mammoth power station, scintillating under the moonlight like a lighthouse in the mist is the hatch door leading to the basement. "Through here," Theodore grunts, overcoming a battle of tenacity and brawn with the hefty door. He leads them across the suspended walkway and down the stairs, into the lengthy service tunnel.

"So, you've done all of this before, Theo?" Henry asks with a snowballing anxiety detectable in his voice. "It's safe down here?"

"I mean, I can't say that no other criminal factions use these structures, many of which are derelict and many of which are still being built. There could be another group with more murderous intent lurking somewhere down here; it becomes somewhat labyrinthine. But…last night I didn't run into a soul besides the Paupers themselves, if that's any comfort to you."

"Um, no. Not really."

He opens the door to the massive, bunker-like basement of the station, indicating the plain white door at the far end to the left. "That's the entrance to The Involute Inn, as the Paupers call it. The tunnel system beneath London is crazy complex and crazy huge…remember that abandoned facility we found under the library in high school, Henry? The one we snuck into during lunch period like every day senior year?"

"Ah, the Musty Bunker, how could I forget that little gem? It wasn't just our secret lunch period hangout; I took advantage of it for most of my PE sessions, too."

"I don't think I ever knew that," Theodore exclaims. "You sneaky, lazy little devil, you. Anyway, the Involute Inn is like that times infinity. And that statement only comes with a dash of hyperbole. So, let's see how far we can make it without me getting us lost. I'm not going to risk our lives to save theirs before getting Vivianne away from that hotel." He opens the milk-white door, ushering the others through and into the damp, fusty darkness of London's underground.

"Whoa," Henry's whisper ripples down the earthy chamber. "It's like we're dust mites in a fucking chimney."

"Shh. Do you hear that?" Francis cups his hand over his ear.

"Hear what?" Theodore asks. A short silence ensues.

"Voices."

They stumble into the abyss, Theodore straining to see anything beyond the ghostly splotches effusing from the mine lanterns into an edacious dark. The farther they penetrate, the more Theodore picks up on what Francis must be hearing as voices, but to him, it's just a gargled mess of noises coming from below. Slowly, he finds he, too, discerns what sounds like a group of men in a lively, galloping banter. The voices warble through the cave, festooning it with eeriness like a colorful cloud of balloons festoons a birthday party.

"It's them!" He nearly shouts at the top of his lungs in his excitement to share with the Pilfering Paupers such a critical message.

"Whoa, hey, Theo! Wait for your future-best-man and the other guy," stammers Henry, plodding along in the darkness behind. Feeling the air pressure rise in parity with the dropping temperature, Theodore reaches the catacombs. Arched brick ceilings toss the voices about, and for a minute, Theodore realizes that if there's another exit to this underground behemoth that the Paupers happen to be taking tonight, he'll never find them in time. It'll be like trying to catch a butterfly in a mirror maze.

"Whoa, this place has some serious infrastructure, man," Francis says. "Is the underbelly of every old city like this?"

"Shh!" Theodore crosses his mouth with his index finger. "Do you hear that?" Seeping in under the trundle of echoing voices is the sound of a senescent jazz song. The very last thing Theodore wants to hear just now.

Henry pauses, panting, and then perks his ears. "Sweet and sour nipples, I can hear that! Now, who would have a stereo down here. I don't think boomboxes were even around back in the 30s."

"That's no boombox, that's the end of the record playing back home. We're running out of time! Let's move!"

They race through the catacombs as the song from another place and time swells from out of nowhere, as if it's coming from within their very minds. It becomes increasingly difficult for Theodore to separate the music from the voices. He begins to panic.

"The voices are louder this way!" Francis exclaims, beckoning them around the hull of an old whiskey barrel and down a narrow corridor.

"Christ man, were you a Labrador Retriever in your past life?" Henry asks. Theodore just keeps quiet and thanks his stars Francis has gifted ears.

As they head through the bright narrow passage, the other voices fall suddenly silent. The ripples of the last few syllables ricochet off the walls, taunting Theodore and then disappearing like the rest. "Well, shit, whadda we do now?" asks Henry, who takes point and shuffles out of the passage. Before he takes two steps further, he finds himself kissing the barrel of a large revolver, with several others looming inches from his face.

"Well, well, well, what have we here? A pack of intrepid Yanks on a midnight expedition into subterranean London?" says one.

"An innocent little venture, I'm quite sure," says another sardonically.

"Or is this but a clever artifice of the Patriciates? Well, if I've ever heard of smoke coming before the fire—"

"Hold that thought, Goshawk," interrupts Theodore. The pointed revolvers all falter slightly in surprise but remain poised and ready to blast Henry's face back to the present at any moment.

"Kestrel, Sparrowhawk, Goshawk, Heron, Snake Eagle, and Peregrine," Theodore says, pointing at each one of them in turn. A frenzy of dubious glances commences between them. "I know you all, we've met before, but I have no time to explain how! I have something very important I need to tell you before we're taken back—"

"Osprey? Is that you?" Peregrine asks, his voice faltering.

"Not exactly." The music rises to a terrifying cacophony around them. "Where's Condor?!"

Steel in his eyes, sweat on his brow, and lips parsed as tight as galvanized wire, Sir Morrow steps out from behind his men. His Luger is poised at

Theodore's forehead. "I pray you accept the cordiality of a simple nod behind the protection of a host of handguns, Yank, for this is the best I can do in this situation. Now, who are you and how is it that you be so keen on the identities of my mates? Bear in mind, one false word—a single utterance I find insufficient—and I squeeze the trigger. You'll forgive the acerbic nature of my greeting, but in the life we have chosen to lead, our enemies outnumber our allies by ten to one. Odds I shan't say I faced even in the war."

"Shit son, you guys look like hitmen in a Hitchcock movie with those old revolvers and those long coats!" Henry's inapposite comment. "And those hats—or sorry, *caps, eh chappies*?" He says in his hammy English accent. "Now, I must say, gents, I'm from New York and I've never to this day been held at gunpoint. You guys shoved like seven of them in my face and I've gotta say, it feels pretty neat. Pretty neat, indeed. There's an immediate-danger aspect to it that makes my skin tingle. My video games could never provide this kind of tension. Never."

"Shut it, Henry," Theodore interjects desperately, watching as the world starts to churn about him. The shapes of the bricks in the walls begin to swirl and mesh together. They're out of time.

"Whoa, whoa, whoa, what's happening?" asks Francis.

"Listen guys, Osprey is compromised; Nithercott and his men got to him." A collective sigh erupts beyond the uncocking hammers of the pistols. "And we've come all the way down here to warn you: this lead you think you've found—the one that's directing you to Marley—it's false. The whistleblower you think you have is actually Nithercott's whistleblower. He's duped you. He's a triple agent and the tip he's given you as to Marley's whereabouts at Doyle and Emerson Metalworks is an ambush. A handful of Nithercott's men are waiting for you right now, and with automatic weapons."

Theodore can't tell the length of the pause Morrow takes before responding. The schism between worlds is opening its maw, and will imminently swallow the three of them.

"What-what is this, Theodore?" Francis' voice is dipped in sheer panic, his arms raising as if he's anticipating a great fall.

"How do you know all of this, Yank? And why are the three of you behaving so strangely?"

"Never mind that, Condor. Just please, heed my words. What I say is true. Stay away from Doyle and Emerson Metalworks."

"Aye," Condor says, taking a cautious step back from them and commanding the Paupers to lower their firearms. They drop their weapons in unison and all stumble backwards, wondering what in the blazes these Yanks are doing. "Aye, we shan't go there tonight. But who are you, young chap, and how might I thank you for your deed?"

"Okay. Okay, Theo?" stammers Henry. "Talk to me, man. I'm not liking this feeling, man. Nope. Feels like I'm on ten rollercoasters at once and they're all taking the plunge at the same time."

"It's okay guys, we're heading back. This happens every time." He yells over the torrent of air that's prepping to suck them right up. "Now, somewhere along the spacetime continuum we're liable to get split up. You're gonna land somewhere in Manhattan, but try to keep your orientation, okay? I probably shouldn't say this until after the jump, but I was dropped in front of a moving taxi the first time—almost killed me."

Francis' eyes nearly bulge out of his head. "You what?" The rest of his and Henry's utterances become a silent movie as they are all lifted from the ground and thrust into the maelstrom of time. The last thing Theodore sees is Henry spring upon Francis' waist and hold on for dear life.

VIII

The ineluctable, frosty grip of the void simmers and broils, like a northern wind through a desert swelter. Theodore feels himself plunge into light, intense warmth, and the now-instantly recognizable state of being, proceeding the vast nothingness between his world and that of the past. In spite of the vertiginous spin his body picked up in the ether, he finds his senses returning even quicker this time than before. As the synapses in his brain fire off warning signals of the inevitable impact, he sees a peculiar shape twirling beneath him. Vivid pockets of green and pink surrounding an item of some complexity, something to which the dawn's light gives no credence. And he's heading right for it.

Brace for impact. Whatever it is, it hits back at his flailing form, hits back hard. But, with a sound like frail bones cracking and shattering, the object gives, submitting Theodore to the firmness of the ground: his final stop. But where is he? All about him the extent of the wreckage becomes clear as splintered bits of wood come raining down upon him. Latticework. He glances left and right, refusing to lift himself from the reassuringly solid and unmoving ground until he's sure he hasn't injured anything. He's in a crumbling jungle of vines, shrubs, and falling cynosures of pink and orange. Some poor sap's rooftop garden?

"Hey, what the…" an innocuous, weaselly grumble seeps over from somewhere beyond the carnage. Theodore grunts, rising slightly and rubbing his head, immediately realizing that, thankfully, his ass is the only part of him that needs tending to after that tumble. Inspecting his glutes, he finds he'd landed on something hard on the inside pocket of his Chesterfield, what was it? He sighs, palming the ceramic facade on his face to realize that, for once, he's managed to keep his doppelgänger from grenading all over the place upon re-entry. He peels it off and shoves it deep inside his coat pocket, groaning.

"Dude...bro," the lackadaisical voice trundles on. Over to the side, practically oozing into the cushions of a weather-resistant sofa is a lanky dude in an oversized New York Giants hoodie, his stick-legs jutting out of a pair of lumpy capri shorts, and the orange glow of a blunt between his thumb and forefinger. Inside the tautly drawn hood is a face which Theodore thinks just might be the paradigm of indolence and hedonism. The kid's vacant, bloodshot stare resumes as his blunt buries itself within his hood and then pokes back out, followed by a healthy plume of smoke.

"Bro, you gotta...you gotta keep it down, bro. Or else the Ice Queen will hear you...and—" A burbling, corn-popping giggle ensues. "And then this Eskimo will have to find himself another igloo. Again. If you...catch my drift, and another igloo means a rent payment on top of college tuition."

"Oh, I'm catching more than just a drift over here, buddy." Theodore grasps the only remaining ledge left in the trellised garden and hoists himself up. He sighs, reaching up and cracking his neck to the soundtrack of the Eskimo's incessant outbursts of badly suppressed laughter. He fumbles his wallet out of his back pocket and flicks the lean wad of bills out onto the debris. "For the damages, guy. It, uh, it won't exactly cover what I've done to the Ice Queen's beautiful garden, but believe me, this heap of collateral damage was made in the name of a very worthy cause."

Being greeted by nothing more than a vapid smile and a flagging thumbs up, Theodore stumbles over to the deck's sliding door.

"You wanna hit, man?"

"Mmm better save it for when you have to tell your mom about the inexplicable wreckage you made, guy." He slides open the door to the stranger's apartment. "Say, where are we? What's your address?" He needs to snag the record once more from The Cat's Meow and he needs to know if it's going to be a minor jaunt or a marathon.

"Dude, we don't—we don't need that gobbledygook around here." His free hand waves around lazily and then flops back down onto his lap. "Time and space, they're constructs man, human constructs. The only purpose they serve is to stress people out—blah, blah, blah, that's all they ever do in this city, man. They're all just a bunch of antsy, wancy, no-fun Nancies, man. Like a bunch of bobble heads down a dirt road who just realized they forgot to pay the gas bill, dude. This here," the Eskimo builds an invisible fortress with his hands. "This here is a no-stress zone, and we don't deal in minutes and hours...or addresses and...distances...we don't have addresses here, man." He hiccups. "But, if we did, I guess we'd be at 47th and 3rd." Theodore pats the stoner on the shoulder.

"Good luck, guy." He descends into the infinitesimal living/dining room. The clash and clatter of cookware tells him what the Eskimo's mom is up too. It's coming from the kitchen, which is just left of the front door. He'll have to slip by her to get out.

"Andy?" the Ice Queen hollers. "Andy, you'd better be getting ready in there or you'll be late for school. Again. And you know that Professor Lundquist really hates it when you're late to kinesiology. He'll give you another big lecture which you hate, telling you that if you had been to class on time you would have learned how to get there quicker." Clatter, clatter, crash. "Two more tardies and it's an unexcused absence. Breakfast's ready!"

It's now or never, Theodore thinks, scudding across the old hardwood of the tenement. He's scooting beyond the dining room table; he's passing the ficus on the hallway credenza; he's slipping by the kitchen threshold...

"Where is that boy?" Eskimo Andy's mom wanders out into the hall, fidgeting with her nightgown with one hand while balancing a cast iron pan in the other; coils of steam billowing from the fresh pancake within. *Shit! Be cool, Theodore, you're an intruder in somebody's home.*

"He's upstairs. Uh…becoming one with nature," he says, diving for the front door as her face peels into a look of surprise. The cast iron pan tumbles from her hand and dances across the floor, leaving in its wake mealy chunks of Eskimo Andy's breakfast. Theodore wrenches open the door and slips into the hall as the Ice Queen begins hollering to Eskimo Andy about how she already told him not to let his degenerate stoner friends into the apartment.

IX

With two gramophone cylinders in the pockets of his Chesterfield, and nothing but sleep—the sweet, felicitous arms of sleep—on his mind, he stumbles up the wide stairway to his apartment. After three pitiable attempts, or maybe more, to climb, he finally slides the key into the lock and closes the door. The requirement for rest after time travel seems to snowball until his system merely shuts down.

His eyelids are iron gates and each time he blinks he's not sure if he'll have the stamina to wrench them back open. He zombie-walks straight to his bedroom, only stopping once after seeing, upon the long convertible sofa, the intermingled bodies of Francis and Henry. Although, he's barely able to tell that it is indeed Francis since his entire form is swallowed up beneath Henry's save for a few stray wisps of orange hair. It looks like they didn't even manage to pull out the sofa so they'd both fit, nor did Henry make it all the way to his own room. They merely collapsed where they stood as soon as they got home. Both of them are snoring like an old couple who have lost too much of their hearing to tell that their significant other sounds like a buzz saw through the night. Henry's face is nestled into Francis' neck; spittle oozing out of his open mouth and trickling down the dress shirt Watters lent Francis.

Were he not so enervated, Theodore would take a moment to realize the irony of the two cuddled so tenderly on the sofa. With the history they apparently have, he imagines they would be more than a little miffed by the position in which they've thrown themselves. Or perhaps not. All three of them have been on quite the journey and he can feel that it's brought them together in a way a simple camping trip never could have. He chuckles, shakes his head, and stumbles on, turning left in the hall and falling into his bedroom door. He doesn't remove the heavy coat; he doesn't pull back the sheets; he doesn't heed the aureate cones of sunlight that are now streaming in through the window; he just lets the heavy, inexorable arms of sleep envelop him.

ACT IV

I

The bus trundles to a disgruntled stop on the main road just outside 745 Tempus Lane. Theodore scoops the six grocery bags he's laid out across a strip of seats and balances them between both arms. He hurries while doing this, not because he's inconveniencing the other passengers, his house is in the middle of—what's that term his dad uses?—*Bum fuck Egypt*. Meaning by the time the bus gets here, just about everyone has disembarked. There's only old Ms. Katherine Corgan, who's planted in her usual spot at the fore of the bus. That's the perch from where she can yammer at poor Hodges the whole way through rural New York, and the bus driver can do diddly squat about it. He spends thousands of miles and at least hundreds of fake smiles entertaining her every year. It's probably been that way forever; Theodore can only attest to the last several years he's been riding to and from school. He always sits farther back where his small frame and muted hoodie seem nearly to disappear against the gaudy blues of the vehicle's interior. And that's the way he likes it.

The real reason he's rushing to get off the bus and get back in his house is because it's 3:47 and Alice has got to be home by now. Any time she's home without Theodore, he just worries, plain and simple. It's been this nail-biting way since their mom left; coincidentally, the same time he started riding the bus for absolutely anything and everything he needs and not only for school transportation. Mom used to be the designated driver for everything since dad became the perennially designated drinker of the family. Theodore can't blame his mom for leaving—not for one second.

Jenny was a beautiful, conflicted, triumphant, tortured woman, and her greatest triumph ever was the day she decided she'd had enough. Dad had been abusing her for years. The coward would get himself just wasted enough to get swimmy and not feel the iota of conscience he must have had while sober. His sobriety the only thing scratching at his brain and exhorting him not to become a monster and thus, the one trifling obstacle in his conquest to eschew any sense of responsibility, any sense of *humanity*, which resided within him. He'd use liquor as an excuse to do whatever he wanted with her, while stopping himself before ever touching Theodore or Alice. Only mom.

No, Theodore doesn't hold Jenny's leaving against her. The one thing he can't help but hate her for is the way in which she left; packing a suitcase full of her belongings, only to be remiss of her most important possession: Alice. Young, vulnerable Alice. He doesn't blame Jenny for leaving him, he's old enough to take care of himself; and besides, he'd leave himself too if he had the chance. But he'll never forgive Jenny for abandoning her youngest. Theodore himself has done his best to fill the parenting void that's existed for Alice ever since, but he can't exactly say he's done a stellar job of it.

When it comes down to the little things moms know, like whether or not Alice prefers the crust on her PB and J, he's miserable, and things like dating advice...well, he thinks Alice is too young to be dating the stupid and callous demographic that constitutes high school boys, but even if she were going out on dates, that's really not Theodore's métier. Then again, seeing whom she ended up married to, it wouldn't exactly have been Jenny's either. And where is Jenny now?

Maybe she's with in Rhode Island with her sister, Jessica, or over in Colorado crashing on the couch of her college roommate, April, who's working in Denver as a civil engineer. For all Theodore knows, she's gotten back together with an old high school boyfriend and moved to Tibet. She's gone and never coming back. Alice needs him now; he's all she's got. And ever since Jenny left, he's made it his young life's work to see to it that she's well fed, well cared for, and most importantly, that she's never subject to the poisons of her father's mind, nor the victim of the dudgeon he holds against life. He's never laid a finger on her but the insidious possibility of it is always lurking in the periphery of Theodore's mind.

He sidesteps down the narrow aisle, nearly snagging the lowest hanging bag on a handrail and nearly losing his six-pack of cream soda to the well-trodden bus floor.

With her hands crossed over an old *Hermes* bag and a placidly inquisitive look on her face, Ms. Corgan says, "Careful there, sonny. I wouldn't like to see the bus floor drinking that pop instead of you." She winks at him. "How's your father doing these days, dearie? Keeping up with his projects around the house? Young men need projects or else they're liable to get into trouble, don't I know it."

Any question regarding his father is an icepick in his heart, and he never knows quite how to respond. "He's, uh...he's good, Ms. Corgan. Same old, really." What projects is she thinking of? Dad hasn't done a lick of work on the house in years.

"And that beautiful little sister of yours, Alice. She must be in high school by now, no?" Her gaze is abstruse—one of concern, like she knows the true nature of their domestic life. Little old ladies are perceptive creatures.

"She is, yeah. Alice is a freshman this fall. She's...she's great."

"That's wonderful, dearie. The sun shines brighter on those who work hard in their youth. I can see greater things coming to the two of you."

Okay, that's creepy. Theodore was young during the days anyone would have called the police—or perhaps a social worker—over a domestic disturbance, and maybe the neighbors were talking all along and he simply never knew it. "Well, thank you, Ms. Corgan. I'll do my best."

He hobbles off the bus and shifts the bag handles to his inner elbows, beginning the long tread down the driveway. The lawn is a pristine sprawl of green, replete with trimmed hedges along the front of the old colonial. While dad refuses to lift a hammer twice per year, he does have the income to hire landscapers. In a sense, the property becomes the archetype of American suburban life. A meticulous and serene exterior cleverly masking depravity and declension on the inside.

He hikes up the steps and fumbles for the key. All seems quiet and still on the inside. *Is dad napping? Or maybe he's still at work? Hopefully he's anywhere that's not here.* Theodore finds himself wishing this often, almost all the time. As the silvery sting of lactic acid builds up in his arms under the weight of the grocery bags, he twists the bolt open and enters, quieter than a church mouse during a sermon. Did Alice miss the bus from school? Usually by now she'd be knocking things around in the kitchen, stitching together something edible. He starts moving past the decorative banister on the staircase and that's when he hears…something. A grunt or a whimper? It sounds human, but it's so brief and low he can't tell. He stands staunchly still. His heart begins galloping in his chest, the bags suddenly becoming a heap of stones in his arms.

Another low whine followed by a sniffle and a series of hitched breaths. It's coming from the living room. Please god, let it be Alice crying over William, or some other boy at school. Please let it be simple, youthful unrequited love and not…the alternative. Someone else is in there, too, he can hear them now; breathing heavily and pacing around. No. No, this cannot be happening. Not after all these years. Theodore takes three interminable steps toward the threshold of the living room—the three hardest steps of his life. Easy does it. His feet are leaden, uncooperative, and all he can think of is running back out the front door, running hard and never stopping, leaving this god-forsaken life once and for all. But no, he won't do to Alice what Jenny did to the both of them. Never.

He rounds the sliding door to the living room and sees a demon made of flesh. Sleeves rolled up, fists clenched and shaking, sweat cascading from his forehead and streaming down his vascular arms. Down below, curled up on the rug is a bruised angel. She's covering her head with both tremulous hands. She's shivering and crying. Blood. A thin stream of blood dripping from her head.

"It's for your own good, you ungrateful little bitch! Women need a little leveling now and again to remind them who's the man, who puts food on the table. And you're old enough now to learn that this is your place." A near empty bottle of whiskey falls from his hand and jangles about his feet. "Get up," he stammers drunkenly. "Take your lesson like a real woman!"

Catatonic, she doesn't respond. She just lies there, sobbing and refusing to pull her hands away from her face. "Just like your mother." He shakes his head, wiping a sweaty clump of hair from his forehead. He paces across the room like an animal. Somewhere deep inside himself Theodore feels an immense fury boiling. It's rising, rising, rising, until he can't take it anymore. Memories of his mother's suffering flood back to him, an unshakeable pall sweeping over his mind. Seeing his little sis like this is too much. He feels his chest heaving; feels his body begin to shake, coursing with a reawakened hatred for his father.

"Fine. You're not gonna take it like a real woman. So, I'm gonna treat you like a fucking dog!" His father lunges forward, hurling his fists upon Alice. In a moment of utter clarity, the mottled storm of rage that's been building in Theodore suddenly clears. The grocery bags fall from his hands. He doesn't hear them hit the floor. He steps forward, becoming the man his sister needs him to be with each and every step he takes. He sucks in a deep breath. "No," is all he says.

He reaches out with firm, steady hands, snatching his father around the neck and pulling with all might against the tyrant who's attacking his sister. He wrenches his father away from her and drives him into the wall, their bodies both connecting with a force that makes the walls shudder. Down goes the monster immediately to the floor where he splays out like a bloated, beached whale.

"What the fuck? Theodore?"

He lunges upon the man—the somatic mess of alcohol-fueled dejection that once was a man—with a fire burning behind his eyes, and in his heart a determination he's never felt before. His father raises his hands defensively, but it's a flimsy redoubt against Theodore's laser focus. He slams his father's head back and begins flailing both coiled fists upon his face. Again, and again and again; he can't stop himself. Little red salvos of blood spray the rug.

"You god damn son of a bitch!" yells Theodore, unleashing years of bridled terror and repulsion into his target. A fearful force overtakes him, and he can't quell the emotional stampede that's driving his fists if he tried. Theodore hits him for the need to protect Alice; he hits him for all the times he caused Jenny pain and for all the times Theodore was too small and too young to protect her; he hits him for all the anguish he's caused the ones Theodore loves; he hits him because he knows a part of Alice and himself has been forever vitiated; the immortalization of his father within them evident in that which he has taken…their innocence, their security, their trust.

Finally, panting and crying, Theodore lowers his arms, letting the physical manifestation of his hurt fall from his body like rain. He stands slowly. He sighs. Never in his life has he looked upon his father this way. Now *he's* the towering one, standing tall and unafraid. As the engine of anger inside him slows to a halt, he finds a discordant stream of emotions overtake him. The fervent, blooming hatred is still there. He knows *that* will never leave for the rest of his life, but it's overshadowed by a penetrative sadness. He pities this shell of a man that lies broken beneath him. He uncoils his fists, simply staring down as this dogged tug of war pulls his mind in two. It isn't until he hears Alice moaning in the corner that his internal struggle breaks.

Between labored breaths he stammers, "If you ever touch her again, I swear to god I'll kill you." Then he falls before Alice, gently prying her hands from her head to reveal a face stripped of emotion and laden with welts. His heart falls. The air evacuates his lungs and he's not sure he'll be able to find it in himself to retrieve any more, not as long as he's looking at her wounded visage. He touches her cheek with an adamant hand still shaking with the potency of love and protection.

"Alice?" She begins to sob, wrapping her arms around his neck. "Alice, I'm getting you out of here. We're leaving right now and never coming back." He finds it hard to muster the words. Rational thought is dawning on the horizon. "I'm gonna go pack a bag for you and...and one for me and we're gonna get out of here, okay?" She barely nods her head in response, but that's all right. For what he's about to commit himself to he needs more reassurance from himself than he does from her right now. "I'll get a job somewhere in the city. There's plenty of work there, so there's gotta be something for a guy like me, with no experience. And you won't need to live through this anymore...Oh god, Alice, we've been living so small for so long."

"Okay," she says. And that's all he needs to hear. He runs upstairs, refusing to glance down even once at the pitiful man on the floor. If he sees his father just one more time, he'll begin to imagine him alone in this big house with only the demons inside his head and a bottle of booze in his hand to quell their voices. One glance, and Theodore's walls might crumble, and he just might stay.

II

Theodore paws at the bedside table, wiping the crust from his eyes and shaking his head. He snatches up his flip phone and snaps it open. Through the window and over the buildings across the wide, cobbled intersection he sees a latticework of aubergine rays cooling the sky. It's early evening; he's slept in a little later than the last couple days. He peers into his phone's tiny screen, squinting. One voicemail from Alice. He grins. This is the one way in which she operates like clockwork. Knowing her as well as he does, he can never predict where she is or what she's doing, but he can always know she'll be checking in on him every day. It's a consistency he appreciates.

"*Bear, I hope you spent the night cuddling up to the priceless antique I let you abscond with yesterday. Okay, the old gramophone isn't exactly priceless, but she is valuable merchandise. Merchandise that Vincent wouldn't have wanted wandering off unless it meant filling his pockets with a little green. So, caress her, cradle her, fawn over her all you want, but for god sake do not damage the old girl. The last few days feel a little weird, Bear. It's like you've got something going on and you don't want your little sis to find out.*

"*Little did you know, I'm quite resourceful and I will discover precisely what's going on over there in your secret lab. Listen, I'm your sister and I love you, but if bulls aren't supposed to run amok in china shops, shouldn't bears be prohibited from doing so in science labs? You're up to something. I feel like I'm usually the one who gets into weird shit and you're typically the one who gets to wonder what's up, and I gotta say, it sucks being on this end of things. Anyways, love you and miss you. Hopefully I'll have my bro back before too long."*

He chuckles, rolls out of bed with the tail of his Chesterfield flapping in tow, and heads from his little bedroom toward the cacophony of voices in the living room. It's an odd scene he stumbles upon. The apartment, which is never exactly the apotheosis of clean, looks particularly ransacked this evening. The only instances of tidying that ever happen are by his hand or Alice's, when she shows up unannounced with a pair of rubber gloves in her hands and the mysterious alacrity in her eyes that she so frequently gets when she decides she's determined to do something. The fact that Theodore's been preoccupied with time travel lately is readily apparent by the state of things. It's like Henry stepped on an IED of snack bags and soda cans and refused to clean up the damage.

Over by the rubble of the kitchenette, stooped over the little high table which Theodore and Henry usually eat breakfast over are Francis and Henry, prodigious mugs of coffee in hand and a shared look of excitement in their bloodshot eyes. They're rapidly gibbering on separate tangents of conversation, and it's unclear whether the one is hearing the other at all or if they're both so stunned by what happened last night that they just need to verbalize their thoughts to the rims of their coffee mugs. But it looks like they've put their disagreeable past behind themselves, and that makes Theodore smile. It's as if, for the first time in his life, he has his own friend circle.

"No, no, no. Dude, the coolest part about it all was not even the massive, old, English orgy we stumbled upon," Henry shakes his head. "And you'd think I'd never say that wasn't the coolest. But the single most bad-fucking-ass thing about last night was the atmosphere of dread, man. It was around every corner; it was in the eyes of, like, every reveler."

"I don't know, man, that masked orgy was pretty crazy. Not to mention just how…different everything felt. It was like watching a movie with a heavy grain filter or sepia tones throughout. It was our world…but not our wor—"

Henry raises a hand with a swimmy, almost-stoned look in his eyes. "Dude, you're like, blowing my mind with your profundity right now." He takes a long slurp of coffee with a rattling hand. Francis glances over at Theodore, his bruise-laden face a deeper purple than it was last night. The swelling is already down, though.

"Oh," he stands up straight and then bows with his arms wide, like a bad impresario at an off-Broadway theater. "Welcome back to the 21st century, fellow time-warper."

"Hey, sleeping beauty!" Henry raises his mug.

"We made time our bitch last night," continues Francis, staring off into the living room furniture as if speaking to himself again. Theodore ambles into the kitchenette; pours himself a stiff mug of black coffee.

"How many pots have you guys made?" he asks, glancing at the remnants of coffee inside the tin.

Henry just giggles into his mug, creating a gurgling morass of bubbles out of the drink's surface. Theodore takes a Viking-swig of his own coffee and wedges himself between them at the high table.

"So, elephant in the room," he says. "Francis, how did you end up serving as Henry's human mattress in our apartment this morning? I only met you three nights ago and I'm positive I didn't share my address with you. Did the spacetime continuum happen to dump you guys at the same spot?" Francis and Henry exchange looks; Francis's is one of loosely bridled excitement; Henry looks like he just bit into a punchy star fruit.

"Not exactly. But we must have been deposited pretty close together because after I landed, I started to head over to the Queensboro Bridge to get back home to Brooklyn. I came upon Henrietta here only a few blocks from where I landed and, in his barely intelligible, post-time travel voice, he told me I could crash at your guys' place. We both traipsed back like the undead in a zombie marathon and we ended up here sometime mid-morning."

"What's so funny about that, Francis?" Theodore asks. "You look like you're going to bust a gut if you hold in that laughter any longer."

Francis props his elbows on the coffee-stained table. "It's about where Henrietta landed, man. I couldn't make that shit up! I had a near death experience coming back, but I'd take that any day over what happened to him. All right, so I was beamed down near Museum Mile, along Central Park East, where a bullet riding a bicycle nearly ran me down. I ended up untouched and totally fine—he swerved out of the way in the nick of time. I, being a magical teleporting pedestrian scared the crap out of him, though, and caused him to hurl his skinny ass into the street and almost into oncoming traffic."

"Serves him right for peddling on the sidewalk in the first place," says Henry stoically, scooting over to the cupboard above the only mini fridge they could find that would fit in the sardine can they call an apartment. He brandishes three different cereal boxes, all of them different flavors. Theodore need not watch him to know that the next thing he's going to grab is the gallon of heavy cream from the top shelf of the mini fridge. "Time for a little pre-breakfast snack, gents."

Henry grabs the biggest bowl he can find, shakes a heap from each box until all the colors of the rainbow are nestled in the bowl, and then he dips the heavy cream over the bowl until the contents spill over the sides. Only when there are chunks of cereal floating around on the counter does he decide it's time to stop the flow. He does this every morning; the mess is just part of the routine, Theodore has decided.

"Pre-breakfast?" Francis leers over his shoulder. "Shit man, the caloric density of that food heap would satisfy a large mule." He shakes his head and Theodore just shrugs, smiling.

"Anyways," Theodore realigns the conversation. "What happened during your re-entry, Henry?" Francis begins to chortle mid-sip, flicking beads of coffee onto his now glistening beard.

"Yeah, what did happen to you this morning, Henrietta?" A deaf person would pick up on the sardonic texture in Francis' voice.

"Well, I uh…I sort of, oh man don't make me relive it, dude."

"Come on…" chides Francis.

"Well, I sort of got to second base with a cougar."

"He landed in some posh, wealthy, old couple's apartment on the East Side; on their bed; in between them; during their…precious coital moment."

"No way!" Theodore succumbs to a real throaty laugh; something he hasn't let himself do for some time. "And I thought I had it bad when I was nearly pancaked by a taxi after night one, or nearly beaten to death by a volcanic little vendor in Chinatown for defiling her wares after night two."

Indignant, Henry shoves a spoonful of cereal into his mouth. "It's not comical in the least. I very nearly got to fourth base with grandpa when I landed, ass-up right in front of him."

In unison, Theodore and Francis color the table with streaks of spewed caffeine. "Whoa, whoa, whoa, let me get this straight. You came down on the bed of this poor old couple, creating a Henry James sandwich…and you were the bologna?"

"It was a nightmare, Theo. I'm talking silken sheets, gilded bedposts, Renaissance art along the walls, and two affluent, old geezers, stripped naked and ready to devour each other. I plopped down right on top of the old chick, diving face first into her sweaty, seasoned bosom, and when I resurfaced, I felt something poke the back of my Chesterfield. I turned to see a dude old enough to remember America before Eisenhower. I'm still hoping it was just his disapproving finger poking my butt cheek while he was yelling arcane obscenities at me."

Francis slaps his knee over and over, trying to contain a convulsive fit of laughter and failing miserably. "So, what was your re-entry experience like Theodore?"

"Oh, after Henry's juicy little anecdote my experience seems rather banal. I landed on someone's terrace garden, had a transcendent discussion with a stoner, and scared the crap out of a single mother in her apartment."

Francis shakes his head and wipes a dish cloth across his beard. "Oh, this is classic! I almost get clipped by a speeding cyclist, you destroy a rooftop garden, and Henrietta motorboats old titties and gets violated by the last dude on earth who can tell you what life in the 1800s was like. You can't make this shit up!"

"So, I'm assuming that in the whirlwind of boobs, bedposts, and bicycles, neither of you managed to hold onto your masks?" Theodore says. One shrugs and the other shakes his head.

Francis rises and approaches Henry, whose acerbic expression softens when Francis throws an arm around him and gives him a good noogie. "Oh, I'm only joshing you, dude. You're far braver a man than Theodore or myself. Now, make me one of those incandescent concoctions that will henceforth be named 'Henry in a Bowl.'"

"Make that Henry in Two Bowls," says Theodore, "We've got a long night ahead of us and my stomach is munching on itself." He reaches into his pocket and, with a care and reverence he would typically use when handling something like the Declaration of Independence, he brandishes last night's prize: the final gramophone record. "I'm going to put the final piece of this puzzle together."

Before he manages even to pivot toward his bedroom, he hears a clatter and turns to see Henry and Francis elbowing each other across the living room like a couple of delinquent kids who've just been released from detention. "If you thought for one second…" gibbers Henry, thrusting a well-placed jab at Francis' cheek, "that you'd be listening to the old geezer's plans—damn dude," he exclaims at Francis, who's snatched his wrist and looks ready to hurl him into the sofa. "You're like a bull on growth hormones, Francine."

He wriggles free and, nearly panting from the turmoil with Francis, smiles at Theodore. "If you thought for one second that you'd be listening to that old geezer's plans without us in tow, you're…well, you're the reclusive Theodore that I thought you were. But that's not happening, bro."

"Yeah man, we're just as invested in this situation as you now. I mean, I was abducted from the lounge, had a sack put over my head, and got tread upon like an old carpet. I get that this whole Bargirl thing is very personal to you, and I respect that, but I think I'm entitled to the inner workings of this conspiracy. I've paid my dues." He points to his gnawed face.

"Oh, yeah, totally. Sorry guys, I didn't consider your part in all this. My mind's a bit of a crazy jumble right now, but you're more than welcome. I wouldn't have any two other people along with me on this adventure. Well, save for a couple of Navy Seals, maybe."

They file into Theodore's room and he readies the old phonograph machine in a manner delicate enough to please Alice were she, too, standing behind him. Henry and Francis stoop over the back of his chair, their hands gripping the chairback with white-knuckle intensity. He places the needle over the cylinder; a fluttering of static warbles emanating from the horn and then an encapsulating silence. Theodore can feel his heart quicken, can hear the squishy thrum of his blood squeezing through his jugular.

"*Hello Future Explorer,*" the distinctly senescent voice of Alger Marley says.

"*If you are hearing me now it means you possess the perspicacity not only to find the proper frequency to open the spacetime rift, but that you have found the first and second of my dead drops as well. You are truly remarkable—an angel sent from above, Future Explorer—and it seems fate has placed you into this most unfortunate of circumstances. Not long ago, I was but a captive in The King's Inn. You must pardon the gravel in my voice, but I need to whisper, for while I am now living in a safehouse far away from that den of corruption, I mustn't grow too comfortable with my surroundings. Even in this new place—the location of which I shan't provide for the sake of both my security and Vivianne's—I must remain vigilant. If you are attempting to ascertain just how it's possible that I am now far from the hotel, and yet somehow this recording found itself waiting for you under Nithercott's floor, the answer is deceptively simple: an associate of mine from across the pond has infiltrated The King's Inn under the guise of a wealthy Englishman. I will refer to him by his codename, Osprey.*

"A loyal friend of mine, Osprey, has agreed to smuggle in a record to my pre-determined dead drop within the hotel. I met him in the city, not far from my safehouse, and if there is a bloke I can trust with my life, I daresay it is Osprey. Alas, I can never be too cautious in my present situation. There is more at stake now than my own humble little life; therefore, I chose a bustling public space to meet him and hand off my record. I warned him at that meeting of the danger involved and still he has agreed to assist me in my greatest moment of need. He knows not of my compatriot, Desmond Morrow, nor of Morrow's Pilfering Paupers, who are sure to be searching for me tirelessly even as I speak. Although, I fear that Osprey's curiosity and sagacity will avail him of my connection to those rabble-rousers, and he might just plan a meeting with them in order to disclose my whereabouts. He feels England needs me. Whether or not he is correct is irrelevant. I have been relegated to this life, Future Explorer. A life of hiding.

"I have much to tell you and precious little time left on the record, so suffice it to say that two summers ago, I discovered that Nithercott was plotting to end my life once and for all. It was only a matter of time before they came to my quarters, blindfolded me like a poor sod atop the gallows, and carted me off into the desolate husk of Gravesend to put a bullet between my eyes. Off to the open ocean would my cooling corpse drift, never to be seen again. Worry not for me, Future Explorer, for when that day came, and I was taken off to be killed at gunpoint by Nithercott's henchmen, I managed to think on my feet for once—mayhap the singular time in my life I've done so—and snatched the revolver from my executioner's hand. Naturally, I fled with the town car in which they brought me. On that pensive drive back to London I came to the heartbreaking realization that, from there on out, all I could ever bring to Vivianne was peril. As I picked up the shattering pieces of my heart there on that unfeeling stretch of road, I realized that if I truly cared for her, I'd let go of her.

"Allow me to explain briefly the circumstances regarding my precious and sweet Vivianne. Like Calliope to the poet's tireless hand, Vivianne has *struck me in the years I have known her. She deserves far greater than the prison into which she was thrust in her youth.*

"Throughout my miserable sojourn at the hotel, I tried multiple times to save the girl. I exhausted every method at my disposal to remove her, and each time had been a dejection worse than the last. My final attempt was but a couple years ago, and we came so close—so very, very close—to absconding from there once and for all. But Alfred is a conniving little devil and, should he deem it be so, not a single incipient thought in a guest's mind might escape those walls, let alone an entire person. Each time he caught Vivianne and me, he invoked some wrath upon her so as to punish me to the highest possible degree. The first two instances his wrath took form of something rather innocuous, such as the enforcement of a strict curfew upon her: forbidding her to interact with hotel guests, and other social injunctions.

"This last retributive act, however, was something so sinister and barbarous that it pains me merely to immortalize its memory into the grooves of this record. By our third attempt, Alfred had had enough of my meddling in his affairs—and you must understand, Future Explorer—that in his own twisted and poisonous way, Alfred cares for the girl; mayhap Dracula cared for Lucy in his own way. You see, Alfred raised Vivianne from a very young age, after all. Therefore, his discovery of our bond proved too much for him to handle, and on our final escape attempt, Alfred inflicted his trademark act of torture upon her. He...he gouged out her left eye."

Theodore feels the fingers of nausea stab into his stomach. He succumbs to a lightheadedness, hitching wildly for breaths. He wrenches the needle abruptly from the record to the sounding of gasps from Henry and Francis behind. "He did what?!"

"Holy shit, man," Henry drops a concerned hand on Theodore's shoulder. Francis just stares wide-eyed at the phonograph machine.

"How could he?" stammers Theodore. "How *dare* he do that to her?"

"I mean, you'd know if he did, wouldn't you, Theodore?" reasons Francis. "You've spent some...intimate time with her."

"Yeah but, she kept her mask on. I've never once seen her without it. And it has this mesh over the eye slits so that you really can't see her eyes. Fuck…"

"Well," says Henry in a surprisingly gentle, mature voice, "if you and Marley are talking about the same girl, then…I guess it's true, Theo." He pats Theodore on the shoulder, who replaces the record needle with a shuddering hand.

"Alas, this is why I knew I must forbid myself from ever regaining contact with her, Future Explorer…it would be an act of insanity to do so. My poor Vivianne…Well, time eludes us once more, and I must yet relate my grand plan to you."

"What's that in the background?" Francis' keen ears have detected something yet again of which the other two were remiss.

Theodore leans in toward the crummy speaker. Suddenly, submissive to Marley's voice is a garbled undercurrent of indistinct noise, inhumed within the static to the point where Theodore almost has to convince himself he's actually hearing…something.

"It sounds like a voice," Francis shrugs. "But there's no way I'm gonna make out what they're saying."

"Probably just some construction guys or whatever outside the window of his safehouse, wherever he is," Henry posits.

"Maybe," says Theodore.

"As I detailed on my first recording, I spent a great deal of my time at the hotel studying Nithercott and his henchmen. They're all remarkably predictable in their patterns. Especially so on the night of a Shibboleth. Thus, I have welded the dial of the Sonophone to deposit you on a future date of the semi-annual event. The only moving piece in this scheme is Vivianne herself, as she is more mercurial in nature than those simpletons. The salient task of finding her will be up to you and you alone, Future Explorer. And so, without further ado, here is my plan…"

"Whoa," Francis' laconic response.

Henry raises him a dumbstruck, "Wow."

"A lot of moving pieces in that plan..." Theodore suggests, anxiously chipping away at his thumbnail with his teeth.

"You guys think we can pull it off?" Francis asks.

"With Watters' guidance and my determination to get Vivianne the fuck out of that hellish place, yes, I think we can. Only, I'm officially making an addendum to Marley's scheme: we're saving Osprey first."

"Theo, are you out of your mind? You heard the old dude. Everything needs to be accomplished just as he says. We can't just go modifying the already-farfetched plan."

"Think about it, Henry. The two of us and Watters were able to get Francis away from Harold and his men. If all three of us plus Watters ambush them like before we can save him. He's not a part of Marley's plan because Marley had no idea Nithercott would discover his real cause and that Osprey's safety would become compromised. The guy suffered so badly last night; we can't just leave him to torture and inevitable death, you guys."

"The only thing is, Theo, it wasn't us *and* Watters who saved Francis, it was Watters who came to our rescue and then Francis's. You and I were goners until he showed up. Doing something similar would just be a calculated snafu, man."

After a ruminative pause, Francis says, "I'm with Theodore. The dude needs our help just like *I* did, and I can tell you first hand, that whole situation was fucked—the most horrific thing ever to happen to me and you guys saved me before I was dragged onto the stage like him."

Henry shrugs, "All right, you suicidal, loony-ass-bastards. We'll do it."

Francis whips out his phone. "I'm just gonna step out and make a phone call really quick."

"Henry," Theodore says, scooping up the phonograph machine and clopping over to the door with the ponderous device. "I have an idea and it involves making use of your tech-savvy ways. Would you kindly get the door for me?"

Henry shuffles over. "You are a curious little man, Theo. Where you takin' that hunk of scrap metal to?"

"Oh, just down the hall. Can you get your door for me now?"

"Oh no, you're not taking that arcane toaster into my Mancave of Technological Marvel, no way! That'd be like plopping a geezer from a Missouri old folks home down in central Dubai, it wouldn't gel, wouldn't feng shui, bro." Henry trundles defiantly after Theodore, who manages to pry open the door to Henry's Mancave of Technological Marvel on his own. Theodore sets down the phonograph machine on the twin bed. "All right. So, I was thinking, you know the garbled nonsense that's barely audible in the background of the record at that one point? There's something more to it than white noise; I can feel it in my bones."

"Okay…"

"So, with you being Mr. Gizmo, I was thinking you could find some way to use modern tech to isolate that noise in a way so we can tell precisely what it is."

"Okay, but what for?"

"Well, what if it is a couple of construction workers on a lunch break? Their conversation might clue us into where Marley is hiding. *Was* hiding, rather."

"Gotcha. But the dude was pretty crystal about not wanting to be found, Theo. For the girl's safety and his own."

"Right. But the way I see it, if we're successful, we'll be bringing her back with us to the modern day, far away from The King's Inn and those monsters inside. She really cared for this Marley dude, and I don't think she'd want him wasting away in some safehouse for the rest of his years. We find him, and we could bring him back just like her: almost a century away from harm."

"In terms of running from vicious antagonists, you can't get much farther than that." Henry scratches the budding little copse on his chin. He's gone over a day without a lick of hygiene. Theodore's gone over three. He brings his hand to his mouth and exhales. Rancid.

"All right man let's do it!" Henry says, with a sudden voracity in his eyes. "You have come to the right place, my friend." He hustles over to the desk and thrusts his arms into the dense tangle of cords and gadgets, an explorer trying to hack through a technological jungle with a dull machete. Eventually, he exhumes from the thicket a corded studio microphone.

"Here's the plan, Stan." He plugs in the USB end to his desktop computer. "While I boot up mission control, you'll find the spot on the record where that little audio anomaly happens. This bad boy will sit right in front of the speaker and record it into my crafty little software program, which is gonna allow me to manipulate the sample of audio and hopefully isolate it."

Theodore winds up the lever on the phonograph and places the needle at about the section in which he thinks the mysterious background noise occurred.

"*This last retributive act, however, was something so sinister and barbarous—*" Theodore scoops the needle off and readjusts the cylinder slightly forward. Henry loads his editing application and presses the big red record button, with a casual thumbs-up to Theodore, who pauses before easing the needle back down. "What's this program called, anyways?"

"Stentorian Sound Suite," says Henry, his usually maladroit fingers looking rather nimble as they clack out commands across the keyboard.

"Fitting name." He replaces the needle.

"*Well, time eludes us once more, and I must yet relate my grand plan to you...*" Theodore sits with his fists anxiously clenched until the mysterious noise fades.

"And that's a wrap," Henry announces, ending the recording and signaling for Theodore to can the audio. "Although that was the cakewalk of the process. I'm gonna be a few minutes here trying to isolate the noise properly. I've done this before, but that wasn't with a phono-whatchamathingy. There's enough ambient interference in that audio to give a deaf dude a headache." The recorded audio appears in the application as a lengthy green bar surrounded by a cornucopia of digital buttons, toggles, and meters. Henry plugs his noise-cancelling headphones into the computer and begins tinkering with what looks like every possible editing tool, shrinking and expanding sections of the green audio bar until it becomes a pixelated accordion on the screen.

"The real bitch," says Henry, without pausing once from his tinkering, "is to separate that sound from the dude's voice. And lemme tell ya, he likes to jabber. Like, there's barely a moment where the mystery sound is there without him blabbing over it." A few minutes elapse before Henry passes the headphones over to Theodore. "What do you think of that?" He crosses his arms over his big belly and smiles exaltingly. He hits the playback button.

Through some miracle of modern technology, Theodore finds he can almost no longer hear Marley's voice at all. It's soft as a rustle of leaves beneath one's feet. The mystery noise comes crashing in after a moment in one long, chunky, static-filled blare, followed by an inscrutable sound that might be someone's voice, and then one more massive blare. "I think those are traffic noises," Theodore postulates. "Someone's honking his horn at someone else and yelling, and then the other dude honks back at him."

Henry snatches the headphones back and resumes conducting his symphony of aural exhumation. Theodore ambles over to the window, peels the shades up, and peers out into the city. The daylight is waning. Moribund columns of light teeter over the tenements across the street, drawing an animated legion of shadows across the Meatpacking District. Perhaps it's due to the abundance of objects that make up this vast city, but the evening shadows never cease searching for another surface to waver upon, their shapes diving onto the cobbled streets and transmogrifying into a series of sinister creatures before creeping upwards and preying upon the crevices between buildings.

The peculiar life Manhattan embodies after dark has long inspired

Theodore. Autonomously, as if his own personal agency has drifted off into the shadows of the street, he reaches for a pen and pad, and begins scrawling a little ode to Vivianne, the girl who defies temporal boundaries; the girl who stole his heart in the past, and whose absence in the present merely magnifies her prominence and unassuming assertions; the girl whose future—

"Got it!" Henry's jarring exclamation rouses Theodore, who turns to see his friend fist pumping the ceiling in his typical celebratory fashion.

"You isolated the noise? What is it, what are they saying?" Theodore cadges the headphones from Henry and does the one thing his technologically illiterate brain can do in a program like 'Stentorian Sound Suite': he pushes play.

"Well, time eludes us once more, and I must yet relate my grand plan to you..." The now-familiar segment plays out once more, but as soon as this enigmatic sound makes its entrance, Marley's voice shrinks to an infinitesimal drone on the track. Henry's manipulated the audio to the point where Marley's narration is but a star in a new constellation of sounds. First, the amplified static erupts, spilling over the track like a round of applause ushering in a stage performer at the Globe, then the main act begins.

A bellowing horn shatters the static, consuming the audio track for several seconds. An entire ecosystem of mechanical noises follows, the slow chug of gears and levers, the blowing of steam through a chimney. This all comes to a standstill, capitulating to the crackle of something distinctly human. A man's voice pierces through the layers of media in which he's been immortalized: the analog record Marley inadvertently captured the voice upon, the digital reproduction of that audio over the studio microphone, and Henry's further remediation of it all through software manipulation. The voice now sounds eerily robotic and manufactured after the technological torture to which it's been subjected, but Theodore has no trouble this time hearing what the man says.

"Mersey Road! This stop Mersey Road! Next stop St. Michaels! All aboard for St. Michaels!" One more massive horn blare and the audio track

continues with Marley's narration once more.

"It's a train conductor!" Theodore grins wide and grabs Henry by the shoulders, shaking him and bouncing up and down in his loafers like a child. "You did it, Henry! I knew I could count on you, man." Henry stumbles to his feet, coming within a hair's breadth of knocking his precious computer right off its stand. The resilient thing wobbles on its stubs and then rights itself.

"I did it!" he announces, locking hands with Theodore and joining in on the plyometric celebration. When their eyes meet and they start to realize what a couple of dorks they are, they immediately break off, averting each other's gaze like two teenagers who've just had their first-date kiss and don't quite know what to do next. Theodore clears his throat and thrusts his hands on his hips; Henry adjusts his glasses and stares at the monitor awkwardly. They look at each other once more, and then do what all embarrassed men who have just caught themselves in a childish display of excitement do. They grumble and shake hands.

Theodore smirks and shakes his head. "To hell with it." He embraces Henry in a big, long overdue hug. Henry reciprocates the gesture, and Theodore thinks he can almost hear a little hitch in Henry's breathing, then feels him begin to sob on his shoulder. He pulls away to see the shine of tears streaming down Henry's face.

"Sorry, Theo, I just—I thought we'd never be friends again." Henry swipes off his glasses, stretches the collar of his shirt, and begins dabbing his eyes with the crew neck. "I thought you'd never wanna spend time with me again, you know? With the way things were headed lately."

"Nonsense, man. You're my Sam Gamgee, Henry. You're the one who puts up with my BS and then saves the day, which you basically just did right now. Now, pull up a web browser and search St. Michaels and Mersey Road stations.'" Henry pinches his glasses back on and does the search.

"We're looking at Liverpool, my dude, not too far from the river it looks like."

"So that's where Marley's hiding, eh?"

"Shh, shh, shh." Henry motions with his hand to shut up. "Is that a girl's voice in our apartment?" Theodore moves to the door and opens it. He hears Francis' baritone voice shaking the living room, and then the softer cadence of a girl's voice in the pauses between. It only takes about two syllables to determine who the girl is.

"Oh, no. No way. This isn't happening." He marches out into the hall. The little balloon of elation that's been floating around inside him since their clever little discovery violently pops and spirals down to earth as soon as he lays eyes upon her. Standing there by the front door is Alice, looking somehow nonchalant and yet sprightly at the same time, as only she can. The one person in the entire world he doesn't want in his apartment right now is standing there at the threshold, her shoes already shed as if she plans on sticking around. She can't be here. Theodore has purposely kept her in the dark these last few days because of the significant danger of the situation. And her lust for adventure would be too great to keep her away if she knew the truth about what Theodore's been up to. She simply cannot get involved.

To add insult to injury, her arms are crossed around Francis' neck. While Francis is a fine guy—less cringe-worthy than Theodore originally deduced when they first met—he's not good enough for Alice. He'd probably end up abusing her or breaking her heart, and Theodore can't have that happen.

Still unaware that Theodore slunk into the hallway, Alice places a delicate finger over Francis' face. Her eyes are swimming with budding tears; her lips pursed with a grave concern as she's taken note of the ginger-haired skyscraper's battle wounds. "What did they do to you, Francis?" she asks, running her hand down his neck. He puts his oafish hands across her lower back. She's looking unassuming and yet spellbinding in her usual blue and white sundress. Her hair is more finessed than usual, and Theodore thinks he sees a hint of lipstick on her face, which is something she only wears on first or maybe second dates with guys.

"Ahem!" Theodore drives a wedge in their tender moment. Alice glances over and her sharp eyes flicker like two headlamps powered by a faulty battery.

"*There's* that brother of mine that's decided it's appropriate to do the vanishing act on me day after day." She stomps over to Theodore with her finger wagging the whole way. Her face is awash with repudiation. "Now, just what did you get Francis into without his knowing? He nearly got killed, Bear! And why did you ever think you could slip this one by me? If what Francis says is true, you guys have stumbled upon probably the single most miraculous device in history. And you thought I wouldn't want to be a part of this?"

Her pointer finger comes mere inches from his nose and lingers there. He gulps. "You—you can't be a part of it, Alice. You were never supposed to know about any of this." He peers past her tensed shoulders over to Francis. "Dude, you might have told me that you were going to call my sister and spill the beans?" Francis shrugs, a grossly insufficient act of contrition for what he's done.

"Sorry Theodore, but you never mentioned anything about your sister, let alone keeping her out of this whole thing. Besides, based on the plan Marley just gave us, she might come in handy."

"Come in handy?" Theodore feels the lid of his pressure cooker begin to rattle, just one more callous comment and it might shoot off. "Alice, you really can't come along with us, it's not safe for you."

"Why, Bear, because I'm a girl? Because I'm your helpless little sister?"

"Because of a lot of things," he finds himself saying. "Why are you so concerned about *him*, anyway?" he whispers, nodding to Francis. "I saw the way you were fawning over him just now. You guys just met the other day. Are you, like, a thing now?" He can't hide the shade of disdain that overtakes his face. Alice recoils, her pointer finger wavering. Her eyes shrink as she scrutinizes Theodore's inner workings in a way only she can. It's like she's peering past his well-guarded psyche and into his very soul.

She scoops up his hand and charges towards the door with him in tow. Henry emerges from the bedroom before they make it out the front door and in his usual fashion says an ill-timed, "Oh, hey Alice."

"Hello Henry," she says, without glancing back. Francis just watches, bemused, as Alice swipes the front door open and drags Theodore into the hallway. She continues her determined march in silence, but Theodore doesn't need dialogue between them to know what's about to follow; he's gone one overbearing step too far again and she's about to lecture his ear off. They sweep past the length of russet brown, peeling wallpaper along the walls of the hallway until they come to the little community terrace at the back of the second floor.

It's a clustered, unorganized, weather-beaten array of lattices overlooking a scenic cobbled side street. Various succulents line the terrace alongside other plants that always have just enough droop to look like they're not getting watered enough. Marcy, the building's landlord, isn't one for aesthetics. Still, Theodore has always found the crummy terrace to be a thing of understated beauty at dusk, and tonight is no different. Sun rays kiss Alice's face through the lattice, illuminating the mystery and ineffability that forever lingers behind her expressions.

"Bear," she says softly. "You're doing it again."

He chooses a stoic response just to play with the tension between them. "Doing what, Alice?"

She eye-rolls. "I saw the way you looked at Francis, the way you looked at me when he was holding me. It's the same way you looked at Corban in high school, and Max after that—the same damn disapproving expression with every guy I get close to."

"Alice, I don't know what you're talking about. I was just surprised that—"

"Bullshit, Theodore!" She never uses his actual name except for when she's irate; somewhat like a mother calling her errant boy by his full name when he's committed a big no-no. "You know exactly what you were doing. You've never approved of any of the guys I've been with, and," she sniffles and wipes her nose, "and I think it's interfered with my ability to find happiness for myself. I mean, you're my older brother, Bear, and yours is the only opinion I've ever put much stock in."

"Well then hear this, Alice, because it's something I've wanted to bring to light for some time now, as a concerned older brother. I think you're spinning your wheels living this frenetic, capricious life, bouncing here, there, and everywhere, refusing to let solid ground formulate beneath your feet. Because you know that whatever normalcy you'd try to spin for yourself would always be predicated upon the horrors of your past, which vitiated your ability to really put your life in the hands of another individual for anything more than a passing 'hello.'

"You're so busy running from your demons, like a felon fleeing the cops across life's turnpike. And you want nothing more than to push the pedal to the floor and hope you can outrun them. But, until you face them head on, they'll always be there in the rear-view mirror, gaining. You'll never move on and start living a real, stable life until you figure out how to come to terms with what you went through...what we went through."

"Exactly," she stammers. "What we went through, Bear. Maybe it's true what you say; that I have tunnel vision on crafting the busiest, fastest-paced life I can for myself so that I can't slow down for one minute for fear of letting those horrific moments back in. But I think you're just as affected by the past as me, and you're refusing to move on in your own disparate way. You've shrunken your world into these bite-sized, manageable bits, and while I may be gallivanting around with too many people, you've effectively sealed everybody out. Where I may be too trusting in a stranger's outstretched hand, you have a pathological mistrust of everyone."

Theodore says nothing. Her words are starting to find their place deep in his gut; what she's saying just might be true. In recent years, he truly has diminished the scope of his world to the tenable confines of his apartment, the comforting embrace of Alice, and the security of his own entrenched perspective of life. And he has certainly always had it out for anybody she gets close to, but this dubiety of his over her love interests was never formed out of spite. He's only ever tried to protect her from strange men. The last thing he's ever wanted was to hurt her. He casts his eyes down, ashamed.

"I've given this a lot of thought over the years, and until now I think I was too young to understand the nature behind this disdain of yours. Until now, I was sure that you were acting this way to spite me, to drive boys away out of some jealousy or insecurity of yours. Like you thought you'd lose me if another guy came into the picture." She sniffles again, the bud of a tear forming in her left eye and coruscating in the dying sunlight.

"And if that's the case then I want you to know, that could never happen, Bear. It's always been you and me. In fact, it's only ever been you and me, little us against the world. And no Francis or Max or Corban, or any other guy could replace the piece of my heart that's reserved for you, Bear. I'm older now though, and the thing that I've grown enough to realize is that this all revolves around dad." Theodore feels his heart begin to gyrate at the thought of John, at the thought of what they went through under his draconian rule. "And when I realized that, it was like I had ripped the window curtains off and let the sun beam in on your sacrifice. It really gave me perspective on what you've had to do for me through the years.

"You were so young and so noble, and you made the choice to step up and be my guardian when dad was such a monster…when he had broken mom down, down to the point where she couldn't care for us…when he finally turned on me."

Theodore's fists clench. They've never openly discussed that pivotal day, nor the myriad trials they faced together after it. And now that they are, he feels something primal stirring deep within him. He can't let her see the tears that are welling in his own eyes now. He sweeps himself away—anywhere but in front of his sis—over to the terrace's edge to stare out over the city scape. She follows him over, her footfalls softer than the pulsing torrents of memories that are flooding back to him. She puts a hand on his shoulder. "You saved me, Bear." She leans in from where she's standing to meet him face to face.

"No one else was there for me in that god-awful moment, no one. Only you. And you could have just up and left. You were old enough. You could have told yourself that the situation with dad was unchangeable, and saving me wasn't worth risking your neck, too; that you should've moved out forever ago, to the city by yourself. And you could have walked out and been gone forever. But you made the choice then and there to stand up for me, to stand up for us after all those years of fear."

"Alice, I never could have left you; you were my world. I'd never forgive myself if I left you with...him."

"You were young, Bear, and young people caught up in a storm like that don't always do the right thing. And you must've known that taking your little sister with you to the city to start anew would be tough. Nobody should have to make the decision to abscond from the only life they know and start all over at such a young age, with a younger sibling to provide for.

"You got a crummy job stooped over a scalding sink washing dishes for twelve hours a day in a dusty old Italian restaurant to support us in our new life. And it wasn't perfect, Bear, for either of us. We struggled like any two children alone in a massive city would. But the truth is that you saved me that day, and I'll never forget it."

At that moment, Theodore raises his head and meets Alice's beatific eyes with his own. His walls are tumbling down about him and he just lets them fall. For far too long he's been holding an emotional load greater than any physical cumbrance could be, and in one long, rattling exhale, he releases it all. An effluence of tears begins to cascade down his face in this long overdue moment of catharsis. Through the sheen of releasing emotions blurring his eyes, he can see Alice's resilient but weathered countenance. It mirrors his own. They lean in and embrace one another, and he begins sobbing for the first time in months. Years. A cool breeze stirs about them, carrying on its diaphanous wings the mottled scents of the city.

Alice pulls away at last, her eyes ablaze with something that looks like alacrity and determination. "I just have one thing more to ask of you

Theodore, one more sacrifice for you to make."

Theodore rubs his eyes. "Shoot."

"I need you to let go now. I'm not the helpless little girl I was back then, I'm a grown woman who can fend for herself. And not every man is out there to hurt me, okay?" He nods. "And if you really love me, really respect me, then you need to recognize that I'm smart enough and capable enough to make these kinds of decisions on my own. Look, I know it's really hard, Bear. It must be so damn tough to go from the way we've been to the way we need to become. We're so closely knit because we're all we've ever had, and you're the only one I've ever needed to rely on. But it's time to let go and give someone else a piece of the burden."

He nods again, slower this time and with more acceptance. "And my being a grown woman means I get to choose to come with you guys on this journey. You know me, Bear," she says, smirking through her sniffles, "I'm a sucker for any kind of adventure. So, you should know there's no way you're keeping my nosy ass out of this one," she chuckles, knocking him on the shoulder. "And hey, Francis mentioned something about a girl being the end goal of this crazy quest? You've actually found somebody that you can tolerate? Besides me, that is?"

He just rolls his eyes and groans, still smiling shakily and wiping away lingering threads of tears. "Guess what, New York City?" Alice shouts, spreading her arms wide and leaning into the spread of latticework. "Theodore's found himself a lady! We haven't felt the effects up on the surface yet, but hell has indeed frozen over."

"All right, all right." He wrangles in her gesticulating arms and peers at the windows surrounding the terrace, fully expecting to see a disgruntled face or two glaring down at them, or for one or two harangues to come wafting down from old Mrs. Bartlett's top floor apartment. Not a single sight or sound to speak of. "If I let you come along will you promise not to tease me about her in front of the dudes?" They walk back in, hand in hand, as wavering pennons of fierce orange light streak the sky above.

"Oh no, now that I *can't* promise," she smiles and squeezes his hand.

III

Henry is skipping down the length of Morton Street with sheer anticipation of the upcoming journey. A few paces ahead of him and Theodore, Alice and Francis are walking hand-in-hand, whispering little love sentiments into each other's ears. And while Theodore is cringing at the sight, he is coming to accept the evolved circumstances between him and his little sister. After all, everything Alice said was quite true and completely sensible. She is her own person, and one of the toughest tasks ahead of him, including saving Vivianne and extracting her from the 1930s, is learning to adapt to the possibility of Alice and Francis being an 'item,' or whatever the other millennials are calling their relationships before said relationships are codified with such terms as 'dating' or being 'social-media-official.'

"All right dudes and dudette," Henry says abruptly, pulling his backpack off his Chesterfield and trying vehemently to unzip it mid-stride. After a few fumbled attempts, he finally gets it, a satisfied smirk peeling across his face. "From the deep, revolutionary recesses of Henry's Mancave of Technological Marvel I bring to you the devices of yesteryear that will serve us on our quest." He brandishes a couple of chunky, jet black walkie talkies, tosses one to Theodore and Francis, goes digging again and tosses one to Alice and then scoops up the last one for himself.

"Not bad," Francis rolls the device over in his hands. "Is this a Wave

Zapper 3000?"

"What's a Wave Zapper 3000?" asks Alice, clicking the transmit button over and over.

Henry gallops over to Alice's side and begins thrusting his walkie talkie in her face, ecstatic at the inquiry and the opportunity to indulge his erudition regarding anything technological. Theodore knows he lives for this stuff. "Excellent question, Alice. The Wave Zapper 3000 can penetrate any obstacle to give you and your correspondent a smooth-as-a-baby's-ass conversation up to five miles away. Wood, stone, slate, concrete, even the peskiest private-sector signal jammers can't compete with the Wave Zapper 3000's sophisticated airwave tech."

Alice smiles politely along as Henry gives the brand's mission statement, nodding along every time his cadence rises with excitement, but Theodore knows that if there's anyone on the planet who gives one rat's ass less about gadgets and tech than himself, it's Alice.

"Good call, Henry," he says. "Our cell phones get bricked during the time-travel process, but as long as there are radio towers in 1931 London, these should work just fine."

"We'll just have to set some ground rules for usage," suggests Francis, wagging his walkie talkie in the air for emphasis. "These little guys would surely attract the wrong kind of attention to us in the hotel—the revelers will think we're from another planet if they see us using modern devices like these."

Theodore nods. "Right. So, we only use them when we're away from any prying eyes. Also, with all the analog sounds, gargles of interference, radio hiss and whatnot, we'll need to make sure our Wave Zappers are buried deep within our coats and vests and dresses. That way, when one of us chimes in, the sound will be as muffled as possible. If we have the need to communicate with each other, let's just make it a rule that we give a brief greeting over the transmitter, like, 'Come in, over.' That sort of thing. If you do that and don't get a response, you can assume that the others aren't in a secluded enough spot to use the walkie talkies."

Theodore finishes his thought and before long they come upon the friable, old brick building that houses The Cat's Meow. Theodore leads the way, perfunctorily snatching the off-colored brick off the wall, powerwalking around back, and slamming the brick in the slot. "All right guys," he says. "When we arrive at The King's Inn, it's crucial that we follow the plan that Marley laid out. Alice, this is your first time doing this, and it's going to be the most bizarre, and maybe the most exhilarating, experience in your life, and you're probably gonna find yourself getting distracted by every little thing you see. But remember guys: as soon as you land, you're going to come find me in the foyer. I still have my mask from last night in my coat pocket, but all of you will need yours, and the foyer's where we'll find them. After that, we assume our positions according to the plan, right?" They all nod.

"Affirmative," says Alice. They move down the staircase to the bar in single file, the crumbling walls scattering tentacles of dust upon them as they go. The metal door viewer slides open.

"Well, well, well," the voice of a too-familiar doorman pours out from the slot. "Luck is just raining down on me today, seeing as I get to interact with this ragtag group of misfits. Just swell. On the left we've got hygienically lacking tubby. On the right is guy-who-knows-squat-about-history. In the middle, Francis, who still owes me a batch of his homemade gin for squeezing him into The Gilded Gopher downtown last week..." He glances at Alice, a sudden edacious glint appearing in his eye. "Oh, and who else to join this motley crew but the enchanting, indescribably radiant beauty...from a couple nights ago, I'm sorry, doll, I can't remember your name."

"Just give us the riddle, Marvin," says Francis, throwing a territorial arm around Alice's shoulder and beaming a sarcastic smile.

"All right, all right, big guy," Jersey Guy capitulates. "I was only playing around a little. My job isn't exactly as exciting as a secret agent's, ya know?" He clears his throat. "Ahem. What was famed armed-robber George Anderson's birth name, where was his family from, and," Theodore groans loudly at the thought of having to answer more than one recondite question from this buffoon. The stress of the rescue mission he's about to embark on is too much to be impeded by petty games. He doesn't have time for this—none of them do.

"And," Jersey Guy repeats, clearly amused with Theodore's repudiating grumble. "What led to his capture after a prodigious $2.4 million-dollar robbery?"

"I call bullshit, Marvin. You're only allowed to ask one question for entry," insists Francis.

"Well, normally that would be true, big guy, but that was before scrawny over there owed me for not providing a proper phone number for the gal. And you still owe me for reneging on the booze you said you'd give me. So, methinks three questions would make us even-steven, eh?"

Theodore and Francis exchange puzzled looks, shrugging. But this intense energy bounces between Alice and Henry, who stare into each other's narrowed eyes. They both smile and Henry announces, "He was born Ivan Dahl von Teler…"

Alice takes over, "And his family was from Denmark…" She and Henry give each other one more bemused look, and then she raises a hand to suggest it's Henry's turn. He shakes his head, "Nah, you go, Alice. I insist."

"No, no, please Henry. You first."

"We'll say it together then," he shrugs. They both shoot a glance at Jersey Guy, announcing in unison, "He was caught when his associate tried to sell gold notes taken from the robbery to a mail inspector."

After a pause, "Dammit. You two are good. Freaky good. Were you both raised by Bonnie and Clyde or somethin'?" A series of clattering bolts ensues and the door swings wide. "Enjoy your stay in our little rumrunner's heaven," he says with a sardonic bite in his voice. They file in, immediately embraced by the swooning serenade of Benny Goodman's clarinet.

"Uh, what did the doorman mean about you owing him a proper phone number, Bear?"

"Oh, uh, well...I'll fill you in about that some other time," he defers. "Let's head to the back of the bar, guys! Time to show Alice what a real adventure is like." He leads them into the gallery of old images, Henry pushing eagerly past him to get the first look at the impossible photo. Theodore glances over his shoulder, ushering Alice and Francis over. "You're going to want to see this, Alice."

Just like history repeating itself—or overwriting itself—there, at the back of the Regal Ballroom are Theodore and Henry, standing side by side in their Chesterfields. Theodore with his gazelle mask on and Henry sporting a hippo on his face again. Just off to their side, awash in the senescent grain of the old picture, is Francis holding Alice in his arms. Instead of the menacing gorilla effigy he had on last night, he's wearing the visage of some sort of lizard tonight. Upon Alice's face is the glaring facsimile of a lemur. Or is it some sort of cat? He can't quite tell.

"Totally sick!" Henry exclaims, fist-pumping in the air. Alice peers intently at the image, silently scanning it with graceful erudition. The exact moment she finds the anomaly plays before Theodore's eyes in the form of a whimsical, childlike grin. She shakes her head, slams her eyes shut, and checks once more.

"That's us...So, you guys really aren't blowing smoke up my chimney after all. How did we end up in this—"

"It's best if we just show you," Theodore asserts, gently peeling her away from the image. He gestures toward the magical device that makes it all possible, perched insouciantly upon the little table as usual. Alice sweeps over to the Sonophone, poring over its every fine detail like a jeweler examining the quality of a marvelously deep blue stone.

"What a beaut! Nothing like *this* thing has ever graced the shelves of my store." She puts her hands on her hips. "So, this is the phonograph machine that—"

"Um, yes," Theodore interjects, motioning to the lone drinker perched at the very dry little bar. They can't risk anyone else knowing about this. "Yes, this is what I wanted to show you. Crazy looking thing, huh?" Francis ambles over to the seated man, whose head is lackadaisically drooping in his hand. He's swirling a near-empty cocktail in idle circles, rubbing his temples and grumbling to himself, a tangled coil of hair persisting through the cracks between his fingers.

"Eugene, what's up, my man?" Francis claps him on the back, receiving nothing but illegible grunts back from the guy. Hunched over the bar, he looks like the paradigm for drunken, defeated heartbreak. "Are you still grieving over Kim Sook, dude?"

"Mhm," Eugene manages. "She's gone, man. Said she wanted a guy who...who wasn't so *cloying*, whatever that means."

"Yeah, well listen dude, I've got some excellent news. She actually just walked into the bar a few minutes ago with longing in her eyes, saying that she wanted you back and all this other sentimental shit. She's over there looking for you right now, bro." Eugene shoots up, straight as a tombstone.

"She what?" He peers into the hall through bloodshot eyes, straining them as if he thinks he'll be able to see her right through the walls.

"Go to her, man! She said something about leaving for...where is she from again?"

"Wisconsin."

"Right, leaving for Wisconsin if she can't repair things with you."

"Oh my god! Kim, I'm coming baby! You don't need to move back home and start over, I'm right here!" He performs an impressive mixture of teetering and stumbling down the hall and into the main bar.

"Well, I know you guys wanted to clear the room before we do what we're here to do but wasn't that a little harsh?" asks Alice.

Francis shrugs. "Meh, when he's not an inebriated mess, Eugene is actually a total asshole. Besides, it's the only thing I knew to do that would get him out of here in a jiff."

Henry chuckles and Theodore shrugs. His mind is a vortex of anticipation and he's just fondling the cylinder record in his pocket over and over again.

Rolling it around as if it might just up and disappear if he were to cease fondling it. He reaches into his outer coat pocket and brandishes the gazelle mask that made the trip back with him for the first time last night. As he's about to don the mask, his hand clinks against something in one of his other pockets. His hand burrows into his coat and comes back with the medieval torture device that he used to retrieve Marley's final record.

He stares at the rotted iron pincers and they stare right back, insisting upon the fact that they journeyed back with him last night. He can't remember having pocketed them, but then again, at the time he was within arm's reach of the madman, so he wasn't exactly thinking clearly. He slaps the pincers on the heel of his open palm. Finding these in his inner pocket definitely explains the reason it felt like he had landed on something much harder than wood flooring on Eskimo Andy's terrace this morning. His body must've driven right down on the pincers. Hell, he slept on them for ten hours today and woke up none the wiser. That being said, he's always so enervated after a bout of time warping, he'd probably be apt to sleep on a bed of nails. Or fire.

"Okay, what uh, what the fuck is that, Theodore?" Francis is pointing at the pincers, his voice lilting only a little, like a sapling vibrating in a storm. Henry gasps and Alice covers her hand with her mouth, astutely recognizing the piece of history Theodore's palming. Henry stumbles forward to investigate, his fingers dancing with anticipation. "I've seen these on the History Channel. Are they the real deal? They look like the real deal. Why do you have tongue pincers, dude?" He leans in, his hand enjoying only the briefest dalliance with the handle, looking as if he assumed it would be hot to the touch.

Theodore shrugs, his tongue poking the inside of his cheek as he mulls over the appropriate response. "It's a long story that involves a little ingenuity on my part to get that Marley record, and some…natural eccentricities on Nithercott's part."

Alice's eyes flicker with an inquisitive intensity, her gentle lips curling to reveal just a hint of her inner complexities; the single iota she deigns to show the world. "Well, between Francis' smart-looking vest and suspenders, your arcane overcoats, and now this relic from an even more bygone era, you guys are just a series of bona fide temporal quilts right now, aren't you?" Alice jests.

Theodore thrusts the pincers back into the depths of the coat and snaps the record into the Sonophone's housing. "So, before we make the jump, remember the plan, guys. Like I said, if we happen to make it out of the hotel alive and in one piece with Vivianne in tow, I have something important to show her and it's gonna take some time. Henry, Francis, are you sure you're up for taking Alice down into the London underground to find the Paupers and warn them of the ambush without me?"

They both nod. "Good. Just remember, the entrance is in the Battersea Power Station. It's the biggest structure on the Thames, you can't miss it."

He turns back to the machine, cranking the lever to its fullest capacity. His heart plays a jaunty little melody in anticipation. They're about to do it; they're about to go back and save Vivianne once and for all. His mind is traveling through the details of Marley's intricate plan, his hope clambering with eager fingers to overcome the distress of all that could go wrong.

"All right, ladies and gents," he sighs, turning from the machine and meeting his trusted allies face to face one more time within the tenable familiarity of their own timeline. Soon, they'll all be steeped in the inimical framework of another, more dangerous world. "Remember the plan as we've discussed it. The audible I've called regarding saving Osprey shouldn't interfere with what needs to be done if we save him in a timely manner."

Alice, Henry, and Francis all nod vehemently. He can practically feel the penetrative force of their mutual understanding, can see the calm grit and determination in the magnetic pull of their gaze. With the gravity of what they're about to do, all the insanity that's led to this moment, he feels like he's marching into the minatory haze of a nightmare and hailing the morning light. He couldn't have asked for a better crew to do it with.

"Don't forget the walkie-talkie protocol and try to make contact with each other as soon as you get a spare moment." He windmills the lever arm of the Sonophone, winding it to its farthest click. He exhales sharply, hovering the needle over the edge of the cylinder. When he turns around, his eyes guide themselves right to Alice. The brightness of alacrity in her face tells him she's ready and eager. He doesn't even glance at the other two before dipping the needle. He doesn't need their tacit approval like he needs hers.

"I can't believe this is happening," she chirps, grabbing Francis' sinewy arm and squeezing it between both her delicate hands. She digs in. *Godspeed*, Theodore thinks, winking at her and then turning away and closing his eyes. Normally, he'd have wrenched her toward him and held her by the shoulders with the protective instinct of a father. But he's got to prove to her that he's ready to move beyond that type of behavior. It takes a mountain of effort to silence the squall of protesting voices within him, to let Francis take his place as her shield. But he does.

IV

A diffused constellation of dusky lights swirls around Theodore's head. The sconces lining the foyer leave ghost trails in his vision that linger even after he closes his eyes to orient himself after the journey.

Hello there, young man, he can easily predict what's coming next.

"Why, hello there, young man. What a fine-looking doppelgänger you have. With that adornment, you've got the air of a man ready for the Pre-Shibboleth Frivolities." He turns around, the world easing to a slow, hazy churn about him. Floating before him are Raven Woman's piercing dark eyes. Like two unburned coals swimming in a sea of egg whites, they pierce right through his own. A soft flurry of motion below, something's nipping at his shins. His eyes dart down to see his coattail wrapping around his leg, the last remnants of centrifugal motion playing around his ankles and then settling behind him.

"Hello, Raven Woman." He brushes past her with a nonchalant wave of his hand. He's a man on a mission and he cannot allow idle chatter to trip up the plan. Alice. *Where is she? Did she make it through all right?* Already winning the battle with nausea, he angles his dominant arm forward and begins boring through the patches of mingling revelers that line the foyer. Any isolated corner of the hotel will do, really any low-traffic spot where he can establish contact with his crew would be sufficient.

347

A vivid blur of movement in front of him and the palm of a limpid white glove appears before his face. He sidesteps to see a tall gentleman in a double-breasted tweed vest, sporting a ferret on his face and a cocky grin below, which frames his crude chin and gives his jowl a temporary lift from the droop it normally abides.

"My, my, where are you off to in such a hurry, young reveler?" The ferret's grin seems to harden upon his face like lava cooling on mountain stone. A cascading, unfitted, gold chiffon dress spins about beside the man, revealing a lady with a neck like an egret, and a fox upon her face.

"Mingle with us a while, won't you?" she admonishes Theodore, pawing at the breast of his coat. Just then, he hears the faintest chirp emanate from within his coat. After, a host of static. *Shit, someone's already using their walkie!* Another chirp, longer this time, and then a stream of static with some garbled verbiage flows out. *Can the revelers hear it, too?* He coughs and crosses one side of the coat tautly over the other, hoping to seal in the noises as much as possible.

"Um, yeah," he says. Another river of white noise and the low, nasally buzz of voices. He raises his voice, attempting to cover the sounds under his own wavering tones. "I'd love to stay and chat, but I have someone I really need to speak with first." He moves forward, but the tenacious ferret bars his path.

"Now, young Yank, there is a certain etiquette to the Shibboleth of which you must have been informed. An etiquette of insouciance and informality. We must take care not to be too brisk in our stride, nor too brusque in our manner. We must strive to be at ease, and plan to live in the moment." Another outburst from the walkie talkie. Theodore coughs as if an entire ear of corn were stuck in his throat. Hopefully the ridiculous display masks the hidden tech. The ferret continues, blithely unaware of the alien device gurgling inside Theodore's coat. "These joyous events take place only every so often, young Yank, and we revelers are not afforded such opportunities otherwise. So please; drink, chat, mingle, and be merry!"

"Now," the man says, gracefully touching the lapels of his coat with two fingers. "You may call me Mister Ferrett and this charming little vision is my joie de vivre, Miss Foxy."

"Very nice to meet you both; charmed I'm sure!" Theodore nods his most enthusiastic nod, hearing Henry's voice blurting something along the lines of "Frodo, come in. This is your pal, Sam, paging you from the verdant fields of the Shire. Over."

It then dawns on Theodore that if he presses and holds the transmit button, he can silence all other transmissions. He honestly can't recall the last time he used a walkie talkie, but he knows that much is true. He thrusts his hand inside his coat and fishes about for the device.

"JK, Theo, it's just me, your pal Henry. Hehehe."

Another voice engages, "Breaker, breaker, one-nine, F-Man is on the line," Click. Theodore silences the loquacious pair on the other end, who, in the excitement of world-hopping, seem already to have forgotten the guidelines he laid out for walkie talkie usage.

"Now, if you don't mind," Theodore says, awkwardly clutching the transmit button on the walkie talkie inside his coat, looking like someone clutching their heart at the onset of a coronary episode, "I must speak with someone about a pressing matter, but I'll be back promptly to…drink brandy and discuss the state of…the state." He tucks nimbly past the pair, pushing through the foyer and taking the first point of egress he comes upon: a right turn into a warmly lit hallway that leads down one of the labyrinthine hotel's dusky lounges. Just past the turn, Theodore can see more revelers dancing and mingling, obeying the unwritten laws of the Shibboleth, as it were.

He pulls away into the junction, craning his neck to verify no one is in eyeshot of him and that he can safely brandish the transmitter. He pulls it out of his coat, but finds himself nervously cradling it against his body, like a paranoid drug mule checking his product near the flashing neon of a border checkpoint. Finally, he dares to release the transmit button under his blanched pointer finger. The frequency chatter begins pouring out of the device just like he knew it would.

"Dudes, I just have to find Jersey Doll. Then I can meet up with you. This is like, super important to the mission, guys. Trust me." Henry's garbled, but edacious, voice announces.

"This...is...insane, guys." *Alice*! She made it through okay after all. Theodore breathes a trembling sigh of relief, then clicks and holds the transmit button.

"Theodore here. Everyone make the jump okay? Over." All three of his correspondents jump on the line one after the other.

"Theo!"

"Hey, man! There you are. We were starting to worry about you."

"I mean, this is like a dream—a wonderful, kaleidoscopic romp through a nostalgic, historical playground—and I must have pinched this same bit of skin on the back of my left hand a dozen times now; it's red as a rose in bloom and throbbing like a bitch, so I guess I can't be dreaming. How could you keep this place a secret from me, Bear?"

"Yeah dude, how could you do that to your little sister?" Henry adds sardonically.

"Yeah, yeah, yeah, I'm the worst brother in the world. Look, I know it looks like a historical amusement park, Alice, exactly the kind of thing that makes your motor run, but let's all remember the danger of the situation, as well as the reason we came." He releases the button, glancing around the corridor's right angle once more. An aureate glow caresses the walls around him from the moody sconces lining the way. The coast is still clear.

"Now it looks like you've all found isolated areas to communicate from, that's great. Just hold tight where you are and listen up. Francis and Henry, you've already danced to this macabre tune, so you're more or less accustomed to the situation. Alice, you're a fish out of water, so here's the deal; you guys are going to make your way towards the front of the hotel from wherever you are. Stop in any coat closet or at any guest kiosk you find and snatch a mask for yourself—super important Alice. Keep a low profile until you've found one; people will be real suspicious of you until you've got your quote-unquote doppelgänger on. Once you have your masks, let's all meet at the elevators. Signage in the hotel is pretty good, so that shouldn't be a problem."

"Gotcha," Francis says.

"Aye, aye, Captain," confirms Henry.

"Affirmative," agrees Alice.

"We have to move pretty fast or else we'll miss our chance to save this Osprey guy, and we need to find Watters to inform him that we're saving Vivianne tonight. He'll likely be at the Pre-Shibboleth Frivolities, which will be under way soon. And don't forget to bury your walkie talkies as deeply in your pockets as you can. And for God's sake, don't blow up the frequency with idle chatter like before; you guys almost made minced meat out of me in the foyer not two seconds after I warped in. Only push transmit for important stuff. All right, troops, retrieve those masks and rendezvous at the elevators ASAP."

He releases the transmit button, carving a fresh silence out of the white noise of the device, and ambles back into the foyer. He just needs to get to the elevator, that's his only mission right now. A wave of anxiety overtakes him as he begins pushing his way through strings of waiting revelers; Marley's grand plan is spinning in his head, like a vicious turbine driving all other thought out. He sucks in two deliberate breaths, reassuring himself that the basis of the plan is to have his friends each place themselves at a different exit and find some way to distract, or incapacitate, the guards there. It's just the sheer number of floating pieces in this scenario that are poking holes in his confidence balloon.

When he's only a few paces from the foyer exit, his eye catches a glimpse of something warmly familiar. A wolf. Halfway across the room, Watters is weaving through the serpentine paths of the crowd, beelining right toward Theodore. As soon as Theodore sees him, his knees turn to pudding and his hands loosen at his sides. He finds himself choking up—nearly crying—at the sight of the man.

Watters saved him, Henry, and Francis from certain death in a daring display of courage and fortitude, he set them on the path to saving Vivianne with his crucial insights, and he's been something of a guardian angel, too, watching over Theodore every single night, tracing his steps and making sure he stays out of harm's way. Theodore finds himself at war with the powerful notion to wave Watters over and embrace him like an estranged father; the type of man Theodore and Alice should have had as a father all along. He needed only to travel back in time to find him. He pauses near the doorway, watching Watters make his calculated approach. He feels the burden of all he must accomplish slip off of his hunched frame like shards of ice sliding off the sagging roof of a dilapidated manor.

Just then, before he pierces the outermost throng of masqueraders—merely steps away from Theodore—Watters freezes. He watches as every muscle in the wolf's body hardens. *What is he doing?* A light pressure forms on Theodore's right shoulder, the gentle vice of a hand squeezing once, twice, three times. A tall and lanky figure swoops into view in front of him; another hand bites down on his other shoulder. He instantly recognizes the crisp, raven-black suit, the greased back hair with one intractable swathe dangling down and vibrating with every small movement, and the inimical rat mask that's now looming inches before his face. What is Alfred doing here? He's never in the foyer before the photo-op.

Theodore gulps hard, not daring to attempt wriggling free of Alfred's grasp. He can no longer see Watters, or just about anything in the foyer for that matter, it's all blocked out by the Master of Ceremonies' oppressive figure. A gelid, prickling sensation swerves down Theodore's spine. Alfred's clutching him firmly by the shoulders, but he doesn't shake him, doesn't haul him away or call the guards to his side, he just stares with those beady, intelligent eyes into Theodore's own. Somehow, Theodore thinks, this tacit confrontation—the austere, penetrative silence between the two of them as they truly size each other up for the first time—is all the more terrifying than any physical conflict could be.

Alfred leans in closer. Theodore's mind, addled with panic, takes him back to last night, to Alfred's penthouse where the monster was so close Theodore could smell his sweat.

He sniffs at Theodore like an esurient animal and then leans back, his eyes darting around Theodore's mask and then down at his garments. Meanwhile, the din of the party trundles on in the background, masqueraders floating about in Theodore's periphery, the sweet swell of jazz music tickling his ear. A host of activity surrounds him and Alfred, and in spite of this, they're completely alone, isolated, pinned down in a gridlock of tension.

At long last, the rat opens its mouth, "Do I know you, chap?"

Theodore says nothing.

"That's a very fine Chesterfield you've got there, I, I swear I knew a bloke who had one himself just like it. Why, Caldwell is his name, Terrance Caldwell. He's a rather tall fellow, too, and so his coat would fit a shorter bloke like a man's glove upon a child's hand." He glances up and down Theodore's body once more, sneering, the milk-white of his teeth showing out of one side of his mouth. "Hmph." Then his face contorts into a wide grin, and he bursts into a burbling fit of ostentatious laughter. "Enjoy the frivolities, my funny little friend, and do be sure to make yourself present at tonight's main event."

Alfred pats him heartily on both shoulders and then slips away into the crowd. The masqueraders welcome him into their arms as if he were a glorified veteran just stepping off the ship and onto Queen's Land soil. Amongst them, one reveler is missing: Watters. Theodore slips into the elevator room, his spirits rising when he sees Alice, Henry, and Francis all arriving at the antiquated lifts just one step ahead of him.

They begin idly pacing back and forth in front of the elevators, scanning the itinerant crowd for any sign of Theodore. It looks like they've each managed to nab a mask. Henry is in his usual hippo, Francis with a horned lizard, and Alice in the endearing, mottled mask of a Siamese cat. She's pacing the quickest, elbows in her hands, observing the passersby with a look of grave concern over her face.

"Miss me?" asks Theodore. Immediately recognizing his voice, Alice pivots, her face turning from a dour pinch into a buoyant gleam. She wraps her arms around him and squeezes until he feels he might burst.

"Oh Bear! I started thinking about everything you've said about this place. All the dangerous people and just the calamitous nature of it. When I found Henry and Francis wandering around the hotel, but saw you were nowhere in sight, I just began to crumble." She cranes her neck across the elaborately festooned lift room, taking in a now-steadying breath. "This whole experience; the masqueraders, the hotel, the nostalgic decadence, the fact that I'm literally stepping through the world of the past, it's all so amazing! But I'm beyond relieved you're okay, Bear."

"Ditto," he says, feeling that she's overreacting just a little. After all, they only just made the journey. He was with her minutes ago at The Cat's Meow. Perhaps their heart-to-heart back at his place awakened within her some unknown depth of concern for him.

Henry's lingering behind her, making a hilarious attempt to be sneaky while trying to pick his nose under his mask. He's unable to properly reach the mark however, and after the first few tries, he gives up. "Well, on the one hand, it's great to be back," he says, slapping an open palm down on the elevator's hailing lever. "And on the other hand," he yanks the lever, which yields one solid mechanical thunk, then he watches as the old brass vessel lurches into motion a few floors above and begins trundling down to meet them. "I keep thinking about what happened to us when we went to save Francis last night—what very nearly happened to us before Watters showed up."

"I know, I know," acknowledges Theodore, biting at a loose peel of skin around his pointer finger. "But this time it's three against two, seeing as last night there was Harold, the dude dragging Francis, and the dude dragging Osprey. We rescued Francis last night, which essentially erases the need for one more meathead to be dragging anyone up there tonight. Which leaves Harold and the guy with Osprey. If we are afforded the element of surprise, we can knock them out no problem says I."

"Three of us?" Alice asks with a hello-I'm-also-here raise of the hand.

"Well, there's no way I'm gonna let you engage in whatever conflict arises up there," Theodore's staunch reply. "These guys are vicious thugs, Alice, and I'd never forgive myself—"

"Remember our little chat, Bear?" She moves forward, her face resolute, the expression speaking to a maturity in her he realizes he had never cared to notice until their talk on the terrace. Her eyes bore into his until he averts them to the ground. "I'm in this as much as you guys now, and like it or not, I'm going to be there every step of the way." Francis pats her lightly on the back; Henry looks at Theodore and makes a whip-cracking gesture. Theodore just shrugs and watches the elevator as it thuds to a stop before them.

The lift gate screeches open, Jarvis' wicked face beaming down upon them. "Going up, young revelers?" His powdered makeup is a drooping canvas of chalk, white splotches melting down and beading on the collar of his red attendant's jacket. Theodore watches as Alice evaluates the oddity looming before her. Her brows furrow as she notices the bloated zipper-like scars that lead from the corners of his mouth to his chin. She almost begins to grimace in revolt but seems to catch herself and turn her expression into a curious smile.

"Why yes, good sir," she says, stepping right in, pinching her dress with the thumb and forefinger of each hand, and doing a little curtsy.

"Third floor, please Jarvis, and step on it. We have business of great importance there," Theodore adds as they all shuffle in.

"Oh my, not one but an entire bundle of Yanks in my lift. Surely this is a first." He closes the gate behind them, sneering all the while, and then squeezes the lever to set the vessel in motion. "I am just bursting with excitement for the Shibboleth tonight!" His maniacal eyes tread a slow course over each of the guest's faces. "Once you discover the identity of the Shibboleth's Guest of Honor tonight, I dare say each of you will be just as piqued as I."

Theodore feels his face pinch. Was that some sort of cheeky jab? Is Jarvis on to them? Does he assume that because they're all American they have some connection to Osprey?

"We're all very excited, too," says Francis. "Ecstatic, actually." Jarvis considers this response silently, his gloved hand rapping over and over on the massive lever to his side.

"Ah, level three. Your stop kind sirs and madam," Jarvis wrenches the gate open, and then bows low to Alice.

"Oh." She puts her fingertips to her lips and dips her chin toward her clavicle in a manufactured display of obeisance. Jarvis smiles wider and scoops her hand in his. Theodore can practically feel the heat emanating from Francis, whose sinewy frame grows taut as he watches the creep fawning over his new girlfriend. With a steely eye contact, Jarvis lifts Alice's hand gingerly up to his blighted lips and pecks each knuckle once.

"Enjoy your stay, revelers," he says at last, and Theodore swears that, through the alabaster makeup, he can see a deepening rouge on Jarvis' cheeks.

"If we come back one more night, we have *got* to find that guy a woman," Henry says, clopping along into the hallway and plopping his hands on his hips.

"Yeah, or else he's gonna find my fists in his face," mutters Francis.

"There they are," Theodore whispers, giving a subtle nod over to the end of the corridor. Just as he assumed, Harold is leading the march with just one servant in tow, who's hard at work vehemently tugging the unfortunate Osprey across the carpeted hallway. "I think we should take out the other guy first, *then* dispatch Harold. His lacky is going to be tired from hauling Osprey across the hotel. He'll be quicker to overpower."

"Right," says Francis.

"Right," concurs Henry. "Dispatch them how? The only physical confrontation I've ever been in was in *Punch-Out!!* on Nintendo. I developed a pretty solid right hook and a wicked right jab, but my left arm couldn't penetrate a pile of pudding."

"So…in other words you've never actually been in a fight?" Francis jeers. "Like you haven't fought anyone man-to-man?"

"I just told you bro. I learned some wicked tools of the melee trade in Punch-Out!!. That's some legit street cred right there. Other than that, there was the fight with these guys last night, but I wasn't exactly conscious for any of it." Francis shakes his head, facepalming.

"That's not street cred! That's like me saying that I became a hugely successful venture capitalist on some bogus internet game and made an apocryphal eight-figure salary that was as real as a unicorn, or a morally responsible GOP." Francis starts chuckling. "No wonder you guys were down for the count by the time Watters came along last night. Not that I don't appreciate what you did, of course." Theodore considers interrupting and arguing that he single-handedly took down one of Harold's henchmen last night, but the grave fact is that he killed the man, and that's something for which he'll never forgive himself, nor will he ever make light of in conversation. Even if returning to the past tonight essentially rewrites whatever he did yesterday, in some way or another, he's still a murderer.

"Boys, boys, boys," interjects Alice, nabbing Henry and Francis by their sleeves and pulling them forth. "Can we call a raincheck on the palaver and focus on what needs to be done? Please? Remember, we're here for a purpose."

Thank you! thinks Theodore. *Now you know what I've been dealing with for the last twenty-four hours.* Crouched low and padding softly across the carpeted hallway, they make their way to the fork. They all peer around the corner. The marching troupe is more than halfway down the hall already, nearly to the door at the end.

"All right." Theodore bites down hard on the loose skin around his pointer finger. "Henry, you, Francis, and I will jump the lacky first. We'll try to knock him over the head with that table clock on the credenza over there once or twice until he loses consciousness, then we pounce on Harold like a pack of wild hyenas. We'll restrain them once they're both unconscious."

"Restrain them with what, exactly, our unwavering smiles and sunny dispositions?" mocks Henry.

"Very funny," Theodore whispers. "And when they're incapacitated, Alice can help us tie them up."

"Oh, screw that, Bear. This is 1931; I'm going to be the first woman on the front lines! I want some action, just like you boys."

Francis shrugs. "Technically speaking, in World War I, Russian women played some pretty prominent combat roles on the Eastern Front. So, I think they beat you to it, babe." *Babe.* The old Theodore would cringe at hearing someone calling Alice, his precious sister, *babe.* But right now, he has a battle to win and his focus is needle-pointed on that and only that.

"Okay, slowly and quietly, guys. Let's do this!"

They slither down the hall; a host of snakes bearing down on a couple of unwitting prairie mice. Theodore swoops over to the credenza, deftly scooping up the hefty table clock, the galloping pulse of his jugular slamming against the left side of his throat as his anxiety builds. Alice, Francis, and Henry fan out beside Theodore as they all descend upon Harold's henchman.

The others exchange quick, agitated glances, expectantly waiting for Theodore to make his move. Henry's breathing becomes raspy and labored. Theodore watches in his periphery as Henry coils his fists into two quivering white-knuckled balls. They're not trained assassins; hell, they're not even club bouncers, and all Theodore can hope as he sidesteps Osprey's prostrate body, is that this conflict goes better for them than it did last night. He brings the clock up toward the ceiling, shaking violently with anticipation. It's now or never.

Thud. The clock strikes the top of the henchman's skull before Theodore even realizes he's released it. He dropped the fucking thing. He was supposed to wallop the guy over the head, not let the unfailing but ineffectual arms of gravity do it for him. The henchman lurches forward, dazed and cantankerous, but far from incapacitated. He releases Osprey and turns, his hands a muddy blur of motion.

"What in bloody hell are you doing?" the man bellows. Behind him, Harold swings about, a wave of stiffness pervading his shoulders as his body enters fight or flight mode. But Theodore hasn't the time to focus on Harold now. He braces as the henchman hurls himself forward, his fists a blaze of violence propelling toward Theodore's face. A swift motion to Theodore's right and Francis dives into the fray, knocking the henchman's arm out of the air in one broad stroke. Obeying Newton's Laws of Motion, Francis' body impels the center of its mass upon the henchman, forcing him against the wall in a violently shuddering slam.

The man is quick, though, and retaliates in a fluid, spasmodic frenzy of limbs. He knocks Francis backwards, all the way into the impending Henry, who was just about to assist Francis in pummeling the man to the ground. The two of them topple over and tumble into the opposing wall, leaving Theodore to contend with the fractious madman. Theodore leaps forth, sending a right jab toward the masked man's throat, but the henchman pivots left and throws a strong right hook towards Theodore's head. Thwack. A throbbing pain erupts from Theodore's ear, disseminating down to his jaw and over to his cheekbone. In a fugacious flash, his vision cuts out, like a tv set with a dislodged power cord. He feels himself losing balance—falling hard and fast.

Someone catches him. Henry? He shoots a glance up to see a blurry hippo staring down at him. Suddenly, his own face feels naked, stripped of its adornments. His mask must've fallen off with the blow. He shakes his head fervently. No time to worry about trivialities now. Up in front again, Francis throws himself once more at the henchman, this time succeeding in knocking the tenacious fighter to the ground. Francis swipes the table clock off the floor and strikes it across his opponent's face. The henchman goes limp as cooked fettucine. The struggle is over.

Theodore rubs his face as a constellation of little stars overtakes his vision. He's dazed but okay. It looks like the guys are okay. *Alice?*

"It seems we are have arrived at a stalemate, eh?" Harold the Pig's voice erupts, booting Theodore from his mushy, concussed state. Harold's standing five paces down the hall with Alice in his grasp. Theodore inhales sharply, every fiber in his body firing off at once. His skeletal muscles writhe and twist under his skin, getting ready for his nervous system's signal to pounce at any moment. Harold has one arm wrapped around Alice's throat, and the other dangling a knife just below her clavicle.

Under Harold's mask, Theodore sees a belt of sallow teeth grinning triumphantly. Just like Theodore, Alice's mask is lying idle on the floor. It must have fallen off when Harold grabbed her. The expression on her face is one Theodore remembers well—one he's had to revisit in his mind lately more than he wishes. It's a look analogous to the one she had whenever their dad fell prey to the monster of overindulgence. Her eyes are saucers, wide and grave, and her cheeks are flush with a rampant fear. But, underneath the terror in her eyes, something comes alive and begins to fight to the surface. A gritty determination mottled with the serene fortitude of self-reliance.

"Whoa, whoa, whoa, buddy." Francis rises, steps forth, his arms outstretched.

"Not one more step, filthy Yankee cunt," Harold spits. "Now, I haven't the faintest clue who you are or what your end goal is, but you blokes have just made a grave mistake by assaulting me and my men." His eyes lock onto Theodore, as if he's determined him to be the chief executive officer of the group. "The poor sod with the bag over his head, do you know him? Did that invertebrate, maudlin chap Desmond Morrow send you over here on a suicide mission to fetch him? Eh?"

Harold begins slowly back-stepping, making his way to the stairwell with Alice in tow. *As long as he's got her at knifepoint, he knows he'll be able to make his escape*, Theodore's mind races. *What are they going to do?*

Francis tries again, "Come on pal, let's talk about this man to man."

"If you bumbling Yanks care one bit about this lass's life, you'll shut your mouths. Now, I am going to make my way out of your sight with her by my side and present her to the Master of Ceremonies himself where her fate will be determined. Knowing my superior, she's liable to become the new Guest of Honor at tonight's events, seeing as you clever little prigs have decided to trade his freedom for her captivity. Oh, and I wish you luck in your attempt to leave this building unhindered."

"That's it." Theodore's face grows hot, his cheeks simmering, his temper flaring. His sister is in danger and he must do something about it. He feels his legs kick into motion. He begins sprinting down the hall before his sense of reason comes into play. "Alice, I'm coming!"

Before he's made it halfway to the door, he sees a flash of motion. Alice grabs hold of the arm coiled around her neck. She stomps down hard on Harold's foot. His head cocks back; he's howling in pain. Alice thrusts her elbow into his side in three swift successions. Harold releases her, his gargantuan frame teetering backwards. She pivots, her dress spinning into motion and blossoming beneath her. She strikes him in the throat. He careens forward, his enervated arm reaching up towards his throat but only making it halfway up his necktie before faltering.

She strikes him once more, deftly stepping aside as he topples down and unfolds onto the carpet, motionless. Theodore just watches her with her fists still clenched, her shoulders undulating with each rapid breath, her teeth barred down hard. He turns slowly to Henry and Francis, neither of whom makes the move to pick their jaw up off the floor. Francis is pawing at his head with one hand, nursing a growing welt on the side of his head. Henry's just gazing past Theodore at Alice, pigeon-toed and head cocked to the side, starry-eyed.

"That...is the hottest thing I've ever seen," he says finally.

"How did you—" Theodore asks.

She turns around brushing her hair back and letting out a rattling breath. "It took all three of you boys to take down one irate Englishman, and only helpless, little me to do the same." She brushes past Theodore, a little more sway in her hips than usual; a well-deserved air of confidence in her stride. *See, Bear? I don't need you to fight all my battles for me, not anymore. I can handle myself now*, her body language screams.

"You sure can," Theodore finds himself stammering, even though Alice hadn't actually said a thing about her ability to take care of herself. Henry gives a slow clap as Alice approaches him. "Where did you learn to fight like that, Alice?" Theodore asks.

"You knew I was taking kickboxing classes at Union Square this summer." She swoops down over Osprey's body and takes his head in her hands with the delicacy and magnanimity of a nurse handling a trauma patient. "And those years of basic karate never really left me, I guess." Theodore remembers karate with Alice, many years ago. He never cared for karate, nor anything with elements of physicality in general, and the only real reason he can recall taking those courses was to be near her. And to have temporary reprieve from what was always waiting for him at home, his father's temper and his mother's helplessness.

Alice removes the burlap sack from the unconscious body to reveal a surprisingly comely young face. Sure, there are a few aubergine blemishes from where Harold and his men have roughed him up, but during last night's torture session, Osprey's face was so mutilated that Theodore would have thought the unfortunate soul that's before him now to be an entirely different person. Theodore joins Henry and Francis, who are crowding around Alice as she gently shakes Osprey's shoulders in an attempt to rouse him.

Henry glances up at Theodore and Francis, extending his fist towards them, knuckles first. "By the way, good job, guys. I think we really showed some quality teamwork in taking that guy down. Good hustle." Theodore looks at Francis and they both shake their heads, ignoring Henry and his inapt timing for a fist bump. Henry shrugs, unfazed.

"Osprey?" Alice hisses, shaking him a little more fervently now. He winces, as if every bit of him is fighting the ineluctable instinct to wake up. Then, his eyes begin to flutter and flounce, finally slamming open. He looks left, at first with little to no expression of which to speak upon his face. His dark hair is in matted tangles on his head, and his lean, chiseled face speaks of youth, but the dark circles under his eyes, and the keen pierce of his gaze speak of a man beyond his years in experience.

As his mental faculties return, and a cognizance recognizing more than alarm at the unfamiliar faces poised over him awakens, he sits up slowly, painfully. "Who…who are you, folks? Where am I, and what—" He jerks onto his feet, stumbling backward as sheer panic unfolds on his face. "What happened to the pig man? And the others who beat me senseless and dragged me here?"

Alice takes point on this. "It's okay. It's all right, Osprey. We're the good guys." Her voice is so soothing, diaphanous in its weight and earnest in its appeal, that Theodore knows she could calm a hurricane. "This man here at your feet, and that man back there, those are the pigs who did this to you. We've just saved you from…" She falters, clearing her throat and continuing in a solemn, gravelly tone. "From what might have been a terrible fate."

He pauses his dazed backwards shuffle. "How do you know about me, about my mission? Who sent you?"

Theodore steps forth. "Alright, Osprey, you're just going to have to trust us. Every second we dally in this hallway is a second closer not only to all our deaths, but to failing Vivianne, too. Listen, I know Alger."

"Alger? Pal, are you tellin' me you know Alger Marley?"

"Sort of. You could call me his…long-distance correspondent."

"Long distance?" Osprey waves his stiff arms around in little pinwheels, rubbing his shoulders and then lightly patting the wounds on his face with his fingertips. "You've gotta be jerkin' my chain, pal."

"Nope. I swear it on that record you hid for him up in Nithercott's penthouse."

"Holy mackerel, you are the real deal, mister. So, I take it you don't know where he's hiding out either?" Theodore shoots a sidelong glance at Henry, who puts forth the perfect, spurious little shrug. Theodore sighs in relief that his less-than-tactful friend didn't expose the location of the labor party's exiled last hope. He mimics Henry's shrug. Osprey seems to be as diehard as Morrow in his cause, if not more so. They can't risk him bungling this operation or inadvertently leading Nithercott's men to Marley himself who, if he chooses to do so, may someday lead the labor party once more to battle against the classists oppressing them.

"I can't say that I do, friend." He watches as Osprey teeters, then collapses onto his knees in a fatigued slump. "Okay, I know you're probably more disoriented than a fish in a terrarium right now, but we have to move. Henry, your phone please." He takes the phone and snaps it open, fervently placing it against his ear. Like lethargic beads of sap oozing down a tree trunk, the notes trickle into Theodore's ear. The woodwinds are ending their intro, meaning the full orchestra section is imminent. They've already wasted at least a quarter of their time in the past. Theodore slips Henry's flip phone into his pocket. He'll need to hang onto it and gauge how much time he has left through the night.

"The Pre-Shibboleth Frivolities are about to commence." He taps his lips with the meat of his pointer finger, pensively sifting through the options regarding Osprey. The guy can't be seen roaming the halls. He's the Guest of Honor tonight, after all, and any one of the many revelers is liable to spot him and cause a ruckus. "Francis, you take Osprey up to the seventh floor to Watters' chamber. That's the safest place for him right now and you're the only one strong enough to carry him in his injured state. Use the stairs—definitely not the elevator—and keep your eyes peeled down each corridor you take. Anyone spots you two and we may all be compromised.

"Once he's tucked away in Watters' room, you come back down and meet us in the Regal Ballroom. Being such a large cog in this bizarre machine, Watters won't miss the first event of the night. He'll be there, I'm sure of it; and that's where we'll find him and inform him that we're saving Vivianne. Then, after the Frivolities, and as per Marley's instruction, we'll split up and execute the escape plan."

"Now just hold your horses there, pal. You...folks, whoever you are, are saving someone else tonight? Is that what Alger wouldn't shut his yap about all those times I met with him? He was yackin' about some broad he left here and how it was just killin' him that he couldn't come back to the hotel, how he couldn't save her."

"All right, buddy," says Francis, throwing a burly arm around Osprey. "You heard the man; we're off. Cradle your head in my chest while we walk just in case we run into any wandering revelers. If that happens, we'll make pretend that you've simply overindulged tonight and can't differentiate your own asshole from your eyebrows."

"Ah, fine, you chumps win. You did save me from these pigs, and I owe you for that, so I'll play along for now. But don't think I won't have a host of questions waiting for you when we get outta purgatory here."

"Ditto," says Theodore. "Welcome to the Misfits Rescue Crew." He salutes the two of them comically, feeling a twinge of something like nausea in his stomach. He has to wonder if he'll ever see either one of them again. Being in the same mindset, Alice brushes past Theodore and Henry and wraps her arms around Francis, bringing her lips to his in a tender, ephemeral kiss. Theodore can see she's shaking, allowing the inexorable rostrum of her passion to break through the wavering hull of her equanimity.

She begins to cry, holding her face against his as if she may never do so again. Of all the dalliances and juvenile romances Alice has had, Theodore's never seen her like this. He's proud of his little sister. If they make it out okay tonight—an *if* that becomes bigger every moment they tarry—he knows now that she'll make it in life. The capricious and ever-searching Alice is finally finding solid ground, and Francis has singlehandedly guided her to it. He'll be forever grateful to Francis for this.

Ever since young Theodore made the decision to uproot Alice from her hell and move her to the city, she's been his beacon of hope, but also his most salient concern. He's felt responsible for each of her missteps to adulthood, and bludgeoned himself with the same questions over and over: did he make the right choice to take her away from the few friends she'd had upstate? Will Alice ever find a wholesome path through the vile overgrowth of temptation and hedonism surrounding her? He may finally stop beating himself up for his own lack of wisdom in guiding her. She's finding her own way.

Francis releases Osprey and scoops Alice up in his arms, whispering a little something in her ear. She nods, tears streaming down her cheeks and coruscating under the corridor lights.

"Okay," she says, letting go at last and returning to Theodore's side. He grabs her hand in his own and squeezes, smiling exultantly at her. She beams a beautiful, pained smile back and reaches over, pulling Henry's hand into her own. Henry gives a surprised glance at the gesture to his side. He slowly looks up and nods at them both. Then they all look on, silently watching as Francis and Osprey limp their way down the hall and out of sight.

V

The Regal Ballroom is a vacillating creature, alive with the swell of jazz. Trumpets crooning their sweet, golden tones; woodwinds piping a rotund melody from wall to wall; a torrid flurry of notes from the brass section assaults every overdressed corner of the dance hall. Party-favors and streamers zip across the room like stocks in a bull market. The concinnity of the scene lies not in the serene kiss of the music, nor the garish allure of the party favors, or the ambrosial scent of liquor hovering in the air, but in all of these elements combined with the frightening energy of the masqueraders as they move like the coiling and uncoiling body of one giant, menacing asp.

Alice teases the edge of the dance floor, spinning to the music, a smile forming under her mask for the first time since she let go of Francis on the third floor. "You know, Bear, it's such a shame that all of this revelry, the nectarous nostalgia of this world, is steeped in such treachery. What did you call it, The Patriciate Party? Such a wicked concept to strip the poor, working class of its necessities while the upper class gets plumper."

Henry shuffles over and bows before Alice. "Might I have this dance, young lady?"

"Why, I'd be offended if you didn't."

"Alice, maybe save observations like that for a safer location," Theodore hisses, watching as she and Henry begin a sprightly waltz before him. *Henry's actually not too bad at the jig,* Theodore thinks, quietly observing the pair. *He's full of surprises.* He looks left, over to the massive double-door of the ballroom. A wolf slips through the door and begins prowling straight towards them.

"There he is," Theodore says, grabbing Henry by the arm. "Watters." The old man approaches cautiously, tentatively, displaying in the reservation of his movements the fact that, for him, this is his first actual encounter with Theodore. Everything they went through last night technically never happened. Theodore will have to take point on this one.

"Watters," he says, clapping the wolf on the back. "Good to see you again."

"The pleasure is mine, young one. I take it this isn't your first journey to London?"

"No. Name's Theodore by the way, this is my fourth sojourn." Despite the raging maelstrom of noise around them and the likelihood that in this environment an eavesdropper would have to be an expert lip reader to discern anything spoken between them, he leans into Watters' ear. A constant wariness has gotten him this far. "I have the records and I'm ready to extract the girl."

Watters blinks through the wolf mask once, twice, thrice, and then leans back, looking toward the door he just ventured through, as if something—some duty—beyond is calling him. "But first you need to know something, Watters. We assaulted Harold and his men, and we saved Osprey from his cruel fate. The bodies of the two men are still up on the third floor; we had nowhere to store them without you...and one of my friends is depositing Osprey in your quarters as we speak."

Watters' stony eyes flare up, his mouth tightening. "You were not supposed to interfere with such affairs, young one. It was your task to save the girl and abscond from here forever. This is a very serious divagation from the course we were supposed to take. I must attend to this matter immediately, lest someone finds the bodies and discovers that the Guest of Honor is missing. Once I have sewn some thread of normalcy back into this situation there is another matter that requires my presence. I will not be here in the hotel for some time tonight, young one, so please be mindful of your environment and do not make a desultory mess of the plan again. You and your friends have gotten this far, so I trust in your abilities and in your sagacity. Fare thee well, young one! Ah! And one more thing."

Watters dips his hand into his vest pocket. Whatever it is he retrieves Theodore can't tell until its already nestled in his own coat pocket. If this wasn't 1931, Theodore would assume Watters was a Cold War agent with the deftness of his actions and his clandestine nature.

"Inside those vials are a particularly potent set of barbiturates. They will go undetected in a stiff drink, and they will take full effect within minutes. I believe you will know what to do with them."

With that, Watters makes for the door and slips out, leaving Theodore to deal with his deflating confidence. *What matter could be so important right now that it requires his leaving the hotel?* Being bereft of Watters on night four is not something Theodore had prepared for.

He feels a soft touch on his back. Alice gives him a hug. "We can do this, Bear. With or without your acquaintance by our side." Theodore watches as the masqueraders collectively hush, the Master of Ceremonies taking the stage in broad, showman's strides.

"Right," Theodore shrugs.

"Francis is back! He made it!" she whispers with a searing alacrity in her voice. She practically gallops over to meet him near the door.

"Hey fellas," he sighs, throwing his hefty arm over Theodore's and Henry's shoulders. He glances at the stage, where Nithercott is busy spouting his saccharine affection for his lovers and friends. "I saw Watters taking off towards the elevators. Did you guys manage to speak with him?"

Theodore nods. "Yup. But I don't think he'll be much help tonight, aside from cleaning up our third-floor mess. He's off to run some errand or something. Said he wouldn't be back for a while."

"Hmm, well at least we only really need four people to pull this off, right?

So being without him shouldn't fuck us over too badly, I don't think." Francis slicks an unkempt, sudorific tangle of hair behind his mask. "So, that Osprey guy has a pretty colorful little story—he filled me in on some things while I was helping him up to the seventh floor."

"Oh?" asks Henry. They all huddle together shoulder-to-shoulder, constricting into as small a group as possible so that no other revelers might eavesdrop. Every so often, the crowd erupts in stentorian applause for their lord and savior, Alfred Nithercott. Francis uses these outbursts to cover his voice.

"Yeah, so it turns out that he moved from the states several years ago and met Marley. A little bromance blossomed between them—"

"That dude's gay?" Henry scratches his head. "I've always prided myself on having excellent gaydar and mine didn't go off at all around him."

"Not an actual romance, you ninny, but they became close buds. Osprey and Marley had similar political inclinations, and Osprey claims that he had a sort of prescience about the Great Depression years before it came about. He moved to England to avoid the economic downturn that he surmised would happen, and that's when he discovered the great divide between economic classes here in England. He decided it was his calling to do whatever he could to turn things around for the working class here, and that's when he met Marley.

"After Marley was taken from the hotel and then disappeared, Osprey snaked his way into this social circle and infiltrated the hotel to observe the ways of the elite class and dig up whatever elicit information he could. Anything he could use against them with a fifth column group. That was a few years ago and he hadn't been back to the hotel since. But I guess Nithercott's men found him hiding out in Southwark and grabbed him.

"They knew he had been a subversive fly in their ointment, but they still aren't sure who he's working for. Nithercott knows Marley got away. I think knowing that Marley is still out there somewhere harboring incriminating knowledge against the Patriciates has haunted Nithercott ever since, and he's deduced that Osprey is an associate of Marley's. As you all know, the Shibboleth tonight is aimed at discovering once and for all where Marley is hiding now."

"Wow," Theodore exhales. "After all that intimidation and torture last night he didn't yield. He didn't once mention that he even knows Marley. Guy's as loyal as they come." Theodore looks over at the masqueraders, the volcanic eruption of their shouts spilling over the ballroom. The space above their heads is fleeced with clinking cocktail glasses and cigarettes. On stage Nithercott bows, pivots, and thrusts his arms up in a fervent cheer as the garish flash of the old camera splashes over the scene.

"Okay guys, this is it. Get into a huddle again. Time to execute this plan. Alice, you take the west exit; Henry, you the main entrance; Francis, the rear service entrance. As you know, there are two guards posted at each exit, and more henchmen blending in with the crowd. As far as we're concerned, these guys could be anyone, anywhere in the hotel, so isolation is always best here. The guard shift changes precisely every half hour, six and thirty-six minutes after the hour. So, whether you're going to try and get them slammed on some liquor or sweet talk them into leaving their post, you're going to want to have as much of that half-hour increment as possible to do your thing.

"Hopefully you guys all go the safe route and get them pass-out drunk. Alice, you showed us upstairs that you could give Bruce Lee a run for his money with your moves, but I implore you, be safe and be reasonable when you deal with the guards. Some of them will be carrying, and I would never forgive myself if something happened to you. I still despise the fact that you're even a part of this." Alice merely rolls her eyes.

"Now, when you incapacitate the doormen, remember to make sure the coast is clear and then drag them right through the doorway and outside. Henry, there are sets of bushes lining the front of the hotel and a streetlamp on the sidewalk to the right that isn't tall enough to reach over the backs of the bushes. Marley instructed you to dump the bodies in the darkness behind.

"Alice same goes for you, except the path out your doors leads to a narrow and dark alley. Pull your two unconscious goons over behind the dumpster to the left. And finally, Francis. Remember that once your cocktail has knocked them out harder than Muhammad Ali's right hook, you're supposed to haul them down the service ramp and throw them into a small equipment shed out behind the hotel. If any or all of you succeed in your efforts, they'll be out cold for a while, but we'll only have the remainder of that half hour left before the shift changes and we're fucked."

Alice, Francis, and Henry all bob their heads enthusiastically. Alice is wringing her hands nervously, and under Francis' mask Theodore can see the ripe pulse of his jugular.

"Are we good, guys? Anyone in the Misfits Rescue Crew want to say anything…you know…just in the off chance this elaborate and impossibly farfetched plan goes awry?"

Henry's face pulls into a confident, prim little smile. "I have nothing to add, other than it's time you go snatch that ring, Mr. Frodo, and drop it right into the fires of Mt. Doom."

"You know what? If this whole thing goes up in flames and that's the last thing you ever say to me, Henry, I'm oddly okay with that." The frenzied expanse of revelers begins swelling toward the double door, each of them eager to commence the search for Nithercott's secret sub-section, and thus the Shibboleth.

"Keep your radios hidden and only use them if absolutely necessary, guys," Theodore whispers.

"What's your plan, Bear?"

"To find Vivianne and slip her out after one of you has achieved your goal but before the guard shift changes." He looks to the double door, watching as the revelers smash, wallop, and bore through each other like an esurient batch of bargain shoppers on Black Friday. He peers beyond, through the doorway, where he can see but a warmly lit slice of the lobby lounge. "And I think I might know just where to find her."

In a cerulean splash of ardent motion Alice's summer dress wraps around

Theodore as she hugs him tight. "Remember back when we were too young to know what it was to be boring adults stuck in a lackluster, humdrum life?" He nods. "Well, the pragmatic part of me is thinking, holy shit, how can any of this be real? While a bigger, self-preserving hunk of me is thinking, run, get out of here, girl, this is an unusual and dangerous place. But the biggest part of my mind is saying, this is it—the moment I've been waiting my whole life for; a moment to be a part of something truly extraordinary. It's like the entirety of history has been carefully mapped by the hand of God himself for this very moment, and he's given us the pen. I know you can do this, Bear."

She pecks him on the cheek and a smile ignites his face, one of those true ear-to-ear smiles that he's had so little reason in life to wear. "I really couldn't have asked for a better bunch of people to come along with me to rewrite history. Good luck, guys, and may the next time I see you be out on the street, falling over each other with exhaustion in our bones and a story in our minds to tell our children someday." Henry shakes Francis' hand and winks at Theodore. Francis gives a venerable and dignified nod to Theodore, who returns it heartily. Like lonely party guests who have overstayed their welcome but find themselves tied to the comfort of each other's company, they reluctantly part ways, with Theodore making straight for the double door.

He brushes through the door to the lounge, which is encumbered with the source of revelers Theodore can only intuit is the bunch that doesn't care to find Nithercott's surreptitious Shibboleth. Cigarettes, booze, smooth jazz, and the lingering glances that lurk beneath each mask are all the excitement this batch of societal elites needs tonight. As soon as he's through the door, Theodore's eyes swerve over to the bar. Bertram the testy mixologist, with whom Theodore exchanged a few words on night one, is tending bar and socializing with a string of indolent guests. Perched on the leftmost barstool, with one hand teasing the nape of a wine glass, and her head cocked insouciantly over the scant slope of her shoulder, is Bargirl herself; the enigmatic little sprite Theodore hasn't been able to peel from his mind since the time he first laid eyes on her, right here, three nights ago.

He'd notice the spark ignite within his heart, like some unused locomotive engine turning over and spinning off a web of dust, were it not for the grim determination he feels now upon seeing her. He must know once and for all if this is her. If the bargirl of his dreams is in fact the Vivianne associated with Marley, and not merely some other random girl who moved into Vivianne's room after she moved on. He must know if this is the girl Nithercott tortured those years ago and kept caged in this hotel like some poor neglected animal. Theodore feels his feet begin to move, conscious thought dragging behind the purposeful step he's now taking.

He watches Bargirl take note of the intense and brooding figure approaching her, he can see the askance look she gives him before causally averting her gaze to the bar top. He sweeps over and plops himself in the creaky stool beside her, making a perfunctory glance to the bartender and then settling his eyes upon the velvet lined-moody oak walls of the bar. Suddenly, he's apprehensive; intimidated by her presence, by the placid self-assurance that her character asserts. He raps on the counter with trepidatious fingers, trying to look like he belongs here and isn't merely succumbing to a coronary episode brought on by stress. He feels a light peck on his left shoulder.

"You've quite the taste in coats, but I'll venture a guess that you find yourself a modicum taller than you stand?" He gulps, turning to see her cradling her head in her palm, elbow poised on the counter and an incisive curiosity in her body language. She's leaning toward him ever so slightly, the coruscant gleam of her pearl white dress beckoning him forth. Being mere inches from her dredges up from the depths of Theodore's self-imposed ascetic nature an unyielding recitation of the moment he shared with her two nights ago, and an unyielding desire to be intimate with her once more. Her perfume cascades from her wrists and plumes over to Theodore; tamed youth, bridled innocence, and fettered confidence.

"That's nothing of which to be ashamed," she continues, her voice is a teardrop of honey dripping from the comb. "Each of the men I've known has had some degree of personal delusion that's shown in some outwardly clumsy way. Most of the time I find it endearing." Theodore smiles, glancing down at his garb. "You must pardon my brash ejaculation, I find myself drawn to strangers and, while you are certainly a stranger to me, I feel as if I've met you before, mister…"

"Call me Mr. Gazelle," he says, pointing to the mask. His hand returns to his lap, where he enwraps it with the other and squeezes tight, feeling the urge to abscond with her right now, just throw her over his shoulder and storm out of here once and for all. Kismet has led him here and he's not about to let a batch of deranged masqueraders get in his way.

"Mr. Gazelle…hmm…" She brings her wine glass to her face and swirls it in cerebration. "I dreamed of a gazelle just last night." She looks down, visibly perturbed. "I was desperately alone, wandering through a caliginous swathe of forest, when I saw this lone gazelle grazing on the grass. It reared its head to reveal a beautiful misty pair of eyes, and it began to chase me. I fled from it out of some intangible instinct cudgeled into me from a life of seclusion, and not out of any explicit urgency or danger. At long last, I ceased running and bade the animal approach. I awoke just as its nose caressed my outstretched hand."

She pulls her gracile chin up towards Theodore again. She chuckles. "You must think I'm mad, relating a story of such inconsequence to you before we've even shaken hands. Still, the resemblance of the beast from my dream to your doppelgänger is uncanny. And I'm sure you understand how dreams can cause you to look differently upon things in the waking world."

"Yes, I do," he studies her pouty lips, her swanlike neck, the elegant curve of her clavicle. "I can also say that some dreams are so vivid, so detailed, like real life dissembling itself into a glossy sheen of images so brilliant that the only reason you know they're a lie is in their utter perfection." His eyes meander down to the soft little hand splayed over her lightly muscled thigh. "And rarely—perhaps once or twice in my life—I've found myself persuaded by the intoxicating perfection of real life that I have to pinch myself."

She nods, the hawk mask bobbing up and down as she continues to study Theodore. "You're American," she says with a tinge of caution mingling with curiosity.

The reality of the situation floods back to Theodore. His mind snaps to Alice and the others. He wonders if they're okay, if they've begun working the guards yet or, God forbid, if the guards are working them. "Yes, I am. Actually, we need to talk about something." He looks over his shoulder, where Bertram is regaling the slew of revelers with a ribald story of his youth in the way only bartenders seems capable. Theodore looks back to Bargirl, covering his mouth with a quaking hand.

"I've met you before," he starts, not knowing precisely how he's going to explain something that cannot be readily related to any sane person. "I've actually been here before, a few times."

"Oh," she says, with the most ethereal utterance of one who believes they're being toyed with. "You have attended one of the previous Shibboleths? I have rarely, if ever, met a Yank at such an event. When did the last Shibboleth take place? I believe it was in the spring," she answers her own question. "Are you sojourning here in London, Mr. Gazelle, or do you have residency in the U.K.?"

"Well, I suppose you could call it a sojourn…" All he's thinking of is ripping that hawk mask off her beautiful face and discovering whether or not she is the Vivianne he's assumed this entire time she is. But such a flagrant display must wait until they're away from pernicious eyes. "Listen, you and I have a mutual friend—well, had a mutual friend."

Her sagacity seeps through her countenance as her social affectations begin to crumble before him. She's starting to catch on. After one more cautious dip of his head leftwards and behind, he continues, "You see, I knew a mister um, Marley." His voice shrinks like the bead of a star in the morning light. "Alger Marley."

As the name slips out of his mouth, Bargirl's expression falters for the most fugacious of flashes. If this girl is in fact Vivianne, a torrent of terrible associations, perhaps peppered through with some fond memories, must be capsizing her mind like a skiff in a squall. But she maintains a miraculously equable demeanor. She sits upright, reaching calmly down and smoothing out an invisible crease in the leg of her dress. At long last, she says, "That is one name that is not to be so carelessly thrown about in this building, amongst people of this import."

"I know, I know. Can we possibly talk somewhere in private?" The seed of a newfound panic cracks open within him and unfurls a nascent root of dismay as he realizes that if this girl isn't Vivianne, she could be any one of Nithercott's closest allies. He might be walking himself right into the belly of the beast with his reckless inquisition.

She holds fast, gently gnawing at her tongue inside her mouth and nearly dipping it into her cheek. "Yes, I think we must." With a calculated swoop, she rises from the barstool and floats to the deepest corner of the lobby lounge. Theodore rises, one hand lingering on the familiar bastion of the oak bar, a significant portion of his being refusing to let go of anything solid. He inhales slowly and lets go, beginning to thread through the lounge in silent pursuit, like a recalcitrant soul wondering whether he's being dragged from purgatory to the gates of heaven or the flames of hell.

He follows her through an unassuming door and up a series of stairs. Neither of them shares a word, nor even a glance, as they ascend, the austere clatter of their footfalls the only shared discourse between them. After several wends, he feels his breath devolve into labored husks, the lactic burn setting into his knees. Up ahead, Bargirl barely shows a sign of exhaustion or of any physical output whatsoever, and Theodore begins to wonder just how many times she's made this climb; just how well accustomed she is to the vermicular nature of the hotel.

At long last they arrive at the ninth floor, where a locked gate prevents any further exploration toward the roof. Bargirl slips through the door, not bothering to look back and see if Alger Marley's ally has obediently followed or retreated back down the stairs and out of the hotel. He knows she doesn't need visual confirmation, as he can't tell if the clack of his shoes or the pneumatic hiss of his breath is bouncing across the walls with more force.

He follows her into the ninth-floor corridor, practically nipping at the evanescent glimpses of her heels under the wavering billow of her dress in anticipation of what's to come. About midway down the hall she stops before the door with no room number displayed—her room. She pulls it only slightly ajar and sidles in, as if the prying eyes in the hallway portraits are allowed only the scantest glimpse inside. Theodore slips in after her, clicks the door shut, and slams the deadbolt.

When he turns, Bargirl is leaning against her ornate ivory desk, the silky lines of her back muscles peering at him from the dual vanity mirrors behind her. She lets out a tenuous sigh like she's freeing herself of some transparent but immense burden. "You should not have come here, Yank," she says at long last. "It is not safe for you, as it wasn't safe for the man you claim to have known."

Theodore barely hears her. He can't take it anymore; his desire for answers eclipses any rational thought. He bounds across the tiny room with both shaking hands poised before him. He grips her mask as she begins to pull away, to bring her arms up in a fruitless retaliation.

"What are you—" she begins, but the cover is removed, the feeble redoubt torn asunder, the doppelgänger cast aside to reveal a naked truth. Under the quivering gape of the mouth, past the alarmed arch of the brow, beyond the cheeks rosy with consternation, is the most beautiful sight Theodore has ever laid eyes on. He's unearthed a shimmering diamond from a bed of pewter ore. The porcelain gleam of her skin which seems somehow to reject the surrounding light and coruscate all its own, the contumacious streak of golden hair that's teasing her forehead, the untamable glaucous sea of her left eye, and the audacious yet graceful peak of her nose.

Nestled above her right cheek is a grey caldera of tissue that once cradled an eye, now serving as a barren and brutal reminder of a past riddled with injustice and horror. It is her. It's Vivianne—it's been her all along. Though he assumed he would, Theodore feels no relief in knowing this; even if knowing that this girl is Vivianne means he can live to see tomorrow, that she isn't another one of Nithercott's henchmen luring Theodore into a snare. He feels no immediate gratitude for his own prosperity; he feels nothing at all but overburdened with a boiling fury that this young woman—this sweet, perfect human—has been shackled in a world of violence, possession, and acrimony.

He feels like stealing away and shouting from the rooftop of this accursed hotel were his knees not about to buckle underneath him. He feels like wringing his hands together until they chafe and bleed, for they are nothing but bits of ineffectual flesh shaking at his sides. He is unable to scrub away the stains of the past, unable to coax a bead of erasure from the impenetrable annals of time. He cannot take back the hurt Vivianne has endured, the fear and uncertainty she has harbored. The fortitude she's shown in the fleeting moments they've shared show a raw puissance he's never known. In the darkest moments of his own past he found the strength only to escape, to flee from his demons. Running was the easy way out and he took it without a moment's thought. Vivianne has owned the pain and the torment, has built a life for herself in the eye of the storm.

Theodore stumbles toward her, drunk with determination, dazed by her presence. He cannot erase what happened to her or her friend, Marley, but perhaps he can bring some closure between them.

"What on earth are you doing?" Vivianne stammers, thrusting her hands over her face in a rush to cover her missing eye. She drops to the ground and paws for the mask, slamming it back against her face. In removing Vivianne's mask Theodore has exhumed her darkest secret, her most guarded truth. He understands the purpose of the layer of mesh over the eye holes of the mask. The imperfection on her face is a living reminder of what she's been through, and she will hide it from everyone she can. The mask is her bastion from the cruel and unfeeling eyes of strangers, which would see only the gruesome, skin-deep evidence. Most would overlook the injury for its truest quality, the forbearance and tenacious spirit that it represents. Theodore knows better than all the other fools, though.

"Why would you do such a cruel thing?" she asks.

"I needed to know for certain."

"To know what? Who are you, and what is your business here? In what capacity did you know Alger?"

Theodore sighs. "It's a very long story and we don't have much time." He brandishes Henry's phone and watches Vivianne's face follow it to his ear in astonishment. In the distance, he can hear the slow drawl of brass instruments pierce the static. The waltz is on. They're halfway through the night—maybe more.

"That's the most curious little device I've ever seen." She leans forward to inspect the foreign object Theodore's holding. He scoops her hand in his, feeling the spark of excitement at touching her again, and places the phone in her hand. She begins turning it over and over before her mask, as if the next rotation might reveal to her some detail that would explain what it is.

"That's my phone—well, it's not mine, it's my buddy's, but still."

"Your *phone*? As in telephone?" She motions to the table against the wall, to a lovely Corian and brass rotary phone.

"Yes, that ugly little thing in your hand is what those ornate and beautiful devices will become someday."

"I say, America truly is a marvelous and utterly different place. I have always wanted to see it with my own eyes."

"Well, it's not *just* that I'm from America, you see, I'm…well, I'm from the future."

A brief silence yields to a burst of amused laughter. "Is this really a time for petty mockery, Mr. Gazelle? First, you allude to your association with a dear friend of mine, a friend that is long gone, and next you swipe my doppelgänger from my face. Then you show me a device the likes of which I've never seen, only to tease me further with such a shoddy explanation of why you're the single most unique person I've ever met." Her cadence slows and then derails as her statement closes, as if she's come mid-sentence to some marvelous revelation about Theodore. "Not a thing about you, from your manner of speaking to the shoes on your feet, adheres to the rules of reality, and I cannot expound beyond that. You're the angel of my dreams realized in waking life."

"But it's true, that crappy phone there and the person standing before you are both from nearly a century in the future. I know I must seem like a crazy escaped from the asylum but there's no time to explain. Suffice it to say that I know Alger indirectly. He hatched a remarkably elaborate plan to get you out of here and I managed to stumble upon it in the form of audio recordings left around the hotel. My friends are downstairs right now trying to knock out the guards at each set of doors so that we can slip out, hopefully undetected, but we need to go now. The guard shift is liable to change soon."

Vivianne absorbs this information with an effervescent half-smile unraveling beneath her mask. He can't tell if the smile is one of satisfaction, as if she'd known someday her prince would come and at long last he's here, or perhaps it's one of incredulity at the madman she's found herself entertaining in her room. Without a word, she glances to a clock on the nightstand.

"The guard shift changes in four minutes."

Theodore takes this as a statement of tentative trust. She's telling him she'll play his game for now, just long enough to see how raving mad he really is.

"Okay, well then I need to page my friends and see if they're okay and if any of them have succeeded in drugging the guards. But we need to move now!" He grasps her hand and gently pulls toward the door, but she withdraws her hand and shrinks back immediately.

"You can't be serious, Yank. The only reason I've entertained your audacious statements thus far is because you claimed to know Alger Marley. But this is a dangerous place—it is not at all what it seems on such an ostensibly whimsical night as this. You can be killed for such recklessness. Or worse. Besides, whatever you know or do not know about my life here at The King's Inn, it is my home and has been for many years. I grew up within these walls. Even if those who would oppose my escape weren't in the equation, it is too much to ask of me to walk right out the door…into the outside world. It is not so simple."

Theodore exhales slowly, trying to calm the freight train of anxiety barreling through his nerves. "Right now, it has to be that simple. Look," he grabs the doorknob with one hand and extends the other toward her. "You have to trust me. I only have a snapshot of what you've been through in my mind, so I can't begin to fathom what you are feeling right now, but there must be some part of you that wants to tear down these walls, or at least say goodbye to them once and for all! This is your chance! And if you feel for me even a modicum of what I feel for you, I know you'd like to get to know me a little better." She remains reticent.

"I get that it must be more than overwhelming for some random guy to come into your life and shake it up so violently, and I know that I'm asking a lot of you. It's not right and it's not fair, but these are the cards we've been dealt! This is our window!"

She takes one step toward him, biting her lip hard. He continues, "I'm only here thanks to Alger. He's behind the machinations that brought me into your life. Did he ever show you his gramophone? The one that looks unlike any other music player in the world? The Sonophone?"

"Why, yes he did. We used to sit in his room for hours every night playing discarded old records. His phonograph became something of a bridge between our worlds…our lives."

"Well, it became an actual bridge between his world and mine, too. I have the Sonophone back in New York City. Did he tell you about his grandfather Walter, who built the machine?"

"Yes. Walter was an inventor from what Alger told me. He was the progenitor of the phonograph machine." She takes one step closer, hovering in the space between the bed and Theodore's hand. Her arm teases forward briefly and then snaps back to her body. "You really do know a great deal about Alger, don't you, Mr. Gazelle?"

"That phonograph machine was no ordinary contraption. It's the time machine that I used to get here. Alger welded the time-travel dial to this specific date and time so someone from the future might save you." He shrugs. "I'm here."

Just then, a burst of static erupts in his coat. His hand dives into the pocket and clutches the walkie talkie.

"Breaker Breaker one-niner, Big Rig transmitting, over," Henry says through an army of electrical interference. "Listen guys, these doormen are as stubborn as a Jehovah's Witness at the doorstop; the fuckers aren't taking the bait. I'm in a phonebooth just around the corner, so I'm out of earshot. Anyone else having any luck with this? Over."

A second layer of static wends across the radio waves. Alice's voice comes through in a dusky whisper. "I'm nearly there, guys. These English elites sure do love an American accent and a little flirtation. They've taken two sips each of my 'Western Twilight' cocktail. That's what I'm calling it, but it's really just a lemon drop with a touch of botanicals and passion fruit. I told them it's all the rage in the states. So, give me a couple more minutes and they should be kissing the carpet. Theodore? How's everything on your end?"

Theodore shoots a glance at Vivanne. "You truly are from the future, aren't you? The mysterious figure of my dreams spun into reality and beckoning me to the phantasmagoria of the future. Take me with you, Mr. Gazelle."

A smile the width of the Milky Way and with all the splendor of the Aurora Borealis peels across his face. He raises the transmitter to his mouth. "We're ready for extraction up here on the ninth floor. Be down in a jiff."

"Righteous!" Henry exclaims, "This feels as epic as that time you and I went to the Buckling Pins bowling alley and those two girls came up to us out of nowhere and…" Theodore pockets the device and takes Vivianne's hand in his own. For a moment as inscrutable as a raindrop in a thunderstorm they're suspended in air, clinging pertinaciously to each other, their bodies static but their hearts dancing to the sanguine rhapsody of love. The energy between them is unstoppable and he knows she can feel it too. Shaking, he draws her to him and brings his lips to hers.

He knows this moment is ephemeral, etched in mere sand, and will fade under the ineluctable tides of time like Ozymandias or the fading Parthenon, as do all of humanity's exploits both great and dull. But despite the destructive waves of time, this moment will eclipse all other of man's memories. The electricity between him and Vivianne will power their love in the future as it does now, and in this sense, their love will transcend the capacity normally allotted to mankind through the constraints of time. Theodore knows that he and Vivianne are setting a precedent for all humanity. Should they make it out of here alive, they will be the first man and woman to have shared a love that surpasses mortal existence, wading across the breadth of two centuries like the waxing moon, standing resolute against the deleterious hands of time like the sturdy oak. In the grand epoch of time, their shared experience will resound with a greater timbre than that of any other moment in man's earthly sojourn.

Still clutching her by the waist, he twists the doorknob and dives into the hallway with the youthful fervor of a newfound purpose. Doubt and dejection bounce off his mind, leaving no seed of influence as they have for so many years. An army couldn't stop him from saving this girl. With his arm drawn tautly about her, he breaks to the left with the goal of taking the rear stairs again and slipping through the lobby lounge to the side exit where Alice will hopefully be waiting for them.

"I knew it," an inimically familiar voice creeps like spreading ice down the hallway. Theodore and Vivianne freeze dead in their tracks. They need not turn to discover who has caught them at the outset of their great escape.

"Fuck," Theodore mutters. Vivianne's hand clasps his and bites down hard. They do a slow pivot in tandem. A stone's throw away, Alfred Nithercott is looming in the hallway under the effusion of a dim wall sconce. The rat upon his face is lopsided, as if he was just about to remove it when he saw the fleeing couple. *Of course*, thinks Theodore. He's done his rounds and he's come up to the ninth floor to practice his speech in his penthouse. How could he have overlooked such an important detail?

"I knew there was something aberrant about you, Yank. Like the portent of a storm brewing in the turgid belly of the sky, I knew there was something different, something cunning and deceitful." Nithercott's posture softens, his mouth uncoiling into a dubious frown. "Vivianne? My dear, my sweet? What is it you think you are doing with this American buffoon?"

"I…I…"

"She's coming with me, Nithercott, whether you like it or not."

After a funereal pause in which Nithercott's whole body tenses, every fiber of his being averse to the idea of losing her, he takes but one step forth. What is it she means to him? Why does he cling to her with such fervency through these years?

"This matter is not yours to decide, young man. I suggest you step aside and allow me that I might put my seedling back into her pot. Lest you try my patience." One more step forth. Theodore pulls her closer to him still. Everything has led to this moment. His whole life he has been on an unrelenting track, spurred on by destiny toward this very moment. He can't falter now.

He says, shaking, "We're leaving, Nithercott. I think you should turn around right now and prepare for your Shibboleth. And while you're at it, consider all the harm you've caused this girl, consider the monster you've always been, and the emptiness your life will suffer for its remaining years, like a ghost ship stirring only the wake of the sea beneath it and never finding a port to pick up another vagrant soul. You're going to find yourself alone from here on, paying for your many sins."

"Alone for my sins, eh?" Nithercott chuckles, meandering over to the wall in a slow yet rigid gait, his muscles expectant of some imminent action. "You know, the greatest quality you Americans possess is your grit…your, your tenacious audacity and your imperturbable will." His hands reach out, hovering over the glass door of a wooden case nailed on the wall. "When you set your minds on something, you bloody well accomplish it with the fiercest alacrity. The Black Hand wove a needle of social and economic dissonance in 1914, a needle which the entire world had already long since threaded, and America put their ingenuity, their spirit, and their resources into the fray. And what do you know, they showed the world's great powers the bitter feeling of genuflection.

"Well, let us see how your courage stands against the patriarchal fury of a man at the end of his tether!" Nithercott draws a fist and smashes the glass door of the case, swiping at the remaining shards and then retrieving a fire axe from within. He plops the neck of the weapon, just below the shimmering steel head, into his left hand and sneers. Vermilion lines trickle down in a gruesome contrast against the stark white of his gloves. He begins cackling like a madman.

"Run!" Theodore stammers, pushing Vivianne behind him and shoving her down the hall. Nithercott starts down after them, flinging the heft of the axe to and fro as he gives chase. Theodore turns, fearing that his knees may buckle in their inability to hold his terrified frame upright. They do not buckle, nor falter in his adamant need, and he launches himself after Vivianne while the thunder of murderous intent clops ever closer behind them.

"This way!" she shouts, hanging a right at the nearest intersection and driving down the length of a nondescript corridor. Some indefinable number of steps behind them, Nithercott's voice eclipses the frenzy of footfalls.

"That's right, flee for your lives. I know every cranny of this building. I shall be on you like your shadow!" Theodore cranes his neck to see the moment the impending figure crests the corner. He can't allow himself to slip and fall, though—which would surely mean a quick and brutal ending, so he only allows the briefest of glances. His eyes dart forward. Vivianne's white dress flaps before him like the rapturous arm of an angel beckoning him forth. His eyes dart back. The silvery glint of the axe shows first, the tall and lanky form following in jerking, maniacal heaves. Theodore's caught between heaven and hell and the only way out of perdition is forward, under the rhythmic propulsion of his legs and the galloping beat of his heart.

"I'll cut you to ribbons, Yank!" Theodore hears several paces back. "But only after I've eviscerated your companion before your waking eyes." Theodore's eyes dart back. Nithercott's stalking after them at a cumbered but steady pace, heaving the axe above his head every few strides, waving it about in vicious, bloodthirsty whirls. His shining swathe of greased black hair flaps madly about. His mouth vacillates between a wide, rapacious grin, and that of utter repulsion at the unfamiliar taste of control slipping through his fingers. Beads of sweat dot his jowl and slide down his chin.

"Follow me," Vivianne beckons him to the right at the hall's end. He watches with awe at her celerity in heels. It's a chore keeping up with her through this labyrinth of corridors, like following a lab rat through the maze it was born in. He dashes along, knowing that if the madman with the axe is able to catch them, all he can do is throw himself in front of Vivianne and take the blow.

"In here!" her voice sinks into a frenzied whisper as she pauses before a door and brandishes a set of keys. Stamping his feet in an anxious fervor and feeling the hammer of his heart in his chest, Theodore glances back. Nithercott hasn't rounded the corner, not yet, but any second now he'll be trundling toward them. Theodore leans over her shoulder; she's scrambling to find the right key to the door, but an unbridled terror is spoiling any fine muscle control she has.

"I don't mean to add fuel to the fire here, but he's gonna round the corner any second!" Theodore glances back. The spectral shadow of their hunter splashes along the wall in gyrating oblong shapes. "We're gonna need a plan B if you can't find that key, Viv!"

"I found it!" She dives the key into the lock and throws the door open, folding her body into the half-open threshold. Theodore squeezes in just before Nithercott's body catches up with his shadow. Quietly, quickly, Vivianne clicks the door shut and collapses against the wall dissolving into a fit of tears. Theodore looks around. She's led them right into a dead end. They're standing in a small hexagonal room with a single table in the middle crowned with an ornate floral display. Nowhere to go and nowhere to hide. Vivianne composes herself, putting her pointer finger over mouth and tiptoeing across the room to a light switch. She flicks it, casting them into a thick shroud of darkness.

Theodore finds himself unable to move; a virulent and unrelenting wave of panic overcomes him as he's lifted from the room and thrust suddenly into the arms of an old memory. The night that his mom hid from their dad in the hallway closet during one of his drunken tirades. He and Alice had been playing with his dad's set of broken old matchbox cars—a present dad dug up from a dusty box in the garage one December in lieu of going to the store and buying thoughtful presents for his kids. Nevertheless, Theodore and Alice got some mileage out of those cheap old toys in their younger years. They were playing in the upstairs hallway just before bedtime, listening to music on an old handheld radio—*Fastball* or *Sugar Ray*, he can't recall which band. What he can remember is that this was one of the only times Theodore hadn't had the presence of mind to hear the ruckus below in time to shield young Alice.

As she pushed a sallow matchbox Mustang, the only car in the assortment she'd play with, mom came brushing past them with an air of severity in her step and a look of terror in her eyes Theodore knew all too well. He remembers seeing the ripe welt of a bruise on mom's cheek before she dove into the hall closet. Alice called to her and when she got no reply she fell into a lugubrious fit, slamming the Mustang against the wall over and over as her young mind got a loose grip on the situation. Theodore darted over to Alice and dragged her into the upstairs office. All he knew to do in that moment was mimic his mother's behavior. He switched off the overhead light and curled up with Alice under the desk, watching the door of the hallway closet and imagining his mother inside, scared out of her mind and defenseless.

He remembers the vacuous silence that ensued, followed by a slow and uneven thumping up the stairs clashing with the pleasing melody that streamed from the overturned radio in the hall. Finally, dad crossed the threshold under the only lit bulb in the upper level, a corona of light playing off his big, teetering frame. Theodore recalls slapping one hand over Alice's mouth and the other over his own, his toes digging into the carpet in fear.

A soft hand squeezes Theodore's shoulder, thrusting him violently from his catatonia. Suddenly, he's being yanked down under the table, where he finds Vivianne's body curled up. He settles down against her and holds onto her with all he's got. *How did they end up like this? Is Alice okay? Francis and Henry? Where are they? Is it all going down in a blaze? Is this how it all ends?*

"Vivianne, Vivianne my sweet, where are you?" He hears the distant crooning of their hunter as he lopes down the hall. Three soft knuckle raps reverberate down the monastic silence of the hall. A shuffle of feet. "Could you be in here, mystery guest?" Three more knocks on a door that can't be ten feet down the hall. Nithercott's just taunting them now. Theodore bites down on the back of his hand and prays their assailant won't choose the right door. "Hellooo?" The haunting voice teases under the crack in the door. He's one room away now. Knock, knock, knock. Theodore's heartbeat echoes the swift rapping on the door. The two black outlines of Nithercott's feet brush across the golden slit of light under the door. They linger for an impossibly long moment. Theodore paws for Vivianne's mouth in the darkness and blankets it with his hand. He does the same with his own until the shadow beyond the door moves on. With its departure, Theodore feels his heart rise from his stomach, like lagan untethered from its buoy.

He digs his knees into the carpet and prepares to rise when the two black outlines muddy the golden ribbon of light once more. "Wait," hisses Vivianne, clamping down on his arm. A low rustling of keys. Theodore squeezes tight against Vivianne, enveloping her constricted body under his coat as best he can manage. The heavy clunk of a key sounds in the lock, followed by the low rasp of the revolving doorknob. The door lulls open, a rectangle of brilliant light splashing across the first few feet of carpet within. Theodore and Vivianne are still shrouded in darkness but their obscurity alone won't keep them safe from their pursuer. *What to do, what to do?*

A lightheadedness overtakes Theodore as he rocks slowly back and forth. He's holding onto Vivianne with all he's got but he feels himself slipping, drifting impossibly away from her. He's back under the table with Alice, watching as his dad staggers in the hallway, clumsily slamming his fist into the wall. He hears his dad's drunken howl as it rattles the pictures in their frames above Theodore's head. He watches as his father angles his body to the hallway closet, stumbling toward it with a foggy determination. Theodore covers Alice's eyes and ears now, knowing what's sure to come next. Just before his wandering hand reaches the closet door, dad lunges sideways, succumbing to the effects of his potent over-indulgence and collapsing to the floor. He emits one more furious grumble before a flatline of buzz-saw snores fills the cavernous silence of the house. Safe tonight.

Theodore feels himself drifting slowly back into the present. The golden cone of light before him, obviated by the long and lanky silhouette perched in the doorway, fades into focus once more. Nithercott moves in soft and silent as a cunning leopard parting the tall grass to pounce on a lone gazelle. *What to do, what to do?* Nithercott begins rounding the center table, his feet falling just inches from Theodore's cheek.

He pauses beside the table. Theodore sees the stark right angle of the fire axe's blade dip into view as Nithercott lowers the weapon to his side. Theodore can hear Nithercott breathing, can see the slight undulations of the axe's blade as it bobs up and down with the taxed breaths of its deranged keeper.

"I can smell you, my pet," he snarls from above. "And I can taste the sudorific beads that glisten upon your forehead, Yank. I can *taste* your fear. It hangs in the air, oh yes, it does, and it leads me straight to you." Nithercott begins moving once more, heading for the light switch at the back. It's now or never, Theodore thinks. He can either remain frozen to the floor and let their demise come to them, or he can do something to turn the tide. He thinks of Alice, and of Henry and Francis. How he wishes they were here to help him now. But they're not; he is all Vivianne has. And he cannot allow himself to fail her, to fail Alice and his friends.

Theodore brushes his nose against the carpet and inhales. He can't move. His legs are lead pipes, his feet are boulders, and he's trapped beneath them, trapped beneath his own history of inaction, his lifetime of dejection. He should have saved Alice earlier, should have taken her from that monster years before that day she had to fear for her very life like her mother did so many times. Vivianne won't suffer Theodore's indolence and inadequacy, not since this miraculous series of events has led him to her, be it by a stroke of blind luck or divine intervention. He shifts under the table as Nithercott's left leg brushes past, almost out of reach now. Vivianne's fingers dig into his shoulder; he swears he can feel the faint thread of her heart beating through her fingertips. He cradles himself onto his back and lifts a languid leg toward their assailant.

Trapped underneath a murderer, each tiny, deliberate movement is like treading the entirety of a rain shadow desert, each shaky breath a knock at death's door. But he holds his leg up against these forces as he paws in the darkness for Vivianne's hand. He gives it two deft squeezes, a tacit implication for her to steel herself under the imminent confrontation. He retracts his quivering leg and propels it forth with all his might.

Thud. The heavy steel head of the fire axe hits the floor first. Nithercott's entire body follows in one slackened lump. Theodore doesn't hesitate. He digs his fingers into the carpet and lunges forth.

"Run, Vivianne!" he shrieks, falling upon the murky outline of their assailant. He hears her scamper from under the table and watches her form in his periphery as she pauses in the doorway.

"Don't fight him, just run!" she pleads. He has no time to respond. He straddles Nithercott with both legs. One hand gropes for the axe on the floor while the other moves to pin Nithercott's shoulder down. The madman is strong, though, squirming like an anaconda and kicking wildly beneath him. He nearly bucks Theodore off, but Theodore stabilizes, pawing frantically at the floor for the weapon. By the time Theodore finds the handle, he realizes that Nithercott's hand is already coiled around it. He lunges back as the blurred shape of the axe flies toward his head. He's tumbling now, falling off Nithercott's body and rolling towards the door. He crashes to a halt on his hands and knees, his brain beginning to swim as tiny aureate dots puncture his vision. He sees a dark figure rise before him, the moonlike glow of the rat's eyes emerging from the darkness. Before he's able to react, a pair of determined hands clasp his underarms from behind and yank him up. Vivianne pulls him out the door and pushes him into the corridor, slamming the door in Nithercott's face as she does it. The heavy slab of wood ricochets off his body and hits Theodore in the back, spurring him onward.

"Let's go!" She grabs his hand with both of hers, avulsing him from the arm that snakes out of the room and clutches his shoulder. Theodore finds his feet and begins slogging down the corridor alongside Vivianne, the muted thunder of their footsteps resounding like the determined thrum of his heart. He does a half-turn to see Nithercott treading after with a rapacious grin on his face and a crimson strand dripping from his mouth. *He's gaining on them. How is this possible?* Burdened under the weight of the axe and pregnant with delirium, Nithercott still has such control of his motor skills. Theodore shoots a glance down. Vivianne's no longer running in heels, she must have kicked those off somewhere back in the maze of halls. She's not the one slowing them down. No, it's him again. He's limping. His left leg. *What happened?* He looks down to see, under the fierce driving locomotion of his legs, a red shimmer on his left thigh and a six-inch tear in his jeans.

Suddenly his leg begins to feel warm; an acerbic sting emanating from his thigh. Nithercott's axe must have clipped his leg as he tumbled backward, and the pain is only hitting him now.

"Fuck, he sliced me," he stammers. Vivianne cranes her neck as they come to a turn in the hall. She gasps. "I'm slowing us down," he continues. "You're dead meat if you stay with me." The cackles of their nearing pursuer build to a vicious crescendo.

"Nowhere to run, my darlings!"

"Go on without me, Vivianne. My friends will be waiting for you…lobby level, side exit…you'll know them when you see them."

"I'm not leaving you! Not after all you've done for me. We're in this together now, both of us fools."

"No." Theodore slows his gait, resisting Vivianne's ardent yanks and howls to keep moving. He gives her a shaky smile and releases her hand. "I'll slow him down."

"No! I love you, you stupid Yank. I don't even know you, but I know that love you and I won't leave you like this," she screams. He gives her a light push and turns to face the monster. Something on the wall catches his eye. It's a largely monochrome scene with a cluster of soldiers in tall fur caps; a single soldier lying dead or injured on the ground as a comrade leans over him. For the briefest of flashes, he sees not the faces of grim, plaintive soldiers cast brilliantly in oil staring down at the body, but those of Alice, Francis, and Henry. He turns, exhaling, with an inexplicable smirk peeling across his face.

The irascible monster in the pinstripe suit is crashing down the hall, swiping the axe from side to side and making ribbons of the opulent wallpaper. Theodore clenches his fists, feeling Vivianne groping at the back of his coat. She's frantic, jabbing at fistfuls of fabric, but pauses when she brushes something hard underneath the coat. Theodore feels the rigid length of it press against his back. *What could it be?* Did he slip a wrench or something, anything that could serve as a weapon, into his coat and forget?

His hand dives into the side pocket, gripping the cold iron of…Nithercott's tongue pincers. He had forgotten about the torture weapon hiding in the oversized layers of his coat. It's far from ideal, but this piece of iron is his only shot at defending Vivianne against the axe-wielding madman. Keeping the makeshift weapon behind his back, he exhumes it from the pocket and squeezes tight. Nithercott is upon them now, a murderous comet hurtling at them from only yards away. Nithercott hoists the scintillating blade above his head, gearing up for one final swipe, his face straining into a grimace that looks hauntingly like a smile.

"She is mine! You cannot have her!" Nithercott shrieks. Theodore inhales.

The axe swoops down. He snaps his arm from behind his back, wrapping both hands around the pincers and bracing for impact. Vivianne shrieks. The shaft of the pincers meets the handle of the axe just below the blade, the resounding clack of wood meeting metal reverberating down the hall. A low-magnitude earthquake carves through the mantle of his radial bones. He staggers back, succumbing to waves of teeth-shattering vibrations. Nithercott lurches forward in a futile struggle against the weight of the axe and the ineluctable momentum of his driving body.

Theodore raises the pincers as Nithercott finally catches his footing. Nithercott moves to lift his weapon, but his battle with gravity is greater, and Theodore has his weapon above his head before Nithercott's is even at hip level. He lunges forward with his whole body, a surge of adrenaline suffusing his bloodstream and the static fuzz of synaptic overload blocking out the sound of his own throat-ripping scream.

Crack. The pincers meet with Nithercott's mask right on the rat's snout. He staggers backwards, howling, his neck whipping back and his mask sliding askew to reveal one widened eye. A patch of red burgeons on his forehead like a flower blossom shooting through cracks of grey stone. Theodore doesn't hesitate. He thrusts the pincers over his shoulder with both hands, Vivianne's fingers fervently digging into his back. She screams again just before he hurls the hunk of iron into their assailant's face.

The dissonant sound of sundered bone and snapping cartilage resounds. Nithercott's splayed fingers grasp his face, retreating almost before they've made contact. He releases a tortured howl; the brief pressure of his clumsy fingers on his nose enough to let him know the excruciating extent of the damage. He crumbles to his knees in a dazed genuflection, his head bobbing up and down endlessly; his cold, orb-like eyes leering upward at Theodore under the elegiac splash of the hallway light.

Theodore lifts the weapon over his head again, barring his teeth and inhaling violently. A potent desire to drop the iron down on Nithercott's head over and over again suffuses his mind, spilling over into his nerves until he's shaking to the core. He brings the weapon down to his side, releases it. The pincers clatter to the floor, giving way to a piercing silence broken only by Nithercott's stifled moans. He's incapacitated—no more harmful now than a snake without its fangs.

Theodore steps aside, trying to slow his breathing and quell the tempest raging within him. His work here is done; what happens to the defeated man is not his call, it's Vivianne's. As his nerves begin to stabilize, the fingers of a leaden fatigue wrap about him, enswathing him in its hefty embrace. He rests his head against the wall and watches as Vivianne steps slowly forth until she's looming right over the villain. She raises her hands as if to touch his tormented face. But she recoils, her hands coiling into fists, the wiry muscles of her forearm tensile and poised.

Alfred's eyes trundle up her dress, exhaustedly climbing to her face. For the very first time since Theodore saw him in the Regal Ballroom on night one, Alfred's features are a lachrymose droop; his eyes heavy and shimmering with tears. Vivianne's hands uncoil, trace a course up her neck. She removes her doppelgänger and tosses it aside, not taking her sight off Alfred once. The face she unveils is a grave, ineffable twist of emotion. Theodore imagines this is the first time in her life in which Vivianne has looked down upon Alfred. He has no knowledge of their unusual relationship, but it wouldn't be a farfetched assumption that her terror and oppression under Alfred have qualities analogous to his and Alice's young lives under their father.

Regardless of the abuse pervading a father-daughter relationship, Theodore knows a certain kind of love will always linger in the abused; a desperate yearning for the abuser to come to their senses and grasp the sanity and the compassion lurking somewhere inside them. For a flash, he sees not Vivianne confronting Alfred, but Alice standing over their father. His mind plays out this somber scenario, a scenario which never came to happen, and never will. He imagines her inner turmoil as the compassionate part of her battles with her voice of reason, trying to reconcile the humanistic qualities she'll always see in her father figure with the monster before her.

"How could you?" Vivianne asks meekly, grasping at the reigns of her voice. "How could you keep me in here like a prisoner all these years? You took me in when I was but a child. You exploited my ignorance and my loneliness, and brought me into your world, making me think that the walls of your hotel were the ends of the world."

"Vivianne…I…you know that I only ever treated you with tenderness and care. I took you in, yes, and kept you here, protected within these walls as Lear did with his offspring. Alas, such peace can only last so long before the foolish progenitor tastes the bitter results of his compassion."

"Why then must I have been your Gloucester?" She thrusts a finger to the hollow enclave on her face that once was an eye. "Your words are the baleful traitors of your cunning deceit. Your care for me was that of the robin as it plucks the struggling worm from the mud. You provided for me not a home but an early coffin in an oversized sepulcher."

"I lifted you from the tenebrous streets of unfeeling London when you were but a child!" Alfred stammers. "You were a vagabond, nothing but street swine, and I gave you *this*!" He lifts his ponderous arms to either side. "This was all to be yours when I was gone, my sweet. My empire for your affection. That was all I ever asked of you. Had I not the grace and the heart to take you in, your fate would have been a lonesome death down some forgotten twist of alley in the dreary winter many a year ago. I saved you from your grim fate and gave you a life, Vivianne. You have always been a daughter to me, and I have cared for none as much as I have cared for you."

"That is the reason for my suffering, the purpose that drove you to entangle me in your life of ignobility?" Vivanne is shaking now, tears coursing down her ruddy cheeks. "I was to replace the child you failed to bring into existence? And that is what spurred your bitter hatred for Alger, is it not?" Alfred's eyes narrow and he scowls at the utterance of the name. "He showed me what it was to have a father, what it was to be truly loved and looked after. In the short time I knew him, Alger had stirred in my heart a love you could never hope to *understand* with your wicked soul, let alone obtain.

Our connection drove you mad and that is what led you for the first and only time to lay a hand on me." She reaches to her cheek once more. "That is why you took him from me and killed him."

Theodore can see the furious quakes of her body growing. She grits her teeth; her hand drives forward, diving into Bertand's vest pocket. It surfaces gripping a glimmer of steel. She looks over the little pocketknife, the weapon with which he damaged her face years before. Like a cowardly animal, Alfred watches the blade bobbing in front of his face.

"My sweet, you will never have even a rudimentary conception of my love for you, my need for you in my life."

"Yes, you have kept me around as the collateral with which you might save your own soul at your day of reckoning. I am the last remnant of any goodness you once possessed. This I am, and nothing more." She grips the knife's handle tighter. "Alas, while you sought to silence Alger and thwart his plans to save me, he has succeeded." She glances over at Theodore. "Even in his death, he has given me a savior."

Alfred cranes his neck, trails of blood wending down his collar. "That little cur is your savior?" He begins cackling wildly. "This effete Yank couldn't save a kitten from the lowest branch. Regardless of what becomes of me, the two of you shan't make it one step outside the door before my men apprehend you and eviscerate *him* while you watch; you ignominious little brat!"

Vivianne releases a fiercely determined cry, her arm suddenly cocking back and then thrusting forward. The knife punctures Alfred's eye; drives right through to the handle. His harrowing howl penetrates Theodore and tumbles down the hall, shaking the pictures almost right out of their frames. Somebody was sure to have heard it; an idle guest lounging in one of the myriad rooms of the upper floor; a stray reveler or two searching for clues to the hidden chambers' entrance.

Theodore watches, feeling his stomach turn as Vivianne—still clutching the knife's handle—wrestles with the wriggling, skewered body of her captor. He gyrates back and forth on his knees as viscid clumps of eye tissue mixed with dangles of blood drip and ooze down his face. It's not long before his convulsions subside and give way to a mild twitching, a final hollow moan slipping from his mouth as the air of his last struggling breath escapes his lungs.

Theodore inches forward, not knowing if the steady acceleration of muted thumps he's hearing are those of a group of strangers approaching or that of his own heartbeat thrashing in his chest.

"Viv," he says tepidly, glancing fervently up and down the hall when he realizes that the thump-thump-thumping is out of sync with his heart. He reaches out and closes his hand around hers, absorbing the waves of spasms moving through her body and down her arm. She's bawling now, trying to force a word or two through the intractable shaking of her jaw.

"Why…why did you do this to me…Why?" she screams at the enervated slump of cooling flesh before her.

"Viv. We really need to move now." Theodore peers left, halfway down the corridor to a bisection in the hall where a squad of shadows plays along the wall. Several people are approaching, and fast. He jerks at the fist clamped around the knife, finally prying it off the weapon and pulling it and the unresponsive body to which it's attached away from the gruesome scene. With both hands wrapped tightly around her upper body he brings his face close to hers. He's about to utter some infinitely insufficient words of consolation to her when the approaching squad reaches the bisection. Six of Alfred's henchmen round the corner, all in uniforms akin to Jarvis the elevator-operator's, crisp white dress pants and floral-red vests under terribly scarred faces.

"What is this?" one of them vociferates. The other henchmen dissolve into a babble of grumbles and alarmed gesticulations.

"Let's go, now!" Theodore tugs Vivianne away from Alfred and down the hall, the sting from his leg reigniting as he enters a solid gallop. Footfalls resound behind them, strings of inscrutable shouts and commands enveloping the corridor in a minatory atmosphere of dread. The stark realization bites into

Theodore as he trundles down the hall with Vivianne that they are doomed. With her in a state of shock and he with his gaping leg wound, they won't make it far before their assailants overtake them.

His hand dives into his coat, fumbles the walkie talkie out of his pocket, and his fingers run wildly over the device until they finally find the transmit button. "Mayday, mayday, we're in big trouble up here on the ninth floor! Anyone copy?" Radio silence. "Hello? A bunch of Nithercott's men are chasing us down the hall. We're outmanned and injured." Nothing. "Fuck!" He throws the walkie talkie back in his pocket and shoots a glance at Vivianne, whose look of horror is laced with the blank stare of one still grappling with utter shock.

Damn, he thinks. *We were so close.* As they reach the hall's end and just before they're able to cut right and head for the stairs, Theodore hears just over his shoulder. "Halt, murderers!" The cold click of metal sounds once, and then again, and again, and three more times, telling Theodore that Alfred's goons are much better armed than he himself was. He pulls Vivianne to a stop at the hall's end, putting his arms up and turning slowly to meet the austere, cyclopean eyes of six massive revolvers staring back at him. He pushes himself in front of Vivianne, having no other shield against the imminent onslaught of bullets than his own body.

"You have just made the gravest of mistakes, bloke," the man in the middle jeers, his shoulders undulating in a sea of belabored breaths. "Vivianne, is that you? You assaulted Master Nithercott?"

A seventh henchman brings up the rear, shrieking, "They've really done it; Master Nithercott's deader than Dickens, he is." A wave of murmurs breaks out amongst the men, two of whom begin glancing nervously back at the dead heap halfway down the hall.

"Are you certain, Hershel?"

"The master's got a finger of steel carving a wee canyon between his eyes, Randall."

The shortest of the bunch clops forth, shoving the barrel of his revolver into Theodore's forehead. "You'll be joining him presently, wanker. And that goes for you too, lassie!" He cocks the hammer back.

"Spare her!" an effluence of words streams from Theodore's mouth of their own accord. "I killed him and I'm abducting the girl! She had nothing to do with it!"

"No," Vivianne draws herself from behind his back. "It was I and only I. Give me your bullet and spare the Yank."

"Enough!" shouts the fractious henchman. "You'll both face justice for this most heinous of actions!" Theodore sighs, placing himself once more in front of Vivianne, his fists uncoiling and dangling at his sides. His eyes flutter shut as an impenetrable fog of memory sweeps over his mind. He sees the impressionable and curious young Alice before him on the front porch of their country home. She's in a white dress caked with mud and grit. The girl never could explore the woods without the most expensive and delicate of her outfits on, much to Jenny's chagrin.

A respectable lady and a rugged explorer all in one, Theodore thinks, *she always effortlessly conflates the two.*

A series of thunderous bangs resounds before him. But he's incorporeal, an intangible tangle of thought and reminiscence. One moment, he's with Henry at the school dance, rolling his eyes at the obnoxious buffoon beside him while safeguarding an irrepressible smile at the new friendship he's found. The next moment, he's stooping awkwardly over the lounge bar downstairs, his eyes falling for the first time upon the effusion of beauty perched on the barstool and gleaming at him under the hawk mask. Vivianne, such a tender and tenable memory in which to lounge for his last moments on earth; a seraph of serenity to hail his transition from this world to the next.

The cacophonous reports of the revolvers pierce Theodore's ears and then fade, tumbling angrily down the lanes of the corridor and dissipating. Theodore exhales. He's still breathing. Is he gone? Is he dead, detached from his world and thrust into the junction to the next? A hand grazes his own, trembling and diffident at first, and then it squeezes him with ardor. Vivianne.

He opens his eyes at last to witness something that so opposes his sensibility, given the situation, that he has to close and reopen them a few times to grasp the situation. Nithercott's henchmen line the floor of the hall, their bodies toppled over and tangled amongst each other like trunks in a felled forest.

Thick twists of smoke curl and tumble about behind the bodies, yielding only a curtain of silhouettes in the background, and for a moment, nothing more. Theodore glances at Vivianne, whose countenance speaks of nothing but terror and surprise. He steps forth as the smoke thins to reveal a throng of sharp-looking overcoats. The tan covert coat of Goshawk; the grey ulster coat of Heron; the grey chesterfield of Sparrowhawk; the black guard's coat of Snake Eagle; the austere and piercing visage of Morrow standing in the middle alongside the wolf. Kestrel and Peregrine tip their bowlers, both smiling and nodding at Theodore.

Lingering anxiously in the background are Francis and Henry. And angling over the height of their shoulders is the fiercely determined, scowling face of Alice. Osprey is just to her left, his battered face speaking of exhaustion and surprise.

"Wha—" Theodore start. "How?"

Not a soul among them so much as twitches a muscle, save for Alice who elbows through, tears swelling in her eyes and her lips quivering with excitement. She leaps over the corpses and slams into Theodore, curling her arms around him and nearly knocking him clear off his feet. She doesn't' say a word, she just holds on.

Henry and Francis thread through the crowd and envelope the two in one great hug.

"Just in the nick of time it looks like," says Francis.

"Two seconds later and you two would've been swiss cheese," Henry chuckles nervously.

Watters approaches at last, with Sir Morrow in his wake. "Surely, you could not have expected me to sit idly by while you carry out this rescue mission of great import by yourselves, young ones." Theodore just stares at him through a sheen of tear-filled eyes, and smiles. "I may not have availed myself of the breadth of Alger's plans, but I am not without my social connections." Watters nods to Morrow. "There are those who would reveal the meeting spot of London's most ruthless and ignoble band of outlaws for no more than a bottle of brandy and a clap on the back."

"That explains why you up and left so quickly earlier. You had to fetch the dragoons," Theodore laughs, feeling a sense of power smoldering within him after reuniting with the Misfits Rescue Crew. He reaches out for Vivianne, who draws herself toward him and nods to the others, seeming unsure exactly what to say in this unprecedented situation. The Pilfering Paupers close in, slowly pocketing their handguns and glancing at the hall behind them, clearly unsettled with the prospect of lingering in the hotel any longer.

Just then, Theodore swears he sees some movement just beyond the wall of gangsters. *Did one of the bodies just move?* Then, before his brain finds his tongue and commands it into action, the topmost body on the heap stirs and rises swiftly. Red-faced and glaring, Nithercott's henchman clutches a dark red patch on his arm and grunts, turning away and swiftly fleeing down the hall.

Theodore finally finds his words. "Contact! Behind you!" By the time the Paupers whip out their guns and pivot, Snake Eagle is only able to pop off one round, which sings just over the henchman's shoulder as he rounds the corner and disappears.

"Blast!" exclaims Morrow, turning to Watters. "We must move and now, lest he spoil our one chance to slip out unnoticed." Watters nods gravely.

"No time for idle chatter now, young ones, we must fly for the nearest exit!"

"This way!" Vivianne breaks away from the pack and ushers them forth, onward to a daring final escape; an escape made all the more desperate now that within moments every single reveler in the building is sure to know of the murderous gang haunting the upper floors. They follow Vivianne; a stampede of anxious footfalls and searing uncertainty. The Paupers pull up the rear, surrounding their leader, guns poised, while Watters holds the middle with the others. Theodore's in front, holding Vivianne's hand as she tackles the wends of the hotel. They throw themselves into the stairwell and cascade down in tight little clusters.

By the time they make it to the third-floor landing, a bustle of commotion below teases Theodore's ears. Voices. Countless irascible voices married with clattering footsteps are bouncing up the stairwell. Vivianne halts, gripping Theodore by the collar and peering down the gap.

"They're upon us!" she whispers feverishly. Watters pushes through, beckoning them to take egress through the third floor. He holds the door as they funnel through, the last Pauper sliding through the doorway just in time for the vanguard of the onslaught—a man in a bear mask as wide as he is tall—to view their escape.

"Through that door!" the man ululates. "The murderers are trying to slip by us!" Goshawk and Peregrine hurl themselves against the frame, with the other Paupers following suit. The cantankerous crowd reaches the doorway, giving it a shove of such force that the Paupers falter, stumbling backwards and nearly acquiescing to the swing of the door. They redouble their efforts against it, leaving the others to pace helplessly in the hallway behind. Henry digs his hands into his hair, yanking out frizzy black clumps as he stares wide-eyed at the door. Francis curls his hands into fists, the sinewy muscles of his forearms bulging.

"If it comes down to fisticuffs, I'll take a few of those bastards down with me!" he growls.

"Should they get through, it'll be a shootout," Morrow says severely to Francis and then turns to Watters. "We can hold them; alas, not for long." He shuffles over to Theodore. "I should have liked to have gotten to know you a little more, young man. Your friend Watters informed me of your daring exploits to save the girl held captive by our greatest of enemies. But we have no time it seems." A tortured smile peels onto his face. He looks like a man who's been running against the wind his whole life—weathered and fatigued—and yet a hint of vigor floats to the surface of his visage, like someone freshly galvanized by some long-unkindled hope for justice and... something else.

"Why are you doing this?" Theodore asks. "You and the Pilfering Paupers? You don't even know us." The shouts and curses from the door's other side surge to a frightening meridian. The far-inferior numbers on this side of the door hurl epithets and curses back at them, holding with all their might, but Theodore knows the crushing force opposing them will soon break the levy.

"Hold, men!" yells Peregrine. "Hold the door like it wasn't your ugly arses that depended upon it, but your wives' beautiful arses, and your children's precious little rumps too."

"Aw bollocks, William," grunts Goshawk, slamming his shoulder into the chattering door. "The Paupers is all the family I've ever had; all the family I need. If this is the way it ends for us, it'll be an honor to die alongside your sodden souls."

"It'll be a final stand against the heart of the tyranny that's sought to oppress us and all the working-class men of England!" shouts Sparrowhawk. The gang gives a resounding cheer that, for but a moment, drowns out the truculent tide of voices coming from the other side.

"I suppose," concedes Morrow to Theodore, "I've staunchly held the belief that it was Marley, and only Marley, who might save our glorious England from corruption and deceit; that the labor party deserves its leader, oh so rightful and just; that our good fortune and prosperity be in the battered yet unwavering hands of labor men, and in the sunken but inextinguishable eyes of those opposing cruelty and subjugation. I've been a myopic fool. And Watters, friend of yours, ally to Marley—and thus ally to The Pilfering Paupers—has shown me that tonight."

Morrow smiles a hard smile, his eyes a gossamer curtain over the dread residing within. He's tired, Theodore can see it plainly. And he cannot blame the man, who's lived a rugged life on the run and now has the impending prospect of death literally knocking at the door behind him. A tight fist of anxiety slams Theodore in his stomach; he knows that this honorable, scrappy league of men are here because of him. Without knowing so much as his last name, they're putting their lives on the line for him and his friends.

"He has shown me that the future lay in the hands of the youth. You see, we are the progenitors of a post-industrial world; the remnants of an acrimonious power struggle whose brothers and sisters have suffered in the name of progress and the ineluctable tide of urbanization. You are the heirs of this world, and if there are any who might save it from the path upon which it treads, it is you."

Watters approaches, receiving a stout pat on the back and a hardy smile from Morrow as he comes, as if the strangers have more between them than a collection of words and a shared ideology—a common desire to watch the aristocracy around them crumble.

"You must leave now, all of you," he warns Theodore. "The entire breadth of Nithercott's followers it seems are tapping at the door. This is your one chance to slip out unnoticed."

"What about you guys?" Theodore's voice cracks. "What's going to happen to you?" Watters places his weathered and yet powerful hand upon Theodore's shoulder.

"The fate of the Pilfering Paupers, and, I suppose, my very own fate, was sealed long ago. To battle tyranny and oppression was our choice, and while we committed ourselves to the battle in distinct ways, there is a parity in our cause and thus in our outcome. It took you but four nights to achieve what the Paupers have attempted and failed to achieve for years. The most salient victory for the working-class across England yet, Nithercott's death just might shift the tide in our favor once and for all.

"I may have dwelt within these walls so long as nearly to forget the bitter struggle of the proletariat, but never once since raising him like a son have I forgotten Alger's ideals, nor his belief in change. Should we fall tonight in the greatest economical coup of our time, so be it! And if we should succeed in holding the horde at bay while you retreat, and then find a chance to fall back ourselves, so *be* it!"

"Aye! I'm ready to die for our cause and I am ready to flee, but either way, I will be taking as many of these slave drivers with me as I might." Morrow raises his Luger to the ceiling concordantly. Theodore knows he could linger here and bask in the bittersweet bond of brotherhood that surrounds him. Never once has he felt so accepted, so united, so intoxicated by the pull of fighting for something noble and great. He knows this and yet, turning to his friends and finding only desperate countenances—wide eyes stricken with terror and dismay—avulses him from that in his heart which compels him to stay. They've made it this far; they can't stop now.

"I wish it didn't have to be this way," he concedes gravely to Watters. "I wish we could take you all with us, but your fight is here." Tears well within his eyes. "Thank you for all that you've done."

Vivianne draws herself to Watters and throws her arms around him in a silent embrace, a shimmer of tears upon her cheeks.

"There, there, child," he says at last, cradling her head in his hands. "You have made it. Alger would be proud of the woman you've become." He holds her embrace as long as the moment affords him. "Now go. All of you, run!" Theodore takes Vivianne's hand in his own and joins the others in flight. He takes one look back to see Watters and Morrow point their weapons to the door. Watters peers over his shoulder one last time and winks coolly at Theodore.

Theodore turns away with a heavy heart, rounding the far corner with the others. As one swift and silent unit, they flee down the stairs and into the first-floor corridor. A distant rumble cascades down the halls; and then another, and another, as both sides hurl bullets at each other. Each round of gunshots lingers in the air like a stark and solemn three-volley salute to the virtuous band of outlaws who sacrificed themselves to save a group of total strangers.

The corridors are one garish blur of light and shadow as Theodore and Vivianne lead the pack. Alice is following right on their heels, while

Francis and Henry are in tow with Osprey slumped over their shoulders. As they thread through the halls towards the foyer, towards the crisp night air, towards freedom, they whiz past the occasional reveler; here and there a wife or a mistress of the pugnacious lot searching the building for the group of murderous escapees. Theodore gives no credence to these agitated revelers as he moves past. No, his focus is a singular determination to get them all out of the hotel safely, to deliver them from this madness enswathing them.

They swerve into the foyer, cutting a sharp angle and making a beeline for the front door. *It's unguarded!* The floors of the foyer are beyond slick. Running across it feels like gliding over a giant pat of melting butter. Theodore loses his left foot, slipping and crashing down on the waxed floors. Vivianne's bare feet maintain their grip, padding softly along, and she yanks Theodore from the floor in one swift motion. Alice gives a little boost from behind and they fly through the ponderous double door.

With Vivianne's hand still tightly wrapped around his own, he throws himself down the stairs, his companions' footfalls cascading behind him and then clacking on the sidewalk as they all stumble away from the hotel. The placid stillness of the watching night yields no comfort, but the gelid fingers of the air, which dig into Theodore's wound and stanch the trickle of blood still escaping his thigh, are a welcome touch. At what must be at least 1 AM, the square is a desolate sepulcher, reticent save for the whine of a low breeze through the dead aspens and oaks. The group flees across its breadth, refusing to stop until they are safely across, beneath the streetlamps on the other side. Under the looming façade of closed shops and three-story stone houses, Vivianne gives pause.

She turns slowly, her chin rising to meet the oppressive specter of The King's Inn, the lights of the many guest rooms glittering against the night sky. Theodore moves to her side, trying to gather his senses and dull his pounding nerves, trying and failing brilliantly. He places a hand, tremulous under the weight of anxiety and the intoxication of adrenaline, upon her shoulder. A rivulet of tears courses down her cheek.

"This was my home," she says, softer than a whisper.

"I know," Theodore replies, staring forth at the laurel of diffused lights emanating from the square.

"Regardless of what that monster put me through; of what he put many unfortunate souls through—I've... I've only ever known this life. My years on the streets, a mere slop of rags overburdened with fear and vacant of emotion, are unfamiliar to me. Those memories are but a distant tune whistled from the deck of a boat that passes by no harbor; adrift in a sea of time I cannot penetrate. This was my home."

"You guys, we really should keep moving," Francis cautions, cradling the wounded face of Osprey on one shoulder and the concerned visage of Alice on the other. Henry's already down the street, muttering nervously to himself.

"You must pardon my ill-timed moment of reminiscence," Vivianne sighs. "But it has been quite some time since I strolled the streets without the shadow of a security escort looming beside my own. It is...ineffably liberating." She turns to Theodore. "If only our timely allies hadn't sacrificed themselves for my freedom." She dissolves into a fit of tears.

Alice moves to Vivianne's side, brushing her cheek with the back of her hand and wiping away the glossy stream. "Honey, you don't need to carry that burden all yourself. They did what they did in order to save all of us. And you're free now, free as you always should have been."

Francis steps in, stroking his beard pensively. "And besides, we don't know what happened in there. There's the chance they were able to hold the maniacs back with gunfire and make their escape unharmed, just like us."

"I'm still waiting to see their figures moving across the square," says Theodore. "We barely knew the Paupers and yet I feel sick to my stomach about it all, regardless of whether they volunteered their lives. And Watters... oh man. We spent a small bit of two evenings with him and yet I care about him like I would my own grandfather." Just then, far across the way and through a screen of moonlit flecks of snow, Theodore sees swift patches of movement. It looks like several figures on the run, but the night shadows are too thick to be certain.

"That may be them across the way now," he says softly. "Or it might be a bloodthirsty search party trying to catch our scent. We need to keep moving."

"Where to, Frodo?" Henry's made his return from his little nerve-wrangling jaunt around the block.

"Listen, you guys need to make your way to a pub clear across London— or at least somewhere there are lots of people around. Get to somewhere distant and lively, but lay low, Nithercott has eyes all over the city. Don't bring attention to yourselves."

"Where will you be?" Alice stares dubiously into Theodore's eyes.

Theodore looks at Vivianne with a severity in his countenance. "There's something I have to show Vivianne before the first rays of morning send us back home."

"Question," says Henry, with one hand clutching the lapel of his coat and the other raised, his pointer finger plucking the sky. "How do you know that Vivianne will be magically whisked back to our time with you when you go?"

"I don't," Theodore concedes. "But both my mask and the tongue pincers came back with me on night three, and they were both in physical contact with my body. Based on that logic, as long as Vivianne and I are touching when I'm beamed back, she should return with me."

Osprey limps over, extending a shaking hand. "I don't exactly know what to say other than thank you. Thank you all for what you've done for me. I'd have been squashed like a bug in there if it weren't for you chums. As long as I live, I'll never forgot the Misfits Rescue Crew," he chuckles. "I figure it'll take a few bottles of absinthe to dull my nerves and peel my mind from this bonkers night we've had, but that's all I wanna do right now."

"Hear, hear!" commends Francis. "Are you not making the leap to the future with us, buddy? If you thought tonight was a shock to your system just wait until you see what's become of American politics in the 21st century," He jibes, shaking his head.

"Or you could compare the way a good thin-crust tastes 86 years after you first had pizza. You're a New York native, right bro?" asks Henry.

"Sure am, kiddo. That does sound swell, and as much as I'd love to run around the Big Apple of the future with you all, I've got family in *this* timeline that I'm not ready to leave behind forever. I've been in this game of subterfuge so long now that I can't say they're exactly waitin' on me, but I'd sure like to see them again. I've got some connections in Camden that'll provide me with a cot for the night, and then I think I'll ride the very next steamboat back west, see what kind of life I can make for myself in a world I would still recognize, and a world that might still recognize me."

"Fair enough," says Theodore, turning to the others. "All right, guys, we're going to need a meet-up spot since the Sonophone tends to dump us anywhere east of the Hudson it sees fit. How about Washington Square Park, right under the arch?"

"Sounds good," confirms Francis.

"Can do, Bear," says Alice.

"You betchyer fuckin' ass," says Henry.

"What is it that you have to show me, Mr. Gazelle?" Vivianne asks.

"I'll let you know when we get there. It's going to require a red-eye steamer across a large chunk of England, but I think the value of what I have to show you will prove commensurate to no amount of money."

"Please be careful, Bear. As you said, Nithercott has people everywhere, and by now they'll know about the squad of anachronistic Americans roaming around the city." Alice puts her arms around Theodore and squeezes tightly. "By the way," she whispers in his ear, "I can see why you went through all this trouble for this girl; she's ineffably moving." She pulls away, winking at him through an onslaught of fresh tears. Theodore turns and pats Francis on the shoulder.

"Watch out for my little sis, will you?"

Francis nods fervently. "Watch your back out there. We'll see you soon, brother," he says.

Next comes Henry. Theodore pauses before him. Something about his old friend has changed. His tired features impart the same characteristics as before, but there's something in the severity of his eyes that tells Theodore he's grown. Were Theodore staring into a pond, he imagines he'd see the same development in himself; the same scrutable and yet indescribable imprint the night's events have etched upon his face. Who can claim to have been through what they have gone through tonight? *Not a soul in history.*

Theodore and Henry, both searching for words and neither yielding anything but tenuous, appreciative sighs, smile big and wrap their arms around each other. As Theodore takes Vivianne by the hand and begins down the street toward Victoria Station, he prays that the next time he sees the three of them it'll be on a sunny October morning in the 21st century, underneath the broad frame of the Washington Square Arch, with smiles upon their weary faces and a handful of wild memories embroidered upon their hearts.

VI

Like a thin layer of tattered sheets laid in careless, rugose clumps over a mattress, a swathe of windswept clouds overtakes the firmament. The train's horn blares roundly several cars ahead as Theodore and Vivianne find their seats in the homey and sparsely populated coach. Theodore slumps into his seat, digging his fingers into the scant cushion. The upholstery is of a rich red gilded with golden crosshatch patterns. Every few rows, an ornate chandelier bounces, bobs, and sways to the fractious trundling of the train, casting a kaleidoscope of warm light upon Vivianne's face.

The first thing Theodore thinks, before leaning into the window to watch the dwindling stars of London's skyline fade in the distance, is that the modern railway systems, with their factory-churned materials and uninspired designs, have nothing on these antiquated lummoxes of conveyance. He feels a tender touch over his shoulder. Vivianne joins him at the window, her nose scrunching against the glass as she watches the darkly brilliant landscape sweep by. For what feels like minutes, she says nothing.

"Marvelous, isn't it?" she states at last, with a lofty childlike wonder.

"What's marvelous?" Theodore asks, a smile playing on his face as he watches her countenance blossom like an intrepid rose bursting through the thorns.

"The naked brilliance of a moment's clarity. My head has been underwater for so long I forgot what it was to breathe," she chuckles heartily. "My life has been one interminable inhale—a ceaseless accumulation of all the woes, all the heartache my demons could muster; while my angel waited in the wings." She half-turns to Theodore, but halts before making eye contact, resuming her surveillance of the slumbering land. A few miles off lie the timid undulations of the Chiltern Hills, their gentle slopes weaving an earthen mask over the low moon.

Vivianne eases back into her seat opposite Theodore. He sees a darkness come over her at once. "Poor Watters. In the years we lived under the same gargantuan roof we shared a paltry few words, but I always appreciated his warmth. I never knew the extent of his relationship with Alger...I really do hope he and the others made it out of that hellish situation. I...I cannot live with the notion that they put their lives on the line for me. It is simply too much."

Theodore nods slowly, knowing any words he could conjure would be a disservice to Watters and The Pilfering Paupers. "I think...I think we could both use a drink or five."

Vivianne nods, still avoiding looking Theodore square in the face. He takes her hand and leads her down the narrow aisle and to the vestibule. A golden plaque reads *To Coach*; *Lounge*; *Upper Class*. They move through shaky vestibule under the heavy clatter of steel on steel, and through another nearly empty lower-class car. Once they push through to the lounge car, they find themselves immersed in a convivial atmosphere. The feeble light from a few dim Edison lamps barely stretches to each corner of the car, which feels somehow wider and roomier than the coach cars. Drifting in and out the door to the upper-class car is a moving mural of businessmen, some in loquacious pairs, others conversing lip-to-stem with their wine and brandy glasses. Plush, high-backed chairs line the room. Most of them are facing away but evincing occupation by the tails of cigar smoke curling out the sides and over the top.

To the right is a partial wrap-around oak bar replete with tufted barstools and a back wall the color of dusky umber wedged between sets of windows. Theodore and Vivianne plop down on the leftmost seats, situated between a wooden partition and a wall of a man in a grey suit and knitted tie, who's bent over the bar muttering lonely sentiments to a few fingers of scotch.

"Oh my," Vivianne gasps, stretching a delicate hand down to Theodore's thigh. He nearly retreats, alarmed at the direction her hand's going, and then realizing what it is she's reaching for. "Your leg, Mr. Gazelle, your poor leg. I completely forgot; how remiss of me." Through the gash in his pants, Theodore sees fresh trickles of blood beginning to coat the dry, blackened stains from before. "It hasn't stopped bleeding. Barman!" A stout, middle-aged man with curly orange atolls of hair surrounded by a sea of scalp grunts, nods, and then shimmies quickly over.

"A clean rag, please. And a bottle of well vodka."

"Aye, miss." He folds a dishrag neatly on the bar and uncaps a small bottle of clear liquid. Vivianne scoops up the bottle and reaches down, audaciously tearing a larger gap in Theodore's jeans until the wound is sufficiently exposed. With the focus of a war surgeon trying desperately to seal a fatal wound on a fading soldier, she begins flicking the bottle over Theodore's leg. Astringent waves of pain assault his lower thigh, like a hot poker teasing at his skin over and over. He clamps his jaw down hard on the back of his hand, watching as the barman leans over the counter with a look of equal parts curiosity and concern.

"Almost there; good sport," she says, her tongue protruding from the side of mouth slightly. Despite the intolerable pain bearing down on his leg and radiating outward, he finds himself focusing on her, becoming more enamored with Vivianne than ever before. He can't take his eyes off her, refusing to miss one intoxicating moment of her presence. He wants to absorb all the minutiae that makes Vivianne who she is; the little scrunch of her nose and the furrow of her brow as she hovers over his injury; the soft effluence of each breath she takes in her stony concentration. Theodore's convinced that the universe pivots on an axis around this girl, that her commanding elegance and ferocious grace alone hold up the very atmosphere around her.

"There." She wraps the makeshift tourniquet over his leg and ties it off, giving his upper thigh a light pat and admiring her handiwork. Her eye travels up Theodore's body and makes a fugacious connection with his. She turns swiftly back to the bar.

"What to drink, young lovers?" the barman asks, reaching up to a gramophone on the high shelf and replacing the dying song with a fresh one. An early Django Reinhardt tune crackles out of the machine.

"Well, let me ask," she says, turning to Theodore. "Since I will soon be living there, why don't you give me an idea of the most popular drinks a lady might order across the pond? I might as well begin familiarizing myself with the culture now."

"Well," Theodore scratches his head. "Honestly, mixology hasn't changed that much. If anything, the art has regressed into a perfunctory routine of attempting to recreate the classics. We've got Pimm's for the summer, Good Tidings for winter, and Hot Toddy's for sore throats. I myself prefer a good Old Fashioned."

Vivianne considers this briefly, the severity of her countenance fading and being replaced by the revelatory smile of one giddy with the knowledge that an auspicious new life is coming her way. "Give me an Angel Face, barman, and do not bother yourself with fingers; drop me a fist of gin, if you please."

"One Angel Face for the lass with the face of an angel," says the barkeep with a cloying smile. Theodore groans audibly. "And for the American gent?"

"Oh hell, give me a Corpse Reviver, barman. I think that might be enough to numb my senses after the night we've just had." The barkeep flourishes a shaker and scoops a prodigious bottle of gin from the shelf.

"I'm afraid to say that I'm on a lighter stock for overnights, Miss. I have an Armagnac from Gascony on hand, a drop of which is smooth enough to tame a cantankerous lion, if I do say so, miss. It might not replace the ambrosial notes of the calvados, but it'd make for a right good drink."

"Tonight, I am drinking to my liberation, barman," she says. "And to a promising new tomorrow." She looks at Theodore. "Armagnac sounds lovely. But bring it over to that cozy little corner by the window, if you will. I've not seen so much sky in many a year, and I do not plan on missing another moment of its vast, insuperable majesty. Come, Mr. Gazelle."

Time passes in one beatific haze. Theodore can only measure the hours in the number of depleted glasses standing on the little wooden table. A light patter has been tickling the windowpane since the train left Coventry Station. The rainfall built in severity in Birmingham and became an impenetrable silvery cascade in the long stretch between there and Warrington, where the locomotive began lumbering westward towards the coast.

Vivianne is curled up on a mahogany-backed leather chair, the toes of her bare feet curling, digging into the seat, and flattening out again as she unleashes a hearty laugh. She reaches into the depths of her dress and retrieves a glint of ivory. She snaps open the little case and plucks at a cigarette—likely the only possession with which she escaped her previous life. Theodore's arm bumbles down to the table between them and he finds his lips kissing the cold rim of his cocktail glass. By the time his gaze returns to Vivianne, she's obtained a match from another passenger and is preparing to take the first pull of her cigarette. Before she lights it, her hand dips down and pinches a dark vial rested snugly between cigarettes, bringing it up to the cigarette and gingerly unscrewing the vial.

She glances over at him, remarkably deft with her hands and cognitively present for the degree of alcohol she's consumed. She snickers. "They say this is so very well practiced over in Paris that it has now become somewhat rote," she states out of the delicate corner of her mouth. "But I relish the idea that it is still somewhat novel in England, something of a party trick." She removes a little glass rod from within and runs it along the length of the cigarette.

"Lean forward, Mr. Gazelle," she commands with a giggle. Theodore obliges. She takes the lit match and brings it sputtering to the smoke's tip, inhales fully, and releases right in Theodore's face. Such a faux pas doesn't faze him; his heart races at the thought of being inches from her face, and an argent lily of smoke blooming right in his face won't irk him in the slightest right now. Much to his delight, however, the smoke that washes over him is no noxious cloud redolent only of chemicals and toxins. It's a rich, dusky scent, brimming with ripe tobacco notes on top and simmering with succulent tones of fruit underneath. *Party trick indeed.*

"It's called *Habanita*," she says, sniffing the lingering ropes of smoke that twist in ethereal shapes between them.

She leans back. Her face is flush with a fresh spirit lent her by the alcohol, and she's tugging mindlessly with one hand at the collar of Theodore's chesterfield. He'd draped the coat over her as they sat down, and it's been refusing to stay perched on her refined and elegant shoulders ever since. Theodore's head is swimming from the booze, and he's nursing a sensation of unrefined joy propelled by the very simple act of admiring every shred of affectation that is drifting off Vivianne as the night unfolds. The intimacy they shared on night two, from her alluringly equivocal nature to the meridian of pleasure and excitement Theodore experienced, cannot compete with the intoxicating qualities of uncovering who this girl really is under the skin.

"Barman, the angels have stopped singing!" she stammers, raising her glass and swirling the trembling remnants of her drink. "Toss your lasso into the heavens and drag another one down to me, if you please! My, I haven't felt this queer in some time." She sweeps her fingers over the pronounced peak of her clavicle. "It's positively delightful."

"Aye, miss. Twirling my lasso even as we speak!"

"Now, Mr. Gazelle," she hiccups, turning lackadaisically back to Theodore, who finds himself almost unable to steady his intractable eyes upon her face. He's had one or three too many drinks. "Mr. Gazelle…I think it's time you told me two things," she giggles, clumsily struggling one pointer finger into the air. "One, what is your true name? I *am* to be traveling into the future with you, after all. I do say I should know your name upon doing so. Your lovely sister only called you Bear, and pissed as I am, I'm *fairly* certain you're not a salmon-shoveling, honeycomb-coveting quadruped. I assume that Bear is merely an endearing sobriquet your sister gave you. It cannot possibly be the name your sensible parents chose for their darling firstborn."

Theodore emits a husky laugh. How odd that they've been through so much, that he feels a shared bond with her unlike anyone who's come before, and yet, she doesn't even know his name. He stumbles to his feet, pitching and yawing with the trundle of the train until he almost crashes into the little table between them. "The name's Theodore." He extends his hand. "It is truly an honor to meet such a...a...dashing drink of water such as...such as yourself."

"Theodore...what a perfect moniker for you. It fits you like a glove." They both erupt into a fit of laughter brought on by nothing more than a prolonged glance; the kind of random gut-buster only drunken souls pierced by Cupid's arrow understand, and any sober onlookers would be left scratching their heads at. "Now, number two. I think you have kept me in suspense long enough. For what could you possibly be dragging me across the entire country before we leave it once and for all—and after such a night, no less?"

The question sweeps away the haze of Theodore's buzz, but he recovers it quickly. "Oh, you know...you'll see when we get there. But like I said before, I really think it will be worth it once we do." He peers out a window burdened with humidity, out into the foggy world. The train lurches around a curve, exposing to Theodore the bobbing forms of the train's other passengers in the cars ahead. Some of the scattered denizens are sipping brandy with their noses buried in newspapers. Some are in tight groups gesticulating wildly and cocking their heads in uncontrollable fits of laughter. Others still are lingering near the vestibules or in breaks in the aisles, hands in their pockets and clouds of pensive thoughts in their minds, their faces awash in the garish filament glow about them. Beyond the coils of smoke coughing into the night sky from the engine car, a corsage of lights dots the landscape as the train hurdles towards the urban sprawl of Liverpool.

"It's my turn for a question," hiccups Theodore. Vivianne nods, a ruddy warmth in her cheeks and an alacrity in her smile. "Why were you averting your gaze from me earlier, before we were drinking?"

Her countenance droops for just a second prior to a nonchalant shrug of her shoulders. "I…I've…well, I've never appreciated the girl that's stared back at me in the looking glass. Not since…*he* did this to me." She points to the spot where her left eye used to be. She emits a saturnine chuckle. 'You have no idea, Theodore, the amount of time I have spent hiding behind that mask." Her lips quiver, and her eye becomes a sheen of glass, absorbing and reflecting the surrounding light until Theodore can no longer discern the iris inside.

"Only in private would I ever remove that cover, whereupon I knew no prying eyes could see what he did to me. This blight upon my face became a part of my identity such that I never managed to retain even a fraction of my youthful disposition, though it was my right to have it. This blight coupled with what the monster did to Alger. I never forgave myself for letting him go that day, regardless of the fact that little inconsequential me wouldn't have been able to intervene. I alone could not stop the psychopaths from taking Alger and killing him," she sighs. "Alas, he's gone, and I've cowered behind my mask ever since, shedding countless tears for none to see. My burden has been mine and mine alone. I've never been the same since."

"But that's where you're wrong," Theodore asserts. Understanding full well the sensitivity of the situation but knowing he can't allow timidity to rule him and keep her mired in the shadow Alfred cast her in, he shoots up from his seat. "From my perspective, you wear your scars with such grace and dignity that you have truly *owned* your circumstances, not the other way around.

"When I first met you at the lobby bar, I knew you as little as I knew my own inner strength—something I've come to learn more about now—but I saw in you something indefinably brilliant. You were standing there, not a downtrodden shell of a girl as you say, but an effluence of curiosity, beauty, and strength. I was the simple pauper rubbing elbows with a fallen angel."

Theodore's hand crawls into his jeans pocket, remembering the little scrap of paper on which he composed the poem for Vivianne in Henry's bedroom. Drunken and stumbling over words or not, he feels this moment is somehow perfect to share. He smooths the dog ears out of the corners of the paper and clears his throat.

"Allow me to share my thoughts in my clumsily contrived way. Ahem." He pauses and gives himself a moment to roll his eyes at the oddity of the concept of him writing a love poem for a girl. The last few days have been laden with many firsts. "Now, I don't normally do this type of thing. So, if what graces your ears isn't a scintillating, gilded stream of stanzas worthy of Wordsworth himself, that's why." Vivianne chuckles and sits upright, an intrigued glare in her eyes.

> *"Wrought with despondence and rotten under wealth of absence,*
> *diseased evermore was my rite of amble,*
> *Brambles of dread o'er my tired soul did tread,*
> *Dread importuned at last to me an offer, as proferred was the grail to Galahad,*
> *Gilded and clad in promises of soft repose was this deal,*
> *Meal of indolence and feast of indifference was my naked plea,*
> *He nodded his head, did this creature named Dread,*
> *Bread did we break, hands did we shake,*
> *Slaked was my thirst for something more, until rumble did the earth and in twine split the heavens,*
> *Leaven was I while from the riven sky floated down an angel in gossamer gown,*
> *Drowned in her beauty was Dread and alas his dissimulation did crumble,*
> *Tumble and wither did this baneful bird's illusion, 'til at length the feathered laurel of the crimson carrion was betrayed, and dissolve to nothing did his ill-got crown,*

Down to Hades did he plummet and forever therein was he bound,
Noun to denote for my angel savior I have not,
Sought though have I for word to describe her majesty humble and
her perfection unbought by avarice or frailty of human birthright,
Unwrite the verb that with feeble arm her agency it does arrest,
Confess do I of a fruitless search, o'er a landscape otherwise fecund
with adjectives of gainful perch,
Verge no label for her might I, alas nary an utterance shall bestow
sense of her true scope,
Elope shall I with the notion of ineffability, and permit the tides of
time to expunge from the quarry of human expression the words
scrawled I meekly thereupon,
Time anon until, whither a word is but a clippéd wing, thither shall
my angel teach my soul to sing."

Theodore's hands quiver as they droop down to his sides. His breath escapes him in a ponderous and tremulous sigh which, had he had knowledge of its existence prior to its passing, he would have stifled with a stiff bite of the back of his hand. The gushy poem has already made him seem a maudlin shadow of a man—a composition so heartfelt and yet so inexorably moody is simply something he has never done for a girl. And his embarrassment *has* to be showing on his face, which was already ruddy with intoxication.

Vivianne remains poised at the edge of her seat, the cushion beneath her just one twitch of the body away from tumbling right off the front. Her brow is a soft arch that speaks not of surprise but of some pensive undercurrent of thought. Her lips are an abstruse plane stretching across the horizon of her face, yielding no sentiment and betraying no emotion. But her lone eye, the inescapable, coruscant sapphire adorning her face, conveys to Theodore the inner workings of her mind, a mind over which the last years she has constructed a near-impenetrable veil. What was just a mere shimmer moments before has become a misty moor. A single tear tickles down her cheek. She opens her mouth for some articulable expression, but the conductor at the front of the car pierces the silence between them.

"Mersey Road! This stop Mersey Road! Next stop St. Michaels, and end of the line at Liverpool Central!"

Threading through the copse of weary businessmen clogging the railway station, Theodore takes Vivianne by the hand up a flight of stairs, past the looming monolith of the Mersey Road Station building.

"What is it, Theodore?! Where are you taking me?" she asks, with expostulation on the tip of her tongue. He ducks down the cobbled lane adjacent to the station and dives with her into the middle of the meekly lit street nearby.

Two interminable lanes of shabby row houses cloister the street on either side. A faint checkerboard of bedroom lights pierces the darkness down the lane, as a handful of residents are just waking up in preparation for the long and arduous day of work ahead. Theodore knows a neighborhood wedged right between the train station and the crummy city center asphyxiating on its own production is replete with factory workers; souls who are more than accustomed to the oft brutal nature of industrialization.

"Now comes the hard part..." he mutters under his breath. "Finding just which of these houses is the right one." The dawn's first rays threaten in crepuscular fragments that pierce the jagged teeth of the pines overlooking the street. Theodore gasps, retrieving Henry's flip phone and thrusting it to his ear. The eerily hollow moan of woodwinds greets him over the line. Back in the present day, the record is spinning out its last few revolutions. *Morning is almost here*! He needs to act fast!

Pocketing Henry's phone and scooping Vivianne's hand into his own, he inhales sharply, preparing to have dozens of doors slammed in his face. His movement is halted before it's even begun, though, and he turns to address the immovable boulder he's now tugging at. He ceases pulling as soon as his eyes meet her expression. Her head is tilted up at a soft angle, captivated by something in a low window on the street's left. It's not merely her head, though, that is suddenly transfixed, but her entire being. Her body has become taut and rigid, tensed as if determining whether it must flee. Theodore follows her gaze, peers at the casement, gleans a meager light coughing its effluence over a kitchen no bigger than Theodore's bedroom back in NYC. A man is stooped over a stove in front of the window, dipping a tin percolator over a mug. A helix of steam escapes the mug and tickles the man's face, upon which Theodore cannot discern a single feature save a blighted flat cap enshrouding a hard and yet amiable countenance.

He turns back to Vivianne, unable to shake her from her desultory spell; unable to tell whether she's even breathing as every piece of her is devoted to what she's found; her eyes lingering, incising the man in the casement. Her behavior seems not so much that of helplessness or hypnotization, but that of sheer conviction that whatever she's staring at will evaporate into nothingness should she look away, should she even blink. It's the stare of the lost and languid traveler in an arid desert, who's certain the shimmering greenery on the horizon is just a mirage.

Finally, a rattled and yearning sigh escapes her. Theodore turns back to the window to see the figure has vanished. Vivianne steps forth, making a slow beeline for the front door. Theodore follows, wondering if she's actually found him, wondering how she could possibly have made something more than Theodore did out of the shadow perched at the window. Just before she arrives at the downtrodden set of stairs leading up to the unassuming row house, the door sways open. She gasps, her shoulders rising and squeezing tightly, her whole frame seizing up like a startled alley-cat. A figure emerges from the tenebrous hallway. The man pauses at the highest step and takes a sip of his coffee, still unaware of the two figures at the foot of the stairs. He sighs and stretches his shoulders, letting the scant streetlight play upon his face and giving Theodore a chance to catch a true glimpse of him.

The hand holding the mug is wrought with muscle and worn as a cherished tome. The forearm jutting from a tattered rolled sleeve shows years of hard manual labor in its rugged cords of muscle, which lead up to a gaunt frame of poised, wiry strength. The middle-aged man's posture is bent in its senescence, but unbowed and unyielding, wielding a dignity Theodore feels he himself has never carried. A narrow taper of neck succumbs to a face with a varnish of early wrinkles that try but do not succeed in diminishing the unquenched fire of youth that lingers in the sturdy mouth. A rocky promontory of cheekbone nestles the eyes, whose weary sag and depth of gaze tell of a vicious battle with sorrow; a battle that has only suppressed the spry twinkle of emerald beneath, but never sapped it of its essence or boyish gleam.

The man finally looks down, his eyes widening at the surprise of the unexpected loiterers down below. A gale of astonishment blows a fresh expression over his face. His jaw drops and he blinks rapidly, mirroring Vivianne's stupor just moments before. The puissant vice of his hand loosens on the mug, which tumbles down and explodes on the step beneath him, sending tendrils of steaming liquid down the stairs and into the skeletal bushes lining the house. He gives no credence to this, refusing to pry his gaze from Vivianne, who also fails to acknowledge the few specks that seem to have flung upon her face.

"Vivi?" he says at last.

"Al?" she lobs back, with all the confidence of someone who has only just found their vocal cords after years of searching. Alger Marley grips the rail and starts down the stairs, gaining speed with each disbelieving step. She leans forward but cannot find her own feet, allowing him to cover the full distance between them. His powerful arms wrap about her and she fumbles her own over his shoulders, unwilling to take her gaze from him long enough even for a hug.

"You're...you're dead, Al," she stammers, the fingers of both hands clasping fervently behind his back. "You're gone, you're gone, you're gone." A virulent tide of sobs takes her, and she thrusts her face into his shoulder, nuzzling and crying, nearly dissolving right into him. "You left me forever; this can't be you! It just can't be!"

Alger palms the back of her head and rocks her back and forth, his bulging eyes drifting skyward and welling with tears. He bites his lip hard, looking truly puzzled, as if he knows mere words won't do here.

"I know, darling girl, I know. Oh, dear lord, you made it out." He brings her closer still, and Theodore knows the man won't ever be able to wrap her close enough in his fatherly redoubt to feel satisfied. His burden is that of the loving adoptive father who's been greeted every morning the last few years with the heartrending knowledge that he'd never see his child again. Knowing this, Theodore's own heart grows heavy. The irreconcilably horrifying, captivating, exhausting, thrilling, ponderous crucible that was the last few days has come full circle in this reunion, and he's just going to let it play out between them. After learning of Alger's remarkable story, unearthing it bit by bit after Theodore first found the Sonophone, he's arrested by a curiosity in finally seeing the man of ineffable brilliance in the flesh. All that might be capable of penetrating this curiosity is the sense of gratitude swelling within him; without the ingenuity of Alger Marley, or that of the late Walter Marley, Theodore would never have gone on this insane journey to find Vivianne, the love of his young life.

"You must...you must tell me what happened, Al," she sniffles, pulling her face away finally to meet his. As when Alger first glanced down to see her a moment ago, a layered expression sweeps his face upon looking at her. His eyes narrow and his lips tremble. Theodore knows this man, who never meant to see her again after escaping his death sentence, could never look upon her again without feeling some sense of guilt. After all, noble though he was in attempting to free her from Nithercott, Marley's actions did lead to the very apogee of her suffering, the disfiguration of her face.

Alger sighs. "When they took me on that most saturnine of winter days, torn from you in one bleak and torturous moment in which I had not the power to fight, nor the pulpit to stake my claim to your wellbeing, I submitted. I was thrust into the boot of an automobile like a lowly sow on its way to the abattoir. When Nithercott's henchmen opened the boot and wrenched me from the metal cocoon in which I awaited my impending death, I found myself in the middle of an infertile old field. Open air for miles, and naught to stave my nerves but the portentous coo of a crow from a sky full of dread."

Vivianne is unmoving in Alger's arms, as still as an infant clinging to every word of her father's lullaby. "With an indifference in their voices that only experience and an austere heart can yield, they instructed me to drop to my knees; two of them, one with an automatic machine gun and the other a revolving pistol. I feigned compliance for but a moment, whereupon I thrust my elbow into the fat sod with the machine gun. I managed to pry his weapon from him and…"

"You pulled the trigger, Al," Vivianne finishes, a glint of astonishment in her eyes as she learns of a courage unknown in her genteel adopted father.

"Oh, heavens no, Vivi. I merely hoisted the thing in front of me and threatened to open fire should the bloke with the pistol attempt anything unwise." He chuckles lowly. "I must have traipsed backwards through that dreary field, with all its cursed undulations and dreaded pitfalls, for the better part of three leagues before I felt safe to turn and flee." He shakes his head. "What a frightfully ponderous moment that was…knowing that should I stumble once—falter even slightly—I would be supper for the worms until the turn of autumn's soil."

"And where did you go? Why did you not return to me, Al? My heart shattered the day they took you. Not a day has passed in the years since last we spoke that I haven't lamented your passing. How could you simply leave me in there, Al? How?"

Alger bites down even harder on his lip, until he breaks the chapped skin. He pulls her against him once more, stroking the blond stream of hair pouring out over the back of the coat Theodore lent her. "Oh, my darling girl, it was the agony of my life when I realized that I shall never return to you. And I understand the impossibility of the task you now have to face, to try and see things from my perspective. But I knew that no matter how I loved you, regardless of the depth of our connection, and irrespective of any cunning I possessed, I was nothing to you at that point but harm. My prior attempts to save you led to your deepest torment and would have led to far worse should I have come back to you. I decided there, treading alone in that dead field, that my life would continue only in such capacity that I would never more bask in the light you brought to it. I changed my name, created a new identity for myself. I moved to a different city and for the years since I've seen you only in the torturous escape of my dreams."

Alger's eyes fall upon Theodore at last. "So, this is the young lad I have to thank for this moment, for allowing an old dog like me one more opportunity to see my angel?"

"Yes, Al." Vivianne pulls away and pivots to face Theodore, extending the little sapling of her arm toward him. He scoops her hand up in his and smiles what must look a weary and downtrodden, but genuinely happy, smile. "This is my knight in shining armor. Theodore." Alger's hands move to his hips. He lumbers forward, looking Theodore up and down with curious eyes.

"You are the intrepid youth that picked up the pieces of my little puzzle." Knowing he's in yet another unprecedented situation in which he has no idea how to conduct himself, Theodore simply pokes his hand out for a shake. Alger glances down and laughs, shaking his head. He knocks Theodore's hand away and takes him in a hug with nearly the lung-deflating strength of one of Francis' embraces.

"That's me," Theodore rasps, patting Alger on the back heartily.

"I cannot thank you enough, Theodore, for what you have done for me. More importantly, what you have done for her." Alger's eyes glisten under the burgeoning morning light. "You must pardon my clumsy inability for words just now…but I am still somewhat agog that my most farfetched of plans found success. But now that I see you, future explorer, I think success is a byproduct of your being. The mere existence of you, however many decades from now, made it an impossibility for my contrivance not to succeed."

"Truly, the honor is all mine, sir. This has been one hell of a ride from the first second your grandfather's machine zipped me back to the past. It's funny, now that I've met you, I can see that he raised you as his own. You talk just like him," Theodore says, alluding to his ally back at the hotel. Alger's face puckers; his brow furrows as the mere insinuation dredges up a host of complex emotions.

"So, you met Watters, that dear old chap? Why yes, he taught me all that I know; made me who I am today. How did the old fellow get along, did he aid you in your quest and make his escape alongside you?"

Theodore considers his response, deciding at last to spare the poor man another bit of unnecessary heartache in his life. "He sure did! He was the best guide I could have asked for through it all." Theodore's visage falters, though he tries so to sustain a neutral appearance. With a staggering intellect lingering behind his gaze, Alger reads Theodore like a signpost.

"He didn't make it through, did he?"

Theodore sighs. "We can't know for sure. He and the Pilfering Paupers sacrificed themselves so that we could get out. There's a good chance they escaped as well, but we didn't stick around to see." Alger's tongue dips into his cheek and he nods slowly.

"You're in workman's clothes, Al," Vivianne changes the subject. "What is it you've been doing in your furtive new life?"

"Why, I work down at Larkin's Coal and Lumber near the riverfront. He's a man of superlative sensibilities, Charles Larkin is, and one who truly cares for the English laborer. He is all that I strived and failed to be, and more."

"Whether he is such things, or if he's a filthy mongrel or even the King of England, you can say goodbye to all that now, Al! I'm setting sail once and for all to the future with Theodore and you shall be our guest of honor on the journey back! He swept me away from the untenable reaches of hell and brought me to you. And now we can live like we were never able, free to be ourselves and live our lives to the fullest! Oh, can you even wait to see the future, Al? I know I can't!"

A sullen gloom sweeps Alger's face; his lips purse at first, and then he commences gnawing on his lower lip under an unexpectedly taciturn gloom. He glances skyward, to the coral-steeped blanket of morning superjacent to the roofs of the row houses.

"I…" he says at last, his gaze succumbing to the pull of Vivianne's alacrity and magnetic presence. As Alger's eyes fall upon Vivianne, his face is a tortured mess. Just then, Theodore discerns a sharp noise from in the dark depths of the doorway behind Alger. He jumps. Vivianne peers behind Alger, whose steely eyes remain fixed upon her face. Another sound emits from behind him, this one more sustained and with a playful lilt. Theodore ponders just what the sound could be when he sees a tiny figure trundle out of the shadows of the house. *Does Alger have a dog?* Before Theodore makes out the true identity of this new presence, Vivianne gasps, her shoulders bunching up almost to her ears.

"Ga ga, dada," the baby calls from the top stair. Without turning from Vivianne, Alger back-steps and scoops the little one, who cannot be more than a year old, up into his arms.

"Vivianne, I'd like you to meet Evelyn." He plucks the baby's tiny hand up and extends it to Vivianne with the veneer of a spurious smile plastered between his cheeks. She recoils as if being presented with the open jaws of an asp. His smile falters and a single tear courses down his cheek.

"You…you have a child," she says with the flatness of one who doesn't believe her own words.

"Vivianne," Alger coaxes from his unwilling lungs. "That chapter of my life—the years spent with you were the most torturous, the most untenable, the most horrendous years because of Nithercott and what he did to me, to my career…to you. Alas, they were also the most precious, salient, invaluable days of my entire life because they afforded me the chance to become acquainted with the only angel the lord let fall from his starry abode. But that chapter of my life had to end. You know now that circumstances forced me to move on, to salvage whatever life I could for myself." A cascade begins tumbling down his cheeks. Vivianne follows suit, her body trembling, rivulets of tears wending down her face.

"Though it killed me to do so, to let the cold fingers of fate immure you in that place, whilst leading me to a salvation I felt I did not deserve. Alas, fate brought me a kind woman, a warm home, and little Evelyn here." He kisses the bald cherub on the forehead.

"You're married, too?" asks Theodore.

"Aye, Helen's upstairs sleeping. The two of you caught me preparing to leave for work. Little Evelyn here woke with me and decided she wanted to play, so I left her in the den with her trinkets. The little lass must've heard voices and that's why she came to the door."

"So," Theodore pries, "your wife doesn't even know the truth about your past, about The King's Inn?" Alger shakes his head firmly.

"I created a new identity for myself and let it consume me. She knows naught about that part of my life." He sighs a ponderous sigh. "This is why you were never supposed to find me, Vivi. My own death forced me away from you, forced me to close that chapter and move on." Theodore's stomach tightens as the weight of his good intentions crashes down upon him. All he wanted was to reunite father and daughter, give them the fairy tale ending they both so deserved. *How wrong was I?*

Vivianne steps forth, slowly placing her gracile hand on Evelyn's little head. She wipes her own face with her other hand, not noticing the interminable stream of fresh tears that immediately take place of the dried ones, and bends down, kissing the baby on the cheek. "Your memories of me—of all this—will fade quicker than the lipstick I just pressed onto your cheek, little one. But you will grow up with the luxury of having such a great man as Al lead you through life. He will watch over you always and protect you as he once did me. And you will have a brilliant life, little one; a life unburdened with pain and strife, and unhindered by the obstructions of cruel fate. And the future is a brightly burning star, little one. Maybe one day your grandchildren will play with my own little babies, as I too have been given the chance at a wondrous new life."

Over Alger's shoulder, Theodore sees a ripple in the sky as morning begins to take hold. He raises Henry's phone to his ear. Nothing but radio silence greets him. It's time.

"Viv," Theodore says softly. "The time has come. Any moment now, we're going to be whisked away from this world." She says nothing, but takes Theodore's hand once more into her own, stepping away from the child, from Alger.

"Before you go, I want you to have this." Alger rummages around in the back pocket of his torn overalls and hands her a folded, tattered piece of paper. She takes it in her open hand and clasps her fingers over it; a little piece of him to have, always. "A little keepsake I thought I'd never have another opportunity to give you," he finishes.

"You'll forgive me, Al, but if I let you take me into your arms once more, I may be unable to let go. Besides," she smiles out of the corner of her mouth, "the distance that will separate us physically can never lessen the thread between our souls." Another ripple tears open the sky. A constellation of dark holes begins to pucker across the houses before them as the world concedes to the inexorable splashes of the future. Theodore leads Vivianne a few steps away from Alger and Evelyn. From the sidewalk, they turn to face the pair at the foot of the steps. "Before we leave you must answer me one question, Al."

He nods, wiping away a sheet of tears from his face and giving no credence to the spectacle unraveling before him. His eyes remain upon Vivianne. "Ask away, my darling."

"Ba ba, dada," Evelyn cries, reaching her little hand out to Vivianne and giggling.

"Are you happy?" she asks, as the pockmarks of the ether begin dissolving the scene. The lower half of Alger's face becomes shrouded in black, but the twinkle in his eyes shines through.

"I have a loving wife, a roof over my head, and a beautiful girl with whom to share my own future," Alger says. "The world of tomorrow is for the young. It is for you, Vivianne. And I know that you will be greeted by a wondrous new place that will take you into its open arms and never let go of you as I had to once before, as I must now. That is all I ever wanted for you; a life full of loved ones that never have to say goodbye. And my dream has come true. How could I not be happy? Promise to watch over her, young Theodore, now and always."

"I will," Theodore says with conviction.

Vivianne cranes her neck as the sheet of black overcomes Alger and Evelyn. But just before his visage succumbs to the impending dark, like a face in a Polaroid as it melts under the summer sun, she smiles at Alger with more veracity and warmth than Theodore has yet seen, her tears streaming off her face and floating into the zero gravity of nothingness. For the first time, she looks truly and uncompromisingly happy. As the blackness spreads from Alger's chin to his mouth, as it crawls down his forehead to his eyes, Theodore sees a flash of movement. It may be just one of the many crackles brought on by the colliding of the two worlds, but he has a feeling it's Alger winking for the last time at Vivianne.

Theodore squeezes her hand as they're lifted off their feet. "Remember," he shouts, "Washington Square Park, under the arch."

Through the raging maelstrom that surrounds them, amidst the crackling temporal storm, Vivianne turns to Theodore, her arms wrapping around him. Suspended between worlds, her lips meet his. The tail of her dress ensconces him, twirling and tangling about, her limbs enveloping him until he cannot tell where he ends, and she begins. He can feel the warmth of her body radiating into his own, can taste the salt of her tears upon his mouth as they coalesce for a brilliant moment in the tunnels of tomorrow. Gradually, she is pulled away—avulsed from his grasp and drawn into the inexorable arms of time and space.

VII

A ripple of naked light too bright at which to gaze, too diffusive to shirk, and too resplendent to deny the eyes, engulfs Theodore's world. A ribbon of hot air attacks him, piercing the depths of his very bones, stabbing deeper and threatening to penetrate more still until it finds no more bone to plunder, then it blossoms out to find its next conquest in the layers of his skin. From the ice-bath of the temporal catapult through which he was just flung to the searing conflagration of re-entry, admission to his own world feels fit for the plight of Icarus, but it lasts only a moment, or what to him is perceivable as a mere moment, before he plunges back to familiar territory.

The scintillating streak of a green road sign whizzes past Theodore's cheek. The fluorescent flash of an SUV's headlamp dashes across his field of vision. Objects all around him, which have no time to materialize gradually before him, zoom forth and populate the scene like a network of blooming trumpeter vines captured on a time-lapse. He hits the pavement, but this being his fourth time returning from the past, he manages to break the fall with his feet instead of allowing his lumbar system, along with a giant dead fish or an unsuspecting wooden lattice, to absorb the impact. He surprises himself when he finds that he's able to land upright without teetering, and even manages to do a little flourish between two passersby on the sidewalk, a move that would have had a true grandeur had he not relinquished his oversized Chesterfield to Vivianne back on the train.

"Watch it, pal," the person on his right, an exasperated little man with a small barrel of liquor cradled in his arms, remonstrates Theodore. On the left side of the human sandwich he's just inadvertently created during his arrival, a lady whose back is bent with age and whose sizeable gray bonnet conceals her face, asks, "Say sonny, do you happen to know where I might find Randall's Pescatarian Palace?" *Vivianne.* Now that he's returned, she is all his discombobulated mind can focus upon. *Did she make it? Did she find the rendezvous point?*

"Uh, Hudson and 12th, ma'am. You're not that far actually," Theodore says, shooting a glance at the nearby street sign. Washington and Charles Street. He's not too far from his destination, either.

"Oh goodie. My son is meeting me there—both of my boys, that is," she prattles on as Theodore makes for the intersection. "What a treat this is, both my boys coming to see me at once. Richard is bringing his grandson, Andy, and he tells me the young sprout has taken to smoking 'the ganja'. Now, if this ganja is what we used to call reefer or Mary Jane, I tell you now, may the lord strike me down where I walk, I will not have young Andy playing around with that marijuana substance. It *is* the gateway drug don't you know?"

Theodore doesn't respond. He's bolting across the intersection, paying zero mind to street signs or moving vehicles, and blazing a path down Charles Street towards Washington Square Park. He reaches West 4th Street and sprints down to 7th Avenue. *Did she make the journey okay? Did she land right in the middle of a busy intersection like he did after night one and get hit by oncoming traffic?* After all, she's not used to motor vehicles that travel above twenty miles an hour or so. She's not at all equipped to handle the pace of this new world.

He flies past 7th Ave, squeezing between two parked Hummers and dashing across the street, disregarding the cacophonous bellow coming from one of the cars' overly sensitive alarm system. *Did Alice and the others get back all right? Did one of Nithercott's many associates find them in a London bar and do god knows what to them?* He gallops past 6th Ave and spots the leafy crowns of a legion of trees lining the park just ahead. His heart is on the verge of exploding in his chest; whether it's from the full-on sprint he's in or the burning anticipation of discovering whether his loved ones made it back from the past, he cannot tell.

He dives into the cluster of trees and cuts his way across the park as the incipient sun crests the tops of the buildings just beyond the park's massive arch, its splendid rays squirming through the space under the arch. Through the glare, he sees three figures looming beneath the monument. The scene is one of beatific tranquility, as if contrived by a higher power; as if the very sun is rising only for them. He closes in on the figures, shielding his eyes from the rising sun to discern Francis' tall, puissant form, one arm crossed before him and his other elbow propped upon it, his hand idly stroking his beard. Beside him is Henry, his hands nonchalantly tucked in his pockets as he watches Theodore's approach with a snarky half-smile; and Alice in her flowing blue and white dress, her hands on her hips and her head cocked to the side, tears churning down her face and coruscating under the sun as she shakes her head from side to side.

Nobody utters a word. They're exchanging far more than words could express in their weary and yet blissful countenances as they gaze Theodore's way. They look older somehow, and Theodore expects he does too—older in mind and body, and older in his soul as well. They've each lost a piece of their innocence these last few days, but they've gained something, too. Their hearts are bound to each other through the crucible they've endured together. This bond is an ineffable but palpable feeling Theodore didn't expect ever to want in his life's quest for solace, but he's relishing it now.

All three step forth and Theodore merely leans in, collapsing upon them in an enervated embrace. A series of arms wrap around him, the Misfits Rescue Crew squeezing tightly and refusing to let go. Like a group of childhood friends reunited for the first time since grade school, the world had seemed so large and unconquerable the last time they were together, and here they are. Somehow older, somehow wiser, somehow different and yet every bit the same. Theodore pulls back, scanning the park through the inchoate morning light. *Did she make it back?* Alice kisses him on the cheek and draws herself away, smiling, and reveals one last figure lingering in the sun's rays behind them; an angelic little form scintillating in the light. Alice waltzes over and scoops the angel's hand up, leading her over to Theodore and placing her hand in his.

Vivianne gazes about the world—from the astonishingly tall, glass paneled buildings Theodore calls sky-sores above to the miraculous pieces of modern engineering flying by the streets around the park. She takes it all in with the look of a blind person whose optical curtain has been drawn back for the first time. Then her focus falls on him. And she smiles. And the group closes in once more, drawing them both into a hug that lasts until the soft caress of the sun's aureate fingers blossoms into a fiery glow that ignites the crisp October sky.

VIII

Two Days Later

"Should I throw some more charcoal on top?" Francis asks, staring into the battered old oil drum, a half-bag of coals in hand and Alice's lissome frame drooping over his shoulder. Judging by the moribund ripples of sunlight streaming across Manhattan and glimmering in little puckers of light on the East River, Theodore surmises it's a little after 6 PM. The whole gang is loitering behind the brick remnants of a long-dead factory just off the river, near the Brooklyn Navy Yard.

Upon waking sometime well into the night of their first day back, Theodore, Henry, Francis, Alice, and Vivianne deliberated—through the vicious effects of time-travel hangovers that neither sleep nor strong black coffee could eliminate—over what to do with the Sonophone. The miraculous, recondite invention that could be the most stunning marriage of meticulous science and preternatural curiosity since the Wright brothers took to the skies.

"I think it needs a little more juice," Francis answers his own question, tossing the remaining hunks of charcoal over the beautiful brass device. It hisses as it begins to dissolve into a brilliantly glowing liquid metal. Theodore pulls Vivianne close against his body, kissing her softly on the forehead. She nuzzles his cheek.

"In a way it feels truly wrong to do this; destroy the marvelous device that brought you to me," she says, her brow furrowed in a pensive shroud. "The device that brought me here." Theodore follows her eyes to the innumerable glittering edifices across the river. Theodore feels the same way. If this machine is handed over to more brilliant minds, the technology could be harnessed and mass-produced in a way that would change not only the world as they know it, but the world as the history books described it, and the world of tomorrow as well. Whether that would be a good thing, they'll never know. Besides, he believes destruction to be the only responsible course of action; the time dials were welded to specific temporal and physical coordinates. Were anybody else with a record containing a similar enough frequency to stumble upon the Sonophone …all that they've accomplished, all they've struggled for could be undone in a flash.

"If you ask me, and I know it's just driving you all bat-shit crazy to know what's going on up in here," Henry says, tapping his cranium with a prim smile. "I think we should have put this thing on the web and sold it to the highest bidder. I mean, we'd own half of everything in front of us right now, Theo."

"That may be so…" Theodore can't seem to wrench his gaze from the glowing effervescence of the melting time machine before him. "Sorry, Walter," he says softly. "All those years hunched over your table, slaving away at the design of your greatest and most impossible invention, the apogee of your genius …destroyed."

Francis shoots up straight, nearly knocking Alice off her perch and into the lake of mud around them. He thrusts his pointer finger at Theodore. "Hey that Walter dude, didn't Alger Marley mention in his recording the fact that his grandfather had a prototype of the Sonophone, one that was quirky but still worked?"

Theodore nods. "Mhm."

Henry concludes Francis' thought, "And didn't he say that they left the prototype in the warehouse in Oldham when they took off for London on that ill-fated night train?"

Theodore looks to the sky as the flames begin to reach higher, a moody rumination overtaking him. He nods once more. Through the golden haze of light pollution that hovers above the city, he sees a shooting star zip across the firmament.

IX

Three Months Later

"Oh please, my love," Vivianne admonishes, extending a delicate hand and caressing Theodore's cheek. "Put on another record. For me?" Theodore weaves across his and Henry's tiny apartment, sidestepping a jagged concourse of boxes filled to the brim with all his earthly possessions. It's peculiar to him how horribly rote, how bland one's life seems when measured only by his belongings. None of these things stuffed hastily away in their containers appeals to him beyond a cursory sense of affection at the fact that they're his. That insane adventure reinforced the notion to him that the narrow perimeter of life he delineated for himself upon moving to the big city years ago was a needed instance of circumspection; a careful, closed off life that he's now outgrown.

He and Alice are closer than ever now, more candid and forthcoming in all matters, and the demons of their past are now their greatest sources of strength and solidarity. He understands that the distant desire in him to see the great pyramids, or to frolic in the crystalline waters of the Caribbean, were never more than a dissembled admonition for something, or someone, of true substance to invade his tightly guarded world. The only item holding any real personal meaning or value to him remains the little phonograph cylinder he still carries in his pocket to this day, the unassuming item that brought him not only another world, but another person—a spirit of kindred nature—with whom to share his own world.

And in a sense, fully welcoming a wonderful new person into his world means forcing important others to the periphery. He and Vivianne are moving up to a quaint and homey one-bedroom in Harlem, which means losing Henry, the friend with whom Theodore now feels a stronger bond than ever, as a roommate. But Theodore's confident that the entire Misfits Rescue Crew will remain close, and living in different points of the same city cannot scrub their miraculous shared experiences, nor stifle their collective desire to combat the loneliness this world so deftly prescribes.

"Okay, but we have to get back to packing up all your knickknacks and stuff soon. The others will be here in, oh, twenty minutes or so to help us."

"What was that word you just used, Mr. Gazelle? Knickknacks?" she chuckles. "I do believe that even back in my time that word was, well, arcane." She beams a brilliant smile at him, biting the corner of her lip and looking ineluctably alluring propped against the counter in his oversized hoodie and one of his tattered, old beanies that she seems to wear more than a queen would her own crown. If anything, he thinks to himself, her presence has given his possessions all the meaning and purpose they now hold.

"So, this is a band that got me through some, should I say, moments of personal turmoil in my late-teens. They released their first album five decades after the night we left London, at a time when clashing ideologies the world over had become such a norm that social and political dissonance caused the building of walls in Europe, and paranoia stemming from counterintelligence and spectral threats became the lyrics of the zeitgeist's song. Everyone was on the defensive, fortifying themselves in preparation for another world war...I told you about the prominence of communism in the 20th century, right?"

Vivianne nods, rolling her eye. "Spare me the history lesson for now, Theodore, and dance with me."

He takes her in his arms as the record begins spinning, the nasally croon of Jim Reid's vocals filling the space. He's not sure how long his lips are locked with hers as they sway to the music, he's only aware of the moment's end, when she breaks away from him.

"I have one 'knickknack' I believe I am ready to tackle now." She shuffles over to their bedroom, retrieving a crumpled, sallow old piece of paper. Theodore recognizes it instantly as the one Alger gave her 86 years ago. He doesn't know where in the bedroom Vivianne stored this closely guarded treasure, but he does know that she has yet to read it and that her hesitation to do so is brought on by a variety of complex factors.

With a tremulous flick of her wrist, she unfurls the paper to reveal an elegantly handwritten note. She ushers him over, her hands shaking too much to hold the note stable enough to read it. Gingerly, he takes it from her hand and holds it so they both can read.

On the morrow I must flee, though thou art the strength in me.

Though once this hand hung limp upon my chest, presently did it refuse to rest, a fist it curled over my breast,
Refused it did, refused to rest, rest there in solemn redress,
The heart within me quivered, quaked, and withered, alas found I my mind it dithered,
and it dallied, Its sole conquest to find some peace, some sullen repose which I might reach,
to stanch this blanched blood my heart now beats.

On the morrow I must flee, though thou art my soul's decree.

Rising now from languid perch, athwart the mantle mine eyes search,
Plunder vainly walls in tatters, vestments besmirched, habiliments scattered,
My fist shakes now, ever unstill but forever silent its cry,

To the casement in a bound I fly,
Unclasp the hasp and hoarsely shout, and curse the heavens this
manly clout,
This terminability, this dead-end route,
This effete nature of man to whom despair is clout,
His loved one gone, immured without.

On the morrow I must flee, hence thou must learn to live and be.

These tattered walls, that gilded mantle, this shattered casement,
alas this sad example,
Of a man abandoned not in the stock, his body unshackled, free as
a gull in flock,
Though dead already be my soul, interred and left to rot,
This cell about me no efflorescent pot, no fecund soil suffuses,
nurtures more than one mere thought:
Failed thee have I, left to do there is naught,
And oh how I've searched, and pillaged, and sought, some recourse
unkindled, unswindled, unbought,
Some winged seraph, some true virgin lot, which supplication might
bring,
Which entreaty has not.
Naked, unbound, words decant from my soul,
Stentorian and clamorous within me they toll,
Yet out from creased lips how silent they roll!

On the morrow I must flee, and ere I go I admonish to thee,
Remember this truth through days yet to be,
Thou hath been the heart of me.

EPILOGUE

The Grand Reopening

"See, this is kind of cool," says Theodore, coming upon the faded printed sign on the pulverulent stretch of wall that holds the hidden key to The Cat's Meow. He's done this so many times now that he barely needs to slow his stride before he's found and plucked the brick from its loosened mold. His hand is a windchime in a blizzard, however, as he can't stop mulling over the possibilities of tonight being the night. "This brick is essentially the key to the door that leads to the mock speakeasy which led me to you."

"You mean the business Alice and Francis purchased a couple months ago?" She follows him down the little alley and around the back of the old building.

"Yeah, I mean Francis was pretty close with the previous owners and when he and Alice decided to buy it, the owners capitulated at the first offer." Theodore slides the brick into the panel with one hand, fondling the gem in his hoodie pocket with the other. He's rather proud of the size of the emerald and he knows Viv places green above all other colors on the spectrum. *She's going to love it.* The ponderous barn doors screech open. He's been saving substantial chunks of each paycheck in the months since escaping Georgian England for an engagement ring, and when he bought it last week, he knew the time to pop the perennially salient question would be soon.

And while he feigns insouciance, trying to carry on a normal flow of conversation with Viv to keep her none the wiser, a particularly intractable frame of thought keeps evaluating if tonight is, in fact, the night. On multiple occasions since Barrow Street, this nagging interloper has nearly given him away.

"So, uh, so now he no longer needs to make his own booze at home in his bathtub. The upside to that is that you never have to suck down one of his experimental cocktails and act like you wouldn't wash your mouth out with motor oil if a bottle was lying around."

Vivianne chuckles, the soles of the new flat tops Theodore bought her clacking down the stairs behind him. "Surely Francis' drinks cannot be as unpalatable as you say. You do have a tendency to exaggerate the most innocuous of things, Theodore."

"Well, let's just put it this way, my dear. I think he'll be tending the books and not the bar at his new establishment." With this comment, Theodore realizes he's trodden the path of insensitivity at a level unusual even for him. It must be a nervous outburst as a result of the diaphanous, and yet oh-so-ponderous, trinket in his pocket. He knocks on the door and waits for the viewer to slide open.

"My, I do love adventuring with you, Mr. Gazelle. Compared to the London of my time, the Manhattan of the 21st century is a panopticon of visual splendor enswathed in a veil of furtive wonder. So much to see on the surface and even more lying beneath."

Theodore mulls this over and shakes his head. "My experience of London in the 1930s speaks to the exact opposite, Viv. In the flashes of time I spent there, I was thrust into a secretive and bizarre masquerade party of societal elites. I loitered about in the London Underground with moralistic gangsters, I witnessed merciless torture and an avaricious sex orgy that would make Dionysus blush…"

With a metallic whoosh, the door viewer slides open. "All right, here's the deal kiddos," the spurious accent of Jersey Guy sounds from the other side. "You answer me one riddle and you gain access to the palace. Simple as pie, eh? A piece of cake, you say, huh? We'll see who's lookin' smug once I've given you the riddle—you're quite a beautiful dame, by the way, quite a beautiful dame indeed. I don't believe I've seen you round these parts, miss." Jersey Guy tips his hat to Vivianne, who blushes and giggles.

"And you're quite the colorful character, Mr. Gatekeeper." She curtsies. Theodore groans.

"So, here's the test, mi amigos; now, this is what separates the men from the boys, real hard-hittin' stuff: What's the real name of the Prohibition Era mob boss who went by the literary moniker, The Mad Ha—"

"Okay, okay, cool it with the interrogation, Bugsy." Jersey Guy scoots over to reveal the sanguine countenance of a slightly buzzed Francis. "These two get a free pass every time. I thought we went over this." He wrenches the door open and before the heavy slab of metal has collapsed on its hinges, he's taken Theodore into one of his asphyxiating bear hugs. He drags Vivianne in as well, who giggles,

"Congratulations on the purchase, Francis." She steps in and does a little twirl. "This place is magnificent!" And she's right. While the design of the bar hasn't changed one iota, its immaterial qualities have metamorphized into something of true value for Theodore. Never in his life has he felt so at home in a place, nor so at ease with those around him, nor so fond of the memories that have taken residence in every corner, upon every surface, and across every wall of an otherwise beautiful but unremarkable space. This bar led him to Vivianne, only it wasn't just her that he found here; he found strength in a dying friendship with Henry, unity in a complicated past with Alice, and possibility in a new connection with Francis. But he also found himself; the real Theodore that was always there lingering beneath the surface, interred within the walls of self-preservation and doubt. He can be himself now and not fear ridicule or rejection.

Theodore takes Vivianne's hand and leads her into the bar. A mellifluous stream of vintage tunes pipes through an assortment of modern speakers, the dance floor a tenable and inviting sea of Francis' hipster buddies, whose faces are all awash with genuine splendor and excitement. With Francis at the helm, The Cat's Meow is fast becoming the worst-kept secret in Manhattan, and Theodore thinks that maybe, just maybe, Alice's adventurous spirit and her hunger for a legitimate social life upon which to predicate a happy and prosperous future will finally be satisfied.

"You made it!" she shouts, emerging from the storeroom behind the bar, her face half-obscured by the hefty box of liquor she's hauling over to the bartender.

"All right, Anthony," she points to a line of sharply dressed customers who are nearly falling over each other to be the first at the tap. "Make sure these lovely guests receive some authentic cocktails that, along with this divine playlist curated by yours truly, will catapult them back to the Prohibition Era."

"But not before he makes our friends their boissons d'honneur!" interrupts Francis, waving them over to the bar with excitement in his hand and an alacrity in his eyes. "Come, come. Come along! I've been through a myriad of shakers and swizzle sticks and about two cases worth of gin and brandy to create my magnum opus…es. Opi? Magnum opi? Oh, whatever, just watch the man and prepare your palates for the most ambrosial of concoctions ever to grace your mouth. It'll be Debussy's bergamasque for your taste buds…or, his arabesques for that matter. Or, well, anything by Debussy, really."

He lives for this mixology shit, Theodore thinks, chuckling at his friend's charming idiosyncrasy. "You know the drill, Anthony," Francis continues, eyeing the bartender's every move like a falcon coveting an injured mouse from the sky.

"You really must excuse my lovably overzealous boyfriend," Alice rounds the bar and embraces Vivianne, pecking her on the cheek. "The art of the drink is his calling and he's never owned his own bar before. My calling is to add a little character to this place; it has warmth enough already. I'm an avid oil painter, darling Vivianne—and I'm not half-bad if I do say so myself—so I've started a little series of Prohibition Era pieces. They're just down the hall to the old Cat's Meow over there. Oh, I can't wait to show you guys! And there's a little something else I've been dying to reveal, and I thought our grand reopening would be the perfect occasion! But it can wait until Francis has given you his gifts, of course."

She motions to Francis as he reaches over the bar to Anthony the bartender, who hands him two cocktails of contrasting color, one hot pink and the other a muted green. *Huh*, thinks Theodore. *There's something I've been dying to show Viv, as well. Either this is going to be the night of nights to lay the question, or it's going to be too crowded with Francis' cocktails and Alice's surprises—whatever those could be—and I'll have to hibernate the issue for a while...Fuck me.*

"Drumroll, please, dear," Francis exhorts. Alice obliges, even going so far as to make the motion of hammering on a snare.

"Oh, they are the cutest couple, Theodore, aren't they?" Vivianne accepts the bright pink drink with a small curtsy; Theodore takes his with a small nod and a smile. He's building himself up for the show of feigned enthusiasm that's sure to follow his first sip. *It'll be hilarious to see Vivianne's reaction upon tasting hers. A real tension releaser.*

"Now, these are both to be featured menu items to celebrate this wonderful, time-and-space defying union between two folks I'm honored to call my friends," continues Francis. "Yours, Vivianne, is the Coral Captivator, for your spirit is as warm and your character as inviting as the color in your cup, and your nature is as captivating as the sweet vermouth lingering in the layers. It's a nice, elegant flavor as well if I do say so myself, to compliment your chicness."

She sips. A beatific smile overcomes her face. "Francis, I must say, this is the most stylish, alluring cocktail I've ever had. I cannot tell you how flattered I am you created a drink in tribute to me." Theodore's shocked. He takes a tentative sip of his own and immediately nosedives into a pit of abashment. The drink is poetry for the palate.

"All right, man, I know you've never considered me the king of mixology, but you don't have to look like you were just struck by lightning from the safety of your couch," Francis laughs a true, belly laugh.

"Oh, no…I never thought that about you, man. Maybe just that your craft could use a little fine-tuning…"

"It's okay, Alice told me how you felt about my homemade hooch forever ago. But after we got back from London, Alice enrolled me in a couple of courses that really honed my abilities and voila! Now, I like to think she did so in a genuine gesture of appreciation for my passion, but I figure she just knew there was no way in hell I'd be building a menu with both our names on it without some extensive training." He scoops an arm around her waist and pulls her into a kiss that would make Sleeping Beauty's prince look as suave as a barbarian during a pillage. *They really do get each other.* And in his life Theodore's never seen Alice so taken with someone. Could Francis be the one?

"Your featured cocktail is to be called the Glaucous Raucous, because, well, frankly since you entered my life it's been one hell of a ride. But mostly in a good way."

"Well, don't forget about the time I accidentally got you killed while pursuing this girl," Theodore chuckles, referring to the fiasco on night two when he left Francis to fend for himself at the bar of The King's Inn while he scurried off to wet his whistle with the Coral Captivator.

"Oh, how could I forget that?" Francis chuckles sardonically. "That event was *definitely* on my mind when I created the Glaucous Raucous. The important thing is you came back to rescue me from causality-loop-purgatory, man." Alice leans in and kisses Francis' cheek. *They really are in love. Now, the Misfits Rescue Crew just needs to find someone for Henry. A girl who will find his quirks and eccentricities charming…*

"What is up, my bitches and my bros?" Henry appears behind them, rocking a *KISS* t-shirt, a pair of capri shorts, and some equally fashionably inapposite Birkenstocks down below. Much to Theodore's surprise, a girl pulls up beside Henry, holding his hand in her own. Her natural beauty is apparent in the pair of cool, green eyes that seem not to reflect the light around her but to illuminate somehow all their own, in the silken swathe of dark hair that cascades down her shoulders, and the simple yet elegant physiognomy that's smiling bashfully at the onlooking group.

"Nice party, Franny, I like what you've done with the place," Henry chortles. "Especially the cases of booze stacked behind the bar. Best feature yet. I'd like to introduce you all to…what was your name again, love?"

"När ska vi dansa på en riktig klubb?" she says in what sounds like a northern European accent. *Maybe Swedish?* Theodore thinks. "Du sa att vi skulle dansa på en riktig klubb."

"Isn't she great?" Henry asks, kissing the girl on the cheek. "Sigrid, that's her name."

"It's nice to meet you, Sigrid." Theodore shakes her hand. She smiles and blushes. "Do you speak any English?"

"Uh, we're still working on that part," Henry says curtly, leaning in and whispering to Theodore. "Isn't she great, man? She's a foreign exchange student. *Very* foreign; she's got that sizzlin' European princess kind of look, huh? I met her down at NYU last week when I was heading over to mooch some fiber internet off their servers. She was standing there on the sidewalk looking like a real damsel in distress when she pulled me aside to ask in utterly destroyed English where the library was. Can you believe the irony? Donde esta la biblioteca?" He emits an esurient little chuckle.

"Well, 1950s perception of women aside, that's awesome, man. But how are you guys communicating, like even on a basic level?"

"Well, a lot of what we've been doing doesn't require *too* much verbal interaction, if you know what I mean," he nudges Theodore on the shoulder. Theodore suppresses a little vomit. "I kid, Theo, I kid. You don't have to look at me that way. I just use this app on my new smart phone to communicate with my bonny lass. These things are nuts. So, I type in a phrase, whatever I want to say to her, in English, and then I butcher the shit out of the translation it provides. Oh, it's a match made in heaven, my dude."

"And once one of you learns the other's language and you can actually communicate with each other it'll be even more romantic," adds Theodore, smiling at Sigrid, who gives a friendly but vapid I-don't-know-what-you're-saying smile back.

"Or maybe she's an ultra-slick, fiercely-proficient spy who speaks English better than we do and is just absorbing Henry's mannerisms and routine before she abducts him and takes him to her homeland for interrogation," posits Francis. "Just messing with you, Henry. You guys are like Tristan and Iseult, you know, without all the pre-Shakespearean tragedy elements. Step this way, Sigrid, I've invented a new drink that I think you might just love."

"Oh, drink. Yes, please, drink," Sigrid manages, "Jag får hudutslag om jag dricker citrus juice."

"It's kind of like a modern take on an Old Fashioned, but with more essence of orange. You're going to fall in love with this drink, Sigrid." They step over to the bar while Alice grabs Theodore by the elbow with that trademark eagerness in her eyes.

"Come, Vivianne, Henry, and you, you old curmudgeon. Let me show you some of the things I've been working on since we got back from London."

"Now, now," Theodore corrects. "That's ex-curmudgeon. I've had the salient and momentous task of showing Viv our world and it's forced me out of my little bubble. By the way, Henry, congratulations." He fist-bumps his friend as they step into the little hallway leading into the original prohibition bar. "She's a hell of a catch, man."

"You're the only person who knows this, Theo," Henry whispers, "but Sigrid is my first actual, ya know, girlfriend. It feels great; I'm starting to understand why you went to the lengths you did to rescue Vivianne from that world."

"Now just think of how much more of that you'll feel once the two of you can actually share, oh I don't know, any verbal sentiment," Theodore jokes.

"Touché, but she's taking English classes. And as you know I have an interest in Scandinavian folklore that reaches beyond the token bits of lore that make their way into tabletop fantasy games ...so about one in every one-hundred words or so I understand. We're on our way, Theo my friend, we are on our way."

"All right, men and Vivianne," Alice interjects as she bores shoulder-first through a wall of tenacious, drunk guests mingling in the hall. "If I may indulge myself for a minute; this is a snapshot of what I've been working on since we came back from London." *And a project of laudable merits, indeed,* thinks Theodore, taking note of eight distinctly moody and impressionistic oil paintings of 1920s hooch smugglers.

On the right is a classic GT car in a minatory back alley; the headlights' cone of golden light splashing over a grimy brick wall where a squad of Faustian-faced gangsters are lugging crates of liquor. On the left, a muggy bar scene littered with poker tables constellated by swirls of cigar smoke. The focus of the piece is in a group of mobsters littering the foreground, lounging in their excessive wealth like rapacious dragons draped over a cache of gold.

Their physiognomies strike Theodore as familiar, ones from the history books he used to show Alice, but he can't put names to the faces. That's why Henry and Alice excelled at Jersey Guy's riddles and Theodore bombed. As they make their way to the back room, a glaring absence makes itself known to Theodore. The photo presaging each night's journey back is gone, its spot on the wall supplanted by another piece in her Volstead Act collection.

He's about to ask Alice precisely what happened to the photo when Viv exclaims, "Oh my! Oh dear, what is this?" She absconds into the old section of the bar. Theodore chases after her, detecting the sly and yet endearing smile inhabiting Alice's face as he does it. The original bar is largely the same, with the obvious exception of the Sonophone and the little wooden table upon which it stood. The ramshackle elements of what was once a vessel for outlawed drinks is still extant, its longanimous frame holding steady through time like the diminishing bulwark of an old ship resting on the seabed. The walls around them are still just a friable mess of mortar and brick, but upon these venerable walls is a series of blown-up pictures. Photos of him and Viv. Candid photos that Alice must have snapped unbeknownst to them during several of their most memorable moments.

Vivianne paces the room, unable to unstick her palms from her cheeks, which are lighting up like sheets of vermilion silk. Tears pool in her eye. Theodore begins to feel queasy; he touches his own cheek, realizing that he too must be blazing up right now. He also fully acknowledges that the previous Theodore—that old anchorite who enjoyed attention as much as bronchitis—would have been vomiting all over the respectable piece of history that is this dusty old room out of the sheer anxiety of seeing his own tender moments captured and made into gargantuan displays for strangers to view.

Alice has simply done a splendid job of showcasing the two of them. The array of photos is masterfully taken and even back lit by strips of warm LEDs. There's one of Theodore and Vivianne chomping on ice cream cones at Lincoln Center; another of them at South Street Seaport—he in a crisp tuxedo and she in a coruscant white dress, meandering hand-in-hand among the wizened harbor buildings. Propped upon the old bar top itself is just the perfect image of him and Vivianne; an apogee in stasis is this representation of the unflinching bond between them. They're in the foreground, holding each other in a soft embrace, as if they knew nothing in the universe could ever pry them apart. And upon their faces are the most honest and candid smiles Theodore thinks he's ever seen. In fact, this is without a doubt the first time he has ever seen himself in such a light; the first time he's ever seen anything, or anyone, give him a reason to wear such an unbridled, genuine smile. In the background looms the Washington Square Arch, out of focus and hazy as it basks in the twilight's resplendent glow.

"How did you take all of these without our knowing?" he stammers, feeling a tear shed from his eye. "I didn't know tonight was going to be a celebration of us…"

"You done good, Alice," says Henry, chomping on an hors d'oeuvres and winking at Theodore.

Vivianne pauses in front of the picture propped on the bar. She seems swept up in a virulent tide of emotion, unable to make a single utterance. Theodore's finger reaches into his hoodie pocket. *This is it,* some persistent and inexorable voice within him insists; this is the moment he's waited for, the moment he believed through the years might never come; this is the moment his tyrannical father manipulated him into believing he didn't deserve; the moment that monster conditioned him in the deepest levels of his being to believe only existed in fairy tales and nothing more; the moment Theodore put on the back-burner in order to take care of his young sister through the unpredictable twists of life's journey—a journey he'd adopted not of his own volition but as a causation of an oppressive and traumatic upbringing.

He gets down on one knee behind Vivianne. He brandishes the emerald ring with a remarkably steady hand and holds it out. The world begins to dissolve around him like it did each moment he left for Georgian England, evanescing about him until all he can see is Vivianne, her back to him as she unknowingly stares at the photograph. Somewhere in the distance behind, Alice gasps. In a murky voice that reverberates like a litany recited between two narrow canyon walls, Henry exclaims, "Holy shitballs!" Vivianne wheels about in response to the outburst. Her gaze falls upon Theodore.

"Viv...will you marry me?"

Her hand covers her heart, a ruddy warmth suffuses her face. The tears that moments before were threatening at the brink of her eyelids bore a path down her cheek. Her look of astonishment is swept away by her smile; oh, that wondrous, invigorating smile that would not only launch a thousand ships but would moor the world itself to the harbor of grace, humility, and love.

"Yes! Yes, of course I will!" She rushes into his arms and he lifts her from her feet, spinning about the room in a harmonious and blissful embrace, fit for all the fairy tales the world can conjure. Henry and Alice crowd about them,

Henry jumping up and down in a fit of hysteria and Alice wrapping her arms around them.

"Great news, guys," Francis calls from the doorway. "Sigrid thought I made a bitchin' cocktail! I could tell so from the thumbs-up and the little smile…that being before she said, 'citrus something something,' and dumped the glass in the sink. So, I'll call it a work in prog…What's going on in here? Did you guys reinvent time travel or something?"

"Get over here, you big lug," says Alice. "Theodore just asked Vivianne for her hand in marriage."

"Hey, hey! Congratulations, you two!" cries Francis, throwing himself amongst them and nearly toppling the whole group over.

Theodore smiles through a dewy haze of tears, taking in the plethora of beaming faces about him. His gaze finally falls upon Vivianne. They turn slowly together, losing themselves in another moment—another sliver of life ephemeral in nature and yet transcendent in essence. His hands on her hips and hers locked around his neck, they lean in and kiss. Only no kiss between them is merely a kiss, but a celebration of forbearance, of overcoming. Every embrace they share, a redoubt against the tyranny of darkness and its regressive hold on the heart.

Life is cruel, it is callous, it's awkward and peculiar; life is tame, it is reckless, it's joyous and familiar; but for all life's vicissitudes, Theodore knows that with these stalwart allies at his side, never again will he walk its annals with forlorn steps. He will hold his head high and embrace the world. For he's found that with every storm of suffering life conjures, it unearths for everyone a bud of Arcadian placidity, of tenacious hope, of propitious joy. One must only sharpen their eyes to such a tender thing before trampling it under foot and passing it by on the wending road of life.

We are not now that strength which in old days

Moved earth and heaven, that which we are, we are;

One equal temper of heroic hearts,

Made weak by time and fate, but strong in will

To strive, to seek, to find, and not to yield.

Alfred Lord Tennyson,
Ulysses

ABOUT THE AUTHOR
ALEC ARBOGAST

Alec Arbogast lives in Salt Lake City, Utah. He received his Bachelor of Science in Writing and Rhetoric Studies at the University of Utah. His debut novel, *The Last Odinian* (2017), has won nine national and international awards, including placing as a finalist in the 2018 International Book Awards and as a winner in the 2018 NYC Big Book Award in the horror category. Alec loves psychological horror. He capitulates to Cthulhu's call as well as the beckoning of pre-war 'weird tales.' His TBR pile is never lacking a few Victorian-era ghost stories, and contemporary fiction and fantasy usually manage to sneak their way into that ever-growing mound of books.

When he's not writing, Alec is taking to the canyons in his Camaro, pondering the next ill-advised decision of his work-in-progress protagonist, and traveling to other worlds in videogames, all while probably sipping espresso from a demi-tasse. *A Night at The King's Inn* is his second novel.

The Last Odinian has also been the recipient of second place in the 2018 Royal Dragonfly Book Awards in the Science Fiction/Fantasy category, Winner of the 2018 Beverly Hills Book Awards in the Horror category, 2018

Best Book Award, 2018 Independent Author Network Horror finalist, and a finalist in the 2018 Reader's Favorite Fiction-Horror category.

You can connect with Alec on Facebook, Twitter, Instagram (@author_alecarbogast) and on his website, www.alec-arbogast.com. In the meantime, turn the page for a preview of Alec's first novel, *The Last Odinian,* availble for purchase in both ebook and paperback format on Amazon and Barnes & Noble!

THE LAST ODINIAN

BY ALEC ARBOGAST

"The boundaries which divide life from death are at best shadowy and vague. Who shall say where the one ends, and where the other begins?"
¬*Edgar Allan Poe*

I twisted and struggled and pulled, pulled hard, but it was no use. I wasn't strong enough and was rapidly growing weaker. All that cut through the dense canvas bag covering my head was the occasional slice of sunlight through the trees. I felt cool blades of grass brush my ankles. The unkempt vegetation had been steadily growing since the woods began.

Two hands were rooted firmly under my armpits. I could tell each one belonged to a different person by the way I was being yanked back and forth, like a trophy being carried by two competitors wanting a bigger share of the prize. They had been pulling me up an increasing terrain for what could have been minutes or hours, it was impossible to tell.

My throat felt stripped and raw from my previous attempts to scream for help. My larynx had to fight for even the most minute utterance, and the pain that incurred from even the slightest jiggle was immense. I figured I had been battered one too many times in the neck, leaving my voice box broken. All I could manage was a moan like a dying seal as I was dragged towards an unknown fate.

My assailants didn't speak to each other, or to me. They hadn't said a word. The sound of breathing and grunting came from every direction. The only noise I could distinguish from inside my burlap prison, aside from the rustling of leaves, was the solid stamping of feet. Feet. How many were there? It was impossible to tell. I focused on the scent of pine and dirt, and tried to steady my breathing, but each slow breath only magnified the pain in my chest.

After some time, the terrain began to even out. I inhaled, disregarding the inevitable searing pain in my rib cage that followed. The earthy smells were still abundant, but were slowly becoming enveloped by another scent. Like the taste of blood—tangy and slightly metallic.

I breathed in one more agonizing time. A foul second layer of this mysterious new scent greeted me. It smelled like I was approaching a dead carcass.

For a moment, the pitter-patter of feet ceased and I was no longer moving. I heard the sound of an old wooden door pivoting on rusty hinges just a few feet ahead, and felt the hands under my arms tighten as I was jerked forward again. The hint of sunlight that had been tickling my retinas disappeared and my world was plunged further into darkness.

The softness of the ground below ended and my feet found cold, hard stone. My center of gravity shifted and, with a cycle of dragging and falling, I blindly stumbled down a stairwell.

The sound of footsteps echoed off the nearby walls, as I was dragged into some sort of catacomb. The stench from before became nearly unbearable, and there was a dampness to it. I was underground.

The stone floor leveled off and I could make out little wavering circles of light drifting by on either side. The warm crackle of flames licked at my ears and shoulders. Where were they taking me, and what did they want with me? Another helpless little groan was all I could muster, paired with two swift but clumsy kicks left and right. They didn't let my flailing disrupt their pace. Whoever they were, they were wearing garbs that flowed back and forth as they walked. The fabric brushed against my bare shins as they escorted me to their destination.

Robes? Could this be some sort of demonic cult? I didn't know. All I knew was that my ability to breathe within the scratchy canvas bag was deteriorating as the oxygen thinned. We were going deeper and deeper down the narrow tunnel. I began gasping for air, my lips puckering, my chest constricting around the remaining air in my lungs.

The strange hands loosened slightly and pulled me to a stop. Footsteps echoed and rattled as the other figures dispersed to my left and right. All I could see were two ominous balls of light in front of me, and I could feel the warmth from other torches bouncing off the walls to the sides. I gulped in air, and once my lungs were satisfied with the new supply, I tried to slow my breathing. My heartbeat eased from a gyrating thrum in my throat, to a quick pulsing.

Breathe in, breathe out, I told myself. I could do nothing more.

For a moment, all was still. The tormenting silence in which they stood yielded to the faint din of a rat shuffling along the floor beside me. I could even discern the sound of its tail dragging on the stone. We were too far into the tunnel for any exterior noises to devise a way in. No more wind, no rustling tree branches. No more birds, squirrels or crickets. Just a suffocating silence.

A horrendous shriek pierced my ears. They must have been carrying another prisoner with them the entire time. At first, I couldn't tell what direction her voice came from. Her screams filled the stone box and refracted off each wall with a jarring intensity. I was able to pinpoint the woman's location after the reverberations died down, and the girl's initial scream turned into softer whimpers.

I looked to the left and saw a blurry, flailing motion in front of torchlight. Why had the girl been silent until now? Had she been drugged, and was only now waking?

"What are you doing with me?" the girl pleaded.

"Crying, into the world I came.

No grave shall there be, to bear my name."

A wall of voices surrounded us, drowning out the girl's screams. Chanting in unison just inches away, the two men holding me nearly ruptured my eardrums with the timbre of their voices.

"The earth, the wind, the rain, the fire.

My life's design, to build a pyre.

The embers of my soul shall kiss the sky.

Return to earth and let me die."

A seething silence followed. The rusty scent that reminded me of death continued to grow. I felt as though I would throw up at any minute, although my mind was too foggy to determine whether my nausea had been caused by the disgusting smell, the lack of oxygen in the chamber, or from the brutal beating they gave me before shoving me in the back of their van.

I attempted to lick my lips and felt my tongue catch between them. They were rough, like two strips of sandpaper, and my tongue felt dry and thick. I smacked it against the roof of my mouth over and over again, trying to coax some spit out of my glands. It was no use.

My heart felt like it could seize up at any second; a pervasive dizziness forced me to close my eyes. Then the screams started again, in tandem with the chanting.

"Crying into the world I came."

The girl's shrieks became more prominent as they dragged her to the center of the chamber, just beneath the two torches in front of me.

"No grave shall there be, to bear my name."

The girl's cries began to sound slightly muffled, but did not desist.

"The earth, the wind, the rain, the fire."

I detected movement directly ahead, discerning the outline of a struggle.

"My life's design, to build a pyre."

I heard the faint shimmering slice of metal on metal, like a dagger being unsheathed. Then, the tearing of cloth. The voices swelled in strength.

"The embers of my soul shall kiss the sky."

The girl's cries sounded guttural now, riddled with raw, quivering tones of desperation.

"Return to earth, and let me die."

As soon as the last syllable in the twisted incantation was uttered, the girl fell silent. Her final haunting shouts of protest echoed through the chamber. Once again, a blanket of silence unfolded across the room. I felt a large hand fumbling at the back of my neck and winced as the sack was pulled off my head.

The first thing my gaze fell upon was the fresh corpse of a young woman, probably no older than her early twenties. She was tied to an upright wooden stake, her hands bound behind her. Her blouse was splayed in two, and jagged strands of it were strewn beneath her feet. Between her breasts and down the soft of her stomach was a rough pagan-like symbol, carved flesh deep into her body.

Blood was seeping out of the wounds and trickling down her abdomen to her white skirt, which was now patterned with thick, red droplets. The pallet of ravaged skin on the girl's torso was not severe enough to have been the cause of her death, but a more surgical, precise gash along her throat was.

Surrounding the body of the victim were men in long black robes with hoods covering their faces. All I could see were their frigid, emotionless eyes floating in the darkness of their hoods. They were all staring apprehensively at the lifeless figure, as if they knew something was coming, but didn't know for sure what that something was.

One of the hooded figures closest to the body held the murder weapon in his fist. A long, scalloped dagger shone under the torches, saturated with blood and bits of filleted flesh. Behind the gruesome image was a sort of shrine, upon which, were propped a couple of ancient looking relics. One of them was an ornate cross that had meticulous etchings carved on its thick, stone body.

My ability to see under the dim and flickering light of the torches was impaired, but I could tell the cross was archaic; it looked like it could have been crafted during the dark ages. To the left of the cross was a more peculiar relic. It was a knight, thoroughly plated in armor, upon a formidable horse sculpted in mid-gallop. The beast was titanic in stature, positively dwarfing the man upon it. The knight had a unique looking sword in his hand that contained little geometrical adornments along its shaft.

I looked to the left and right. My veiled guesses had been relatively accurate; I was in some sort of underground tomb. Along the surrounding stone walls were large rectangular cutouts, and in each space were caskets large enough to fit human bodies.

Who built this catacomb of death? A chill descended upon me when I considered there may be an empty casket waiting for me.

An undercurrent of grunts and murmurs spread amongst the robed men. As they whispered, I began to feel a bud of pressure in my ears. At first, it was so subtle that I barely took note, but it rapidly developed into a virulent gust, as if my whole body was being yanked forward by an unseen force. The men around must have felt it too, briskly falling into silence around me. The stench I had managed to forget during the murderous event was growing even stronger, like my nose was buried inside the gut of a dead man.

At once the torches began to quiver, their flames dancing and sputtering. An icy gale burst into the tomb and threatened to blanket us in total, suffocating darkness. I could not only feel the change in pressure, but could hear the whistle of air as it stampeded from behind us and propelled towards the center of the room.

All around me, I saw the ghostly silhouettes of the men in the lingering light stumble forward and collapse under the pressure; their robes flailing and twirling madly. There was a swooshing noise followed by a deafening crack. The torches wavered and died, enveloping the tomb in a terrific blackness.

I couldn't see a thing. My unsteady breathing and a deep throbbing in my head was all I could focus on. Soft curls of air brushed my shoulders as the two men who still held me tightly exhaled. I felt something squirm over my foot, a rag of coarse hair massaging my ankle, and kicked. I heard a rat squeal and scurry away.

The utter silence caused a frenzied panic to pervade my mind. The hairs on the back of my neck stabbed like needles. I realized something else was in the room with us. A devious presence had crept into the chamber; something that seethed with malice, and simmered with hatred. I could taste it; that same metallic scent that stung my nostrils earlier now fell upon my tongue.

The fingers of a new fear poked at my mind while the torches reignited all around me. Everyone's focus hastily gathered to the center of the room, where, looming behind the body of the dead girl, was a ghostly figure.

The fear in the room was palpable; everyone's eyes locked upon the figure. When it exhaled, two tendrils of air shot out of its nostrils and bathed me in a frosty embrace.

"Bring her to me." Its menacing timber, which was disproportionately large for its body, rattled the chamber. The two men clutching me with trembling hands, clambered forward.

"We..." one of them stammered. "We lost the child back in the forest, my lord."

CHAPTER ONE

THE MAN IN THE ROAD

His fingers danced across the grooves of his jacket, the corduroy, soft and plush against his skin. Fingering the seams of an outer pocket, he brandished a box of cigarettes and pulled one out. Before raising it to his face with a shaking hand he paused, realizing his lips were still kissing a lit cigarette. He stared for a long moment at the little paper box in his hand and thumbed a tattered corner. The familiar logo, "Golden Light Cigarettes," seemed to dance under the warmth of the dim fluorescent light, and the image of a lighthouse printed on the front of the box swayed in the shadows.

A gruff voice broke the silence.

"Hey mister uh, Koh-nig, was it?" Waking from his trance, he fumbled for the pocket of his jacket and buried the cigarettes inside.

"Koenig," he said, out of the corner of his mouth that the cigarette wasn't occupying. "Pronounced Kay-nig." He had a commanding voice. One that wasn't particularly deep or refined, but had a gravelly tone that never shook or stuttered. He turned to face the officer behind him. "Although Edward will do just fine. Easier to pronounce."

"Koenig, that's exotic. What is that, Swedish? Dutch?" Sheriff Grady asked. He was a tall man with a rough complexion and a receding hairline accentuated by the grey hair that he slicked back. With a stern face that was likely aged beyond its years, he looked like a man who had seen a great deal of action. But the softness in his midsection suggested that it had probably been awhile.

"German, actually." Koenig faked a smile. "Although, I do have a lot of Swedish and a little Dutch in me, along with a smatter of blood from of the rest of Europe. Pretty good guesses." Grady extended an arm toward him and he obliged. The man's rough and calloused hand was certainly not that of a pencil pusher. Koenig could tell that Grady was a man accustomed to taking charge and getting results rather than frittering away with small talk.

"Well guessing the correct continent is close enough for me," he chuckled. "Welcome to Pinemist Bay, mister uh, Koenig, pleasure to meet you. I'm Sheriff Robert Grady." Grady had a harsh, scratchy bark for a voice, and he heaved when he spoke; like his lungs had to work hard to get anything out.

Let's just get on with it. I've had a long night, Koenig thought to himself, faking a smile at the sheriff.

"Nice to meet you Sheriff Grady. This is a lovely town," he said.

"Aw, well, thank you. One of my assistants said there was an outsider who had requested to speak with me, said you needed some refuge from that downpour, and that you had somethin' to report to me." Grady barked as he led Koenig into his office; the wooden door creaking as it opened. Everything in Pinemist Bay seemed sprawled out, disjointed, and eerily quiet. If anything broke the silence, even a small sound like Grady's office door, it didn't just graze the ear, it pierced it.

Following Sheriff Grady into the room, Koenig heard footsteps echo down the hall to the right, and the low grumble of voices as the late-night staff floated around the station. The crew was sparse tonight.

"Come on in, sit down. Make yourself at home. That corduroy coat must just soak up the rain," Grady chuckled.

"This helps." Koenig nodded, propping his drenched umbrella against the chair as he sat down. Grady walked around his large oak desk and let out a sigh as he seated himself. Koenig heard the clacking of footsteps approach the door and he heard it moan once again, sending a little shiver down his spine.

"Anything I can get for you Sheriff?" a woman's voice asked. Koenig turned to see Grady's secretary holding the door open and leaning inquisitively towards them. She appeared to be in her mid-thirties and had thick glasses on her face. Her hair was a red that nearly matched the burgundy colored blouse beneath. Koenig could tell that her eyes were hazel, but under the shadows cast by the dull hallway lights, they glowed a much darker, sultry shade of green. Koenig found himself lost in her eyes. This woman had a gentle, simple beauty that captivated him unrelentingly.

"Get this gentleman a coffee, Darlene. He needs something to warm up his bones," Grady said. "How do you take it, Edward?"

"Black with a sugar cube, please," Koenig said, and then looked away so as not to make the woman feel uneasy by what was becoming a prolonged stare. He took a long drag of his cigarette and stamped it out in the visitor's ashtray. The only light in the room came from a desk lamp beside Sheriff Grady, which caused a mosaic of shadows to bounce across the room. Underneath the lamp was the sheriff's own ashtray, upon which was propped a slowly burning cigar. The smoke trailing from its tip looked ghostly under the light.

"And for you, sir?" she inquired.

"Black, if you will," Grady said, while ushering her away with a wave of his hand. When the door closed behind her, the air inside the room grew still and quiet. It was as if Grady's office was a giant vacuum, siphoning out all the chatter of the station. Through an open window to the sheriff's left, a breeze was stirring behind the pines. The scent of rain and earth tickled Koenig's nostrils.

Leaning back in his chair, the sheriff's eyes fixated on Koenig.

"Well, Edward, on behalf of the entire county of Pinemist Bay I'd like to thank you for making the trip up to our quaint little town. We're a pretty good stretch from Chicago." Grady tapped his fingers on the desk. "I trust the trip went alright?" He lifted his hand and motioned briefly at Koenig's head, where a bruise blossomed like an aging purple lily. "What's that on your forehead?"

The wind howled menacingly and rain slapped the windshield of his car. The wipers moved like a pair of frail, bony arms of a drowning man, waving frantically for survival.

Koenig had never been a nervous driver. Climbing up this steep mountain road on any other day would have been like a regular trip to the lake. Today, however, there was something menacing in the air. For the past several miles, the road was largely fixed on the edge of an ever-climbing mountain, and Koenig could barely see the valley below through the torrents of rain and wind, and a curtain of fog that blemished the mountains. To the highest peak ahead, he had a hard time making anything out. *How can that be? How can there be such dense fog with this much wind and rain?*

The dashboard of his restored '76 Mustang glowed ominously as night began to fall. Beside the instrument cluster, the hands of the clock read 7:06.

How do I get myself tangled up in these situations? Koenig thought, and slapped the wheel. *Oh god Edward, you're in it now and there's no going back, not with Dalla's voice screaming inside my head.*

As the car lurched around a curve on the edge of the precipice, a raw, gyrating pain assaulted his head. He slammed on the brakes and centered the wheel as the ponderous car began to over-steer. It was happening again.

Ever since he left home earlier that morning, he had been having bizarre seizure-like episodes where his vision would blur and a violent, pulsating pressure would encompass his head. The sensation was so great that he needed to pull over every time it occurred and wait out the storm. The feeling would arise out of nowhere, and during the occurrence, his four-year-old daughter's voice would inexplicably echo in his mind.

As if in a dream, she called to him, beckoning him towards Pinemist Bay.

"Daddy," Dalla said, and as she spoke, a searing pain shot up his spine and resonated in his skull. *"Come find us in Pinemist Bay. Mommy and I need you..."* Her voice, and the overwhelming sensation in his head, attenuated and his vision stabilized. He rubbed his temples, surprised to find them damp with sweat, and rolled his eyes to the left. He took an edgy, trembling breath.

The edge of the cliff was not a foot from his left tire. If he so much as opened the door and stepped out, he would be a dead man. Peering downwards, he could clearly see the bottom of the chasm far below. The terrain was riddled with pine trees that looked like flakes of pepper from such a height. He shook his head, rallied his nerves, and eased back onto the road.

As he continued up, the ground began to level out. The path slowly diverged from the side of the cliff into the meat of the mountain and became unforgivingly windy. The pine trees now closed in overhead and the world suddenly seemed smaller.

Without having seen a single signpost or marker, Koenig had no idea where he was. He could have been twenty miles up the mountain, or sixty. There was no concept of time in this no man's land, no indication that time even existed, except for the slowly moving hands on the clock atop the dashboard.

Koenig had switched off the radio near the bottom of the canyon when the reception had become too spotty. This was the first time in a while he had been truly alone with his thoughts, which, in the current state of things, was not good. He rubbed his tired eyes as the big eight-cylinder engine roared under the hood, catapulting him ever onward into the unknown. Koenig found himself stretching forward in his seat, attempting to see the sky between the blur of tree branches that passed above the car, but to no avail. The fog was too thick, and even if the air had been devoid of haze, he still would have failed to see beyond the dense pines. It made him uneasy to be encased in the dark womb of nature, and it was agitating that he couldn't make anything out beyond even the first line of trees in front of him. Rocks, boulders, shrubs, droopy branches and languid trees; everything appeared abruptly and then flowed past, disappearing into the darkness behind. Then, something unexpected came into view.

At first, Koenig couldn't tell what it was in front of him. There was a small white flash and an object appeared directly ahead, too small to be a tree or a signpost, and too narrow and upright to be a deer. Koenig squinted, then slammed on the brakes and cranked the steering wheel. For a mere moment, the object came into view under the Mustang's powerful fog lamps and Koenig thought he saw the pinkish-yellow of skin. His brain was unable to process more before the big, heavy car lost control and, with a piercing screech from the tires, careened off the road. He felt the lap restraint constrict against his legs as he was lurched upward, and then the shoulder harness bit into his torso as he was thrust forward with ferocious momentum. Koenig's head met the steering wheel with a crunch.

All went still.

With some effort and a long groan, Koenig slowly lifted his head. The engine rumbled in front of him. *Good. At least the motor is still running,* he thought. He immediately touched his hand to his forehead and winced from the pain. No wetness, though—no blood. Just a sharp bump. *I knew I should have put the damn airbag back in after I restored this thing*, he shook his head. The only airbag Koenig did put back in after the restoration project was the one on the passenger's side, for when his little girl rode along. Letting out a sigh of relief, Koenig looked into the rear-view mirror of the car and unbuckled his seat belt. The fog behind was churning in ghostly circles.

"What the fuck was that?" he grunted to himself. The muggy air was too thick for him to make anything out. Normally, Koenig would have immediately gotten out of his car and inspected it up and down for body damage or a popped tire. Something was holding him inside though; a fear or dread that he couldn't shake. It was like the feeling he got as a child when he walked by a mirror in his house and saw something in the reflection that didn't belong there. Some abhorrent shape would appear and then vanish, or something might dart by the corner of his bedpost in the reflection. But every time young Koenig's eyes returned to the mirror, whatever he saw would be gone. He continued to gaze into the rear-view mirror, his stare unwavering.

Come on Edward, you're 33 years old, shake it off. He didn't dare peel his eyes off the mirror. *Whatever was back there, you're probably in no danger,* he comforted himself. The fog behind the car that had been tumbling from the commotion was finally settling down and beginning to thin out. Koenig saw a figure slowly materialize in the road. It was a human being. At least, it looked like one from his vantage point.

Koenig rubbed his eyes with cold, sweaty fingers, half believing the figure in the road would be gone when he looked again. It remained. He was sure now that the figure was human; a man, standing, but slightly hunched over. Koenig was curious, but apprehensive. Feeling a tremulous chill sink deep into his bones, he stepped out of the vehicle.

The man in the road remained motionless, facing slightly away, as if he was transfixed by something, during Koenig's slow approach. As far as Koenig knew, the man hadn't moved a muscle since Koenig narrowly avoided hitting him with his car. He couldn't even tell if the man was breathing. The man just stood there, looming like a statue in a graveyard. As he approached, and the thinning layer of fog between them dissipated, Koenig saw that the man was naked.

"Hey man, sorry about that." Koenig startled himself when he realized his voice was shaking. "I, uh, I didn't see you standing there...I almost hit you." The man remained still. Making sure there was a comfortable distance between them, Koenig walked around to meet him face to face.

The man was old and sinewy. His bald head coruscated as rain drizzled down his cheeks to his shoulders. Goose bumps were poised all over his old, saggy flesh. Koenig cleared his throat.

"You're sopping wet old man, what are you doing out here?" Koenig pulled his jacket off and turned it around to wrap the old man in it. Right as the jacket was about to embrace him, the old man came to life and burst into a frenzied rambling. Startled, Koenig stumbled backwards and nearly lost his footing on the drenched road. The old man was speaking at a blisteringly fast pace, and Koenig couldn't understand what he was saying through the ramshackle phrases. He couldn't tell if the man even knew where he was.

Koenig wiped his eyes with a soaked and trembling hand, and watched as the old man's head began to shake violently. The ramblings eased and he slowly lifted his head to look into Koenig's eyes, but with the violent tremors the man was experiencing, it was impossible to establish eye contact.

"Edward...Koenig," the old man spat between inane grunts. Koenig felt the air escape his lungs and he clutched his chest with an unsteady hand.

How the fuck does he know who I am?

Koenig's heart was hammering against the wall of his sternum, and he began to feel dizzy. *I must be dreaming; I have to be.* The old man's jaw started to open and close repeatedly, as if he was struggling to find his own tongue.

"What...what did you say?" The words came out this time, but were soft enough that a gentle breeze could whisk them away. The old man did not seem to hear Koenig, and he didn't reply. His ramblings slowly subsided, but his head continued to spasm violently.

"Edward...Koenig. You must...listen to me." The old man fought with every word, as if it pained him to speak.

"I don't understand!" Koenig interrupted. "How do you know who I am? I've never met you before in my life. This must be some kind of dream..." His eyes stayed on the old man's face. Although he desired to, Koenig could not bring himself to return to his car and leave the man to the elements, not before hearing what he had to say.

"There is not...much time, and they are listening...always listening." The wind started to whine between the trees. Behind the old man, the pines began to wave their arms and sway from side to side. The gale strengthened, carrying a stench that crawled into Koenig's nostrils and made him cringe. It was similar to the foul smell of something dead and decaying, accompanied by a rusty metallic scent; like a big rain-soaked nail buried in the flesh of a wet dog. Koenig looked around nervously; the fog surrounding them was lifting.

"You are here, now…so what is set in motion cannot be undone," the old man said. "But, maybe you can still vanquish him…"

"Vanquish who?" Koenig asked, feeling the hairs on the back of his neck stiffen. The old man's head wobbled from side to side, as if he was scanning the nearby woods for someone, or something.

"When did you last speak…to your family?" His focus returned to Koenig.

"Right before I left," Koenig said after a brief pause. "What do they have to do with any of this? My wife and daughter are in Chicago."

"Listen to me…do not let the Vucari find you. If you walk the year, true darkness will reveal itself to you."

Do not let the Vucari find you; if you walk the year, true darkness will reveal itself to you. Koenig was trying to memorize the old man's instructions, even though he was nothing but baffled by the entire situation.

"Will you…remember that, Edward?" the old man begged.

"Yes. Who are you?" Koenig thought this was the most pertinent question.

"All in time, Edward." The old man's head momentarily stopped moving and his cracked mouth upturned into a grin that looked sincere but tortured. Koenig entertained a twinge of compassion, even appreciation, for the old man.

"Now, you must leave at once…return to your car and continue to Pinemist Bay, and remember what I have told you."

Koenig took a long last look at the old man, desperately craving to pursue the many questions in his mind. Then, he turned toward the side of the road and slowly walked to his car. Deep in thought, he climbed in and took a long breath to steady his nerves. He cradled the shifter in his palm. Before clicking it into reverse, Koenig looked into the rear-view mirror, still worried about the old man alone on the road. But the old man, and the fog, were gone.

Koenig watched a trail of steam escape from Grady's mug and swell under the warm light of the desk lamp. He felt the heat from his own cup in his hands and, feeling somewhat more relaxed, let out a sigh.

"Well, Edward, it's not too often that we have outsiders around here, given that we're so isolated. We're a simple, but kind folk. So…why is it that you stopped by my station before headin' into town?" Grady asked.

The sign for the sheriff's department had been the second one Koenig came upon after leaving the old man. He had driven further up the winding road until it leveled out, when the ominous glow of the "Welcome to Pinemist Bay County" sign materialized. It had been partially overtaken by foliage, but Koenig could still make out the image of a shimmering bay cradled under a nest of pine-covered mountains. A few hundred yards later another sign reflected in his headlights, "Pinemist Bay County Sheriff's Department." It was an old printed sign lit up from underneath by two powerful halogen lamps.

He had rushed in to the sheriff's department because he needed to inform the authorities about his bizarre encounter on the road. Koenig was half assuming that the old man may have been one of the escaped crazies from a local asylum, and half assuming that what he saw was a figment of his imagination. Altitude sickness was known to cause hallucinations.

Now, sitting in the sheriff's office, Koenig had wanted to tell him about the old man in the road, even if just to restate the events and confirm his sanity. But he couldn't bring himself to do it. He was well aware of how crazy his story would sound, and more importantly, he didn't know or trust anyone in this isolated town. It didn't help that the sheriff's demeanor was rubbing him the wrong way. Something intangible about Grady put Koenig off.

"I wanted to come in and warm up," Koenig said, biting his lower lip. "My eyes were getting pretty weary after tackling that windy canyon road. I figured maybe you'd have some coffee on!" He raised the mug for emphasis, hoping the sheriff would believe him and move on.

"We've got the best brew in all of Pinemist Bay County here at the station!

We get it from Blackrock Café in town; be sure to visit there during your stay if you're a fan of coffee!" the sheriff said. "So what is it that you do, if you don't mind my askin'?" Grady leaned back in his chair and rocked it from side to side with his feet.

"Corporate analyst for a pharmaceutical company based in Chicago." Koenig hadn't thought of his job since starting up the road to Pinemist Bay. His mind had become a convoluted mess ever since his daughter's troubling messages began, and the old man in the road had escalated it.

"Ooh we got a pill pusher in our little town, run for the hills." Grady's coarse voice let out a laugh, and he raised a gimpy hand. *Grady thinks himself a comedian. Sad thing is, in a county with 7,536 people, he may be the town funny-man.*

"So, what's the name of the company you work for?" Grady asked, returning to his line of questioning.

"Hammond and Wilkes, LLC," Koenig stated. "You've probably heard the name, we're the supplier for about half of the drugs along the west coast. We've got a large distribution network in California."

"No, no," Grady said, shaking his head firmly. "I've never heard of that company. But, and don't take this the wrong way, mister, here in Pinemist Bay, we take a firm stance against drugs of any kind. You see, we believe there are other ways, safer and better ways, to connect with our spiritual side." Grady's voice grew louder and his eyes widened.

"And we don't cover up our flaws, our God given traits, with some synthetic, phony-baloney, mind trickin' voodoo substances." Grady hit the desk, knocking his cigar off the ashtray. At first, he just stared at it, as if he had surprised himself with his outburst. Then, clearing his throat, he gingerly picked the cigar up by its butt and placed it back on the ashtray, leaving behind a charcoal colored smudge on the desk.

"Anyways, Edward, what was the purpose of your comin' here?" He changed the subject. Feeling even more uncomfortable in the man's presence, Koenig shifted in his seat.

"Well, I rarely take real vacations and I thought to myself, why take another boat out on Lake Michigan, or stay in town and check into another hotel in the Chicago Loop? Why not go somewhere you have never been? And I remembered how my father had come through here very briefly on his way up to Vancouver for business. He had told me that the Cascade Mountains really helped him to relax. He mentioned this place in particular."

What he said was only partly true, his father did travel to Pinemist Bay once when Koenig was a teenager. George Koenig was frequently out of town for work, but after the fateful trip to Vancouver, he was never the same. He returned a changed man, a broken man. George kept to himself far more than usual after visiting Pinemist Bay, and developed a debilitating drinking problem that worsened through Koenig's teenage years.

Koenig began to find it hard to live with his father after that, but he and his mother stood by George's side and attempted to maintain a degree of normalcy in their lives. George continued to harbor a deepening depression, but over time, he divulged some details of the fateful business trip that changed his life. Whenever he spoke of his journey up the Pacific Northwest to Canada, which he only ever did when he was drunk, he would whisper it to young Koenig—a warning.

"I want you to promise me something, Eddie. When you grow up and move out of the house and explore the world, which you will do someday, it's the way of life, promise me you will keep your wits about you if you go to Pinemist Bay. It is a dangerous old port town. Somebody may try and take you there, or to convince your family to go, but don't let them. Remember what I'm telling you. Can you promise me that, Eddie?"

He remembered nodding in reply and thinking to himself that he would likely never travel that far from their hometown of Rochelle, Illinois. Through the years, however, Koenig's mild curiosity about Pinemist Bay developed into a hunger. He starkly remembered watching his father's casket being lowered into a grave at the Rochelle Public Cemetery, and thinking to himself that, one day, he would discover what it was in Pinemist Bay that broke the strongest man in his life.

Before he even made it out of Illinois, he met his future wife, Eveline. They settled down in the burgeoning Chicago Loop and had a beautiful daughter together. The mysterious old port town sat on the back burner for a while after that. The image of the deflated man that it turned his father into did not. It became inhumed in his psyche indefinitely.

"Well, Sheriff Grady, it's been great meeting you, but it's been a very long night and I'd like to change out of these wet clothes and get some rest." Grady glanced at the clock on the wall and stood up.

"Yes, Edward, I completely understand. It is a long drive all the way up here from the airport." Grady chuckled as he leaned over his desk and took Koenig's hand in another firm shake. "Thanks for stoppin' by," he said. Koenig could smell a mixture of cigar smoke and coffee on the sheriff's breath, but another scent lingered equivocally behind them; like an afterthought in a writer's mind. Whiskey.

As Koenig stood and leaned over Grady's desk, a light scintillated off something behind it. He hadn't noticed from where he was sitting, but the lower drawer of the sheriff's desk was half open, and inside lay a half-full bottle of amber liquid: "Mt. Hood Single Malt Whiskey."

Taking care not to look too long, Koenig's eyes met the sheriff's again, but too late. Grady glanced down inquisitively for what might have caught Koenig's eye. He couldn't tell if the sheriff noticed that his drawer of debauchery was open, but a momentary look of unease painted Grady's face. He cleared his throat, looking back at Koenig. The sheriff's grasp on Koenig's hand tightened more forcefully now, and he pulled him closer.

"Thanks for stopping by," he repeated, this time with a labored intensity behind his eyes. "I like to know what goes on in my town, ya know, keep a close watch." Grady's eyes were slimmer now, as if he was studying Koenig. "I'm the jurisdiction around here, and nothin' gets past me. Anyone that comes in, anyone that goes out, I'm aware of it. I've got eyes everywhere."

His tone changed to a more conversational one and his grip loosened.

Koenig could feel cool air kiss his sweaty hand. "So anything you need, you just let me know." Grady grinned. It was an ugly, self-serving grin that revealed only one or two teeth in the middle. Mustering a smile, Koenig pulled his hand away.

"Thank you for your hospitality, Sheriff Grady. I'll be sure to let you know if I need anything."

Grady rounded his desk, his big belly grazing the edge, and led Koenig out of his office.

"My assistant Darlene will show you out." Koenig had forgotten about Darlene. He looked to his left and there she was, sitting unassumingly in her booth to the left of Grady's office. He motioned to her in an awkward gesture and she smiled back.

"Would you like her to show you around town, Mr. Koenig?" Grady asked. "It's a pretty small place, but I bet you must feel like a fish out of water."

"Oh no, no that's fine," Koenig said, thinking of his wife, Eveline, and how their situation was already delicate. "I'm sure I'll get along just fine by myself, thank you."

"Alright mister. Well, you can stay at the Pinemist Hotel. It's the only lodging around here for outsiders," Grady said. "And they're plenty accommodating. I had better get back to my work." With that, Grady's door moaned shut, leaving nothing but a frosty silence between Koenig and the girl.

"Let me walk you out, Mr. Koenig." Darlene maneuvered out from behind her desk. Koenig fought hard not to stare. They slowly made their way down the halls of the sheriff's department to the soundtrack of their own echoing footsteps. The building was nearly empty now.

"So, how long do you plan on being here, Mr. Koenig?" she inquired.

"Please, uh, call me Edward. I'm not really sure how long I'll be here, I just wanted to get away," he said.

"So, have you heard of the disappearances?" she asked, with a softer voice now.

"Disappearances?" *Did a senile old man happen to go missing recently?* He looked over at Darlene. The equanimity of her facial expression didn't mask the fear beneath it.

"They're saying that it's not safe to go out at night, at least, not until the situation is figured out." She looked around cautiously as if she didn't trust someone who might be lingering in earshot. "That's one of the reasons we're all here at the department right now. Normally things here shut down at around eight or nine o'clock. Everybody's working overtime trying to figure out what's happening in Pinemist Bay. Things like this haven't happened in a peaceful town like ours in quite some time."

Maybe that's why Grady seemed so suspicious of me. They rounded a corner and continued down a long hallway, which led to the station's entrance. About halfway down the hall, a janitor was meticulously mopping along the grooves of the tile floor. He slowly lifted his head as they walked by, but it was difficult to see his face through the shadows cast by his baseball cap. All Koenig could make out was a toothless smile following them as they walked by.

Koenig yearned to know more about the mysterious disappearances, but he couldn't bring himself to ask Darlene. *Why is she telling me all of this?*

"Well, Mr. Koenig – Edward." She was blushing. "It was nice meeting you."

"You too, Darlene." He couldn't think of what to say. "Uh, thanks for the coffee."

"My pleasure, I hope you find the hotel all right." He began down the steps and opened his umbrella, already getting pelted by unsavory slices of rain. "And be mindful of the lights in there. That building is old, and the wiring is pretty bad." And then she said with a hint of emphasis, "In the darkness, you may not know if someone's coming for you."

Koenig paused mid-step upon hearing Darlene's advice and thought of what the old man had said. 'Do not let the Vucari find you.' Was he being paranoid, or was there some kind of connection? Could she be hinting about the same danger the old man warned him about? He pivoted to face the doorway, but she was gone.